I0841075

ΛΛΖ

LORDS

OF
WRATH

WE *KEEP*
WHAT'S *OURS*

SAMANTHA RUE
ANGEL LAWSON

THE ROYAL HOUSES OF
FORSYTH
COUNTS
BARONS
COUNTS
TO THE VICTOR
F
DUKES
PRINCES
LORDS
LORDS

For the rogues.

1

THE DAY AFTER

THE HOUSE IS quiet when I get home from practice, walking in the door to complete silence. There's no music coming from Rath's hovel upstairs, probably because he's still sulking. Not a sound from Tristian, either, who's likely shut in his room plotting some kind of twisted, fucked up revenge on our enemies.

No skin off my back.

I don't need to look to know Ms. Crane has already settled in for the night, but I'm starving badly enough to fend for myself. Practice kicked my ass from one end of the field to the other. With Homecoming two weeks away, Coach is worried we'll get distracted from his goal of a perfect season, and with the way I was playing today, he's right to be. I need to un-fuck myself, and fast.

I drop my stuff in the hallway just outside the kitchen. Dinner, I discover, is in the refrigerator, covered in plastic. She's a pain in the ass, but that cranky old bitch isn't a fool. She knows exactly how to work us and exactly what we need. I know when I go upstairs, I'm going to find my mattress stripped of the blood-stained sheets, like nothing ever happened. I doubt she even flinched at the sight, loyally cleaning up the crime. Knowing her, she probably whistled as she was doing it.

I place the plate on the counter and hear a small shift behind me. Glancing back, I see her. Story. My stepsister. The reason I was so drag-ass on the field today, getting drilled repeatedly. She's standing in the doorway, arms loose at her sides, eyes shuttered. I know it's probably all in my head, but as I look her over, I get this thought. She looks different now that she's not a virgin. I still remember the sight of her beneath me, those plush lips falling open in equal parts shock and pain as I forced myself into her tight, virgin cunt.

Christ.

No wonder I couldn't focus today.

If I wasn't thinking about how it felt to fuck her last night, then I was thinking about waking up to an empty bed, her dried blood still on my dick. She was gone, but the evidence all remained. A dirty reminder of what I took. What she *owed* me. How poetic.

"I can make that for you," she says, stepping into the kitchen. I move aside, but monitor her, not so hungover on her pussy to think it changed anything between us. If anything, she probably hates me more. I wouldn't put it past her to poison me. She opens the refrigerator and pulls out a beer, flipping off the top and sending the bottle cap through the air. I catch it deftly in my hand, watching as she places the bottle on the table. "Sit. I know you're tired."

There's not an ounce of kindness in her tone. Just obligation. Fine by me. She knows full well that I fucked her because it had to happen. She wasn't safe. The Counts and the Barons drew that line when they kidnapped her and tried to steal what belonged to us. But that wasn't the only reason.

I won her. *Won.* Fair and fucking square. Even if she hadn't chosen me personally—the true mark of victory—The Game's score still would have still added up in my favor. I didn't play it safe like Tristian and Rath, with their petty mind manipulations. I've owned her ass since the day she moved in here— longer than that, even. Since the day we met, years ago.

I watch as she presses the timer on the microwave, getting an eyeful of the cuff on her wrist that marks her as LDZ property. She pushes up on her toes to peer inside the door, giving me a pleasant view of the cotton shorts that barely cover her ass. She's come a long way in the last few weeks. Less combative. More compliant. Look at that move, calmly choosing me as the winner last night. She didn't even fight me when I laid her out on my crisp white sheets and finally claimed what's always been mine.

"How was practice?" she asks, turning around.

I stare at her, wondering if she actually cares. "Hard."

Of course she doesn't.

"Ms. Crane wanted me to tell you your suit's in your closet for the press conference this week."

I nod and down the rest of my beer in one long, tense swallow. She passes me to go to the refrigerator, sending a wave of her scent across my face. All I can think about is being between her legs, the way she looked when she came, quivering around my cock, that little divot in her forehead as she cried out, like she felt so goddamn good but was really pissed off about it.

I reach down to adjust myself.

"Do you want another—"

"No." I shoot her a glare just as the microwave beeps. Seeming unbothered by the curtness of my tone, she removes the plate and sets it in front of me. Like a servant. Like a *Lady*. Pulling in a hard lungful of her scent, I say, "The food is fine. You can go."

I wonder if she still has my come inside of her.

She folds her hands, voice flat. "Are you sure? I don't mind—"

I snap, "Go upstairs and get ready for bed."

She pauses, eyes flicking to the clock on the stove. It's only nine. "You… want me to go to bed?" That tone—uncertainty laced with disbelief—is the first actual glimpse of her I've seen since last night.

I stab my fork into the casserole and blow on it, calmly announcing, "You'll be sleeping in my bed from now on."

"But…" Her expression freezes, that mask she's been trying to wear crumbling beneath the spark of alarm in her eyes. I watch as she tries to put it back together, smoothing out her features. "Can I ask why?"

"Because I told you so." I shove the food in my mouth and chew slowly, already anticipating finding her there, curled up in my sheets, sound asleep. My dick's been throbbing all day at the thought of it. "Be there in two hours. No later. And don't go crying to the others about it. They already know."

She wants to argue. I can hear it in the way she shifts her weight, like she's bracing to push back. Instead, she turns on her heel and silently, *obediently,* leaves the room.

I'm not stupid. Last night, I fucked her like she was someone worth savoring. I fucked her like I wanted it so intensely, I didn't even care if she realized it. I fucked her like I was getting a prize.

All of that was true.

Now she needs to understand what that means. Her virginity might be off the table, but she's still under our rule—under *my* rule—and now that I've gotten a taste for her, I'm not letting go.

2

BIG BROTHER

WHEN I RAN to Colorado, I stopped caring about myself. My hair got weird, and I never wore it down. I got too skinny, too pale. I never did things like wear makeup or buy pretty new clothes. I lived out of a duffel bag, uncaring of how it looked. In short, I survived.

Since being back, it's been different. I put in the effort—not because I care about looking pretty, but because looking pretty is now a part of that survival. The shiny hair. The makeup. The clothes. These are tools. When I first came here, the sight would meet in the mornings like an alarming surprise each time I looked in the mirror, this new awareness that I'm playing a part.

But at some point, that awareness wore off.

Now when I look at my reflection, I just see someone who's squirmed their way into a costume they've forgotten they're wearing. In books and movies, there's the thing a girl does when she loses her virginity. She looks in the mirror, searching for a physical change, some tangible mark of the transition from girl to woman. It's dumb, and it's not real, but I find myself doing it anyway, trying to reconcile this person I've become; the girl who walked into my stepbrother's room last night and emerged this morning a woman.

It took me a long time to see it, but now that I do, it seems like having sex with Killian was always strangely inevitable. It was right in all its wrongness, just like these clothes I'm wearing—inappropriate yet perfectly tailored. After all, we've been drawn to one another like the hammer to a head of a nail since the night we met over dinner with our parents. The prize of my virginity was something I leveraged to protect myself, but I knew that would run out, and I'd have to give it to someone. Who better than the man I hated most? Yes, that's perfectly fitting.

That's not what's spinning me around. Not the pressure of Killian inside of me, pushing past the barrier I'd held intact for so long. Not the fact he was kind of nice about it. Not even the fact that, despite all my resistance, he somehow made it feel not horrible. No, that's not what's changed me the most.

It's finding out how hard they played me.

I agreed to be their willing slave, but knowing I've been an unwilling pawn in their stupid, childish games has lifted a veil. I was foolish enough to think that, despite the contract and abuse, we'd developed a bond.

That's what I see in the mirror. The reflection of a fool.

Every encounter I've had with the Lords was fake, from the meals Tristian so painstakingly chose for me to the soft, comforting safety of Dimitri's bed. Sure, I've been hiding my motive for coming here—for protection from my stalker, Ted—but I signed that contract and I agreed to be their Lady. I stopped fighting back. There for a minute, it'd really felt like things had shifted. It'd seemed as if Dimitri—*Rath*—and Tristian were men I could curl up against, count on, *trust.*

How unbearably pathetic.

I stare at the woman in the mirror. The one who just made Killian dinner. The one who's dressed for his bed. I'm wearing white, sheer lingerie picked out by one of these three sociopaths. I force myself to see the authentic person under the makeup and lace; a woman who knows how to survive.

The Lords aren't the only ones with secrets. I've put up with their deranged behavior because I need them. Ted is out there somewhere, and when I got the package at my mother's house, I realized he'd found me. *Again.* I'd met Ted back when I was playing as a sugar baby in high school. I only did it because I was trying to escape Killian and his pervy father, Daniel. Ted worshiped me. Stalked me. Tormented me. He was obsessed with having me and he would go to any length to keep me pure.

Jack, my old roommate, is proof of that. When Ted found out we were close, he killed him, which is why I knew sending him that text last night was firing the first shot.

Ted now knows what Killian took from me, that he made me bleed. And I'm not exactly sure what he'll do to the Lords, but I know it'll make them regret toying with me. Until then, I'll keep to the rules of the contract and be their Lady. I'll play Tristian's mind games and help Rath with his schoolwork. I'll even spend my nights in Killian's bed.

And then…when Ted is ready to make his move, I'll watch them burn.

However misguided and stupid it was, until twenty-five hours ago, Rath's bed had been my psychological happy place. Always so comfortable, plush, and inviting. Killian's bed is different. Firmer. Colder. His room is a touch too tidy, giving it an eerie impression, as if everything is staged. I lie under the blankets and stare at the perfect line of his shoes against the wall beneath the window, and I shiver, tugging the blanket up. There's no music. The only noise I can make out is the faraway hum of traffic. I'm not sure how long I lie there, listening. Waiting for the sound of his footsteps. Wondering what he's going to do to me. Wishing there were somewhere safer in this house to be, even though any bed here is an invitation to shame and hurt.

I don't mean to fall asleep.

It shouldn't be so easy here, in this uncomfortable bed, in this cold room. And yet, curled on my side, I find my eyelids falling, the phantom tug of exhaustion pulling me under. It's effortless to give into it, to hand myself over to the mindless drum of slumber. I don't know how long I'm like that, but I know I dream.

I dream of quiet breaths that tickle the skin below my ear. A cloud of masculine scent, so thick that I might choke on it. A fingertip against my bottom lip, parting my mouth. Sounds of ticking clocks and rustling fabric. The brush of a hand against my thigh. Cold air and the prickle of my gooseflesh. I dream of whispered words I remember all too well.

"Yeah, you fucking like it."

His voice floats up to me quieter than it was last night. Barely audible. More distant. And then it morphs into something a little different. New words, spoken from behind me. *"I bet you're nice and wet for me already."*

The dream is thick and hazy, so full of sensation that I can't help but arch into it. I'm aware I'm dreaming of Killian, of his breath on my neck, of his body being so close that the heat radiates from his skin. I should be disgusted, revolted, cringing away and rousing myself, but the last thing I want to do is wake up. This is the only place that's safe anymore, lost inside my dreams, letting myself acknowledge the desires that only ever seem to bring me shame and suffering.

Barely half-conscious, I reach down to push my fingers between my thighs, sucking in a breath at the much needed friction. It says something about my life now that I mindlessly pause, some fundamental part of my hindbrain acknowledging that this isn't allowed—not without their permission.

There's a rustle, the whisper of a hard exhale, and then Killian's voice behind me. "You're dreaming about it, aren't you?" he's saying, something both warm and cold—a tongue—grazing the skin above my jugular. "You're dreaming about being split open on my dick."

My belly twists with want at the words, at the memory, and I sink deeper into the phantom hands on my body, teasing and toying with my nipples. I can sense the strength in the fingers that tuck below my bottom, fisting into the crotch of my panties, yanking it aside, exposing my heat to the cold. Knuckles against my backside. Fingertips sliding through my folds, prodding, exploring. I unthinkingly push back, seeking the warmth and touch, my breaths coming faster. It's a good place to be, indulging in the build of my thrumming pulse, the quiver in my thighs, the softness of the whispered words against the shell of my ear.

"Because you're mine, now."

I don't really understand it at first—the pressure against my entrance, the heat of all the skin pushing against my back—until the first sting of pain comes. I think I make a sound, but I feel it more than I hear it. It's small and pained, but mostly surprised. This is supposed to be a better place. A place without the hurt and agony.

"Shh. You're still dreaming," the voice is saying, the pressure digging deeper. "Your pussy's fucking soaked. That's how much you want this."

A hand grabs my thigh from behind, pushing it forward, rolling me almost completely to my stomach. He shifts on top of me, and with one powerful, lurching shove, pushes the rest of the way inside. The intrusion is shocking and sudden, sharply painful in a way that makes me aware my flesh is tearing. *Again.*

My heart pounds and my eyes fly open, scrambling to acclimate to the dark. The first thing I see is the orange and purple Forsyth flag. The next thing I feel is the punch of a cock—*his* cock—thrusting in and out of me. I know it's him. His room. His bed. His scent. His pelvis against my ass. His need for absolute control.

Nothing about this is a dream.

He's huffing these short, hot exhalations against my neck, his dick relentless in its pursuit as his hips push into mine. "So many times," he whispers, scoring my shoulder with the drag of his teeth. "I've thought about doing this so. Many. Fucking. *Times*." The words punch out in time with his hips.

I slam my eyes closed and, like a coward, play dead. It hurts and I can't process what's happening fully, the weight of his body surging into me, the way his hand looks, fisting into the sheets beside my pillow, the sound of his panting breaths, the way he's using my body.

But mostly, I can't process how good it is.

The arousal from earlier doesn't fade. Instead, it just builds and builds, swelling inside me until it becomes a struggle to remain limp and passive. I allow myself a little bit—a writhe against him, sleepily wedging my arm beneath my body to touch myself—and hope he doesn't realize how awake I really am.

Luckily, he doesn't. "That's right," he says breathlessly. "You're dreaming about this. You want it. You can't fucking wait for me to fill you up." His pace increases, the relentless drive of his powerful, athletic body into mine. All-consuming. Completely controlling. Ruthless.

He unleashes with a sharp, guttural growl—the sound of an animal catching his prey. It's a sound I'm now familiar with, one that will end the physical pain but still leave a wound. He pushes into me hard, shoving me against the mattress, and it makes the heel of my palm grind into my clit, sending me over the edge.

It's a gentle sort of orgasm—almost painful in its quiet intensity—but it somehow clears the fog of the moment, leaving me with a vivid awareness.

My mouth parts on a soft gasp. *"Dimitri…"*

Killian goes rigid, even as his cock begins to soften inside of me. His chest heaves as he suspends there, nothing but the sounds of his harsh breaths filling my ear. There's a long moment where nothing happens, and then he shifts, slipping free and falling away, landing on his back at my side.

The anger radiates from him just as plainly as the cum dripping down my thigh, and for the first time in days, I let myself smile.

It hardens just as fast.

"I've thought about doing this…"

Flashes of Killian in my room flicker through my mind. The sensation of being watched. Him sitting in the chair. Jerking off. Standing inches away. Things that I've always assumed were dreams, a lot like this one, but far more vague. Killian holding himself, *stroking* himself, tracing my mouth with his fingertip. The sensation of a tongue against them. Waking up with sticky lips and tasting salt and flesh on the back of my tongue.

It's going to take more than another man's name on my lips to even this score.

3

REVENGE

RATH MIGHT BE a midnight cuddler, but Killian is anything but. He spends the entire night eerily still, contained to the other side of the bed. He doesn't snore. If it weren't for the rise and fall of his chest, I could almost imagine he's dead. It's the only reason I'm able to sleep at all.

My escape from his room the second I'm anywhere approaching awake is swift and silent. I leave him there in the bed, naked and as motionless as stone, and slip out before his alarm can wake him.

I take my time in the shower, washing the scent of him from my skin. His dried spunk from my thighs. The phantom feel of his lips from my neck. Inch by inch, minute by minute, I gradually reclaim my body. Funny how this used to be a process that took me months, days, hours, but now I can do it in the span of a single shower, stepping out of the steam and back into the skin Killian has borrowed.

When I open my closet, I see immediately what to discard. The tight pants. The cute dresses. Instead, I go for something straight out of the Tristian Mercer collection—a low-cut top and a short, pleated skirt.

Downstairs, I pause outside the dining room, the scent of eggs and bacon thick in the air, and eavesdrop on the discussion they're clearly in the middle of.

"…acting like a child because you're still fucking salty that I won the game," Killian is saying, the sound of a fork on ceramic loud and startling, as if he's stabbing whatever's on his plate.

"You didn't win the game," Rath replies, voice flat. "*I* won the game. Plus, what's there to be salty about? We all know why she chose you. Nothing special about factory-sealed pussy, anyway."

There's a small clang, and then Tristian's voice rings out. "Would the two of you focus on the big picture for one goddamn minute? There's another game going on here—a bigger game—and it's more important than our little competition to pop a cherry." There's a momentary pause, tension thick in the air, and then Tristian says, "We need to retaliate."

"And what the hell do you suggest?" Killian responds, voice hard.

Tristian offers, "There are a few options on the table. We go after Perez directly, just like he did to Story, or we go after something that belongs to him. The Countess. His beloved G-Wagen. His pretty fuckboy face." Tristian's voice lowers, tinged with a quiet intensity. "I can make this happen tonight, but I need your go-ahead."

"Can't do it," Dimitri says, sounding bored. "I have a mandatory rehearsal for the alumni event during homecoming."

"Killer?" Tristian asks.

"Who are we, the Dukes? We can't just walk up to him in the courtyard and string him up by the balls. We're Lords. We take the time to do it right." A fork clinks on a plate, and Killian adds, "Plus, this is a bad time. We've got more shit to do this week than ever. Like Rath said, it's homecoming. You know there are a ton of obligations for me. Both on the field and in the frat."

After a tense beat, Tristian's chilly voice responds, "You mean like forcing our Lady into your bed at night?"

The dining room goes silent.

There's a burst of quick breaths I recognize as Killian's quiet, humorless chuckle. "Neither of you seemed to have a problem with that yesterday. Rath obviously gave the green light because it's his way of punishing her."

"Fuck you," Rath snaps. "You don't know what's happening in my head."

But he does—I know he does. It's so unavoidably, malevolently *Rath*. I don't know how I didn't realize it before. My chest swells with a slow-burning fury, remembering all too well the way he looked in that video, smirking up at the camera as my head bobbed in his lap. I used to think Tristian or Killian were the worst of the three, but now I know better.

Killian might be a monster, but he's never worn a mask to conceal it.

Tristian might be a creep, but he's never dressed it up in pretty lies.

Rath is the kind of evil that infects you. He gets inside your blood and hides there, wounding you in places that won't become apparent until he's done with you. He's an internal catastrophe you don't see coming.

He's by far the worst.

"Please," Killian scoffs. "No one knows you better than we do. But I had wondered what Tristian's angle was."

"This isn't about an angle," Tristian argues. "If she wants out of your bed, she'll tell us. This is about you getting distracted during the play because you already scored the trophy."

"I'm not distracted," Killian insists, sniffing. "Parameters needed to be set. Her status doesn't change because I popped her cherry. She's our Lady. She needs to be reminded of that."

Neither guy argues with him, which pretty much proves where they stand on it.

"Look, I don't want these guys to think they're off the hook," Tristian says. "The longer we wait, the weaker we seem. Do we really want the Lords—and the Lady—to come off like pussies here? We need to do this now."

I take a deep breath, squaring my shoulders as I step into the room. "You're right." All three gazes rise to mine, faces showing varying degrees of surprise. "I'll go with you."

Killian's eyes narrow. "Like hell you will."

It's hard to meet his eyes, knowing what he did to me last night, but that's exactly what I do. I lift my chin and shrug. "Why not? I'm the one they hurt."

Killian plants his palms on the table, pushing slowly to his feet. "Because this is Royal business. You were just a pawn in a bigger game—a game you don't even understand. The last thing any of us need is for you to cause more problems." There's a flash of warning in his eyes that I pay no mind to.

Yeah, I know all about their fucking games.

I look to Tristian. "I'm not going to cause problems. I can help. I'm not some pathetic little damsel who can't take care of myself. I survived on my own for two years." *I've survived the three of you*, I don't say. "I've been through more than any of you know."

"Like what? Never learning basic fucking gun safety?" Killian snorts. "Because if that's how you learned to take care of yourself, you're going to need a few more lessons."

"Fine!" I snap, feeling my blood heat. "I don't know how to use a gun. But that doesn't mean I can't take care of myself."

It rankles, knowing that he had to save me from Perez and the others. I'd been so grateful at the time that I hadn't thought to really consider how it looked. Like I was just some pitiful little girl who needs her master to protect her.

The part that pisses me off most is that it's true.

Rath pushes his plate aside and shoves out his chair, rounding the table only to stop in front of me. "Killian's right." He reaches out to touch a lock of my shiny hair, gently tucking it over my shoulder. It's probably meant to seem affectionate, but now that I know to search for it, the cool glint in his eyes gives away the lack of sincerity. "It's not your problem. It's ours."

I curl my hand into a fist, barely restraining the impulse to slap him across the face.

"Car in three minutes," Killian says, giving me a dark glance as he and

Rath walk out of the room.

"They have a point," Tristian says, cutting off any more arguments. "The Royals are more than just regular frat boys. It's bigger than that."

"So I've gathered."

He wraps my breakfast in a napkin and looks up at me, eyes sweeping from head to toe. "Well, it seems like you're in one piece, but we didn't talk yesterday. Are you okay?"

"I'm fine."

He approaches and slides a palm up my thigh. "You look sexy today." I manage not to flinch when he dips his hand under my skirt, gently cupping my center in his large palm. "Sore?"

Swallowing, I meet his icy blue eyes, knowing the sincerity there might have nothing to do with me. He probably just wants to know when he can have his turn. "Yes."

His mouth slants unhappily. "We told him to give you a break for a few nights, but you know how he is."

"Yeah," I say, my mouth feeling dry. "I do."

"I know it's been a rough few days, but things will go back to normal."

I laugh. "What's 'normal', Tristian? Not getting kidnapped, or just the regular Lords-inflicted torment? I'm kind of lost on what's 'normal' anymore."

His eyes shutter, hand falling away. "Normal is you remembering your place, Sweet Cherry."

I swallow back the rage I feel for them. As depressing as it is, Tristian is the closest thing I have to an ally right now. I can't afford to tarnish that. Plastering on a rueful grin, I say, "You're right. I'm sorry. I'm taking out my frustration on you. They really scared me the other day, and the thing is? I want to make them pay, Tristian." Looking away, I grimace. "Plus, there's all the stuff with Killian…"

He reaches up to touch my chin, forcing my gaze to his. "I know he didn't leave any visible bruises, but was he too rough? Did something else happen?"

It's almost worse when he's like this, all gentle and worried. As if he cares. As if he didn't take part in the bet or agree on my sleeping in Killian's bed, knowing all the while what would happen.

"It wasn't…rough," I admit, hearing the distant sounds of Killian's truck roaring to life. "But it still hurt."

A wrinkle appears between his eyes as he searches my face, like he's trying to find the truth. He never will. The last thing I'll openly admit is that fucking my stepbrother wasn't the worst thing that's happened to me.

Tristian tilts my head upward and gives me a kiss—sensual and unhurried—his soft lips coaxing against mine. "It'll get better," he says, voice smooth like velvet. Like this, I can almost imagine he cares about me. And then he gives me a smile, adding, "We just need to break you in a little more, that's all."

That effectively shatters the illusion.

The ride to campus is quiet, bad country rock blaring from the satellite radio. I sit in the back, suffocating as I breathe in the same air as these liars. Twice I catch Killian's eye in the rearview mirror. Both times, my eyes dart away. I can't help but think about it now—what his reaction will be when he comes face-to-face with Ted. I wonder if he'll be more angry than scared. I know neither of them will make it painless.

It's the first day I've returned to campus since the kidnapping, and I sense the looks the second I climb out of the truck. Usually, we have a routine wherein Killian will immediately walk off, leaving Rath and Tristian to handle my instructions for the day.

This time, he drags me roughly into his side.

I go stiff against him, nearly tripping in my surprise. Tristian loves kissing me on campus, pushing me up against a wall and staking his claim. Rath is less flashy about it, but he's been known to lead me around with his arm slung around my neck. Unlike the other two, Killian has never made a public display with me.

Never.

Today, he reaches down to cup his wide palm on my ass, leading me toward the campus. Dumbly, I follow, face going hot at the sudden increase of attention. We're flanked by Rath and Tristian, who seem aware but uncaring of the eyes on them, strides loose and purposeful at our sides. The three of them move like a single malevolent entity, dragging me along in their wakes, and the other students part for them, giving the Lords their berth.

"...more than just regular frat boys."

I guess everyone is aware of that much.

Mutely, Killian walks me all the way to the building that houses my classroom, his hand on my ass like a brand with the way it squeezes when we pass a group of rowdy underclassmen boys.

The three of them stop at the steps and the hand clenches almost painfully as Killian jerks me close. I stumble into the solid wall of his body, the bulge in his pants unmistakable.

His fingers fist in my hair, forcing my gaze up to his. Blinking at his intense stare, I know we're on display. Obviously, he wants everyone to know who owns me. He'd be less subtle if he whipped it out and pissed on me. I wonder if Ted has found us yet. I wonder if he's watching this. I wonder how seeing this makes him feel.

"Don't speak to anyone or walk anywhere alone," Killian demands, eyes pinging down to my mouth. "Don't trust anyone, including those Royal bitches."

"I won't."

For a second, I think he might kiss me.

He doesn't.

"Good girl." He gives my ass another little squeeze, looking away to say, "Tris, you're on Story duty. I won't be home until late."

I have to twist my fingers in his shirt to steady myself. I hate myself for needing to ask. "Do you want me in your room again?" He'd given me the order last night mere hours before bed. It'll be better like this, knowing what to expect, being able to anticipate it and prepare myself.

He looks at me, the sharp edge of his jaw going tight. "Eleven. Before that, you can do whatever you want."

Swallowing, I nod. "I'll be there."

He stills for a moment. There's something contemplative about his eyes, even though the hard lines of his face remain unchanged. "One more rule, though." This, he leans down to say into my ear, voice low and cutting. "From now on, you come to bed naked."

My pulse stutters, but I'm getting used to the wash of shame that follows the hot twist in my belly.

He releases me, and it's obvious that they expect me to walk into the building while they wait. I feel their eyes on me as I climb the steps, wondering how long it'll take until Ted makes his move. Until then, I'll have to carve out my own plan.

These three aren't the only ones who can play games.

"I HAD THEM hold the sprouts," Tristian says, sliding the tray in front of me. We're in the dining hall, where I've waited at the table while he ordered our food. "I know you hate them."

"Thank you." I pick up the turkey and avocado sandwich and take a bite. "What did you get?"

Tristian is getting better at knowing what I'll eat—what I like—and I've gotten better at seeing it as one of the scant benefits of my Ladyship. Word has it that the Princes coddle their Princess. Apparently they wait on her hand and foot. They pamper her. They *worship* her.

The Lords will worship nothing but themselves, but this may be as close as any of them get.

Taking a seat next to me, he removes the lid off a container, revealing a bowl of brown mush. "Lentil soup. It's high in protein. I'm trying to bulk." He holds out the spoon. "Want a taste?"

I pull a face. "No thanks. It's all yours."

"How did the morning go?" he asks. "Did you see any Royals?"

"No." But that's not entirely true. "Well, I saw Sutton, but I turned around and went the other direction."

He throws an arm over the back of my seat, scoffing. "You don't need to be afraid of her."

"Oh, I'm not afraid," I reply, my jaw going tight. "I'd actually really enjoy bashing her face in. But Killian said I couldn't approach her, so I guess I have to follow orders." I give Tristian a look that tells him exactly what I think of this.

He smirks, taking a big bite of mush. "He's just being cautious."

I roll my eyes. "I told you, I'm not as stupid and fragile as you guys think I am."

"So you've been saying," he says, giving me a calculating glance. "I'd heard you ran away from the boarding school. Why?"

Why? Well, a letter was waiting for me on my pillow that included a creepy note and current photos from my stalker.

Tell me? Are you still a virgin? I hope that by being at the all-girls school, you're able to stay pure. I want to be the one that claims you. Now that I know where you are, I'll be waiting and watching for my opportunity. I can be patient, for a bit...

I had to get the fuck out of there—*fast*.

"I just didn't fit in," I lie, picking at my crust. "I hated the teachers and the elitist attitude. An all-girls school meant constant drama. I just wanted out of there."

He arches an eyebrow. "Then why didn't you just come home?"

I glare at him. "Gee, I wonder."

His mouth stills mid-chew, like he's remembering. He's apologized for what he did to me that night years ago. Forcing me to my knees. Making me swallow him down. But even though he's said the words, it's hard to believe he's changed in any actual way.

"I was in a bad place…"

No one knows better than me that 'bad places' can pop up at any time. What happens next time Tristian finds himself angry and insecure? I can't let myself forget that even though he's nice now—even though he's caring for me—Tristian is a razor-sharp edge that could cut me whenever the whim strikes him.

"Okay, but we'd graduated by then. Killian was out of the house. We were out here banging sorority pussy." He shrugs. "You could have come home and picked back up where you left off."

That was exactly the problem. Ted would have predicted it. Plus, Killian wasn't the only Payne under that roof who proved to be an issue.

I push the remains of my lunch aside. "I wanted to be on my own."

"You're lying," he says, sounding unimpressed. "Something happened. Something changed." When I give nothing but a vague hum, he changes tack. "What did you even do when you left the school? Where did you live? *How* did you live? You were…what, barely eighteen?"

I think about lying here, too, but I don't see the point. "I went to Colorado. Found an apartment with a couple of roommates. Got a shitty job waitressing at a diner in town." Shifting uncomfortably, I add, "It wasn't pretty, but I made it work."

He leans back, mouth spreading into a devious grin. "A waitress, huh? Did you wear one of those cute little uniforms? Blue? Green? Mustard yellow?" He reaches down to…*adjust* himself. "Please tell me you served hot, delicious pie."

My face screws up in distaste, even though my cheeks heat. "Shut up." After a beat, I wryly add, "Like you'd ever lower yourself to eat something as trashy as diner pie."

"Not in a million years," he says, dragging a hand up my bare thigh. "But if I did, it'd be a nice, hot slice of cherry."

I give him a bland look. "Really? This kind of flirting usually works for you?"

"Oh, Sweet Cherry," he mutters, fingertips tickling my skin, "you have no idea."

It's pointless, anyway. If Tristian wanted me, he could have me. I wouldn't have a choice. I'm at his mercy, always watching for a signal, waiting for the moment he forces me to my knees—to the place that's haunted me for years now—looking up into his cold, emotionless eyes as he ruthlessly takes his pleasure from my mouth. It makes moments like these all the more fraught, as if some part of me will always be waiting to meet that harsh, malicious boy again. Sometimes, I wish he'd just get it over with. Rip off the Band-Aid. Free up some headspace for far greater worries.

Clearing my throat, I say, "Then the girls you go after really must be dumb."

"Your tips were shitty, weren't they?" His lips quirk into a smirk. "I bet they were. You've got a pretty bad attitude."

"I'll have you know my tips were excellent."

"Hm, maybe." He squeezes my leg. "You *are* a pretty fast learner, and I know from firsthand experience that your dedication to serving others is…" His eyes sparkle, mouth quirking. "…top notch."

I hate the way my skin tingles from his touch. I'm mad at him—at all of them. They lied and manipulated me with their stupid little game. They got me to do things I never would have. Degrading, exposing, violating things. Yet all it takes is a little flirting and a gentle touch and I'm caught like a fly in a web. It's stupid and reckless. I didn't make it this far just to be the fly.

I want to be the spider.

"I'm a survivor, Tristian. That's all. I get up every day and try to make it to the next. I work, study, *serve*. I do what I need to, even if I'm not always proud of it." I peer across the room at a table of Royals. They're beautiful and poised. Controlled. Tristian follows my gaze, and I don't hide the sharp, steely thing that must harden my features. "I had to do things to make it on my own—primarily, not letting assholes get in my way."

"Sounds like you were handling it." He lets his hand slip away, reaching for his drink. "Why come back at all?" Despite the question, he sounds more surly than curious.

Shrugging, I say, "I wanted to take my life back," and it's not a complete lie. "Then Daniel offered me a chance at a college education, and it seemed stupid to pass up the opportunity."

Tristian looks at me for a long moment, his features so sharp and painfully beautiful that I pick up my sandwich again just to give me something else to focus on. "You're right," he says, voice decisive.

"About what?" I ask around a mouthful of turkey.

"You are a survivor," he answers, something firm and resolute coming over his features. "And if you want to get back at those bastards, you should get your shot."

Pausing, I wonder, "What about the guys? They both said no."

"Eh," he says, draping his arm around the chair. "They don't know you like I do. We'll start small. Baby-steps."

"What?" I stare at him wide-eyed, refusing to acknowledge the part about him knowing me best. "You mean it?"

"Yeah."

"When?" A flicker of adrenaline licks up my spine and I clutch onto it for dear life.

He looks away, forehead creased in thought. "Tonight. After dark."

He digs back into his soup, and suddenly I find my appetite has returned. Sitting around the Lords' house, playing the victim, waiting on Ted's next move, is going to drive me insane. This is real. It's action. I have no doubt there will be consequences for what Tristian is proposing, but I'm tired of looking weak. I'm tired of *feeling* weak.

It's time the Royals of Forsyth learn I'm not completely pathetic.

Especially my Lords.

"THIS IS YOUR car?"

There's a shiny black Porsche idling at the curb in front of the brownstone. Tristian is behind the wheel, looking sexier than ever as he pops the door open and steps out.

"Yep." He rounds the front, stopping at the passenger door. "Got it when I graduated. I keep it at my parents' place, because the parking on campus is so shit-tier, but occasionally I take her out to play."

I run my hand down the sloping, sleek exterior. It's a glorious piece of machinery, no doubt. It's clearly been impeccably kept. Carefully maintained. This is something Tristian values. "How many horses is it?"

He raises an eyebrow at the question. "Six-forty."

Damn. I'm so focused on the car that I don't take in Tristian's clothing until I'm a foot away. He's dressed in a tight, long-sleeved black shirt that's stretching over his broad chest, and black jeans and boots. He grabs a black stocking cap and covers his fair hair with it, and for a moment, I'm at a loss for words.

Tristian always looks like such a golden boy around campus. No one knows better than me that it's a lie. His blond hair and blue eyes, the charming grin, all his swagger and chilly politeness—these are all a predator's bait.

But *this*? The dark shirt that outlines his lean, toned muscles. The frost in his eyes. The sharp lines of his jaw and the way he moves, economically and controlled.

This is the hook.

"I see you found something to wear." Propping an arm against the roof of the car, he hems me in, one fingertip tracing the collar of my shirt. He hums in thought. "Remind me to have you dress as Cat Woman for Halloween. You look sexy as fuck dressed like this."

I fight down a shiver, at least grateful that I'd managed not to completely embarrass myself. I'm wearing a mixture of Lords' purchased clothing and my own. The black ripped jeans are mine, along with the scuffed, worn combat boots. But the shirt is from the closet—Rath's choice, most likely—tight enough to fit like a second skin. Tristian pulls a matching cap out of his pocket and tugs it over my head, gently tucking my hair underneath. After giving me a once-over, he steps back and opens the passenger side door, sweeping a hand out.

I enter the car with far less reservation than I should, inhaling the scent of expensive leather and Tristian's cologne, waiting for him to settle behind the wheel before asking, "Don't you think this is all a little overkill?"

"Oh, sweetheart." He cranks the engine, giving it a couple revs as he smirks at me. "I always know just the right amount of kill." A chill runs down my spine at the cold, predatory flash in his eyes.

His hand grips the gearshift, and then he punches the gas, peeling out. Music fills the car, but it's not that country shit Killian plays. It's something dark and rhythmic, the bass squirming its way into the pit of my chest. Butterflies flutter in my stomach.

"So when are you going to tell me your plan?"

"First, we need to pick up a few things," he says, getting on the highway and driving away from campus. Forsyth University is in town, but not *downtown*. "Basic supplies that can't be traced back to either of us."

He slams on the brakes and mutters, "Fucker," at a car in the lane next to us as we're merging off the road. The Porsche hums beneath us, smooth and with the barest vibration.

"She drives like a dream," I say, running my hand over the dash. "You ever take her out on the road? Push her to her limits?"

"You're one of *those* girls, huh?" His mouth quirks into a grin and he shifts gears. "My dad has a place out in the country. All back roads. Maybe I'll take you sometime."

He passes through the touristy part of town, with its quaint restaurants, specialty stores, and boutiques, to the side of town where the streets grow uneven and narrow, the buildings a mix of industrial and low-income housing. We pass a group of kids on the corner, and then a homeless encampment tucked under a bridge. In the middle of all this is a massive house—more of a mansion, really. It sits behind low walls and a gate, warm lights glowing like a beacon in the windows.

"What the hell is that?" I ask, peering out as we cross.

He looks over and chuckles. "GussyZ built that monstrosity for his mother. It was in foreclosure for a while but, but now it's," he tosses me an expression I can't decipher, "a private business."

Snorting, I joke, "You keep up with the South Side real estate market?"

He shrugs. "A little. We have diversified interests, but at the end of the day, we *are* Lords." Giving me a grin, he elaborates, "Territory, little Cherry."

It feels foolish to be down here in a car this flashy, but Tristian obviously knows where he's going, zipping quickly down the streets until he makes a sharp turn into a dark warehouse parking lot.

"We came *here* for supplies?" I ask once we're out of the car.

He turns on the car alarm with a sharp *beep.* "Yes." He takes my hand like it's nothing unusual, tugging me toward the building.

I glance between his strong, shifting shoulder and the warehouse. "What is this place?"

"Storage, mostly," he replies. He approaches a door and deftly enters a password into a keypad lock. Seems a little upscale for the shitty surroundings, if you ask me. I know the Lords are involved in some kind of South Side 'business'. Is this where it takes place?

The inside of the warehouse is dark when we enter, but Tristian reaches out knowingly, easily finding a switch. When the harsh flash of dim fluorescents blinks to life, I find we're not in the larger building, but instead a smaller, square room.

Quietly, he orders, "Wait out here."

I stand nervously as he turns away, striding into the room, and I can't help but peer into the doorway. The room smells musty with oil and dampness. I watch as Tristian heads straight to a tall shelf against the wall, picking mechanically through supplies. Whatever this place is, it seems like he knows it well, not having to rummage much. As I follow his sure movements, the nearest shelf catches my eye. It's stacked with identical little boxes, tidy and painstakingly organized, almost like something you'd see in a store. This doesn't seem like mere supplies. It looks like a stockpile. I don't need to go too far into the room to make out the large numbers and letters on the boxes.

It's ammunition.

I jerk back, spine rigid as I watch Tristian heft a bag over his shoulder.

"I think I've got what we need," he says. He's carrying a gas can and a bottle of lighter fluid. God only knows what's in the bag.

I eye the gasoline as we walk back out, feeling antsy and uncertain. I know Killian has a gun, of course. I've held it in my hand, have touched the cool metal and the heavy weight of it. But I just figured it was a macho power-trip thing.

I shiver at the sound of the door locking behind us. "You're going to burn down their house?"

Tristian turns to me, arching an eyebrow. "Who's overkilling now?" Shaking his head, he clicks the key fob, making the car chirp. "As much as I'd love to burn the Counts' house down, I think this calls for something a little more subtle and a little less 'attempted murder charge'." The trunk opens, revealing a large plastic tub. He places the gas can and bottles inside. "I think just his car will do."

The flicker of a memory, more like a rumor, makes me pause. senior year after Genevieve cheated on Tristian—a few days after he…

Well. The laundry room.

There was a fire down at the marina, and I heard the boys at school joking about it. They'd called Tristian a 'firebug'. I left town a few days later, but now we're here, and I have to ask, "You're serious about this?"

"As a heart attack." Slamming the trunk, he turns to me, face melting into an indecipherable silhouette of a sharp jawline. His head tilts as he watches me. "Is this too much for you? Because you told me you could handle it."

"I can." I frown down at the closed trunk, remembering that shelf of bullets. "It's just…"

His fingers are warm on my jaw, his broad palm cupping my cool cheek. "Sweetheart, they hurt you." His thumb moves against my skin, right in the place I was bruised. "They took you from us. They tied you up. They wanted to…" I see, feel, and hear the harsh exhale he releases at the idea of Perez raping me. "They wanted to damage what belongs to us. I'm a Lord, Story." He tips down to press his lips to mine, chaste and gentle. "I'm *your* Lord. That means I have to make them pay. But if you'd rather me drop you back home first—"

"No," I say, cutting him off. A ball of heat burns in my chest. It's wrong, and I know it's stupid, because these men don't see me as a person. They see me as an object, as something that's important only because they own it. Much like Tristian's Porsche, I'm a possession he means to have impeccably kept, carefully maintained. It's dehumanizing. But the Lords are also the only people who have ever fought for me.

And Tristian is the first who's allowed me to fight for myself.

Taking a deep breath, I say, "Let's do this."

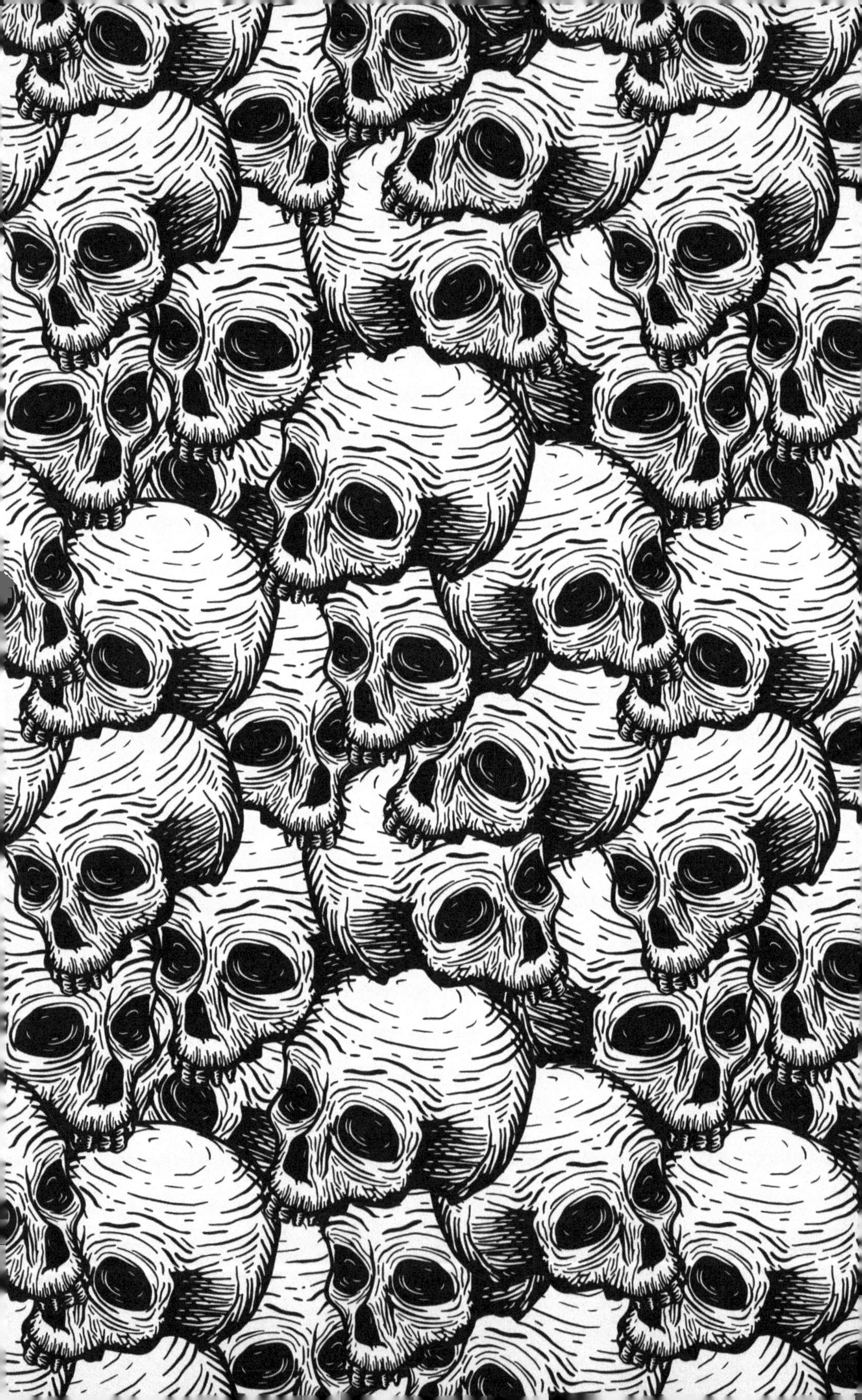

4

PLAYING WITH FIRE

TRISTIAN PULLS THE Porsche into a dark parking lot. I recognize it immediately when I look across the street and see the bar I went to with Killian a while back. It was inadvertently the cause for so much of this mess, my spilling the secret of my virginity to Sutton—the Countess—over what had seemed like a private, comforting moment.

It seems a little too on the nose, and for a time, I worry he's pulling a prank on me.

Or worse.

"See that red G-Wagen over there?" He points to a boxy-looking Mercedes SUV across the way. "That shit is getting lit."

I blink at the vehicle parked in the lot's corner, at a diagonal angle. It takes up two spots. "Aren't those super expensive?"

He reaches across me, forearm flexing beneath his sleeve as he opens the glove compartment and pulls out two pairs of black gloves. He hands me one. "Starting price? A hundred-and-fifty grand. But knowing Perez, it's probably fully loaded. He just got it last week."

Perez is the Count who kidnapped me, tied me to a bed in some rundown house, and then threatened to rape me. Even almost a week later, I'm still afflicted by the memory of his hands on me. Anger churns in my chest as I look at his obnoxious car, simmering with the injustice that guys like him get away with it, every damn time.

"And you want to set it on fire?" I ask, remembering the last time I'd vandalized someone's car. That time had been Perez, too. Rath had slashed three of the tires on his sports car, and then saved the last for me. I guess this is what happens when a guy like Perez gets his tires slashed. He just buys something new.

Disgusting.

Tristian's laugh is low and tinged with darkness. "Oh, no, sweetheart." Leaning over, he noses into my neck, planting a sucking kiss into the skin there. "*We're* going to set it on fire."

When he pulls back, he reaches for the edge of his stocking cap and rolls it down, revealing a full ski mask. My heart hammers at the way he looks here, nothing but the blue of his eyes giving away the reality of the man beneath the mask and dark clothes.

Heart hammering, I remain still as he moves to do the same to mine, tugging it carefully down my head.

This is real. We're really doing this.

"Last chance to back out," he says, hand resting on the door handle.

But I shake my head, adjusting the mask. "No. I want that fucker to pay."

There's a spark of something malicious and delighted in his eyes. "That's my Lady," he says, chucking me gently on the chin.

It's dark in the parking lot, illuminated only briefly by the soft, interior light of his opened trunk. Tristian grabs the gasoline but hands me the lighter fluid, snatching a box of matches before closing it all up. We wait a moment in the dark, taking in the energy of the surrounding air. The music coming from the bar is muffled and muted, but still somehow settles frantically in my bones. Two cars pass by, and then Tristian jerks his head, not sparing me a look as he strides toward our target. I follow him across the street, ducking behind an old minivan and crouching when he does, steadied by the weight of the touch he reaches back to pat my thigh with.

Voices echo off the pavement, coming closer to the car than I'm comfortable with. If we get caught back here, dressed as we are, holding gasoline and accelerant? We're definitely fucked. The footsteps sound ridiculously loud—close. Tristian grabs my hand and raises his eyebrow, giving me a chance to back out.

Again, I shake my head.

My knees ache and my feet start to cramp, but finally the footsteps fade, and then disappear altogether. We wait another full minute before Tristian stands and scans the lot. "It's clear," he says, pulling me off the ground.

His motions are fluid and purposeful, not unlike a cat, as he strolls to the SUV. He unscrews the gas can along the way, only glancing back once to ensure I'm following. With smooth, almost mindless movements, he circles the car, leaving a splashing trail behind him. The air fills with the heavy scent of gasoline, thick and suffocating. Tristian makes this look effortless, as if it's something he's even done before. For a moment, I get this weird, inexplicable flash of pride. I know it's just another way they've got my hindbrain all twisted up with their mind games, but the thought strikes me that the Lords are better than the Counts. It's deranged and oddly possessive, but so strong that I shiver.

I might be theirs, but in some deep, fundamental way, they also feel like mine.

Mine to know.

Mine to injure.

Mine to beat.

Inspiration tickles at the back of my brain, and without thinking, I climb on the bumper and shuck off my glove. Carefully, I douse it with the accelerant and then look at the hood, pristine and shiny. I take some time to trace out the design, but I have a good reference strapped right to my wrist. I don't stop when Tristian places a hand on my hip.

"What are you doing?" he asks.

"You'll see."

As soon as I lift the glove, his hands are on my waist, powerful arms lowering me gently to the ground. Wordlessly, he pulls me out of the range of gasoline on the pavement. "Ready?" he asks, pulling out his matches.

I give a nod, heart hammering as I get my matches out, too. "Yes."

On the count of three we strike them across the strip of sulfur. The flames spark to life, flickering hectically when we toss them to the ground. His lands on the circle around the base of the car, but mine goes straight for the hood.

I watch, transfixed as the flame zips around the design I created.

Tristian tilts his head, adjusting his grip on the empty gas can. "Is that a…"

"Sure is."

It's the outline of a skull, crude but still visible. It's bizarre, my sudden affinity for the symbol that's shackled me. The flame flickers higher and higher, casting the lot in a shadowy glow, until the skull is all but consumed by a wall of it.

"Beautiful, isn't it?" he breathes, eyes reflecting the fire. He watches it for another long beat, but I grab his hand and pull him away.

"Someone will come," I explain, and it seems to snap him out of it.

We run across the lot, crouching behind cars and scanning the distance for eyes and ears. Luckily, there are none. Tristian throws his trunk open, carelessly tossing the cans in before shucking off his gloves and mask. I follow suit, but can't deny the adrenaline rippling between us. When he shoves me roughly against the car, the bulge of his erection pressing into my lower belly, I don't fight. His hand sweeps behind my neck, and then he yanks me forward, crashing our mouths together.

Tristian's private kisses are always a little different from his public ones. He enjoys being watched—that much I know—and he does his best to give people a show. But when we're alone like this, he's always a little greedier. That's how I know it's for him.

This kiss is just as greedy, but it's all the more *searing*.

He licks into the seam of my mouth like he physically couldn't take no for an answer. His breaths are hard and quick, and when he surges into me, grinding the hardness of his erection into my hip, all I feel is a liquid-hot spike of need that makes my knees tremble.

When he releases me, it's only to wedge a hand between my thighs and gruffly ask, "Still sore?" I wouldn't need the words to know he wants to fuck. The wild, unhinged look in his eyes is enough to broadcast it.

Breathlessly, I lie, "Yes."

His jaw goes tight and sharp. "Too bad," he says, letting his hand fall away.

I lick my lips and nervously offer, "I can drive if you want. I'm pretty good under pressure."

His hair is ruffled from the ski mask, messy in a way I'm not used to seeing on him. The playful look he gives me makes the knot of anxiety in my chest unwind. "Let someone else drive my baby? Not a chance." He closes the trunk, stalking to the driver's side and opening the door. "Let's get the fuck out of here before the fire trucks come."

Tristian starts the car, not with a rumble but the soft purr of a well-built machine. My body thrums—from the sensation of him against me, from the insanity of starting the fire, from the knowledge that he wants so badly to fuck me—but mostly from the satisfaction of watching Perez's car engulfed in flames.

People start pouring out of the bar, crowding around to see the fire. Tristian pulls the Porsche out of the parking lot just as Perez is running toward the G-Wagen. The look of apoplectic horror on his face is priceless.

"Fucking asshole," I mutter. "Should've lit *him* on fire."

Tristian's chest bounces with a laugh. "Oh, we're not done with him yet, sweetheart." He shoots me a crooked grin. "But yeah, that was fucking satisfying."

I can still see the bulge in his pants.

We pass two fire trucks and Tristian's eyes keep darting in the rearview mirror to make sure no one is following us. I'm still jittery with nerves and adrenaline, something I've missed since returning to Forsyth and agreeing to be molded into the perfect Lady. Tristian punches the gas, but I'd give anything for him to go faster—to heighten the energy bubbling under my skin, to prolong this sense of *being alive*.

I don't think I'm ready to fuck any of them—not willingly. Tristian could make me, just like Killian did. He could pull over somewhere, and I know just how it'd go. He'd look stony and impatient, could give me some line about this just being a part of the job I agreed to. He could take me into his lap and rip my pants off, spread me wide and force his way inside. Perhaps he'd look like Killian had that night he took my virginity, tense and powerful as he fucked into the cradle of my thighs. It wouldn't even be bad for me. I'd hate it, but I'd like it all the same.

I shift restlessly in my seat.

"You okay?" he asks, eyes flicking over.

But Tristian isn't going to do that. He's going to wait until I'm whole. I might be a possession to him, but Tristian isn't careless about his things. Just like this car, he prefers me shiny and without flaw. Impeccably kept.

He might want me to do other things, though.

"Yeah. It's the adrenaline." I reach out and run my fingers over his neck, bolstered by the quick, surprised look he shoots me. "Thank you for letting me come along."

His knuckles go white around the gearshift. "Feel better?"

"I shouldn't," I say, keeping with the act, "but I really do. Those guys are the worst." We're coming up on the highway and I tug at the hair on his neck. "Take the back road back to the house."

His eyebrow quirks. "What for?"

"Take the back road," I repeat. "Since you've been really good to me the last few days and let me tag along, I thought maybe I could...express my appreciation."

One of these days, Tristian is going to make me get on my knees for him again. He's going to want me to swallow him down. He won't even be mean about it. He'll probably be doing me a favor by asking me to pleasure him with my mouth instead of taking me the way he wants. The way they *all* want.

His hand grips the gearshift, and at the last minute, he swerves off the highway ramp and back down to the access road.

"How exactly do you plan on showing your appreciation, Sweet Cherry?" His voice has dropped an octave, but I can hear the pleased anticipation in it, can see the way he shifts restlessly.

I lean over and lick a hot path up his neck, the tip of my tongue sliding over the tightness in his jaw when he hums appreciatively. I slide my hand down his chest, over his hard abs. He inhales sharply, but I keep going, moving my hand down between his legs. I squeeze the rock hard bulge in his pants, wondering, "Did setting that car on fire turn you on?"

"Fuck," he breathes, head falling back against the seat. "Maybe watching you strike that match did." I massage his cock, feeling it grow harder under my hand. "Cherry, I'm going to blow my wad if you keep doing that."

I breathe against his neck. "That's sort of the point."

There's a pause before he lifts his hand from the gearshift, placing it over mine. He pushes it into his hardness. "Yeah? You going to jerk me off?"

"No."

I watch as his eyebrows climb higher. "I thought you were sore."

"I am." I thumb at the button on his pants and lower the zipper, whispering, "But my mouth is fine."

Tristian's chest dips with a long exhale, expression collapsing. "Fuck, don't tease me."

I reach into his pants, fingertips hesitant until I touch the hot, velvety length of him. But there's not enough room to wrap my palm around it. "I'm going to need you to lift up."

"How about I pull over?" he asks, voice low and rushed. "We're far enough from the bar."

I wouldn't be able to do it if I had to look into his eyes. If I had to remember that night in the laundry room. If I had to do what he told me. "Tristian Mercer," I say, running a finger up his shaft. "Of all people, I'd think you would be into road head."

A slow grin spreads across his mouth, both of his hands clenched around the steering wheel. It's a challenge not to ask how many points that might be worth, me going down on him in the car. Eighty points? A hundred? Bitterly, I wonder if he'll brag about it later over whiskey and a laptop, admiring his new score.

Still, I say, "Let me thank you properly, my Lord." We're in the desolate outskirts of town between the South Side and the University. He takes his foot off the gas for a minute and lifts his hips. I shimmy his pants down and his cock bounces free, hard and angrily flushed at the tip.

I've started to reconcile the two sides of the Lords. They're cruel and manipulative, but I'm not blind to how dangerously hot they all are. They might think they've taught me subservience and deference, but mostly they've taught me I enjoy pushing my sexual boundaries. I like the sense of control it gives me to know just how much they want me. Perhaps I always have—even back in that laundry room. The dampness between my legs is evidence enough.

That doesn't mean Tristian deserves to get his cock sucked while he drives down the road. But right now, I'm playing a game just as much as he is. He'll get points. I'll build equity. One day I'll burn them all down, just like Perez's prized car.

"Just don't kill us, okay?"

He licks his lips. "I'll do my best."

I lick my palm and wrap it around his base, gliding up and down. He shudders, but other than the slight buck of his hips, remains still and composed. The second I duck down, his hand rests on the back of my neck, thumb massaging into the muscle.

The tip of his cock is salty and warm on my tongue, and the second my lips close around it, Tristian releases a rough groan, sliding his palm to the back of my head. Gently, he pushes me down. I don't fight. I know just who I'm dealing with.

I take him in and he releases a loud breath, his palm letting up the pressure in exchange for what can only be described as petting. "So good," he mutters, voice husky. When I pull back, only to plunge back down, he breathlessly asks, "Did Rath teach you that? Or did I?"

My only response is a low hum that makes his thighs tense and release. I get the sense he'd be fucking up into my mouth if he didn't need to keep his foot on the gas.

He gives a ragged chuckle. "Who knew you'd go from that shy little virgin to such an eager little cocksucker, hm?"

I don't let his words faze me, teasing and taunting, licking down the side of his shaft before taking him in again. His hips thrust upward, and then his hand presses down, and down, and *down*, until the tip of his cock is pushing into the back of my throat. I make an alarmed sound, unable to breathe.

"Sh," he soothes, pressing his fingertips into my scalp. "You can take it. You know I wouldn't hurt you."

Squirming, I try to relax, even though my eyes are filling with tears at the way I'm choking. But true to his word, he lets me up before it can get too much. I gulp in a frantic breath, chest burning, and try to suck my saliva away.

"See? You're such a good girl for me," he gasps, petting me again. "Unbutton your pants," he orders. I do as he wants, nervous but pleased at how he's responding to me. The car vibrates smoothly underneath us, and he removes his hand to shift gears. "Touch your pussy, sweetheart. Show me how wet you are."

I'm already warm between my legs and I push my hand down the front of my pants, feeling the slick heat of my inner folds. When my fingers brush against my clit, I release a whimper, and Tristian groans while his foot slips off the gas. I have to pull off his dick to smirk at how flustered he is, but that only annoys him, and he growls, slamming his foot down to accelerate.

I feel the weight of his hand on my head again, but this time I'm prepared, sucking in a big breath before he pushes me down and chokes me on his cock. It wasn't like this with Rath. Rath likes it slow and deep, and I've learned that he needs a rhythm. But when Tristian shoves me down onto his dick, he trembles, his thick length jumping with a surge of pre-cum that tastes salty on my tongue when he finally lets up. Tristian likes it like *this*, me coming up wildly gasping for air. He lets me bob up and down his shaft long enough to catch my breath, and then he does it again, holding me down as his fingers fist in my hair.

I push a finger in my pussy and move in the same rhythm, grinding against the heel of my palm every time he plunges me down. His cock thickens and expands, his breaths turning erratic and gritty. His foot slips off the accelerator again, this time for a long, extended moment.

His voice comes out reedy and rushed. "You ready for my come, sweetheart?" I try to nod, but it's hard with so much of him in my mouth, pushed into my throat. His foot slams down and the car lurches forward at the same time his release rips through him. Warm come floods my throat. He groans, fingers pulling at my hair, and I struggle to swallow without choking on it. My vision sparkles at the edges, but before I can panic, he yanks me up, the last of his release painting my tongue.

My mind grows fuzzy, forgetting where we are and what we're doing. It must be a lack of oxygen, the way warmth spreads through my body and across my limbs. I buck against the heel of my hand, cresting the wave of my orgasm.

"Show me," he says, practically buzzing with the satisfaction of his release. "I want to taste you, Sweet Cherry. Show me how much you liked it."

I take a moment to gather my bearings enough to understand what he's asking for. Pulling back, I remove my hand from my panties and sniffle away the tears, showing him my glistening fingers. Not sparing me a single glance, he takes them into his mouth, hooded eyes trained on the road as he tastes my release.

He hums, tongue looping elegantly around my fingers, and then lets them fall free, sucked clean. "Good girl." He says it like I'm a dog—like I'm his *bitch*—but when he finally looks at me, he reaches up to cup my cheek, thumbing away the wetness of my tears. When he kisses me, pushing the taste into my mouth, I feel as sweet as my release.

And as bitter as his.

5

ICE CREAM

Being a Lady is starting to really suit her.

That's what I'm thinking about as we sneak into the house. It's taken some time, and sure, it hasn't been all daisies and sunshine, but Story just set a car on fire and then sucked my brains out through my dick at seventy miles per hour.

We're not like the other houses. Most have a clear preference for what their girls should be, but there have been a lot of opinions over the years as to what a Lady is. Submissive and deferent like the Countess? Delicate and sweet like the Princess? Dark and mysterious, like the Baroness? Every LDZ iteration has had their own flavor. Charlene, last year's Lady, was cold, slutty, and painfully agreeable. Not our type at all. Even though Killian would swear up and down he's more of a Countess type, I know better. Killian Payne would probably prefer a Princess. Someone soft and cute who bruises easily. Rath would be all about a Baroness vibe. A girl he can hole up with to suffer alongside him.

But me?

My perfect Lady is loyal, above all else.

"Wait," I say, pulling her to a stop. We're in the first floor hallway of the brownstone. I point to her chin. "You've got a little something right here."

"Oh." She reaches for her face, but I get there first, bending over and licking the melted ice cream away.

Obviously, road head deserves a treat. Something to get the flavor of my spunk out of her hot, skilled mouth. She picked peanut butter and chocolate. I got blue raspberry. Now I've got the hint of chocolate on my tongue. It's almost as sweet as her slick fingers had tasted.

She ducks her head, cheeks heating, which makes my mouth curve into a grin. Weird of her to get bashful now, considering she had my cock crammed down her throat thirty minutes ago. She takes a bite out of her cone, crunching it as we pass the den, and I get a flash of awareness that Killian would cream his pants at the sight of her like this, all sweet and shy and reluctantly pleased.

"Where the fuck have you been?!"

Well, speak of the devil...

Story jerks to a stop, eyes flying wide at the fury in her stepbrother's voice. I don't miss the way her hand trembles around her cone. I narrow my gaze at the tell, but keep composed despite Killian's obvious rage. I was prepared for this.

"We were out," I say, holding up my cone. "Just getting some ice cream."

"You? Eat ice cream?" Rath gives me a cold, blank look. "If there's one thing we've learned from your fucking annoying nutrition rants, it's that dairy is bad for the digestive track and sugar is a cancer on society."

Shrugging, I toss my cone into the bin by the door. "Well, tonight was a first. For a few things." I turn to Story and wink. "Wasn't it, Lady?"

She stands a foot behind me, eyes darting anxiously between the guys. I want to tell her it's okay, that I wouldn't let either of them punish her for this. But in the room's light, I can see soot smudged across her forehead. We'd gone directly against Killian's order, and she knows there will be a consequence.

I take her hand, dragging her into the curve of my body. "Don't worry, sweetheart. I've got this."

"Lady," Killian says, going all scathingly formal, "go upstairs. Now."

She flinches at his tone, but I hold on to her, tossing him an exasperated look. When I lean in to lick at the crease of her plush, cold lips, it's mostly just to show all three of them that Killian isn't the boss here. If I want to taste her, I will. If I want to reach down and give her tight, plump ass a squeeze, no one will stop me. If I want to hold her chin and thumb at her mouth, then that's what I'll do.

She stares at me, unblinking, as I push my thumb between her lips. It takes her a moment, but she closes her mouth around it, eyes dropping as her red cheeks cave with a hesitant suck.

My dick twitches. "Good girl." She looks up at me through her lashes, so quick and demure that it could have been tailored for Killian himself. That's the irony of it all, that Story unfolds so sweetly at the one thing Killian would never bring himself to give her; a simple word of praise.

I can tell she knows it's not just about this specific moment. It's been a good night, having her at my side, so eager and willing. I let my thumb slip from her mouth, dragging her lip as I retreat. "You can go."

Killian watches her exit the room, his eyes narrowed into angry slits as they fix on her ass. "What the fuck did you do, Tristian?"

I walk over to the armchair and sit, spreading out. "I told you. I took our Lady out for a treat." I raise my eyebrows. "Seemed like she deserved a break after the last few days, if you know what I mean."

"That's strange," Killian says, teeth clenched, "because I just got a text about a car going up in flames at the bar."

"Which bar?"

"Don't fucking try me," he growls. "The only bar we go to."

"Oh. A fire, huh?" I ask, badly feigning interest. "Well, I guess that's not a surprise. It's a shitty part of town."

Killian glares at me. "It was Perez's brand new G-Wagen."

"Really?" I snort back a laugh. "Ouch. I have to say, it couldn't have happened to a better prick."

"Jesus Christ, Tristian," Rath says, lurching up from his seat. "This is fucking serious." He shoves his phone in my face, the screen showing a photo of the charred remains of Perez's SUV.

"Poor bastard," I sigh, head shaking. "That was a sweet ride."

Rath stares at me, clearly not buying my bullshit. "Care to tell me what you see on the hood of the car?"

I pretend to peer at the photo as though I didn't see it light up like a bonfire in person. But there's no fire in the photo, only the aftermath. Something about it is hard to miss, though. The red paint is completely gone off the hood, but what remains is pretty defined. Story's skull. *Our* skull. God, watching her light that match and toss it on without a care in the world?

Sexiest thing I've ever seen.

And that includes the sight of her choking on my dick ten minutes later.

"Looks like someone is trying to set us up," I remark.

There's a sudden crash, Killian having chucked something off the mantle of the fireplace. "Don't fucking play us, Mercer! You reek of smoke and gasoline. As if we don't know about your hard-on for setting fires?" Killian takes a breath and shoves his fingers through his hair, clearly struggling to compose himself. This guy's short fuse is going to give him an aneurism one of these days. "Goddamn it, Tristian. I'm not surprised you went off half-cocked, but I can't believe you'd risk taking Story with you!"

"Sorry, Killer," I toss back at him, "but I don't know when you decided you're the one who makes all the decisions around here. Was it when Story picked you as her first fuck? Or was it when you realized she wanted you *least*?"

Killian lunges for me and I hop up, coiled to strike back.

Rath jumps between us before it can come to that, holding his arms out to keep us apart. "Guys, chill," he says, trying to deescalate the two of us. "We've got an actual fucking problem here."

Will I fight Killian if I have to? Sure. Do I want him to bruise my pretty face? Not if I can help it. Still, I don't back down.

"Is that what this is about?" Killian asks, eyes calculating a way to get around Rath. "The two of you just can't handle that I'm fucking her, and you're not."

"Maybe one of us could," I volley back, fists curling, "except you fucked her last night, so she never had a chance to heal up."

Killian doesn't look the least bit bothered. "That's my right."

"You're wrong," I argue, jerking my chin toward Rath. "Story belongs to me and Rath, too. Just because you got your dick into her and are making her sleep in your bed every night doesn't change that."

"He has a point," Rath says, turning to level Killer with a stare. "We all agreed we'd give her some time."

"Well, I'm sick of waiting!" he snaps, veins popping in his forearms. "You've been waiting a couple months. I've been waiting for *years*."

"None of this has jack shit to do with getting revenge on the Counts," Rath cuts in, raising his phone. "This is going to come back on us."

"Whatever, it's a skull," I point out flippantly. "So what? Anyone could do that. Perez isn't exactly short on enemies, and neither are we."

Rath's jaw goes tight as he turns to me. "We don't need the heat. This was dumb as hell, Tristian."

"I'll tell you what it is," I say to him, snatching the phone from his hand. I hold it up, showing them the picture. "This is only the first strike. I'm not finished. *We're* not finished. They tried to defile what belongs to us. And yes, I said *us*."

"Just one problem," Rath says, plucking his phone back. "It's not the first strike. It's the second."

Killian's gaze slowly moves to him. "The fuck does that mean?"

He takes in a hard breath, shoving his phone into his pocket. "I had a little run in with Perez a while back." Sniffing, he casually adds, "I got mine."

"Got your *what*?" I ask.

"Slashed his tires." He says it like it's the most obvious thing in the world. "Well, three of them, at least. Story got the fourth."

"Excuse me?" My eyebrows hike up my forehead. "When the hell did that happen? Were you ever going to tell us?"

He tosses back. "Were *you*?"

"Un-fucking-believable." Killian's staring at us with wide, infuriated eyes. "The two of you are just flying off the handle and taking our goddamn Lady with you?" He gives a low, humorless laugh. "I hope that stunt was worth it, because we've been called to the South Side. First thing in the morning. Your little act of rebellion is going to come with a price. So tell me," he raises his chin, "who's going to be the one to pay it? Because it sure as fuck won't be either of you."

It's in that moment that I understand Killian's rage. Payback on Perez was compulsory—he knows that bastard deserves it—but Story wasn't on the South Side's radar.

Not until I brought her with me.

"Killer," I try, "she wanted—no, she *needed* to be a part of this. We were careful."

"No, you weren't." He shakes his head. "And you didn't give a fuck about what she wanted. This was about what you wanted." Tilting his head, he gives me a cold smile. "Did it work? Did she fall on her knees for you?"

Technically, no…

"Fuck this." Rath grabs his leather jacket from the couch and heads for the stairs. "We'll deal with this bullshit tomorrow. Go ahead and rip each other to shreds over some pussy, I don't care."

Neither of us moves until we hear Rath's bedroom door slam shut, two floors above us.

It's me who breaks the silence. "She sucked my dick on the way home." I watch his eyes go hard and shuttered. "I didn't have to make her. I didn't have to ask her. I didn't have to wait for her to be unconscious. She did it because she wanted it, and she had the time of her fucking life. So when you're up there tonight, trying to sneak your dick into her, you remember the reason she's so wet." On my way up the stairs, I call back, "You're welcome."

6

CONSEQUENCES

She's naked.

Whatever I'd been feeling with Tristian before—anger, resentment, concrete resolve—gets snatched up and tossed into oblivion at the sight of her in my bed. It doesn't matter that it happened last night, too. This is still fresh enough that my blood turns to lava just seeing her there, all nestled into my space like a small, vulnerable animal.

For a day that started off fan-fucking-tastic, it quickly devolved, ending up in the shitter.

Story was gone when I woke, the memory of what I'd done to her during the night an ache in my balls. The thought of finally—*finally*—having her the way I wanted, like a rag doll in my hands, fueled me during my morning jerk in the shower. I expected some kind of backlash over breakfast. Tears, yelling, or her crying to one of the guys. But she didn't. She was cold, but that's nothing new to me.

I thought about her all day—about what it was like to be inside of her, to have complete control and dominion over her body. And when I got home and found out that she and Tristian had gone off somewhere…well, that was fine. I'd told her what she did before I got home was her business. And then that photo of Perez's car came through the text. Immediately, I knew it was Tristian. Psychotic fucking firebug. He's been setting them since we were kids. It's probably a miracle he's waited this long.

But looking at her, all of that annoyance melts away.

I've always had a penchant for tidiness. Compulsive, some might say. But nothing ever feels quite right until everything is in its place. I get this annoying, nagging fucking awareness when something is out of sorts. Can't help it—don't want to. Because that moment when things slot together, falling into how they ought to be, is better than sex. It slides down my spine like a warm caress, settling into the center of my bones and twining around the marrow.

That's how I feel right now, seeing Story in my bed.

This is her place.

This is where she belongs.

Why can't anyone else see it?

I think these last couple nights have been the only time that nagging, out-of-sorts awareness has completely left me. When she disappeared all those years ago, I teased apart the tendrils that entwined us, and it seemed easy. Her mom. My dad. Our shared bathroom. My routine of sneaking into her room to watch her. Her locker at school, always plastered on the inside with glittery stickers. Her seat at the dinner table. The laundry room…

I methodically removed her from them, mentally. She was no longer a thing that required a place. She was gone. Null. Empty space and silence. It seemed easy.

Now, I realize it never actually worked. Now, she's in my bed, curled around my pillow, and I'm getting that settled-marrow feeling so acutely that it makes my hands tremble. Now, she's mine, and it doesn't matter that she doesn't want me back.

Now, I've won.

I stalk silently toward my prize, watching how the glow from the window falls over her bare skin like a blanket. She's such a fucking tease, too. Didn't even get under the sheets. Didn't even bother to cover herself, just wanted me to walk in and see that she followed my orders. She probably did it spitefully—bitterly—imagining that she was throwing it in my face.

Instead, it just looks obedient and alluring. A shiver of anticipation zings through my balls, but I take my time with this, walking around the bed, soaking in the sight of her. Last night, I'd been impatient and greedy, slotting right up against her ass and taking my fill. Tonight, I reach out and run a single fingertip up the smooth line of her leg. So much better than last night, with that ridiculous lingerie Tristian had picked out for her.

I wouldn't mind sharing her with them if I thought they really appreciated her. But they're both so goddamn intent on dressing her up like a little slut. They want to erase her softness and sweetness, and replace it with red lips and lace and artificial bullshit. Girls like that are a dime a dozen. It's like buying a premium steak, and then cooking it well-done and squirting ketchup on it.

So wasteful.

She sighs in her sleep, nuzzling into the pillow, but doesn't wake as my finger ascends her thigh, her hip, the dip of her waist, the tender side of her heavy, full tit. I linger there for only a moment, watching the gooseflesh spread over her skin, and then I undress.

She's not in my bed willingly. I know that. I want her uneven and grappling for a sense of control. The fact she talked Tristian into taking her with him to burn that car proves the power she has over men, even the Lords. She's always been like that. With the sugar daddies. With my father. She gets under people's skin. She makes them want her. She makes us want to *hurt* her.

My dick's been halfway to hard all day, my mind constantly returning to this place. How limp she'd been. That little crease between her eyes as I fucked her. The sleep-twitch of her fingers as I pinched her nipples.

Fuck.

I could do this every night for the rest of my life, and it still wouldn't be enough.

She's nice and pliant when I touch her shoulder, easing her onto her back. I never had the guts to do this back then, too afraid she'd wake to bother with stuff like posing her, opening her up for me.

Tonight, I wedge a hand between her knees and gently pry them apart. They fall open for me easily, and she barely stirs when I spread them wider, bending her knees to give me room as I climb on the bed between them.

Her skin is as ethereally pale as always, but all the best parts of her are a fervent, rosy pink. Her perky nipples. Her pretty little pussy. Her full lips. Her adorable, sweet cheeks. It's a struggle to choose which one I want to indulge in first.

Bracing over her, I choose her lips, parted in slumber. I trace them with my tongue, feeling the warm wash of her breath as she breathes evenly. I keep my kisses shallow and slow, ghosting a palm over her side, cupping the weight of her breast in my hand. Last night, she came with Rath's name on her lips.

Tonight, it'll be mine.

"You know who you belong to," I whisper into her ear, gently thumbing her nipple. "Say it."

She breathes in and out, and says nothing.

"That's fine," I tell her. "I've got all night."

I sweep my hand down to her belly, her muscles twitching as I drag lower, simultaneously eager to discover how slick she is and dreading the knowledge that it'll be for Tristian.

When I dip between her legs, fingers sliding through her folds, I pause, shuddering.

Jesus Christ, she's fucking soaked.

I press my mouth into the cave above her collarbone and exhale jaggedly, pushing a finger inside her pussy. So subtly that someone else might have missed it, her walls clench around me.

"You're not sore, are you?" My finger pumps in and out. "You were just saving it for me. Tell me." Dragging her earlobe through my teeth, I demand,

"Say my name."

Nothing.

She lays so still when she sleeps. Even when I'm knuckle deep inside her. Even when I'm rubbing my thumb into her swollen clit. Even when my lips are pulling at hers, soft and sucking and *taking*. Story lays perfectly motionless.

Even when I push my cock into her tight cunt.

I have to stop for a second to catch my breath, buried halfway inside of that wet, perfect heat. She hasn't gotten much looser. There's no way the stretch isn't hurting her.

Her only response is the shallow wrinkle in her brow.

I drag my hips away just to plunge deeper, and just like the other times, I get this white-hot moment of utter chaos inside my brain. It's the part of me that wants to fucking rip her apart. It wants to dig my fingers into her flesh and mark her with my bruises. It wants to fuck her hard and brutal, make her bleed with how badly I need to claim her. It wants to take her apart, piece by piece, until it can be covered with her.

And then it wants to put her back together again.

So, so carefully.

I know this is the part of me that scares her. Fuck, this shit scares me, too. There's nothing worse than not being in control, guided like some mindless slave by the wild, thrashing thing that wants to hurt and stroke and own. It's the reason she can never want me—love me—accept me. If she knew how many times I shoved it down, curled my fists and let her go, then maybe she could forgive me for the times I couldn't.

But probably not.

That's how I fuck her, like a man on the edge of breaking free, holding on so tightly that it's physical ache not to give in to it. Her body barely jostles with how carefully I fuck her. This is probably how she thinks she wants it. Slow and sweet and cautious. Tristian and Rath wouldn't fuck her like this. Rath would go hard and relentless until she was shaking and begging. Tristian would probably wrap his fingers around her neck until her face went blue. I'm the only one who can do this, holding my mouth to hers as my dick glides in and out of her.

When I push down, as deep as I can go, she finally makes a noise. More of a breath, really. She digs her head back into the pillow and gasps, and I know she's about to say it. I can tell from the pucker in her brow, the way her thighs flex around mine, the jump in her throat, that she's going to speak.

"Say it," I demand, dragging my dick in and out. "Say my name."

There's a stuttered breath, her fingers curling, and then a low, sleepy whimper. "Tristian."

I freeze, my pulse kicking up as I watch his name fall from her lips. My vision goes red, and suddenly that wild, thrashing thing is breaking through, reaching up to grab her jaw and wrench it toward me. "Wake the fuck up!"

Her eyes fly open and then she's *looking at me*, and goddamn it, this isn't what I wanted. Why can't anything ever go the way I fucking want? I squeeze, fingers digging into her jaw, and then slam my dick into her, watching her teeth clench in a hissed breath.

"Why," I growl, fucking into her, "do you have to be such a fucking bitch?"

Her brows crouch low, eyes flashing with a malice that I doubt she's even capable of. "Fuck you," she growls back, clamping onto my biceps, nails digging hard into the muscle.

My balls pull up tight, but I stave it off, ratcheting up the power of my thrusts until my headboard is slamming against the wall. With every sharp 'bang', that divot between her eyes gets a little sharper, a little deeper, until her face screws up, eyes sliding shut.

"Open your eyes!" I snap. "I want you to see who's fucking you."

The second she does, I regret asking. The anger and hatred are probably still there, buried under the surface, but eclipsing it is something nervous and pinched.

I'm hurting her.

I freeze, panting through gnashing teeth as I look down into her pained grimace. She came in here wet, open, and ready. Probably wouldn't have even taken much to push her over the edge. Now, she's all coiled up and closed off, pushing me away.

"Goddamn it!" I jerk away, dick slipping out of her, and the second I've got one foot on the floor, her knees are snapping shut. I take a moment to drive this pissed off, violent thing away, because it wants to keep fucking her like that. It wants to tell her this is her fault. If she would have just been thinking of me one fucking time, I could have kept it under lock and key. I could have fucked her gently, could have made it good for her.

She's looking at me now. I can sense the weight of it on my neck as I tug at my hair, jaw clicking with the grind of my teeth. I take a long breath, trying to work the tension from my shoulders. This is what I get for waking her up. Hard as nails and nowhere to put my dick.

When I look back at her, she's watching me warily, slowly dragging the blanket over her.

Fuck that.

I shove the blanket away and return between her legs, wrenching her thighs apart. She makes a startled sound, muscles seizing, but I shoot her a look.

"Just fucking relax."

She doesn't, digging her heels into the mattress.

It doesn't stop me from bending down and licking a hot stripe up her slit. She goes rigid beneath the hands I've got planted on each thigh, prying her open for me. But it doesn't last long. As soon as my tongue reaches her clit, the tendons under my palms go pliant and slack. I look up to watch her, blinking wide-eyed at the ceiling as I lick her cunt. I can tell she's fisting the sheets, can feel her toes curling against my side, can see her chest rise and fall on a greedy inhale.

I spend a few minutes there, working her back to where she'd been before. I wonder what she'd say if she knew she's one of only two girls I've ever done this for. The first was merely an experiment to see if I'd like it. I didn't, so I never did it again. Not until the night I took Story's cherry.

It takes a while, but eventually she begins moving with my tongue, her hips twitching beneath me, seeking, restless. Despite not having liked it with that other girl, I find myself hungry for it from Story, grabbing her ass and tipping her up to me, moving down to slide my tongue into her pussy. She tastes like flesh and girl and something vaguely metallic, and when I let loose a satisfied rumble, she makes the sweetest little sound.

"Oh my god," she gasps, letting go of the sheets just to fist those fingers into my hair instead, and *yes*. Fuck yes. This was what I wanted. Her writhing beneath me, nose scrunched up in pleasure, lip trapped between her teeth as she whimpers and holds my mouth to her. It's better than her being asleep, this mindlessness, driven by her own cunt, not even caring who it is, so long as I keep making it good like this.

It's not long before her thighs are shaking, mouth gaping open with her soft cries, hips bucking into my tongue. She's wide open now, legs splayed without needing to be pushed apart, and I know when she's going to come because her shoulders start curling, fingers tearing at my hair hard enough to sting.

I can feel it fluttering through her, right on the pointed tip of my tongue. Every muscle in her body clenches tight, and her chest hitches with a gasp.

It's released in a short, sobbing exhale. "*Killian.*"

I lurch up, grabbing my dick and thrusting it inside. Her walls are still clenching with her release, the delicate body beneath mine shuddering as I force my dick into it. It takes everything I have to keep it shallow and quick, but she's so wet again—wet for *me*—that it barely takes a dozen pumps before I'm stiffening, coating her insides with long, shuddering surges of my come.

When I open my eyes, she's staring up at me, forehead glistening with a fine sheen of sweat. There's a dazed sort of softness in her eyes, like she's wondering how she got here.

I roll away before she remembers.

Slinging my arm over my eyes, I catch my breath and try to avoid her presence beside me. There's a fan going on the other side of the room, and for a long time, that's all I hear.

I don't realize I'm halfway to dozing until her voice rips me away from it.

"Why do you do those things to me when I'm sleeping?" Her voice is contemplative, made up of equal parts confusion and disgust.

Why?

Because it's hot as hell. Because it's the only time I've ever felt in control with her. Because it's the only time she won't say no to me. Because it means she's not looking at me with that cold, distant hatred in her eyes.

I don't lift the arm from my eyes. "Because I fucking want to." The room falls silent again, but I can practically hear her dissatisfaction with the answer. It goes on long enough that she probably expects nothing more. Hand clenching into a fist, I add, "It's the only time I can do that without hurting you."

It's not an explanation.

It's a warning.

There's a long beat of silence, and then I can hear a gentle shift—her head turning. "Why?"

This time, I don't answer, letting the air cool my overheated skin. It's only then that I realize the sound of a muffled piano is creeping down through the ceiling. Rath. There's no chance the two of them couldn't hear that headboard banging against the wall. They're probably pissy about it. Fuck if I care, seeing as how I have to haul it down to South Side tomorrow to clean up their messes.

"Can I...go now?" Story shifts, rolling like she could be out of the bed in the space of a heartbeat.

"No."

She pauses. I don't need to see her to know she's covering her bare chest. "Aren't you done?"

Finally, I lift my arm from my eyes, snapping "Go to sleep!"

She flinches back into her spot, face creased with a frown. "Can I at least go take a shower?" *Take a shower.* That means she wants to wash away everything I just put into her body.

"No."

She inhales briskly, clearly annoyed. "It's...*on my thighs*. It's going to get all dry and flaky and gross." She's talking in this sharp, nasty tone that makes my temples throb.

Fuck's sake, can't a guy enjoy a little goddamn afterglow?

Biting back a snarl, I jump out of the bed, stomping to the door and wrenching it open. I slam it behind me, knowing that I don't need to tell her to stay put. I walk to the bathroom, stark naked and far too tense for a guy who just had a really nice nut. Wetting a rag, I run it over my own junk first, glaring at my reflection in the mirror. Just had to wake her up, didn't I? Couldn't have simply enjoyed the moment with her limp body. Now I have to *handle* her.

She's sitting up when I return, the blanket clutched to her chest, wincing as I barge through the door. I pause at the uncertainty in her eyes, the way her shoulders are drawn high and tense.

Shuttering my features, I walk to the bed, telling her, "Lay back and spread your legs."

Something in her expression collapses at the order, but she does as she's told, slowly lowering herself to her back, throat bobbing with a swallow as she lets her knees fall apart. Clearly, she doesn't want it. Doesn't like me there. Doesn't want to be touched. Doesn't want my eyes on her.

This, I want to say. *This is why I do it when you're asleep.*

Instead, I crawl between her legs and push them apart, fixing my eyes to her pussy. It looks red and well-used, and my dick gives a feeble twitch at the sight of my spunk dripping out of her. God, how long did I dream of this? Those long nights watching her in high school, standing over her bed, lurking in a corner, feeling her lips against the head of my dick…

And now she's so full of me, she's dripping.

As if in a trance, I reach down to where it's leaking out, gathering my release up with the sweep of a fingertip and pushing it back inside. She goes tense, her thighs closing, but I keep my finger there, halfway into her cunt.

I stare into her nervous, alarmed eyes, and the confession is pulled out of me like an exorcism—surly and stilted. "I wasn't trying to hurt you."

She blinks at me, lips pressing into an unhappy line. "Since when?"

My face hardens, because she has no fucking idea—no goddamn clue—how much I *don't* hurt her. But I'm plugging her up with my finger to keep my come inside her cunt, and I don't think that knowledge would be welcome at this juncture.

I go through the motions of cleaning her, running the rag over the inside of her thighs, gentle as I work it over her red, inflamed center. She's stiff but obedient, fixing her eyes to the ceiling as I scrub her clean of us. Story's got really delicate skin, so smooth and soft-looking. I like her best when she's freshly showered, sweet-smelling and new, free of the others' touches and grime. But this is almost better, knowing that she's full with me, carrying me around inside her, all night and all day.

Just then, her stomach releases a loud, demanding rumble.

Her hand flies to her belly, cheeks blossoming pink. "Um..."

My eyes narrow and I grow even more pissed at her little adventure with Tristian. She must have really worked him over if he took her out for ice cream and little else. This is supposed to be his job, worrying about how much she eats and how clean she is. And here I am washing her.

Here I am, pulling on my boxers and leaving the warm comfort of my bed to go downstairs and find something to feed her.

Jesus Christ.

There isn't anything prepared—Ms. Crane doesn't exactly plan for late night post-sex snacking—so I make her a sloppy peanut butter and jelly sandwich, fuming with every slather of the knife. This isn't what I do. I'm supposed to find her in my bed, use her like my own personal toy, and then fall asleep, tired, fucked-out, and happy.

Instead, I'm stomping up the stairs with a plate in one hand and a glass of milk in the other.

What kind of fucking twisted Prince-flavored bullshit is this?

She's gnawing on her thumbnail when I storm back through the door, using my foot to slam it behind me. Just like before, she jumps at the sound, drawing her knees to her chest. I don't pause this time, but it still annoys me. I've never hurt her before.

Except that one time.

Well, those two times.

Whatever, those were special circumstances. This is just me being put out and too tired to care about keeping a cool exterior. She can fucking deal with it.

I set the plate and glass down beside her on the end table, biting out, "You tell Tristian about this and he'll put you on some dumb fucking cleanse."

She stares at the sandwich with this loose, dumbfounded expression, but doesn't say a word as I go to my desk, opening the laptop there. I try to ignore her as she picks it up, but I don't miss the sniff or the way she glances at me, suspicious and unsure.

I answer a couple emails as she eats, shifting uncomfortably at the thought of crumbs in my bed. That's when I see the new addition to the spreadsheet. It's useless. The Lords' game is over. Story's virginity is gone. The only points that matter anymore are the ones between houses.

But Tristian has entered 'Blowjob' with a variant of 'Road Head', giving himself a solid hundred points. My lip curls at the number, knowing that he's only entered it in to provoke me. It doesn't work. In fact, it's just proof that I'm the winner here. He hasn't fucked her yet. I'm the only man who has. Glancing up, I watch her tear a piece from the sandwich before placing it in her mouth, looking unsettled but relaxed.

For now, she's mine and mine alone.

I wait for her to finish, gulping down the rest of the milk, before closing the laptop. She looks less twitchy than before as I lumber to the bed, settling back into my place. I wedge my arm behind my head and try to sink into the exhaustion of the day, avoiding thoughts about tomorrow. Forsyth, The Lords, South Side...everything is a game here. I'm good at playing them, but sometimes I wish I didn't have to juggle so many.

There's a dip of the mattress before our skin meets, a cool cheek pressing into my shoulder. It startles me, my muscles tensing at the sudden invasion, but for some reason I can't do anything but lie there as Story nestles into my side. My eyes fly open, gaping at the top of her head as she settles against me, a knee dragging over my thigh, her soft tits pressing into my ribs.

"Thank you," she whispers, resting her hand on my chest.

I stare at her hand, at the raggedly bitten thumbnail, at the wrist cuff that marks her as our property, at the way her fingers curl against my skin.

And my tongue won't work.

It's stuck to the roof of my mouth, melded in some impossible fucking way, because in no universe would Story be *cuddling me* right now.

I get this instant, lightning-fast swarm of thought. Maybe Tristian was right all along. Maybe Prince tactics work. Maybe all it takes is the smallest act of kindness, even made in spite, and she'll latch onto it with a death grip. Maybe we've broken her. Maybe she's dumber than I thought.

Maybe she could be mine.

Slowly, reluctantly, I slide my hand from behind my head and ease it around her, daring to skate my fingertips across her bare back. It's a wary, testing movement, more about me than her. Is this even something I want? Do I want to feel her, warm and sleepy against my side as we sleep? Do I like it? Is it good?

Well.

It's not *bad*.

Quietly, she asks, "You wouldn't let anybody hurt me, would you?"

"What?" There's this pebble of wonder at the question, but it's overtaken by the way she feels, curled all small and vulnerable into my body.

"If someone wanted to hurt me," she clarifies, "you'd protect me?"

Baffled and lost, I turn my gaze away from her smooth body and shiny hair. "I did before, didn't I?"

There's a stretch of quiet, and at some point she begins tracing the tattoo on my chest, hand barely moving with the scorching circuits. "But if someone did. If they hurt me. You would..." She trails off, voice floating away on a thin exhale.

Pressing my palm to her back, I inhale the scent of her hair. Softly, I answer, "I'd fucking kill them."

She nuzzles her cheek into my shoulder. "Okay."

Okay.

It gives me an uneasy feeling, like I've just signed a contract I don't know the terms to. It's just so hard to care when she's falling asleep against me, not flinching away at my touch.

7

RESTITUTIONS

KILLIAN SNORES. I hear it all night under my ear as his chest rises and falls. I didn't realize he'd be so easy. All it took was some pretend sleeping, whispered names, a show of weakness, a little vulnerability, and some sweetly offered gratitude.

He fell asleep smelling my hair and skating his fingers up my spine.

I sleep in fits and bursts, unwilling to move from my spot against him. It's the first time I've been touched like that—satisfied like that—and felt no remorse or shame. Killian didn't trick me. I tricked *him*. I manipulated him into pleasuring me, and my stepbrother may be a monster, but he's good at burying his face between my legs and bringing me off. My bones still feel mushy and full of phantom tingles.

Idly, I hope I can make him do it again.

Soon.

I leave just before dawn, not because I want to, but because it's what he'll be expecting. Truthfully, I could play with him a little more, see if I can get him to do that thing with his tongue again. But it wouldn't do to put it on too thick.

I finally get my shower, standing under the steam, and it's different from yesterday morning. I don't feel like I'm reclaiming my body. It was never anything but mine. It's a thrill so intense that my hand wanders down, wet and slick, to the place between my thighs. I exhale into the steam as I push against my clit, replacing the memory of Killian's tongue with my own touch.

I freeze when I realize what I'm doing.

I think I might be horny.

Not because some creep is forcing me to be, but just because it feels good. I wait for the rush of humiliation and shame, but all I feel is the thrum of my heartbeat, eager and waiting.

Still, rules are rules.

That's what I tell myself as I duck out of the shower, reaching for my phone. But this has nothing to do with obedience. I open up the group chat and type out my request.

Lady: *Good morning, Lords.*

Lady: *I need permission.*

I was up earlier than them, so I have to wait a few minutes to get any response. I spend it choosing my outfit for the day, almost regretting that I'd destroyed all those cute dresses Killian had chosen for me. It would have been the perfect play, dressing for him after what happened last night. That may be too much…

I dress for Tristian again, instead.

Finally, my phone dings with a response.

Lord Tristian: *Permission for what?*

Lady: *I'd like to…enjoy myself.*

Lord Tristian: *Are you asking if you can get yourself off?*

Lady: *Yes. Please.*

Lord Tristian: *Can I watch?*

Lord Dimitri: *denyed.*

I stare down at Rath's badly misspelled message, anger swelling hot in my chest. He's still mad that I chose Killian over him. If I plan to get my revenge, then I'm going to need to smooth that over. The idea of bowing and scraping to him makes my stomach roil, though. It's harder with him than it is with the others. Tristian has a cruel streak that I don't want to see myself on the wrong side of, but in his own strange, twisted way, he cares for me—even if it's just as a prized possession. Keeping Killian close was always going to be a tall task, but the more I do it, the less terrifying it feels.

But Rath was the first to break a little piece of my heart.

Since I won't be getting off any time soon—and I'm not stupid enough to believe they wouldn't know if I did—I check my old email out of habit. I've been refreshing the inbox for the last three days, waiting for a response from Ted. I'd sent that picture hoping to provoke him. I'd cuddled up to Killian last night to make sure he'd still be a viable defense against him. I've made a dozen small, yet monumental moves to position the four of them at each other like cruise missiles. It's a dangerous game, a decision made impulsively, but there's no backing out of it now.

My blood still turns to ice when I see the email in my inbox.

I drop like a sack of rocks to the foot of my bed, and the spots at the edge of my vision are the only thing that alerts me to the fact I'm holding my breath. I let it out in a choppy exhale, thumb trembling as I open the email.

Did you think I'd be surprised, Sweet Cherry? I'm not. Of course you're a whore. You could have been cherished, but you'd rather be used like a cheap hole. I saw it in you all those years ago. Always flaunting yourself around, giving your body away to all those old men, making eyes at the younger men. Foolishly, I thought I could sway you to reason. Now I know the truth. You're no better than the other trash.

Such a waste. You really were such a sweet, pretty thing. Now you're just another slut looking for your next deposit. You want to know what I plan to do about it? Very well.

I take my restitutions in flesh.

TED

I read it over three times, the reality of it all becoming too real. This isn't some intangible strategy that's been brewing in my mind. This is playing with something hotter than fire, sharper than a blade. For a brief moment, I'm overtaken by a wave of pure, bone-numbing terror.

It doesn't last long.

This was always the way it was meant to be. Killian, Tristian, Rath, Ted… they all deserve whatever fate awaits them. If I can keep playing the game, then there's a chance I can win. And if I lose?

It's better than rolling over and just accepting defeat.

THE GUYS, ALL of them, are gone when I get downstairs. It's mostly a relief, since I'm still off balance from receiving the email, and I've completely lost the thread of action regarding Killian. How should I act around him? Should I sit in his lap? Should I give him a kiss? Somehow, I doubt either would be welcome or subtle enough to go under the radar.

"They're off handling Lords business this morning," is what Martin tells me as I take my place at the table. Whatever the rush may have been, it didn't stop Tristian from making sure I get a nutritional breakfast.

"Here," Ms. Crane says, dropping a plate of something white, green, and gross looking in front of me. "Don't ask me what the brown slop is. Ignorance is bliss." Watching me, she says, "Well? Down the hatch, missy! I'm not about to hear that fucker's bellyaching when he finds out his precious little fucktoy didn't get her minerals and vitamins."

"Any chance there's a Pop-tart in the kitchen?" I ask, pulling a face at the bland egg white omelet. I pick at it with my fork, revealing spinach and some kind of fake meat substance. That must be the slop. "Even a toaster waffle? A bowl of cereal?"

"This is what I was told to serve you," she says.

"And you always do what you're told?" I ask, genuinely curious. "That doesn't really seem like you." The more I think about it, the more I wonder about the dynamic. Ms. Crane doesn't have a problem back-talking them, and they don't have a problem taking it. Yet, she still follows their orders.

She gives me a smile that's more derisive than anything. "Having ourselves a little rebellious streak, are we? How cute."

Shrugging, I offer, "Maybe it's not rebellion. Maybe it's just about integrity."

"Integrity?" She barks a rough laugh. "God, spare me from another pretty fucktoy crying about her integrity. Want to know where integrity will get you? Nowhere, doing jack shit. People in the gutter have *integrity*. I'll take a roof over my head and a safe place to sleep, any day. Survival means sacrifice. You should know that better than anyone at this point, little girl."

She's probably right.

I pick up my fork and stab it into the gummy eggs. The menu is only half the problem. Ms. Crane isn't a very good cook, so the eggs are overcooked, the spinach is a wilted gray, and the brown slop is not remotely identifiable. I'm about to take the first bite when the fork is yanked from my hand.

"Just forget it." She jerks her head, her wrinkled lips all pursed into a scowl. "Follow me, little fucktoy."

She moves quickly, and I jump from my chair, rushing after her into the kitchen. She dumps the plate into the sink and enters the pantry. The Lords' pantry isn't a standard small closet lined with shelves of food. It's an entire room with enough food to feed an army barrack. It's not surprising. She feeds three ravenous men, plus the rest of the frat several times a week. She might not be a good cook, but she still has to do a lot of it.

Ms. Crane stops at a shelf holding industrial sized packages of basics like salt, sugar, and flour. She reaches behind a container of rice and flips a small lever. A moment later the door swings open, revealing a second room.

"What's this?" I ask, following her in. The room is cozy, with a comfortable-looking chair and a nice TV mounted above a desk. Bookcases line the wall. There's a small, separate kitchenette, and doors throughout—perhaps a bedroom and bathroom. She walks over to one cabinet and pulls out a cheerfully colored box of cereal.

"Milk is in the fridge," she grunts, grabbing me a bowl and spoon. I open her refrigerator and pull out the carton, marveling at the living quarters. She nods at everything set up on the counter. "Go on, fix yourself a bowl." Lower, in a grumbling tone, she adds, "Getting fucking soft."

I do as I'm told. "Do you live here?" I ask, pouring a generous bowl of the sugary cereal, then covering it with milk. The first bite is a burst of precious, sweet, unhealthy heaven.

She nods at another door. "Through there."

Shoveling more cereal into my mouth, I muse, "I didn't know this house had secret rooms and stuff."

Her eyebrow arches. "There's a lot about this house you don't know."

She's right again, although I learn more every day. Like the cameras and the locks that don't actually work. I chew my cereal slowly, savoring the sugary mix. "Is there anything else I should know about? You know, to help be a better Lady to my Lords?"

She shrieks an abrupt laugh. "Don't bother putting that act on for me, girl. I'm not a dick-brained frat boy." Shaking her head, she pulls a pack of cigarettes from her cardigan, tapping them on the small table. "They're men. Men are simple. All they want is a nice pair of legs to spread and a mouth that opens for something other than yammering. They want nice tits and a tight, slippery stroke to their egos. Be a pretty little fucktoy for them. They'll eat that shit up with a spoon."

"I wish you wouldn't call me that," I say, putting my bowl down. The title is quickly destroying my appetite.

She mockingly puts a hand to her chest. "Do you want me to dress it up,

Lady?"

"No," I argue, stomach sinking at the meanness. "I just like to think I exist for something other than…*that*."

"Not to them, you don't." She plucks a cigarette from the pack, pinching it between her two forefingers. She uses it to point at me. "You take the parts of yourself you like—the parts you want to keep for yourself—and you lock them away when those dogs are around. You become their little fucktoy, and you get good at it."

"That sounds so…" I grimace, pushing my cereal around in my bowl. "Awful."

"You know what your problem is?" she asks, sitting in a chair. "You think it's bad. You look down on it because you're stuck-up. You think you're better than the other fucktoys. This is all very beneath you, isn't it?"

"I don't think—"

She cuts me off. "Of course you do. You're not stupid, are you?" The arch of her eyebrow is shrewd. "Truth is, I say it with affection. Probably the highest compliment I can lower myself to give. The most power you'll ever have over a man is when you're on your knees for him. Get his dick hard and you've got him in the palm of your hand. That's what I was meaning before about using that thing between your legs." She points her cigarette toward my crotch, sniffing. "You got that young pussy. Might as well put it to use while it's still fresh and interesting. Quality cunt's got a shelf-life, believe you me."

I gape at her, my face blooming with warmth. "You're kind of crass, you know that?"

"I don't need you to tell me I'm crass, little fucktoy. I know." She looks at me, eyes full of something that could only be called softness on her, and I possibly see it now. The affection in it. The compliment. Holding my gaze, she admits, "I know a lot about what goes on around here."

Swallowing thickly, I'm startled by the awareness in her eyes. "Like what?"

"I change the sheets, girl." She gives me a dark smile, uncaring of the way my face pales. "I collect their dirty laundry, and then I wash it. You can take that as literally as you please."

In that heartbeat, I realize the truth of it. She does know everything. Every sordid detail. She knows about the game they played for my virginity and what Killian does to me at night. She knows about Rath's manipulations and Tristian's control. But she must also realize I'm a survivor, just like she is.

"Oh."

She flicks a hand dismissively. "Nothing shocks me anymore. He tear you up? God knows he's been riding you every night since."

Stuttering, I answer, "I-I'm fine."

She clicks her tongue. "Young pussy might be resilient, but I'm still seeing some blood on those sheets. Don't bullshit me."

"Look, no offense," I tell her, shifting uncomfortably, "but this is kind of… private."

She rolls her eyes. "You think I want the gory details about that meathead fucking you raw? I might have a bit of a soft spot for him, but I could do without it." Sniffing, she picks up a lighter. "Like we've already established, I do what I'm told."

I realize then that she's been ordered to ask me about this. By whom— Tristian, Killian, or Rath? From the brashness of her gaze, I doubt the question would be answered. "It's a little rough," I confess, throat dry. "But I think…I think it's getting better."

"Finally learning how to tame your stallion, eh?" She cackles a laugh. "Good for you. Better give that thing a rest for a night, though. And if it gets— hey! Look at me, girl." Her voice is firm, brooking no argument. She waits until I meet her gaze to say, "If it gets *too* rough, you come down here and tell me, you hear?"

Face flaming, I mutter out a quick, "Yes, ma'am."

She opens a drawer and pulls out a small plastic container filled with white powder, pushing it next to my bowl. "Run yourself a warm bath—*warm*, not hot. Add this to the water and let it dissolve. I'll help with the swelling and any tearing."

I nod. "Thank you."

"Eat," she says, never lighting the cigarette, "and don't tell that big blond prick I gave you something out of a box. I'll never hear the end of it."

"Yes, ma'am." I scoop the last few spoonfuls into my mouth, eager to leave. "Thank you."

I CLEAN UP and grab my school bag, searching the house for Martin. I've never gone to school alone and after already disobeying Tristian's food orders for the day, I don't want to make any missteps.

I find him in the library, talking to a guy I recognize as a LDZ member. He's also one of Killian's teammates, and I take a moment to remember his name; Marcus. They're standing by a white board mounted to the wall. It's organized into a grid with names in one column and stars in the others. Each name has a different number of stars—some have none, some have a couple, and others have a dozen. A number is totaled at the bottom.

"Last night," Marcus is saying to Martin, his mouth spread into a grin. "It should be worth a solid ten points."

Points.

An unsettling churn builds in my stomach. The Lords accrued points to determine who won my virginity. All of their points were earned by manipulating me—getting me to do things, sexual acts, favors, kindnesses. I had no idea it was going on until after I had sex with Killian. That's when I saw the spreadsheet on his computer. I stare at the whiteboard, unable to avoid the memory of that night. The betrayal and shame. The knowledge that I'd been duped.

This chart is similar, but different. Bigger. Is there a larger game going on?

Am I still part of it?

Unnerved, I turn to leave the room, bumping into an end table in my haste. A plaque topples over and clatters loudly against the wood.

Fuck.

"Ah, Lady," Martin says. "I was hoping you'd find us." I turn, knowing the surprise must be registering on my face. He wanted me in here? "Marcus will escort you to campus today since the Lords are unavailable."

Marcus waves, and I give him a tight smile. "Great. Thank you."

"Are you ready?" he asks, lifting his backpack off the ground.

"Yes, whenever you are."

I take one last look at the board, trying to get a better sense of what game they're playing, but it doesn't have any specifics—just a lot of code. I shouldn't be surprised. The Lords aren't dumb enough to leave valuable information out in the open. At the same time, it doesn't exactly seem like they're keeping a secret.

Marcus drives a truck like Killian, and as I sit in the front seat I build up the courage to ask, "What was that board for in the library?"

He glances over, fast and wide-eyed. Anxious. Could be from being near me, the Lord's prized Lady, or from the question. "Oh, that? Just a frat thing."

"It looked like a points system." I keep my voice even. "Is it a game?"

"Yeah, kind of." Marcus is a handsome junior who's almost as physically intimidating as Killian. Unlike my stepbrother, however, he has a soft face and kind eyes. "You know how the different Royal frats have a rivalry, right?"

Scowling out the window, I mutter, "Intimately."

"Well, every year the frats compete against one another," he explains, not seeming bothered by the explanation. His anxiety must be about me. "Points are given for different things."

"Like sleeping with girls?" I ask, feeling sick. "Virgins?"

He cuts me a glance, forehead creasing. "Uh, there's a tally for that, sure. But it's small fries in the grander scheme."

Strange. That spreadsheet I saw didn't seem like small fries at all. He could be lying. I doubt he'd want to be the one who informs me just how much of a little fucktoy I am. Curious, I wonder, "Then what do you do to earn points?"

"The Lords haven't told you about all this?" he asks, looking more confused than anything.

"There's been a lot to take in," I say, smiling bitterly.

Shrugging, his words come out casually. "Some stuff is just tradition. Stealing something from a rival's house. Sabotaging a Baron ceremony. Winning the annual boxing match against the Dukes. Sneaking a girl into the Prince's masquerade party. Every frat has their thing."

I blink at him, completely lost. "Their thing?"

"You know, like how the Lords have territory. The Barons have their freaky, dark shit. The fighting Dukes. The Princes and their—" He gives me a sharp glance, lamely finishing, "Prince…stuff."

There's something he's not telling me.

There's *a lot* he's not telling me.

Narrowing my eyes, I ask. "What's the prize?"

"Internally?" He looks nervous again. "The top three winners get to be the reigning Lords, live in the house, and keep a Lady."

"And externally?"

"Well, duh," he says, laughing. "The people leading the winning frat get to be the Kings."

"The Kings of *what*?" I worry at first he won't answer, what with all the anxious fidgeting, but oddly, this answer comes easier than any of the others.

He pulls onto campus, tossing me a smirk. "Everything."

8

POSTURES

EVEN IF I didn't have my earbuds in, I wouldn't have to worry about talking to the guys on the way to the South Side. The cab of the truck is silent. Killian is still pissed at Tristian for disobeying him and putting Story at risk. Tristian is holding a grudge that Killian's been nailing her every night. I'm pissed at both of them. Tristian for getting us called down to the South Side *and* Killian for using Story as his personal fuck every night.

That's not how this is supposed to work.

Killian parks the truck in front of the late 70s-era renovated office building. It's beige with brown trim, and the first floor is windowless. There are no signs identifying what kind of business operates inside. Daniel bought it for his real estate headquarters, which works out nicely, as it's tucked up right on the edge of South Side. Presentable enough for clients and investors while still being close enough to the heart of his territory that he gets to monitor things.

"No one mentions Story, do you understand?" Killian says when we arrive. He turns to glare at me over his seat. "Not a single fucking word."

Tristian impatiently replies, "We should just tell him what they did. If anyone would understand the importance of keeping what's ours, it'd be him."

"He does need us to win," I point out. "He'll still be mad, but he'd get it."

"What do you think is going to piss him off more?" Killian's jaw goes sharp and tense. "Retaliation, or the fact we let them get a hold of our Lady in the first place?" He looks between us, even though the question is rhetorical. We all know the answer to that. He jabs a finger toward the building. "You're both so fucking concerned about her? Fine. She's off-limits in there. Otherwise, we're dragging her into a clusterfuck that she couldn't even begin to comprehend."

Despite the tension between us, no one disagrees. Daniel has to know by now that Story is our Lady. After the football game and dinner with Killian and Story, there's no way his dad missed the bracelet. Knowing Killer, he probably agreed to dinner that night to show her off to him, stake his claim, make it known. The pissing contest these two have had over her is legendary.

We take the elevator up to the top floor, silent and tense. Killian looks like he'd rather be shoving needles into his balls than attending this meeting, which is probably fair. I almost feel bad for him. *Almost.* I'm sure getting massively laid for the last three nights in a row is dulling some of the sting. Hopefully Ms. Crane can suss out how bad it is. I'd pulled her aside before we left and asked her to see to Story's...condition.

Whatever the fuck that may be.

Eventually the doors slide open to a lobby.

Vivienne, Daniel's secretary, looks up when we walk in. "Oh, if it isn't our strapping boys!" She pushes her hair blonde hair back over her shoulder. "I heard you were coming in."

"Viv," Killian greets, giving her a tight nod. "Can you tell him we're here?"

"Sure thing." She picks up the phone and speaks softly. Once she hangs up, she says, "Can I get you some coffee?" She looks at Tristian. "Tea?"

"No, thank you," Tristian says, walking over to her desk and propping himself on the edge. She's sitting in her chair, giving him a perfect view of her tits. They were naturally big, but that wasn't enough for Daniel. He told us one night over cigars that he paid ten grand for those babies. Five for each side. "You're a vision today, Miss Viv. Love that necklace."

Her hand flutters to the chain around her neck, the pendant nestled obscenely in her cleavage. "Aw, thank you! It was a gift."

She doesn't have to say who it was from.

Vivienne was one of twenty applicants Daniel interviewed when he opened the office. He wanted someone local. Someone who understood the South Side and would be loyal to his interests. Loyal to *him*. Vivienne was young back then, having just graduated from high school. Daniel showed us the video of her interview before we did our own with the prospective Ladies. Imparting wisdom, he called it—as if we needed it. Now, being that she's his right hand, she's basically the queen of this whole scene, and I can't look at her mouth without getting hard.

The phone buzzes on her desk and she picks it up, listening for only a moment before telling us, "He's ready. Go on in."

Daniel is sitting behind his massive desk when we enter the room. Framed black and white photographs depicting the South Side decorate one wall, and a series of flat screens occupy the other. A massive window fills the wall behind his desk, overlooking his territory—*our* territory. On a shelf is an award made of crystal, announcing him as Civic Leader for the prior year. Daniel grew up three blocks away in a housing project owned by the city. He was raised on the streets and watched his friends either go to jail or die young and hungry. He didn't want that. He got an education. He clawed his way out, ruthless as ever. Then he came back to take care of the people left behind. Despite the antagonistic relationship between him and Killian, he's determined for his son to have a vested interest in the community. There was never any other option for Daniel's son. Killian was born to be a Lord. To own. To have. To keep.

"Gentlemen," he says, in a deceptively professional tone. "Thank you for coming down so early."

Killian drops in the chair across from the desk. With his wide sprawl and inked arms, he's a stark contrast to his father's formal demeanor and crisp suit. Tristian and I both greet Daniel, but neither of us sits. The power play between

Killian and his father is unique and twisted. We learned a long time ago not to get in the middle of it.

Until high school, Killer had been more than happy to follow in his father's footsteps. If Story had never come into the picture, I'm betting things would be different. Killian might have been a preppy little business major, just like Tristian. Instead, he's chasing NFL dreams and LDZ glory. It'd probably make any other dad disgustingly proud, and to his credit, Daniel plays the part. He always attends the home games. Donates handsomely during fundraisers. Hangs his jerseys and displays his championship victories. But the four of us know better. Football was a statement, which is kind of hilarious to think about. Most kids rebel by fucking up their lives, not becoming NFL hopefuls on track to stardom. Classic Payne energy.

Despite his shows of support, all his father wants for him is *this*.

Killian Payne, Lord of South Side.

I think he'd rather let it topple than do it on Daniel's terms.

"I'm not sure we had much of a choice," he says to his father.

Seeing the two of them across from one another brings back the memory of the first time they got physical with one another. Killian was fourteen and had gotten into his dad's coke stash. Daniel revealed a side of himself I didn't know he had until then. He's always so calm and methodical, downright Machiavellian, but there's a simmering rage buried underneath that cool exterior that no one wants to see.

Killian inherited the rage, but not so much the ability to hide it.

Daniel regards his son with a flicker of annoyance. "Your choices evaporated when I got a call from the chief about that fire last night."

"Yeah," Killian says, stretching his long legs out. "You sent the picture. I'm not sure what this has to do with us."

It's a ballsy move, playing it off. There's no chance Daniel doesn't know it was Tristian. He's a total firebug. Killian could save himself a shitload of grief by throwing him under the bus, but he won't. Even if he's pissed at Tristian—

even if he thinks it was reckless and stupid—he's still got our backs.

"I wondered the same thing until I learned that this particular car—a very expensive Mercedes—belonged to one of the Counts." He turns to his computer, sending a photo to the flatscreen on the wall beside us. It's obvious from where I stand that it's the shell of a G-Wagen. "Didn't you boys have a run-in with them lately?"

Daniel is the kind of person who makes everyone's business his own, not just here in South Side, but also with the people he has professional dealings with. Since he's our LDZ supervisor for the year, that doesn't just include the Lords. It encompasses it.

Of course he's perfectly aware of the shit going down with the Counts and our Lady.

"That's been handled," Killian lies.

"So you didn't burn a skull into the hood of the Mercedes as an act of revenge?" He leans back in his chair, leisurely inspecting the photo. He shakes his head. "This is some sloppy, sloppy work, boys."

Tristian cuts in, "Daniel, look—"

Killian cuts him off. "That area has so many criminals, one sweep by the police would bring in half-a-dozen solid suspects. Perez was a fool for taking a car like that down to the bar. He was asking for it." Killian's voice never wavers, face hard as stone. "If you brought us down here for something, then cut to the chase. We all have busy schedules."

"As do I," Daniel states, pointing at the photo. "In fact, it's become much busier now that there's an arsonist on the loose in South Side. The business community is unsettled—understandably, since more than half the members pay for my protection. Tell me, does this look protected to you?" He looks between the three of us, waiting for an answer. When none comes, his expression hardens. "I've got the media champing at the bit for any excuse to question the safety around here. I've got the feds pacing outside the city lines, waiting for any opportunity to investigate my assets. Most importantly, I'm in the middle of re-launching my most lucrative venture, which means this is all attention I can ill afford. And then I've got the three of you," he adds, eyes darkening, "pissing in my goddamn corn flakes with your shoddy revenge schemes."

I try, "We didn't—" but my voice clips off at the glare he shoots me.

"You're lying to me, which tells me you know just how idiotic that stunt was, but I don't actually give a damn. Even if you weren't responsible for the fire," his expression implies heavily that he knows we are, "you three are cleaning up the mess."

"Now?" Killian asks, mouth pressed into a tense, annoyed line. "It's a bad time. We've got homecoming to deal with. Coach is riding my ass." He looks back at me. "Rath has to perform for the alumni, and Tristian's heading up the frat while we're busy. We don't have time for this."

"Your responsibilities to your coach are so far down the list of priorities, they barely even register a blip." He's watching his son with a curled lip, his words oozing with condescension. "But if it means so much to you, then you should have thought of that before running off to terrorize my city," he says, holding up a list. "You know how this shit works. You go in early, before everyone is awake, while the kids are at school. Collect money, assure our clients the area is safe, shake wallets, shake hands, shake dicks—whatever it takes. If anyone pushes back…well, you know what to do then, too."

Killian opens his mouth to say something, but Tristian steps forward and takes the list. "Yes, sir. We'll get this done immediately."

It's clear that we've been dismissed, and Killian takes the lead, looking fully prepared to storm out in true Payne fashion. But before we can leave, I hear Daniel call Tristian's name. When I glance back, he has an arm slung around Tristian's shoulders and his phone clutched in his other hand.

"Before you go, I need to show you something."

He thumbs something on his phone and another TV flickers to life. The video is a jerky loop, but it's obviously from a security camera. The room is shadowy, but two things are clear; it's a male and a female, and one is holding a gasoline canister. He pauses the screen and looks at Tristian, who's stiff and trapped by his arm.

"Whoever started that fire used my materials. They brought an outsider into my warehouse—a girl, from the looks of it. They compromised my organization, I assume in some effort to get between her scrawny little legs." He squeezes Tristian's neck, hissing into his ear, "That road head better have been worth it. Right, son?"

"Yes, sir," Tristian replies, and even though his poker face flawless, I can see the flash of dread in his eyes. How the fuck would Daniel know about Story giving him road head?

Daniel releases him with a barely restrained shove before stalking back to his desk, tossing the phone with a clatter. "You remember that little talk we had your senior year, Mercer?"

Tristian dips his chin in a nod. "I do."

"I hope so," Daniel says, pinning him under a glare. "Because your inability to choose pussy has caused more property damage than a goddamn wildfire. You're still in my debt for covering up that incident with the boat. You just remember that, too."

"I will," Tristian says, the corners of his eyes tight at the mention of his ex-girlfriend, Genevieve. It wasn't a boat—it was a yacht—and the primary fuck-pad for our high school softball coach. Tristian had fucking lost it when he found out Genevieve was screwing him behind Tristian's back. In hindsight, we're probably lucky it was a yacht that got torched. His throbbing rage-boner could have burned down this whole fucking city.

Tristian leaves, squeezing past me, and I take one last look at the screen. Even I can't tell it's Tristian and Story, but Daniel has a way of knowing.

He always has a way of knowing.

9

LEASHED

My Lords never show up on campus. I check in regularly, texting them my whereabouts, asking if everything is okay. Their answers are short and non-committal. It's obvious shit is hitting the fan on account of what Tristian and I did last night. Revenge was sweet, but ultimately fleeting. I don't even glimpse the Counts on campus, so I miss out on the rush of satisfaction I'd get from seeing their pissed off faces. Most of all, I'm annoyed that Killian was probably right. We should've listened to him and waited for a better moment. That's definitely the worst part.

It's weird being on campus without them. You'd think I'd appreciate the freedom; no Tristian hovering around, forcing his nutritional lunches on me, or sneaking his hand under my skirt. No Rath, who would occasionally let his guard down long enough to let me watch him practice or help him with his work, but flipping on a dime, too moody and erratic to ever feel truly at ease.

And then there's Killian. Normally, I barely see him during the day anyway, but he's still a constantly ominous presence, lurking like a stormy cloud, threatening to terrorize anyone who crosses his—or my—path.

Even with them gone, I'm not alone. Marcus sticks to me like glue, hovering closer than the guys. For most of the day, he doesn't speak or look me in the eye. I don't blame him. I don't want to look him in the eye, either. I know he was in the room that night when Killian forced me to my knees and made me suck him off in front of the whole frat. I doubt he cares about that. He's probably been threatened with castration for even thinking of crossing some kind of line with me. That doesn't make me feel any better about walking shoulder to shoulder with a stranger who's seen me at my lowest point, debased and humiliated.

When classes are over, Marcus pauses on the quad. "Do you mind stopping at the Archer building? I need to pick up something from Coach."

"Fine by me." I'm not in a hurry to get back home and deal with the consequences of our impulsiveness the night before.

We head down to the athletic building, passing Mercer Field. The oval stadium holds a hundred thousand fans, and even empty, it's impressive. Marcus leads us to the building's main entrance. This part is purely administrative; tickets, fundraising, recruiting. I dutifully follow him down into the lower floor, where the air turns sour with heat and sweat. The players' gym is down here, along with the trainers and coaching offices.

"Are you okay waiting for me?" he asks, looking harried and impatient. "I'll just be a minute."

"That's fine." I glance down the hall at the rows of team photos. "I'll be out here."

He ducks into the office, and I study the photos on the wall. It's interesting, watching the eras roll by as they shift from black and white to color photographs. I spot Killian at the end. The most recent photograph. It's not a flattering picture of him, obviously taken after a practice. His face is red and his eyes are hard like steel, hair dark in its dampness. Even here, he stands out amongst the team. A little taller, a little bigger. Arms decked out in ink. Jaw set, chin high. He looks like a criminal dressed in a disguise.

I guess I'm one to talk.

Still, it's strange seeing him like this, knowing that mere hours ago I'd been tucked into his side, our naked skin melding together. It wouldn't have occurred to me at the time, with all his stiffness and blank-eyed looks, but I see it now for what it was. Possibly, that was as soft as Killian gets.

At the end of the hall, there's a small, open room with a trio of vending machines. Eager to clear my mind of Killian's sharp version of softness, I allow the brightly colored candy to taunt me from behind the glass. It's silly, but living with Tristian's strict dietary concerns has turned my appetite into that of a twelve-year-old's. I have a dollar in my purse. No one, not even Tristian, would be the wiser.

Feeling like a child sneaking into the candy jar, I find the crumpled bill and quickly shove it into the slot. It zips in and back out—rejected for being too wrinkled. I smooth it out and try again. Rejected. And again.

"Having trouble?"

"Just can't get the machine to take my dollar," I grumble, glancing back. The blood drains from my face. I barely feel the dollar slipping out of my fingers, falling at the feet of the man before me.

Saul Cartwright.

"It can be a little fussy," he says, opening up his wallet. He thumbs through crisp bills and pulls out two ones. "Try one of these."

"No. Um. No, that's okay." I take a step back from the man. He's the Athletic Director at Forsyth; the second highest paying job, only below the president. He's also one of my old online sugar daddies. But worse? He could be Ted. "I-I didn't need candy, anyway."

"Don't be ridiculous. Everyone deserves a treat every once in a while." Winking at me, he shoves a dollar in the slot. It accepts it instantly. But that's not what has my attention. It's the big, obnoxious gold ring on his finger. I instantly know it's a frat ring, just like the one Killian and his dad wear. Instead of a skull, the icon in the middle is a bear's head, jaw opened wide, fangs glinting. Around it are three greek letters.

DKS.

Delta Kappa Sigma?

Dukes.

"What are you interested in?" he asks, perusing the machine. "Chocolate? Something chewy? Something to suck on?"

My eyes dart up in stunned horror, but he's focused on the row of snacks like it wasn't even meant as innuendo. When I don't answer, he punches in a code and the item drops to the bottom with a sharp clank.

"How about a good, old-fashioned candy bar." Cartwright bends, head hovering mere inches from my breasts, and then shoves his hand through the little door, feeling around for the candy. He smiles up at me and a memory bursts into my mind—one from back in my sugar baby days. Him, on the other side of the computer screen, asking me to show him how I'd suck a dick.

"Use your water bottle," he'd instructed. "Show me how you'd take care of my big cock, gorgeous girl."

I faked my way through it, licking the sides and sucking the top. I moaned like I'd seen the women do in porn videos, but I just wanted the money—was desperate enough for it that I played it up as well as I could. Nevertheless, I had no idea what I was doing. He sure did, though. He jerked off while I fellated it, telling me all the while how beautiful and sexy and *mature* I was.

I was sixteen.

He straightens and holds out the candy bar. All I can think about is what his face looks like when he comes; flushed and slack. "Take it," he says, expression friendly. "My treat."

I'm speechless. Nauseous. Because I have no doubt this is a game—one orchestrated by a master manipulator. Is he Ted? Or did Ted set this up? It seems too implausible that he simply chanced upon me here, the one time I'm alone.

"Personally, I like salty stuff. Chips, nuts, popcorn. It's terrible for my health, but you're so young you don't have to worry about that yet." Cartwright looks at me again, but this time his eyes narrow, head tilting curiously. "You look familiar. Have we met before?"

"No," I blurt, taking a step back. "I don't think so."

"You're probably right. I'd definitely remember a pretty little—" His eyes catch on something. My wrist cuff, I realize. Seeing it makes his lips turn up at the corners. "—*Lady* like you." His attention is drawn to something over my shoulder, and I whirl around at the sound of footsteps. I'm so relieved at the sight of Marcus loping toward us down that it makes my head spin. "Your boyfriend?"

"No," I rush out, taking another step. "Just a friend."

From the look in his eyes, he already knew the answer. "Be careful with these boys," he says softly, eyes tracking my slow retreat. "We spoil them in the football program. They're not used to hearing the word 'no'." Quietly, he adds, "Payne, especially."

Marcus approaches then, nodding in greeting. "Sir."

Cartwright squares his shoulders, plastering on a big grin. "You ready for the homecoming game this weekend, son?"

"Yes, sir."

Cartwright gives him a firm nod. "Good to hear. You two have a pleasant afternoon."

I don't breathe until we're back in the stairwell, trying to shake the tremors from my hands. I push the candy bar at Marcus. "Here, take it."

Marcus looks confused, but does as he's asked. "You don't want it?"

I shake my head and start up the stairs. "I think I've lost my taste for sweets."

THE GUYS ARE all in a mood when I arrive home, but I'm expecting it. Tristian barely looks at me as he climbs the stairs to his room. Killian sits in his leather chair, his hot, furious eyes tracking my path across the hallway, as if our time together last night never happened. The only one who even deigns to speak to me is Rath.

"Come on," he says, jerking his head toward the library. "I have a paper due tomorrow and my head is already throbbing."

So that's how I spend the next hour rigidly helping Rath with an essay on Robert Frost's thematic use of nature. They weren't kidding when they called the gen. ed. Lit requirement a coast. I'm pretty sure I covered this in ninth grade. I probably still have a similar essay saved somewhere in all my old things—provided my mother kept them.

I'm just grateful that he's not making me go up to his room, still remembering the way he looked in that video, sprawled out on the bed, smirking up at the camera as I sucked him off. I'm not sure I'd be able to maintain composure if he tried another one of his 'I need an orgasm before I can focus' acts again.

Tristian and Killian filter in eventually, working on their own stuff, which makes the tension that much heavier. Killian's anger has always been a heavy, palpable thing, and I can feel it now, like a weight bearing down on my shoulders. Suddenly I feel like an idiot for thinking I'd made any headway with some sex and barely consensual cuddling.

Rath is quiet and difficult to read, and I struggle not to look at him, bitterly searching for the fakeness I'd seen that night on video. All I see are the bare angles of his face, his snake bite piercings bobbing and shifting when he rakes his teeth over his lip, lost in thought.

"She's putty, dude. The punishments don't pay off, but you know what does? Being nice!"

"Wait." He looks agitated and pinched as he rubs his temples. It's getting late, and he keeps whining about a headache. "This is making no sense. I'm done trying to read this shit." With a flick of his wrist, he flings the book across the table—not that he was reading it, anyway. I've been reciting the staple poems aloud. "My head is killing me. Just tell me what to write."

I stare at him. "You want me to tell you what to write."

He stares back. "Yes."

"And then write it for you."

His tongue peeks out to prod his lip ring. "Yes."

"And then read it aloud, so you know what it says."

He sweeps out a hand. "Exactly."

Sighing, I push the laptop away. "Maybe I should turn it in for you, get the grade, and collect your whole fucking degree while I'm at it." It's too sharp—too insubordinate—but I can't seem to get a handle on these *feelings*.

I hate that he was able to hurt me so badly.

I hate it more than I hate him.

From across the room, Tristian makes a sound, low and strained like an aborted chuckle.

Rath fixes me with a tight look, asking, "What's got your panties in a twist?"

"You have to put in some work here, Rath!" There's this instinctual response to the way he straightens, a grim darkness falling over his features that makes the hair on the back of my neck stand on end. The spite pumping through my veins overpowers it. "I've made this as easy as possible, but you're not even listening. You probably couldn't even tell me what the last poem was about." Annoyed, I shut the laptop. "You can't just coast through life by manipulating people into pleasing you. I'm not some starry-eyed co-ed you can con into doing all your busy work. I'm your *Lady*. Maybe it's time you started treating me like one!"

There's a dangerous glint in his eye, and I don't need to look at Killian to know he's giving me the same threatening stare.

Rath's lips part, probably to tell me he was fine making other people do this for him. He's not wrong. He'd only agreed to be tutored because I browbeat him into doing it. It doesn't make it any better. He's taken advantage of it quite enough.

Before he can voice whatever mean, barbed thing is sure to emerge, Martin sweeps into the library. "Lady," he says, lingering at the door. "I wanted to remind you about your meeting tomorrow afternoon."

"Meeting?" I look over at Tristian, who's still staring at me with some unholy mixture of proud displeasure at my outburst.

"The Homecoming preparations?" Martin looks at the guys, exasperation tinting his features. Clearly, they were meant to inform me of this. "It's a gathering, of sorts. The Royal girls are meeting to coordinate the weekend's social events—primarily the annual Forsyth carnival, which is the biggest fundraiser of the year."

I look around the room, all too aware that my little fit of temper has soured the mood even further. "Let me get this straight," I say, feeling rigid and far less fragile than I should. "You want me to get together with the bitches who lured me into getting kidnapped so we can…what? Plan a party? You've all lost your goddamn minds."

Rath gives me a long, snide glance. "You want to be treated like our *Lady*? Well, here it is, Sour Cherry. This is part of the job. Deal with it."

"You can't be serious!"

Killian shifts in his chair across the room, propping his elbows on his knees as he pins me under a glower. "It's tradition. You're the Lady of this house, which means you have to represent us." After a moment of watching me gape at him, he looks away. "Trust me, none of us are happy about it either."

"Then get me out of it!" God, I'll look like a fool showing up around those girls after what happened. The kidnapping was bad enough, but the fact I was fooled by a bunch of girls with fake tits and expensive shoes? That's another level of humiliation. I lived on my own for two years. I'm not some spoiled country club cunt. "What if they try something again?"

"There's no getting out of it," Tristian says, mouth pressed into a tense, unhappy slant. "But you don't need to worry. In fact, we've worked out a plan to keep you safe."

Rath sinks back into his seat, pinching the bridge of his nose. "I think the royal 'we' is overstating our agreement a bit."

I look between them, noting the agitation. "Are you going to give me a gun?"

"What?!" Killian looks at me like I suggested he skin a cat. "Fuck no! Are you insane?"

"Maybe," I snipe back. "Attempted rape might have a way of doing that to a person."

An ominous shadow falls over Killian's features. I've seen it before, the way his jaw goes tight, knuckles a stark-white as he clenches his palms together. My stomach turns uncomfortably at the sight.

"Marcus told us Cartwright approached you at the athletic building today."

Shit.

So that explains why Killian is so pissed at me. Freaking Marcus. Should have known he'd be their eyes and ears.

"It was no big deal," I insist. "It's not like I approached him."

Tristian closes his book. "Story, you being approached by any man is a big deal, but one of your former daddies, to boot? That shit isn't flying."

Killian jabs a finger in my direction, eyes sparking. "And you haven't spoken a single fucking word about it. We've been here for hours, and what do we get? Fuck-all."

"Nothing happened!" But the truth is, I was scared. It's against the rules for me to speak to other men, but I still don't know how to handle it. Just turn around and walk away? Look like a fool? The situation was unbearable enough without having to navigate my limitations as their Lady.

In a calm, measured voice, Tristian asks, "Did he say anything inappropriate?"

"Not really." I shake my head, giving him a hapless look. "I don't think he even remembers me."

Tristian arches an eyebrow. "Are you sure?"

No. Not in the least. "Yes."

"It doesn't matter," Killian says. "We've got busy schedules coming up, you included. There's shit you'll need to do without us glued to your side all the damn time—like the homecoming prep."

I deflate at the resolve in his eyes. "So, what are you going to do? Are you going to send Marcus with me?"

Rath scoffs, cracking one eye to glare at me. "You think we're the only house with rules? None of them are going to send their girls to a meeting with some rival frat member lurking in a corner."

Tristian shakes his head. "We came up with a better solution. Something a little more…permanent."

Permanent?

A chill of unease creeps up my spine.

"You and Killer came up with a solution," Rath corrects, throwing them both a look. "Don't bring me into this." To me, he gives a blank, dead-eyed look. "Consider my conscientious objection a willingness to do some of that 'busy work' you think so highly of."

I swallow thickly, wondering, "What kind of solution?"

"Martin," Killian says, thrusting his chin at the man. "Has Ray arrived yet?"

Martin nods. "Thirty minutes ago. He should be about set up in the basement."

"Basement?" I stand, knocking back my chair. "What's going on?"

My heart thumps hard against my ribcage, lungs feeling suddenly constricted. I haven't been down to the basement since the night Killian punished me in front of the whole frat. The settings of all my nightmares used to be our old laundry room, but now it's definitely that room down there, all dim and full of the memory of their cheers and taunts.

Tristian appears in front of me, reaching up to frame my face in his wide palms. He searches my eyes, and whatever he finds makes him frown. "There's nothing to be afraid of, sweetheart. We're doing what we need to do to keep you safe. You understand that, don't you?"

The last time they wanted to keep me safe, I'd gone upstairs to lose my virginity to my stepbrother.

"I'm not going into the basement." I try to inject my voice with as much determination as I feel, but it cracks, coming out plaintive and pathetic.

"You will," Killian says, standing from his chair and stalking forward. "You can either walk or I'll carry you, but you're going down there."

Impulsively, I make a dash to the door. It's laughably futile. I don't even get out of the room before muscular arms wrap around my upper body and lift me off the ground.

"If you'd calm the fuck down, we could talk this over!" Killian grunts, biceps bulging. "Fuck it. Rath, get the door."

"No!" I shout, squirming against him. "Killian, please don't make me go down there. I'll do anything. I'll sleep for you! I'll write Rath's paper, I swear!"

He pauses so briefly that I might have missed it if I hadn't been looking for an opportunity to get away. It doesn't last long enough to try. He hauls me out of the library and down the hall like I weigh nothing, barking at someone to, "Open the fucking door!"

The door to the basement.

"Wait, wait, wait!" I try, arms aching from his grip. "We can talk, okay? We can talk it over, I'll listen, I promise."

Killian must decide the time for that has passed, because as soon as Tristian swings the door open, he's hoisting me down the stairs. I fight, using my feet to drag along the walls, but he just tightens his grip, making curt, annoyed sounds at every thrash.

"You're being fucking ridiculous!" he spits.

The first thing that registers is that the frat isn't waiting for us in the meeting room. The second thing that registers is that someone else *is*. There's an old guy standing next to a table that's padded and sterile-looking. His gray hair is slicked back into a ponytail, and he doesn't look the least bit bothered by all the commotion I'm making.

A table with metal instruments waits nearby.

"Where do you want her?" Tristian asks.

The guy answers, "Put her on her back."

"No!" I strain toward Tristian. "Please don't do this to me. Whatever it is, please don't. Please?"

"Hey, hey," he says, stepping in front of Killian. He touches my chin, giving it a soft stroke with the pad of his thumb. "This isn't a punishment, sweetheart. We're doing this because it'll be best for you. But the harder you fight, the more difficult this is going to be. Settle down, and it'll be over quick."

My legs give out, but Killian has me crushed so tightly to his broad chest that I just hang there, limp. Tristian is a lost cause. Rath lingers by the door, arms crossed, eyes fixed to his shoes. Conscientious objector or not, he won't be my savior. Instead, I twist my neck, trying to catch Killian's gaze. "You said you'd protect me," I cry, grasping his forearms. They're as immoveable as steel.

If I hoped my mention of last night might spark something sympathetic in him, then I'm sorely mistaken. His reply comes out harsh, forced through gritted teeth. "That's exactly what I'm fucking doing!"

That's how I know that whatever is about to happen can't be good. It'll be pain and humiliation and a long night spent licking yet another wound. I rear back and fight against Killian with all my strength. Naturally, it's useless. He plunges me onto the table and plants a palm on each shoulder, pinning me down.

"Hold still," he barks, "or we'll have to tie you up."

I pause, chest rising and falling as I try to settle my breathing. "Please don't tie me up."

Tristian strokes my hair. "Can you promise to behave?"

I nod, no longer able to hold the tears back. "W-will you at least tell me what you're going to do to me?" All sorts of horrors crowd my mind. Gruesome, sexual, invasive things.

Tristian wipes a tear off my cheek, his blue eyes holding mine. "Ray's going to put a GPS tracker under your skin—just behind your ear. That way we'll always know where you are."

My breath stutters to a standstill, filling my lungs with an ache. "What?" Of all the things that came to mind, that wasn't among them. I'm not twisted enough to have thought of it. "You're implanting me with a tracker? Like I'm a goddamn dog? This can't be legal!"

Killian's palms are heavy and unyielding on my shoulders, and when he bends down to look me in the eye, it's only to hiss, "Maybe if you weren't talking to shady old perverts like a bitch in heat, we wouldn't have to treat you like one."

My jaw goes slack, both at his words and the naked malice in his eyes. For Tristian, this isn't a punishment.

For Killian?

It is.

I get my hand loose and slap my stepbrother across the face, palm stinging with the force of my strike. I watch as his head jerks—just barely—and then his eyes are suddenly blank.

Empty.

Terrifying.

Rath appears between us, wrenching Killian away. "Don't," he snaps, putting a hand on his chest. "Remember last time? Remember what you said?"

"Tie her down," Killian snarls, trying to lunge past Rath, who holds him back. "Tie her the fuck down or I'll do it myself, and I promise you, I won't be gentle."

"Fine," Tristian says, holding up his hands in surrender. "I'll tie her down, but you need to get the fuck out of the room."

His eyes narrow into vicious slits. "No."

"Yes," Rath says, pushing him back. "You're too pissed off. You're going to lose your shit and fuck everything up. Get out of here. We'll take care of it."

Killian glares at the three of us but ultimately turns on his heel, storming out. I don't take another breath until I hear the door slam at the top of the stairs.

Softly, Tristian says, "Sweetheart," and strokes my hair back. "We're going to have to do this. I know you're upset, but we're not doing this to hurt you. I know how it looks, but we're not even doing it to control you. There are some bad people out there who have hurt you before and may hurt you again. You understand that, don't you? You understand that I just want to keep you safe."

The fucked up thing is, I almost understand. Tristian takes care of his things, and that's what I am to them. A thing. A possession. A shiny trinket. A prized fucktoy. This and the occasional sugary treat are as close as Tristian probably gets to showing affection for someone.

Sighing, he adds, "I don't want to tie you down, Story."

My lip wobbles under the inevitability of it all, another tear making a track down my temple. Tristian catches it before it falls. "Will it hurt?"

Tristian looks over his shoulder at Ray. "He's going to numb you up first, so it's just one quick shot. You can handle that, can't you? You can be a good girl for us?"

From his spot by the door, Rath shakes his head, muttering, "Give me a break."

Sniffling, I stare up at the ceiling, feeling brittle and stiff. "I'll…be good."

He looks relieved, bending to pluck a slow, chaste kiss from my lips. "That's our Lady. I'll get you something nice, okay?"

I don't answer, taking the time to gather myself up, just like Ms. Crane had said. All the parts of me I want to keep—I lock them away, tight and safe. I'm not this girl who's about to be leashed to three monsters. I'm the girl who's engineered their fates.

This isn't a punishment.

It won't be a defense.

I'll make it into another weapon for my arsenal.

"SHE'S DONE," RAY says, stepping away from the table. In the end, taking away my freedom was just as quick as Tristian promised. A couple of pricks behind the ear to accompany the couple of pricks waiting by my side.

I didn't even flinch.

Tristian helps me sit up, but I shrug him off. The room is quiet while Ray packs up and prepares to leave. That doesn't take long either. Idly, I wonder how much he's getting paid to force implants into helpless women. What's the cost of someone's autonomy, per billable hour?

Even after he's gone, I don't move—staring at my hands, my shoulders feeling slumped and heavy. All the fight has been sapped out of me, leaving me hollow and cold. The spot behind my ear doesn't hurt. Not yet. But I almost wish it would. It'd be a reprieve to feel anything other than this gaping pit of hopelessness.

"Come on," Tristian says, easing me off the table. "Let's get you upstairs, clean you up."

Freezing, I finally feel the seed of something panicked and desperate. "Don't make me go to Killian's room. I can't…not tonight." Even the thought of playing dead while he fucks me makes my stomach heave.

Tristian shoots Rath a look. "It's fine. You can go to your room," he tells me.

I lift my chin, meeting his gaze. "No. That won't work. He'll just…" I swallow, knowing that my eyes must be glassy and red. "He has a key."

Nodding heavily, Tristian offers, "You can—"

I cut him off before he can finish. "Can I stay with you?" I ask Rath.

If he's surprised at the request, it doesn't show. He gives Tristian a look before agreeing. "Okay," he says, tucking his hands into his pockets. "Just come up when you're ready."

Tristian watches me as Rath leaves, his boots loud and heavy against the stairs. "You're mad at me," he observes, head tilted as he searches my eyes.

When he reaches for me, I flinch away. "Don't."

His eyes go shuttered, that flawless mask of his clicking firmly in place. "Be mad, if that's what you need. I'd rather have you mad than constantly at risk."

Jesus, he really believes that, doesn't he?

He doesn't stop me when I leave the basement, going up to wash my face and collect my toiletries. Earlier, I'd been awash with dread at the thought of going into Rath's room again. Now, every room feels tainted in one way or another. I spend a long time in my bathroom—not even bothering with a lock—sweeping my hair back to look at the injection site. I have to peel back a bandaid to get a look, but when I do, it's almost disappointing. Something so significant should leave more than a piddly little dot of a scabbing flesh.

I don't leave for Rath's room until over an hour later. I skitter past Killian's door like the little mouse they've always accused me of being, climbing the stairs to the third floor with a racing pulse, as if he were behind me, trying to catch me by the back of my neck.

I give Rath's door two knocks before pushing it open. It's dark inside—darker than it used to be—messier, too. But just like always, there's music playing. The melody is bittersweet and haunting. I tiptoe over the threshold, peering around the space. But he's not in the bed or at the piano. There's a flicker of light that draws my attention to his bathroom door, cracked open to reveal a soft glow.

I approach it nervously, still feeling ill at ease from my journey through the halls. Peeking through the gap, I see the flicker is actually a candle. Three, maybe more. Moving closer, I hear a soft swish of water, daring to push it open and step inside.

I've never been into Rath's bathroom before. The mornings I awoke in his bed, he always claimed it first, leaving me to go back to my own. It didn't bother me. I enjoyed having a place of my own, for all the flimsy privacy it offered.

Now, I see I've been amiss.

There's a large claw-foot bathtub at the end of the room, illuminated by only the light of the candles and the moon shining through the open window. The air is heavy with steam—steam and pungent smoke.

Rath has his head tipped back. His eyes are closed, arms draped leisurely around the lip of the tub. In one hand, he's pinching a blunt between forefinger and thumb. The fingers of his other hand are rising and falling against the porcelain, as if he's following along to the melody coming through the speakers. He looks loose and unguarded, hair so haphazardly damp that it's clearly the product of his wet hand having pushed through it at some point.

I get this ironic and completely misplaced notion that I'm intruding on a personal moment. Considering I'm recovering from a biological AirTag, the thought pulls a scoff from my throat.

Rath's eyes blink open at the sound.

They're so black in the darkness of the room that he looks like a demon, the rings in his lips glinting like fangs. Without breaking my gaze, he brings the blunt to his lips, sucking a slow inhale. He holds it in his lungs, watching me with those demon eyes as he lets it out in a lazy plume of smoke.

"Water's still warm."

His voice is quiet and rough.

An invitation.

It's a long moment before I decide whether or not to accept it. When I see the carton of Epsom salt at the foot of the tub, it dawns on me that Rath had been the one to tell Ms. Crane to take care of me. To ask after my wellbeing. To make sure I wasn't hurt.

It doesn't change anything.

I wind that fact around my heart like barbed wire as I reach for the hem of my shirt, lifting it over my head.

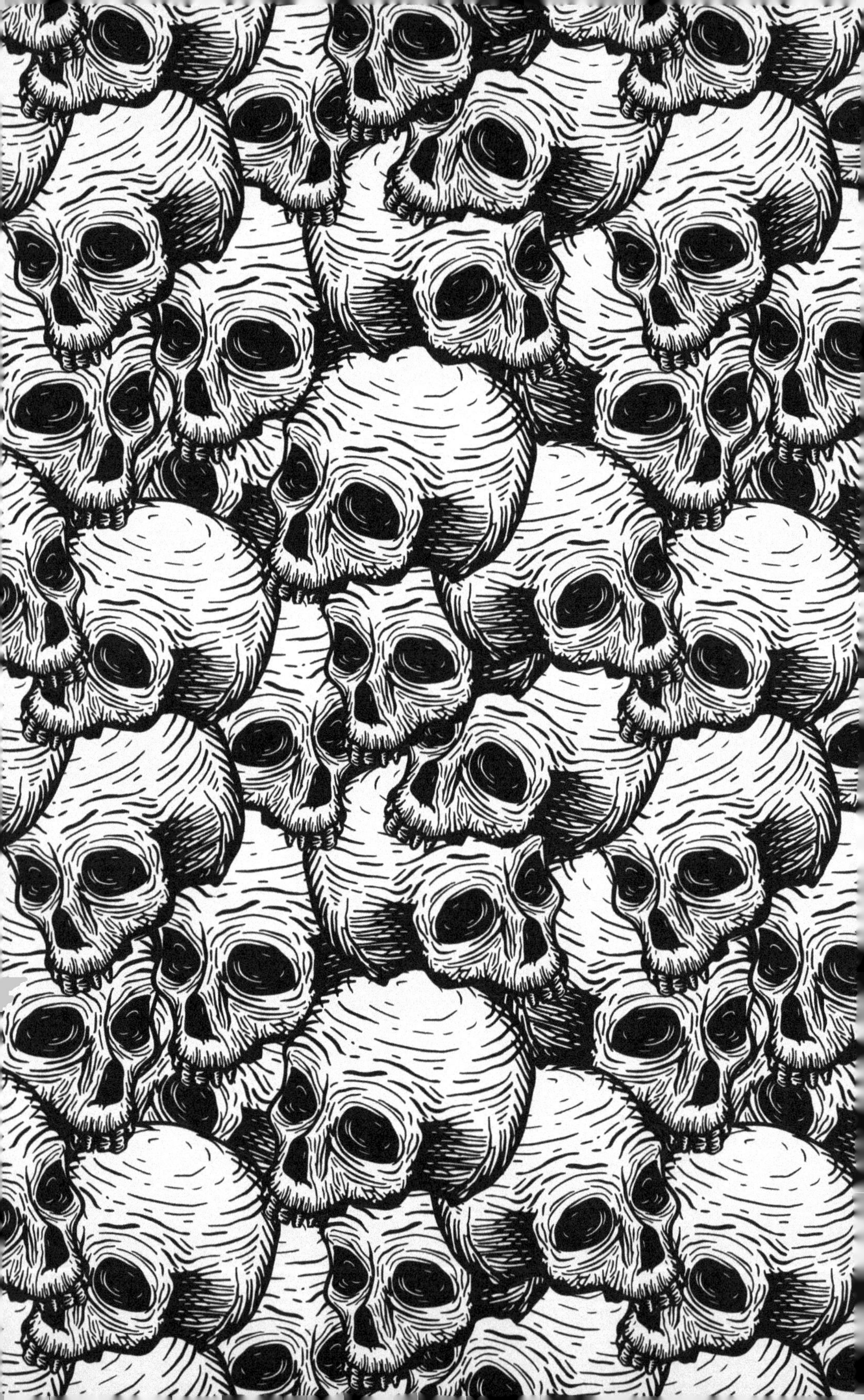

10

MILES TO GO

SHE UNDRESSES WITH no fanfare, slipping out of her skirt and panties like it's nothing to bare herself before me. She's still a fucking vision, though, standing there all pale and delicate-looking, those full tits of hers looking perfectly grabbable. I rake my teeth across my lip at her approach, my eyes dragging down her body to that sweet pussy.

I gesture to the Epsom salt, explaining, "Ms. Crane sent that up." It was meant for Story, but hey. A long soak is good for the muscles.

I make space for her between my legs, watching as she steps into the water. I'd rather take a dive off a tall structure before admitting it, but I think I might have missed her these last few days. She was interesting. Fun to toy with. Nice to wake up to. Warm. Sort of nice, really.

And then she chose Killian.

I've been white-knuckling my grudge about it for so long that it wasn't until a couple hours ago that I realized she's nursing one of her own.

I just don't know why.

She avoids my gaze as she settles herself into the water, her ass against my rapidly growing cock. Killian's been abusing that pussy, that much I know. Sore, Tristian had said. Ms. Crane hadn't seemed worried, but she had threatened my testicles in a variety of creative ways if I tried to stick my dick in there a second before it was healed proper.

I didn't need that cranky old bat to enlighten me to the fact I'm not getting any tonight. The way Story's got her knees all tucked to her chest, tense and closed off, is evidence enough.

Sighing, I go to hit my blunt, only to realize the ember's gone out. I hold it out to the candle, re-lighting it. "You ever smoke weed before?"

She turns only enough for me to make out the curve of her cheekbone. "Yes."

I raise an eyebrow. "Really? When?"

One of her shoulders curls toward her ear in a loose shrug. "Back in boarding school."

"Private school girls, huh?" I shake my head, explaining, "It's the only thing that seems to help when I have a headache. Well, that and turning off the lights." Drawing another hit into my lungs, I ask, "Did you like it?"

She hums in response, tightening her grip around her knees. "It was fine."

Well.

Enough of this shit.

I reach out to stroke her shoulder, gently pulling her back. She's resistant only for a second—stiff, like an impulse—before sinking back to rest against my chest. I'm probably just stoned stupid, but I can't help but notice how perfectly she fits into the curve of my body. I exhale a stream of smoke as I look down at her chest, watching the water flutter over her pink nipples.

"Here," I offer, holding the blunt in front of her lips. She stares at it for a moment, frozen, so I add, "You can say no. More for me."

She doesn't.

Her lips wrap around the end, sucking in a short drag, and I pull it away, watching her inhale. It's released with a slow, steady stream of smoke.

"Tastes like ass," she whispers. Despite that, I can feel her body loosening, head lolling back on my shoulder.

I take the opportunity to sweep her hair back from her neck, getting a look at that ridiculous fucking tracker. Tristian was dead set on the thing. Any other time, I might have been able to talk Killian into seeing sense.

And then he found out about Cartwright.

Killian's got a lot of hang-ups when it comes to this girl, but one will always be front and center, sending him careening right over the edge of reason: Story receiving, seeking, or accepting any amount of attention from pervy older men.

I run my finger over the spot. "Does it hurt?"

She fixes her eyes to something across the room. "Yes."

Right. Stupid question. If anyone in this house understands how it feels to have metal pushed through their skin, it's me. "How about…" I walk my fingers down her arm, sliding them down her belly, beneath the water. I give the patch of skin above her clit a light tap. "…here?"

She turns her head away. "I don't know. A little."

Tristian and I have both been wondering what's going on in Killer's room at night. Story has been going willingly—at least seemingly so. There haven't been any marks. We've been careful about making sure. But I should have known he'd find a way to throw her some hurt.

Jesus.

"Killian is such a fucking *fuck*." I let my head fall back against the tub, eyes sliding closed. After a moment of processing the anger, I tell her, "I would have made it good for you." I feel her weight against me, skating my fingertips lazily over her shoulder. "I had all these plans…"

Her voice is dry when she repeats, "Plans."

"Yep." I skim my fingers over her arm. "I had a playlist. Couldn't let my Lady lose her virginity to shitty music, could I? I was going to wear a condom—ribbed, with lots of lube. It was going to be in the morning, because…" I pause, having to think hard to remember why that was a detail. "Well, because we're just really good in the mornings, right? I was going to eat you out for a while. It'd have to be a weekend, so we could take our time. Now that I think about it, I guess it wasn't really anything elaborate. Still, probably would have been better than what you got."

Her head turns back toward me, but I don't open my eyes to see her expression. Her voice sounds flat. "Maybe."

I hit the blunt again, feeling some of the tension bleed out of my neck. Fucking stress headaches. The worst. "For what it's worth, I was against the tracker. Bunch of police state bullshit, if you ask me. But…" I crack an eye then, finding that she's watching me back, some unreadable emotion swimming in her eyes. "They might have a point."

The unreadable emotion instantly turns to ice. "I'm micro-chipped like a dog, Rath. Like an *animal*. There's no 'point' that could make that any less of a violation."

I reach up and touch the line of her jaw. "People chip their pets because they're important to them. Because they're precious. Because they care for them." Sighing, I offer her the blunt again, and it's kind of funny to watch her pull a drag from it with that pinched, angry expression. "I'm not saying it's the best display or whatever. Just…" Shaking my head, I lose myself in the scent of her hair, letting my muscles go lax. "Shit. We're busy people, Story. Not like… schedules and chores kind of busy. The kind of busy that just doesn't stop. We have our hands in a lot of pots, and almost no one likes it. Trust me, there are worse people out there than Perez."

"What does that mean?"

Lifting the blunt to my mouth, I take another drag, thinking. "It means the woods are lovely, dark and deep. But we have promises to keep." Exhaling, I open my eyes to meet her stunned gaze. "And miles to go before we sleep."

"Robert Frost?" She gives me a slow blink. "You were listening earlier?"

I reach out to snuff the blunt into a nearby tray. "Who wouldn't listen to a beautiful girl reading them poetry? Just had this bitch of a headache. Like I said…"

She looks away. "Oh."

I get my hands in the water then, feeling up her sides, gliding over all of that soft, ripe skin. I run the tip of my nose over the shell of her ear, wondering, "Feeling any better?"

She certainly feels more relaxed.

Or she does until my fingers brush over the side of her tits. Then she's going all tense again.

Fucking Killian.

I reach down and lift the plug, draining the water out. "Come on," I say, nudging her. "Let's get you dry and tucked into bed."

When we step out, she takes the towel I give her, wrapping it tightly around her middle.

"You bring something to sleep in?"

"No." She finally looks up at me. "I can wear something of yours. If that's okay."

"Sure." I'd prefer her naked, but I doubt the suggestion would be welcome. I head out of the bathroom and go to my dresser, finding an old t-shirt. It's gray with a black Lord skull on the front. The cotton is soft and worn. I'd gotten this thing my junior year of high school. That's how in-the-cards this whole thing has been.

When I turn, she's standing just outside the bathroom, pulling her panties up her legs. Her eyes are glued to the bed, like she's seeing something that hurts to look at.

"Drop this," I say, tugging at the towel. She fidgets for a moment before untucking it, letting it fall to the ground. I scrunch the shirt up to the neck, holding it out. I get a bemused look at the gesture, but she lets me push it over her head, threading her arms through.

It looks good on her.

It makes my dick hard.

She reaches over her chest to clutch her elbow, looking small and weirdly vulnerable for someone I just watched slap a quarterback clean across the face.

"I can, um…sleep on the couch."

I'm halfway into pulling on my boxers when she says it. Freezing, my head snaps up, eyes narrowing. "The couch?"

Excuse me?

She nods, ducking her head. "Yeah."

I may be a bit lost when it comes to a lot of things in life, but there are some things I just know.

I know I smoke too much, and the creative side of my brain works best when I'm full of vodka and too tired to see straight. I know that Van Morrison is a legitimate god, Debussy is overrated, and electronica can be really good in the right hands. I know that Killian and Tristian give me a dozen reasons to hate them every day, and that I'd take a bullet for either of them in a split second, without even having to consider it. Most of all, I know that wanting something and not being able to have it is nothing more than the mark of failure.

Sweet Cherry is freezing me the fuck out.

What I know, I know.

Time to grease these goddamn wheels. "Okay. Can I do something for you first?"

She pushes her hair out of her eyes, looking shifty. "Like what?"

Goosebumps rise on her flesh as I trail my fingers down her arm, watching her body clench in response. "Let me give you a massage. These fingers are good at more than playing the piano."

That earns a surly remark. "I've been made aware."

"I'm not talking about anything sexual," I insist, although…let's face it. *We'll see.* "Come on, we've got a nice buzz going. I know you're still upset, but at least let me help you relax." Leaning in, I whisper into her ear, "Use me, *Lady.*"

Possibly I'm still smarting from her earlier remark about treating her like a Lady.

She eyes me suspiciously. It's well-founded. I'm not known for the spirit of giving, Tristian loves to dote on Story with food and gifts, like she's his little poodle. That's *his* game. Baths and massages aren't my style. I'm not good at the whole attentive nurturing thing. I strongly doubt my ability to sell it. But I've got to find out what the issue is, or I'll lose ground.

I'll lose *her.*

"Come on," I say, sitting with my back against the headboard. I pat the mattress between my legs. "Sit here and I'll ease some of that tension."

She considers it for a minute, like she's wondering if it's a trap. That's fair. It's not *not* a trap. Finally, she relents, moving so that her ass is against my crotch and her back is in front of me, just like in the bath. My cock twitches, but I will it to stand down.

I start at her neck, pushing aside her hair and taking care not to touch the small spot where the tracker was implanted. Working the tight muscles with slow, deliberate motions, I make myself think of this like a symphony, different movements, each drawn out to make something whole.

Maybe she just needs to feel in control, even if she isn't. That's probably why Tristian took her with him to set that fire. He wanted Story to feel like she has power, even though, ultimately, she belongs to us—body, mind, and soul.

My hands travel over her shoulders, then down to her arms. I knead her little biceps, then rub down her forearms and lower, taking my time on her wrists, her palms, every finger. Then I start over and do it all again. Slowly her muscles unwind, and her breaths coming deep and even.

When she shifts, sinking back into me, her ass grinds against my dick, which is hard as nails. It's been a minute since I had a mouth on me, but I've heard her down there with Killian, soft cries and a banging headboard.

Yeah, I'm panting for it.

She tenses right back up at the feel of my hardness.

"I'm not going to do anything with it. Promise." At her skeptical look, I add, "Ms. Crane would garrote me with a piano wire, girl."

She exhales and nods. "True."

I make the same pass again, starting at her shoulders, moving down her back, over to her arms and hands. "Lean back," I suggest, and she complies, resting her body against my chest. Her sweet-smelling hair is under my nose. I work my fingers up the long column of her neck, threading into the hair above her ears, massaging her scalp, her temples.

She releases a drawn out groan, going limp.

"When did you start playing piano?" she asks, her voice drowsy.

I'm surprised by the question, but answer easily, "When I was six. My family didn't have much money. It was just me and my mom at that point. My older brother, Alessio, was already graduating high school."

"You have an older brother?"

"A lot older," I stress, feeling her limp against me. "My mom had him young. We were never close or anything." Alessio got out of South Side and never looked back. Not at us.

She nods into my palms. "So the piano…"

"My mom, she had this thing about wanting to provide for us, the way rich people provided for their kids. She was convinced if we learned to play an instrument, it could be our ticket out. She made a deal with our neighbor, Mrs. Budd, who had a piano, that Ma would do her laundry if she'd teach us piano. Alessio was awful at it, but I took to it pretty quickly." I knead the back of her shoulders, working out a little knot of tension. "It's the only thing I've ever been good at."

"You were good at soccer back in high school," she points out.

"True, but that was a team thing. Playing instruments…that's something all of my own." She flinches as I needle her back, but it's obvious she likes how it feels. "Can you keep a secret?"

She stills. "Yes."

"I've been saving up money for my own piano for a while now. I want a really swank one." It's selfish and greedy of me, considering my position with Daniel, but it's all I've ever really wanted. Tristian would buy me one in a heartbeat, but it doesn't feel right to let him. Not for this.

She looks across the room. "What about that one?"

Scoffing, I explain, "That thing? It belongs to the house. It's supposed to be down in the library, but I had them bring it up when we moved in." A couple of the pledges still hold it against me to this day, and it's hilarious.

After a pause, she wonders, "How much have you saved?"

"The one I want costs forty grand. I have about twelve saved." I close my eyes and think of the baby grand I want, and what Story might look like bent over the top, cock buried deep inside her cunt, crying out my name. Quietly, I ask, "Why'd you stop calling me by my name?"

She's boneless here, head lolling around as I work it between my hands. "Wha…?" she asks, forehead creasing in either pleasure or confusion. "I call you by your name."

"You used to," I answer, gathering her hair in both fists and giving it a slow, gentle tug. The motion makes her shudder, mouth parting. "I liked it. No one else really calls me that. It's always 'Rath'."

I can see when she realizes what I'm talking about. Her slack jaw lifts, throat bobbing with a swallow. "Habit, I guess."

Bullshit of the highest order.

A few days ago, we were sharing a bed and fucking around and looking at each other without all our muscles going taut. She'd begged me to let her help me with my schoolwork, and even fell for easing my tension with some of the best blow jobs of my life. She'd wanted it, asked for it, which is exactly what made it so fucking hot. Now she doesn't even want to sleep in the same bed with me?

Only one thing has really changed over the last few days.

"Is it Killer?" One palm descends, rubbing into her clavicle as the other continues the soft hair tugging. My lips move against her temple when I ask, "Was he giving you shit about it? Telling you to keep your distance? Because I know he's the jealous type, but—"

She shakes her head. "No, it's not him."

There's an ambiguity to her reply that I don't particularly care for. We're still in the middle of our game, stakes are on the line, and *shit*. I actually do need her help with reading. She's the first person who's ever really taken the time to help me and not just pass me along or mock me. But beyond that, I don't like being on this side of things.

This shit has got to change.

Her tits rise and fall as she inhales and exhales, and I see her nipples pebbled under the soft cotton of my shirt. Running my hands down her sides, I drag my nose over her pink cheek. "You used to like sleeping here. It was good, wasn't it? We were good."

She stutters out a dazed, "I-I…"

"Something happened," I muse, hands gliding over a spot that makes her squirm against me. Over the fabric of her shirt, I graze her soft belly before my fingers climb up her ribs. Her hips shift minutely, and I have no doubt that she's aroused. Probably already wet. Fuck, I want to dip my fingers between her legs and find out. I don't. "Whatever it was, it doesn't seem to apply to the others. A guy could feel a little hurt."

"He could," she breathes, eyelids rising and falling with a heavy blink. "But he won't."

I watch her face closely. "Why's that?"

She doesn't answer until my hands have risen again, framing the underside of her tits, caressing the skin stretched over her ribs. "He'd probably have to care first," is her low answer.

I pause, hands going still. "You think I don't care?" When she doesn't answer, I think *fuck it*, and sweep my hands up to cup her tits, giving them a long squeeze. In a hushed voice, I ask, "You think I haven't missed you?"

She stiffens, but her back still arches into my hands. "Me? Or the things I do for you?"

Well, that's hardly fair. The two are unavoidably linked. "So you're pissed at me because…you're feeling neglected?" Well, she *has* given me some premium head, and I *did* send her off to handle herself after.

"I'm not pissed at you." She's clearly lying.

Jesus, she's fucking infuriating. Push too hard, and I spook her. Don't push hard enough and things are too one-sided. What the hell does it take with this girl?

Biting back my frustration, I run my hands over the curve of her hips, to the inside of her thighs, dragging them apart. "Just relax," I say when she tenses.

"What are you doing?" she asks, planting her hands on the bed.

"Treating you like my Lady." The taste is sour on my tongue. Who the fuck is she to tell me how to treat my own Lady, anyway? "If tit-for-tat's what you're looking for, then we can settle this right now. I pay my debts."

"I-I don't want—"

"Yes, you do." I can hear it in the stutter of her breath when the tip of my thumb grazes the edge of her panties. "You just had a nice, warm bath. Got a good buzz. A massage. Who wouldn't want to get off after that?"

"You said you wouldn't." The words come out small and accusing.

I correct her, "I said I wouldn't do anything with my dick, and I won't." I run my thumb up the center of her panties, scraping a blunt nail over her clit. "But I can still make you feel good."

She sinks her teeth into her lip. "Rath…"

I feel my face go dark at the name. Suddenly, it clicks together. It's possible that, for a minute there, I'd been something better than a Lord to her. *More* than a Lord. But now it's looking like that's all I am. I don't know when it happened or why, but I can feel the certainty of it. Somehow, I'm back to square one with this girl.

At least I know how to navigate *that*.

Tipping my mouth to her ear, I softly ask, "Would it be easier if I made it an order?"

Her jaw goes taut, gaze dropping. I know what she's about to say a moment before her lips part. It's in the flash of shame that fills her eyes. "Yes."

Fucking called it.

"Spread your legs, Lady."

Her thighs open for me. That's the thing about Story. She likes what we do to her. She gets off on it. It feels good enough that she always comes back, skirting the edges of our awareness, waiting around for someone to pounce. She just can't handle feeling accountable for it. A few months ago, this knowledge would have amused the hell out of me.

Maybe it's this new realization that I'd actually achieved something greater, but tonight, it just strikes me as unfortunate. It doesn't matter that I arrived there by using Lord tactics. We had fun, the two of us.

The inside of her panties are warm and already damp when I dip a hand inside, running my fingers through her slickness. In an instant, she's putty in my hands, head thrown back on my shoulder. Her breathing is shallow and her muscles are relaxed, down to the bend in her knee that parts her creamy thighs. "Oh…"

Oh, is right.

I close my eyes against the wrenching impulse to flip her over and drive my dick deep inside, claiming it for my own, if only for tonight. That won't do, though. I make it about her instead, getting her clit nice and slick with her own wetness before setting a rhythm. I know I'm hitting it right when her thighs fall open wider, her little hands clamping onto my legs.

I hum against her cheek. "You like that, baby?"

Her mouth is all slack again, a crease forming between her eyes.

She doesn't answer.

I let my other hand creep under her shirt. "I would have let you be on top," I tell her, remembering all my plans. I palm her tit, flicking my thumb over her stiff nipple. "I was going to show you how to ride me, nice and slow. Let you set the pace." Her breath hitches, hips bucking. Oh, yes. She likes that idea. "I was going to play with your clit, just like this, until that tight little body of yours started trembling." Smirking into her flushed cheek, I note, "A lot like how you're shaking now."

When I pull my hand from her panties, she gasps, "Rath…"

I shush her, rubbing my palm into the soft inside of her thigh. "We'll get there."

She was right on the edge of coming. The fine tremors in her thigh muscles are evidence enough, but the way her hips squirm confirms it. I give it a moment, make her back off that steep precipice, before grazing my knuckles over the cotton of her panties.

"You want more?"

She bites her lip, nodding.

"Then maybe we should take these off, hm?" I hook my fingers into the elastic of her panties, fighting back a smirk when she lets me drag them over her hips, down her legs. I tuck them beneath my pillow as a little treat for later.

Some of that anxious tension starts coming back, which is how I know it's time. I pull her thighs apart and get back to work, watching as my fingers work up and down her wet slit. She's watching too, those brown eyes of hers heavy and hooded as I rub tight, deliberate circuits around her swollen clit.

"I would have made you come on my dick," I tell her, enjoying the way my fingers look against her rosy cunt. "Then, when you were all loose and sloppy-wet for me, I would have rolled us over and fucked you right." She shudders when I pinch her nipple. "I wouldn't have torn you up. But I would have made sure you felt me the next day."

Jesus fuck, how long had I been thinking about taking her virginity?

Apparently, I'd put a lot of thought into it.

When she starts shaking again, I take my hand away, pressing a low, "Shh, baby," into her neck when she groans, writing up into thin air.

Possibly, I'm still holding onto a little piece of that grudge.

She makes a plaintive, breathless sound. "What are you doing?"

I knead my fingers into her thigh some more. "Just edging you a little.

It'll feel good, but you need a little patience." She looks the exact opposite of patient, her dark eyes shining with a dazed sort of confusion. I tug on the hem of the shirt. "Maybe we should take this off, yeah?"

She doesn't argue, letting me shuck it up over her head.

Now I've got her exactly where I need her; horny, naked, and writhing on my boner.

Good show.

"Ready for some more?"

She's nodding before I even finish the sentence.

I drag in a soft hiss when I touch her again. She's blazing hot down there, so wet that she's probably got my blankets all kinds of forfeit. When I lay my fingers over her clit, I can practically feel her pulse through it. She bucks into the weight of my hand, chasing any bit of friction, and I don't make her wait.

I make this touch light, the muscles in my arms going taut and sharp as I glance the flats of my fingers over that bundle of nerves with tight, furious flicks of my wrist. "I was going to keep my eyes open," I say to her.

When she grinds up against it, I pull it back, keeping the touch nothing more than glancing. It makes the tendon in her neck go rigid and pronounced as she digs her head back into my shoulder.

"I would have watched you the whole time," I continue, my voice going rough like gravel. "Made sure you felt good."

"Please," she gasps, chasing the friction of my hand.

Finally.

I take my hand away, hugging her close when she whines in response. "Almost," I assure her. My dick could probably drill a hole right now, but there's something I need to hear before I can let her fall to pieces. I turn to watch her flushed face, reaching up to brush her chin. "Come on, baby," I say, nudging her toward me. "Give me your mouth."

She complies mindlessly, lips parted as her head lolls to the side, allowing me to lick into the seam. Her tongue is shy and lazy, barely pressing back against my own as I kiss her. I take what's mine anyway, crushing our mouths together as my hand returns to her center.

I feel her hand come up to wind in my hair and then swallow her gasp as I rub hard and insistent against her clit. Fuck, I missed this, too. Story has the most docile kisses, sweet and lax no matter the rhythm or heat of the moment, like she's content to be tongue-fucked.

That's exactly what I give her, licking in and out of her mouth like I own it—and I suppose, in some way, I do. My own words come breathless when I say, "Right before I came, I was going to pull out and take the condom off."

I can feel her body starting to clench up, so close to breaking that she's quivering.

"Don't," she says against my lips, begging so sweetly. "Please don't stop."

"I would have wanted it off so I could fill you up." Maybe I'm shaking a little, too, but most of it is restraint. Not enough of it, though. My voice is growing too hard—too harsh—teeth scraping against her lip with a snarl. "I would have buried my load so far inside of you that you could *taste* it."

I time my retreat perfectly.

The sound she makes when I pull my hand away is high-pitched and wounded. "Rath, *please*." It's a long sob of a breath, full of frustration and agony.

I brush her hair back, forcing down the wild, aggressive thing that's boiling beneath the surface. "You know what I want."

She does.

I know she does because she won't look at me.

Not even when she says it.

"Please…" Swallowing, she gives it to me. "Dimitri."

It's worse than never hearing it at all. There's no kindness to it. No softness. Used to be, she'd say my name and I could feel the lightness of it. I hated it at first—resented the way it made me want to look at her mouth, watching the shape of it made flesh—until it just became a part of the bubble between us, quiet and so still that I could have covered myself in it and disappeared.

Now it just sounds hollow, reduced to cold bilabials and sterile consonants.

I tip my head back against the headboard and finish her off in exactly the same way. Mechanically, like it's nothing more than a task. Even when she's arching against me and coming apart, mouth opened on a cry that the others are destined to hear, I just press my fingers to her soft places and feel nothing of it.

I leave her on the bed, breathless and red-faced, forehead shining with sweat, and disappear into the bathroom to jerk off.

On my way out, I grab the wrist cuff she'd removed before getting in the bath, and then throw her a rag, not watching as she silently cleans herself up. Her eyes follow me around the room as I grab a couple blankets from the closet, laying one on the bed for her, and the other on the couch.

For me.

She stops me when I go to grab a pillow. "Wait."

I look down at her, and I'm pissed off because I've apparently lost all my ground with this girl, and I don't even know why or how. But there's something else underneath all the ire.

I think this must be what rejection feels like.

It makes me want to strike out, to tell her she's a whore for letting me do that when she clearly doesn't want me. I want to tell her to go back to her brother, who'll tear her open and manhandle her, but is apparently more appealing than me. I want to tell her she's not that special, anyway, and that I've had better, easier, prettier girls than her.

All the lies die in my throat at the look of bald panic in her eyes.

"Are you…mad?"

Maybe she doesn't want me like she had before, but she can't afford to have another one of us looking to use and taunt and *hurt*.

So I shove the feeling down, reaching down to take her hand. Her arm is limp when I raise her wrist, gently snapping the cuff into place. "We're good," I say, knowing all the while that we're not. "Go to sleep."

11

SUPERSTITION

THE MEETING IS held in the student center at a table near the front windows. At least it's nice and public. I'd spent twenty minutes beforehand scoping it out, panic and humiliation clawing at the back of my throat.

The worst of the Royal girls—Autumn, the Princess; Marigold, the Baroness; and Sutton, the Countess—sit across from me. Everything is stiff and tense with the act we're putting on, as if these three hadn't led me into a trap a week ago. The only one present who wasn't involved that day is Bianca, the Duchess.

Luckily, with a stack of folders in front of her, Bianca seems to be the one in charge. As she passes them out, my phone buzzes with a text from 'Lord Tristian'. Discreetly, I open it under the table, completely unprepared for what greets me: a picture of his erect cock.

Lord Tristian: *T-Bone misses your pretty mouth.*

I fumble the phone, stiff with shock. After a moment, another text rolls in.

Lord Tristian: *Maybe when you get over being mad at me, you can finally collect your treat.*

I shouldn't be surprised. Tristian is exactly the kind of guy who thinks a girl wants to see his cock in the middle of a meeting—even when she's irate with him. The same kind of guy who is likely to fingerbang you in a crowded room. The same kind of guy who thinks his cock qualifies as a 'treat' worthy of wiping away any resentment at being forcibly micro-chipped.

Horny fucking psycho.

"Phones up," Bianca says, cutting her eyes at me. I slide it back in my pocket, knowing that my face must be glowing red. "I'd like to get this meeting over with as soon as possible. I have a rotation at the hospital this afternoon and a Duke to patch up at midnight."

"Are you allowed to put your phone away, Story?" Sutton asks, batting her lashes. "Or is that against the rules?"

The other girls laugh, and my jaw goes tight. "I don't know, Sutton." I bat my eyelashes back. "Are you allowed to be around other women without stabbing them in the back like a sycophant, or is that against *your* rules?"

She gives me a barbed smile. "I make exceptions where necessary."

Whatever. They're owned by their Royals just as much as I am. Sutton's always worn a necklace, high and tight around her throat. I used to think it was just jewelry, but it doesn't go with all her outfits. I realize now what it really is. It's just like my wrist cuff. A mark of ownership.

A collar.

Turning to Bianca, I grapple for any sense of an ally. "You're patching up one of your Dukes? Did he get hurt?"

"Duh." She gives me a look that says this should be obvious. "They're Dukes. You know, raging chaos goblins?" At my slow, confused blink, she explains, "They're fighters, Lady. They always need patched up."

"Oh," I say, head snapping back. Marcus' words come back to me.

"Some stuff is just tradition. Stealing something from a rival's house. Sabotaging a Baron ceremony. Winning the annual boxing match against the Dukes…"

Clutching onto that, I wonder, "When's the annual boxing match, anyway?"

Bianca brightens at the mention, like a flower turning to the sun. "January.

No offense to your Lords—Payne is totally jacked—but my boys are *for sure* going to win. The Dukes almost always do."

Smiling tightly, I offer, "Maybe I'll see you there."

Bianca doesn't seem put off by the friendliness, even though I now understand that she can't be trusted. I'll take artificial civility over the way Sutton and the others are looking at me right now.

"For those of you who are new, here's the deal," Bianca begins, squaring her shoulders. "Every year, we put on a carnival during homecoming weekend. The sororities might have their holiday formals and lame mixers, but this is the biggest jewel in the Royal women's crowns. We have to do it up right. You're all here to represent your houses, but as a unit, we come together to represent Forsyth." Opening her folder, she explains, "The carnival is meant to be fun, but don't be fooled—this is a serious event that's meant to underscore the Royals' charitable efforts. It's the legacy that keeps our houses' heritage intact."

"Wait, wait, wait," I blurt. "The Royals do this for *charity*? You're kidding."

None of these guys have a charitable bone in their bodies.

Autumn scoffs, appearing uninterested. "You should know, *Lady*. The Lords are the biggest fundraisers out of all the frats. The work they do with the South Side Community Center has won national recognition. Last year, they raised half-a-million dollars."

Bianca nods and Sutton rolls her eyes at me like I'm an idiot. I might *feel* like an idiot if I hadn't spent the last few weeks doing anything other than surviving and experiencing their less than charitable attitudes first hand.

"In your folders is a detailed summary of your responsibilities for the carnival. Countess, you're in charge of food and beverages. Baroness, you'll take games and prizes. Princess, you'll organize the schedule and set up. I'm going to handle the rides, and Lady, you'll be in charge of securing permits for the location."

I stare at the information on the page. Apparently, there's a big lot just outside of South Side where this sort of thing is normally held. I see the contact information for the property owner and deflate.

Daniel Payne.

Fucking perfect.

"It seems like a lot of work, but the guys will do their part," Bianca says once she's finished outlining responsibilities. "It's tradition, and there's nothing these frats love more than upholding all their rituals. They'll provide the manpower, with the pledges contributing most of the heavy lifting. Everyone really gets into this, so don't be overwhelmed. Take your time. Do it right."

Soon after we're dismissed, I step outside and lean against a column, anxiously texting the guys my status.

Lady: *All done.*

I keep the other Royals in my periphery, suspicious and on edge. It's Tristian who responds.

Lord Tristian: *Be there in a few minutes. Then you can get your treat.*

I stare blankly at the phone, stomach sinking. *Great.* Now I'm going to have to suck him off and act like I don't want to rip it off with my teeth while I'm doing it. This entire day is a disaster.

At least I got to sleep alone last night.

Well, sort of.

Rath slept on his couch, leaving me in his big, comfortable bed. It was a good sleep, too. The kind of sleep I probably wouldn't let myself get around Killian. A soothing bath, some weed, a massage, and…

God.

That orgasm.

I was dead to the world for eight solid hours for the first time in a long time.

The issue is, he knows something's shifted between us, despite all my efforts to remain impassive—which was the best I could possibly aim for, considering. There's no doubt in my mind that the knowledge of him toppling down the points-based totem pole with me has made him furious. They're all hyper-competitive egomaniacs, after all.

What I've come to discover about Rath is that he doesn't hurt me when he's mad.

He managed it just fine when he wasn't, though.

I scroll through my phone until I hear Autumn and Sutton talking on the other side of the column.

"Did you get any news about Perez's car?" Autumn asks.

"Definitely arson," Sutton replies, voice wry. "The bar had cameras outside, but the assholes had masks on."

"That sucks."

"It does, but it's not like we don't know who did it." Sutton sniffs haughtily. "It doesn't matter, anyway. Word is that their boss is *pissed*. You know how he is about the South Side. They crossed a line in their own territory. Whatever he's going to do to them is probably better than any payback the Counts could come up with."

Autumn wonders, "So what, Perez is going to drop it?"

Sutton laughs. "Doubtful. You know how he is. That's twice now they got the best of him. But my boy is patient. He'll wait it out, nice and steady."

The conversation shifts back to homecoming planning, and I stay hidden until they're gone. Knowing that Perez still plans on getting revenge makes my palms sweat, and for the first time I don't mind having this tracker lodged under my skin. The Lords definitely have a way of making enemies. The Counts, they know about. Ted, they don't.

I wonder which one will get to them first.

Tristian chooses that exact moment to pull up. His windows are too tinted to see inside, but the instant I open the door, his music blares through. He reaches over to turn it down, patting the passenger seat. "Hop in."

Rigidly, I comply, giving his crotch a baleful glance. The ironic thing is that suddenly, I wish it'd been Rath to pick me up. Every day here has been like an agonizing set of monkey bars, swinging from least-hated Lord to least-hated Lord. My brain keeps tallying up the score, the winner changing faster that

I'm able to parse. With each transgression, I'll think *this is it*—nothing could possibly make him seem anything less than the worst evil. But I'm constantly being proven wrong.

Sometimes, it's that one of them shows me something soft and incongruous, leaving me to face the reality that perhaps everyone—even these harsh, cruel men—are made up of both light and dark. But sometimes, it's that one of them hurts me more, better, more perniciously, lowering the bar with every act of brutality.

This is an odd mixture of the two.

I'll never see myself forgiving Tristian for putting the tracker into me, but at the same time, last night had complicated my feelings for Rath. I'm all too aware of his ability to manipulate me, but the way he'd been in the bathtub, so ready to gather me up and hold me close, didn't seem artificial at all.

Neither had the somber look in his eyes when he told me goodnight and left me there in the bed, exhausted and confused.

Tristian's got a pair of sunglasses perched on his nose, wrist slung loose over the steering wheel. "How'd it go?"

My answer is short. "Fine." I'm wondering if he'll drive somewhere so I can give him road head again. We're too close to the brownstone to bother getting anything started on the way home, but he could make a detour. Somewhere crowded, no doubt.

He pauses, watching me from behind the glasses. "Still mad, then?"

I look out at the campus, remaining silent.

Sighing, he grabs the gear shift and yanks it back, peeling out of the lot. "You know, I could be mad, too." His mouth is scrunched into a tight, unhappy line. "You've never—not once—slept in my bed. You'll sleep with Rath. You'll sleep with Killer, even though he fucking hurts you. But me?" He shoves the gear shift up angrily, and I wince. "I get fucking nothing. And you know what's fucked up?" He actually glances at me like he expects an answer. We'd be here all damn day. "I'm the one who takes care of you. *Me*. Everything I do—and it might piss you off, but it's true—*everything* is because I want to keep you."

Keep me.

Not keep me happy.

Not keep me safe.

Just keep *me*.

I give a loose, unconcerned shrug. "Why don't you just make me sleep in your bed? That's what Killian does."

He slams his palm on the steering wheel, roaring, "I don't want to make you!"

I flinch so hard that my entire body jumps. Aside from that fight with Killian, I've never heard Tristian yell before. It makes something hard and panicked rise in my throat. I watch with wide eyes as he sucks in a deep breath, nostrils flaring.

He lets out a soft curse, reaching up to comb his fingers through his blond hair. Gently, he says, "I'm not Killian."

I'm not sure if he's talking about the yelling or the order to sleep with him, but I say, "Okay," and don't feel any less unmoored.

He takes off his sunglasses, shooting me a look I'd call apologetic on anyone else. "I shouldn't have yelled."

Gulping, I fix my eyes out the window. "It's fine."

"No, it's not. I scared you, and that's…" He turns onto the street that leads us home, and I can see him glancing back and forth, from me to the road. "You were right yesterday. What you said to Rath, about being treated like our Lady? There are some things you can call us out on, you know."

I give a weak laugh. "There are a lot of things I can't."

"Yeah, there are," he agrees, turning into the spot in front of the house. "But this is one of them."

I watch him from the corner of my eye as he puts the car into park and kills the ignition. He lingers there, looking out the window, and his face is tumultuous and pensive, like maybe he's got more to say.

Or like maybe he's hoping I'll say something myself.

I get this…awareness. If I reached over right now and bridged the gap, I think he'd be relieved. Happy. Because right now, he is distinctly *unhappy*.

Somehow, the way I act has the power to do that.

How odd.

I'm not sure why or how or when that happened. It's perfectly clear that Tristian cares for me more as an object than a person. Why should it matter to him whether I'm hot or cold?

Testing this theory, I reach for the hand still on the gearshift, gently resting my palm over his knuckles. He remains still, but I don't miss the flick of his eyes to our hands, that sulky crevice between his eyebrows disappearing instantly.

Jesus.

So easy.

He flips his hand, knitting his fingers with mine. "Hey," he whispers, giving my arm a light tug. When I turn to meet his gaze, those blue eyes blaze back at me. "Forgive me?"

"For yelling?" I ask. I don't even need to lie. "Yes."

His eyes fall to my lips. "And for…the other thing?"

I stare at him. "Do I forgive you for forcing me to undergo a micro-chipping that effectively strips away the thin veneer of freedom I've been clinging to for my own sanity?" Smiling, I answer. "No, and fuck you for asking."

His eyes harden. "I did it for your—"

I put my fingers over his mouth, cutting him off. "I don't want to hear any more about it being for my own good. I get to be pissed about this, Tristian. You can't force me not to feel something and you can't talk me into seeing whatever twisted logic is eating a hole in your brain." I let my hand slip away, willing him to understand. "This is the part of me you can't control. You're just going to have to deal with it."

For a moment, I think I'm crazy for trying to reason with him at all. It's a straight shot to more hurt and debasement. The tracker was obviously one of thuse things I'm not allowed to call him out on.

His eyes search my face. "But I don't like it."

Some of the tension drains from my spine at the response, spoken so plainly. "You're free to feel that way, too. But I think if you wanted some gutless little Stepford robot as your Lady, you would have chosen someone else."

"You're right," he says, after a long, pensive moment. He lifts my hand, holding my gaze as he presses a kiss to the cuff around my wrist. "You'll let me give you your treat, though?"

My face falls. "Oh." He looks confused at the reaction, and then even more confused when I reached for his fly, asking, "You want it here?"

He captures my wrist, frowning. "What are you doing?"

"Didn't you want…" I look at him, baffled. "You said you wanted my mouth."

His expression blanks out, and then he chuckles, low and mischievous. "Sweetheart, of course I want your mouth. But that wasn't the treat I had in mind."

My face flushes in embarrassment. "Oh."

"Come on," he says, looking excited as he opens his door. "I'll show you."

I stare at it for a long time, unable to move.

My chest swarms with too many emotions to process all at once. Disbelief, because he must be mistaken—there's no way this is mine. It's a joke, a trick. The actual surprise is waiting inside, and it won't be nearly as appealing. Then I feel a wave of suspicion and fear, because I can't even imagine the conditions that must be attached to this. After that comes the heartache. A sorrow so thick that I think I could choke on it. Because *god*—I want it.

Tristian's arms wind around my waist from behind, a kiss pushed beneath my ear. "Do you like it?"

"I-I…"

I'm speechless.

He buries a smile into my shoulder. "I spent all day looking for the perfect one. I knew the second I saw that dark cherry red, it belonged to my Sweet little Cherry."

"Mine?" I ask, tongue feeling dry and heavy. "Really mine?"

"*Really* yours," he says, slipping away to walk to the car. It's not all red. In fact, it's mostly a flat, matte black. But there's an elegant stripe that sweeps along the doors, slashing down the hood and along the roof, that's a deep, vivid red. Tristian looks at the car, eyes sparkling with satisfaction. "Admittedly, the muscle car called to me because I'm a red-blooded man who likes the growl and speed, but you seemed to like my Porsche the other night. Not like girls usually do, either. You didn't care that it was expensive and shiny. You just liked the power beneath the hood." He turns to me, giving me a knowing look. "Isn't that right?"

I can't believe he even noticed that.

It's nothing like my old car—the only thing I regret abandoning in Colorado. That one had been a beater. Old and rusted, but fast and true. It was the only thing that kept me together some days, roaring out along some deserted highway, feeling so free that my chest ached with the possibilities.

This one is like something out of a magazine. Sleek and flawless and…

"It's a Dodge Charger," I say, still stunned. He could have given me a pile of only semi-drivable rust and I would have been just as shocked. But this?

He spreads his arms wide, looking deviously handsome. "Pretty sweet, right?"

"Tristian, this is…" I shake my head, fear rapidly becoming the winning emotion. "This is too much."

I can't earn this.

Whatever he wants me to do in exchange, it won't be worth it.

Probably.

"For you?" he asks, coming to stand in front of me. He reaches up to tuck a lock of hair behind my ear. "Never."

Swallowing thickly, I have to ask. "What are the strings?"

His eyebrows knit together as he watches me. "I get the tracker is a violation to you. I just wanted you to understand that it's not all bad." He tilts his head toward the Charger. "It can help us give some of your freedom back, see?"

After a moment of gaping at him, I hedge, "So, you're saying…I've already paid the price?" and he gives me a puzzled look.

"There's no *price*, Story," he says, grabbing my hips and tugging me close. "This is a gift, because that's what a Lord does for his Lady. If you're asking if I expect something in return, then…well, you're right." My stomach sinks like a brick at his words, too disappointed to do anything but stand limply as he presses a kiss to my neck. He lingers there, whispering, "You have to smile."

I cock an eyebrow at him. "Smile."

Nodding, he assures, "That's it. The only thing I'm asking of you is that you enjoy it. A sweet ride like this needs a Lady who can properly appreciate it, don't you think?" He reaches into his pocket, pulling out a pair of keys. He dangles them there in front of me, waiting.

My palms sweat with the possibility that he'll snatch them away, so I reach for them stiltedly, preparing for the inevitable, giving him too many opportunities to pull the rug out from under me.

When my hands close around the keys, something inside of me sparks to life, my pulse quickening.

Somehow, Tristian sees it, his lips curling into an indulgent smirk. "Come on. I know you want to give it a spin."

It's not that I don't see it. This is probably another manipulation tactic. Having something I want just means they'll have something to take away from me. It'll give them leverage. Control. I shouldn't get hopeful or attached. I should treat it as the bribe it's clearly meant to be. It'll come back to bite me. I just know it.

But life is harsh and cold and cruel, and I think it might be like I am with the guys, constantly having to untangle to the dark from the light, clutching any bit of goodness close, just to make it to the next monkey bar.

This is light.

This is good.

I look at the keys, feeling my face crack with a reluctant grin.

"There it is," he whispers, brushing a knuckle under my chin. "Lay it on me, hm?" He taps his cheek, grinning like the cat who got the cream when I bounce up to give him a peck. "That's my good girl. You think you can handle this thing?"

I pluck the sunglasses from the collar of his shirt, putting them on. "I think I can manage."

He doesn't make me ask, laughing at the barely restrained impatience on my face. "Go on. Be back in an hour. I'll cover for you with the others." He gives my ass a slap and sends me on my way.

When I open the car door and reverently slide behind the wheel, I notice something in the passenger seat, waiting for me: A dozen sunny daisies. There's a skull hanging from the rearview mirror, ornamental and brand new, marking this as a Lady's ride.

Okay, maybe Tristian isn't the *worst*.

For now.

THERE'S ONE FUNDAMENTAL difference between this pregame party and the first. Thanks to Killian forcing me to blow him in front of the frat, every guy here knows intimately who I am. They also understand that I am completely off limits. No one hassles me as I walk through the party, still feeling buzzed off the drive I'd taken earlier.

The car is sex on wheels.

Pure, undiluted power beneath the palms of my hands.

I'm not proud to admit it, but if they'd asked me yesterday whether I'd be willing to take the tracker to get the car, I might have had to think about it.

Hard.

I'd gone to the back roads, really opening it up, getting acquainted with it. With every press of the clutch, I was saying, "Hello, my name is Story," and with every shift of the gears, the car was saying back, "Pleasure to meet you, Miss Story." When I adjusted the mirrors, I was saying, "I think we can be the best of friends," and when it responded to my foot on the pedal, it was responding, "I think you're right."

I'd still be out there now, exploring the back roads I'd barely gotten acquainted with in my youth, except that I have duties tonight.

Rath's in the corner of the main room, jaw working lazily around a piece of gum. I know him well enough by now to realize he's craving a cigarette, but doesn't want to leave the laptop and the music to move outside to smoke it. I'm still a little uneasy about last night. About the way he treated me. About him clearly being mad, but not making me take the brunt of it. If I'd never found the videos, I think last night would have pushed me into a canyon of feelings that I'm grateful to have avoided. Obviously, it's better to have the veil lifted, but part of me wishes I could have accepted the lie. I could have chosen him that night. The plans he had for me…

They would have been perfect.

We could have had sex, just the way he wanted to, and I can see perfectly how it would have unfolded. The two of us in his bed all day, rolling around, learning each other's bodies. After, when we were tired and messy, maybe we would have taken a shower—or a bath. Ms. Crane might have brought us up something to eat. Maybe Rath would have played me something on the piano as I stole food from his plate. Perhaps we might have talked, quiet and close, secrets pressed into sweaty, tender skin. I would have emerged from that room a changed person. An attached person. A person so close to the edge of falling that it would have been impossible to walk myself back.

It would have been wonderful and exciting and so horrifically fake.

Rath doesn't see me coming until I'm slipping into his lap, so caught up in the music that he startles at the invasion. There's a flash of irritation in his eyes that gets zapped away in an instant when he realizes it's me.

He greets me with a low, "Sour Cherry," but despite the words, his arm snakes around my waist, holding me to him.

"I've decided to be sweet tonight, actually." I hand him the beer I've brought, still cold enough that's it barely begun to sweat.

He tips it back, eyes dropping to my cleavage as he swallows. I don't know how Tristian can accuse me of playing favorites with Rath and Killian, considering that I seem to dress for him every day.

"I bet you did," he replies, adjusting his grip on my waist to pull me up his thigh. His dark eyes scan the room, even though he pitches his voice low enough that only I can hear it. "I could have bought you a car, too, you know."

"Really?"

Scoffing, he sets the beer down. "Fuck no. Mercer money is bottomless. Rathbone money has both a floor and a ceiling, and not much room in between."

My eyebrows rise in revelation. I always just assumed he was as wealthy as the others. "Well, I don't think I need two."

"Hm." His expression is exceptionally broody, even for him, so I decide to give it the test. The same one I'd used on Tristian.

I cup his cheek, turning him to me, and then press our mouths together. I keep the kiss just as sweet as I promised to be, plucking gently at his lips between the piercings. He responds by yanking me close and prying my lips apart with his tongue, greedy as he plunges into my mouth. He tastes like beer and cinnamon, and when I feel the gum trapped beneath his tongue, I steal it for myself, pulling away.

"Thanks," I say, giving the gum a few smacks as I slide away.

His eyes follow my retreat with a dumb look that I'll be smirking about for hours to come.

I walk into the game room next, where Tristian is dealing cards at a table beside the bar. He's holding court around a group of pledges that look starry-eyed and stupid, which means he's probably taking all their money while he's at it.

Tristian catches my eye and holds it, shuffling the cards with a precise, expert flick of his thumbs. "Might as well pack it in, boys. My secret weapon just walked in: Lady Luck."

One by one, the pledges turn to watch me. It's a little easier with them. None of the pledges were in the basement that night, so the only thing they know about me is that I'm untouchable. Every single one of them stands when I approach, however, which catches me off guard, making me tense. It's a bit startling, actually. I think for a moment they're about to flee, but instead, they simply…wait. For me. To sit.

They're not fleeing.

They're being *gentlemen*.

One of them even takes his fucking hat off. It's a quick, panicked gesture, like he's not sure if he should or not, but he's deciding not to take any chances. The scene is so surreal that I just stare at them for a long moment, unable to think of anything to say.

Tristian takes me by the wrist and pulls me in, dragging me into his lap. Like a switch has been flipped, they all sink back into their seats. I watch for a while as Tristian skillfully parts a freshman with two fifty-dollar bills. Once he's gone, a baleful sophomore tries his hand, losing three twenties so fast that I barely catch sight of them before Tristian's tucking them into his pocket. Every now and then, he'll lean in to press a kiss behind my ear, or stroke the hair laying against my back.

Once the last victim has lost his money, Tristian calls the bartender over and says, "Try this." He holds up a drink. It's ruby red and has two cherries floating on top. "It may be your signature cocktail."

"Oh, I-I probably shouldn't," I stammer. Lowering my senses around these guys seems unwise.

"Just a sip." He takes one first and licks his lips. "I think you'd like it. It's sweet, just like you."

Loud laughter bounces across the room, and I glance over. Killian is surrounded by three girls over by the fireplace. They're different girls from the last party, but still perfectly the type he goes for. Blonde, tanned, big tits, short skirts. My exact opposite. One leans in and whispers something in his ear, and a flicker of irritation crosses over me.

"You've got to be kidding me," I mutter.

Tristian follows my eyes, tsking at the scene. "Cherry, you can't get worked up about Killian and his pregame stuff. He's crazy superstitious. It's almost crippling."

My eyes narrow before I look away. "After the week I've had, Killian shouldn't get to break the contract—no matter what kind of loopholes he added in."

"It doesn't work that way," Tristian says.

"Of course, it doesn't. Since when does anything about this fucked up situation work in my favor?"

I grab the drink from him and gulp it down in one big swallow. It's sweet on my tongue and spicy going down my throat—cinnamon, like the gum. I pluck out the cherries and pop them into my mouth before pushing the empty glass back in his hand. "Got another?"

His eyebrow lifts, and he hands the glass to the bartender. A moment later, I have another drink. It tastes better than the first. I drink it quickly and hold it out. "More."

Tristian gives me a disapproving look. "Sweetheart, you're going to get shitfaced if you keep going like this. Look how tiny you are. You probably have the metabolism of a gerbil."

"Mercer," I say, using his last name, "in the last week, I've been kidnapped, lost my virginity to my stepbrother, set fire to a hundred-and-fifty-thousand-dollar car, had a fucking tracker implanted underneath my skin, and was forced to organize a stupid homecoming charity event with the bitchiest girls on campus. Name one person here who deserves to get wasted more than me."

His eyebrows crouch low, like he's about to argue. But he doesn't. "Okay, you've got me there," he concedes and looks at the bartender. "Make the next one a double."

"A triple," I say, already feeling the buzz. I take one more look across the room at Killian and his whores and loop my arm around Tristian's neck.

"You know what his problem is?" I ask, eating another cherry and licking my fingers.

Tristian looks amused at the gesture, fixing his gaze down my shirt. "I'm sure you're going to tell me."

"He's spoiled, entitled, and so goddamn obsessive."

He arches an eyebrow. "Pretty sure you just described every man in this room, Cherry. The difference with Killian is that he's obsessed with *you*. He has been for years."

I roll my eyes, feeling the warm heat of alcohol under my skin. "He hates me. He thinks my mom swooped in and destroyed his perfect, spoiled little life by splitting his daddy's attention. He's not obsessed with me. He's just obsessed with punishing me."

"You know the saying," he runs his nose down my neck, "there's a thin line between love and hate. Killian Payne is riding that line even harder than he likes riding you."

The liquor hits my bloodstream, and the room grows fuzzy. I feel weightless and loose for the first time in a while—even more than the weed last night with Rath. *God.* Fuck these guys with their trackers and bribes and games.

I look at Tristian's flawless face, sharp jaw, and blue eyes. "How come you haven't fucked me yet?"

His eyebrows climb to his forehead. "Do you want me to?"

"I don't know." I shrug, plucking the cherry out of my glass. "I just figured once Killian popped my cherry, you would have taken me for yourself. I keep waiting for one of you to pounce. It's making my head hurt."

There's a beat of silence before Tristian rises my chin, forcing me to meet his gaze. "Oh, I've thought about it. Repeatedly." He pitches forward to steal a slow kiss. The chaste nature of it is belied by the words he speaks next. "I've thought about tossing you on my bed and driving into you so hard that you cry out my name. I've thought about bending you over the edge of the couch— the one right over there—and making the other two watch as I take you. I've considered doing it a million different ways."

Those scenes flash in front of me, warmth pooling in my stomach. "So why haven't you?"

"Maybe I'm waiting for you to heal up." He licks at my mouth, his tongue darting against mine. "Or maybe I'm waiting for you to answer my question with a 'yes' instead of an 'I don't know'."

Tristian Mercer, caring about my consent?

His lips tip up at my sudden peal of laughter. I don't realize we're drawing stares until his amused gaze shifts around the room, pinging from person to person. "Is that funny?"

I nod, wheezing. "Oh, my god, it's hilarious." I clutch my side, hardly remembering what was so funny, but knowing that it was.

He shakes his head, chuckling. "Okay, you are well and truly hammered. Up we go."

I stumble when he stands me up, but his arms are there in an instant, catching me and dragging me close. "Oh, no." I palm my head, vision swimming. "Everything's all wonky."

"I'm sure it is." He's talking to me like I'm stupid. Like I'm a child.

We've just reached the staircase when I ask, "Why don't you just do it now?" I think I could do it like this—get it over with. Stop feeling like it could happen at any time. Finally get the smallest sense of peace. "You could fuck me tonight. I'll say yes."

He lumbers up the stairs, practically carrying me now. "That's your massive blood alcohol content talking, sweetheart."

He assists me down the hall toward the stairs, but my legs give out. "Oops."

He lifts me up and turns into the library, where he helps me onto a leather chaise. He covers me with a soft blanket draped over the chair, and my eyes flutter closed. I guess this is probably way better than sex, anyway.

I feel his lips on my forehead, a soft kiss pressed into my skin. "Soon, Sweet Cherry. You'll be mine, soon."

1 2

ROUGH

"Are we going to go upstairs?" Monica asks. Her tight body is glued to my side, hips undulating with the beat of the music. The room is packed, everyone excited to be out on a Thursday night. Monica's tits rub against my side while another girl offers me a beer. I've been playing all of them up all night. My reputation was very close to taking a hit last time, when I couldn't get it up. I haven't had that problem again—not since I broke my dry spell with Story in the upstairs hall, nor since I claimed her virginity.

I'm not ready to commit to monogamy, but only one girl is getting my cock hard these days.

And isn't that the bitch of it? The only girl who gets me hard also gets me so fucking furious that I can barely stand to look at her. I was such a fucking idiot, thinking she was cuddling to me the other night because she might want me. I see it now for what it was. Just another ploy. A mere thirteen hours later, Marcus was telling me about her mixing it up with that old pervert, Cartwright. Old habits die hard, huh?

They must, considering all it took for Tristian to fall back into her good graces was a forty thousand dollar car. The whore really doesn't fall far from the whore tree, does it? After all this time, she's still looking for some fool to throw money at her. You can bet your fucking ass it won't be me.

So whatever, I'll take her glares and cold shoulders. Watch her sit on Tristian's lap and giggle like a bimbo. Lay in bed at night knowing she fucking ducked and chose to sleep with Rath instead.

I'll get what's mine.

"We can stay down here if you want," Monica says when I don't answer, taking my hand and settling it just below her tits. "Oh, hey! What about that hot tub out back?"

I look down at this girl. Her blonde hair. Her bronze skin. Her green eyes. I haven't been with her before, but I can tell from the way she moves that she walked in here tonight, confident about being the one to please me. What she doesn't realize is that girls like her can't fix a guy like me. Used to be I'd give it a whirl, see how it shook out, but I get it now. I need something else. Now that I've actually lived my fantasy—had my stepsister beneath me, pliant and warm and wet—there's no going back.

Anyway, I have a new pregame ritual, and it doesn't involve any of these bitches.

"Thanks for the offer, but I'm out for the night." One pledge passes by and I grab him, jerking my chin at the girl. "I bet my boy Tucker here would love to show you three a good time, though." The other two girls look pouty and crestfallen at my rejection. Being one of my pregame fucks is an honor. I pat Tucker on the shoulder. "Isn't that right?"

Tucker looks like a kid who just got handed a golden goose. He grins, this charming little smirk that I'm sure has helped him pull a hundred girls before, and says in a slow drawl, "I'd be honored to entertain you beautiful ladies."

There's no doubt Tucker is going to be nicer to these girls than I would be, so I hand them off and cut through the crowded room in search of Story. She and Tristian had been over by the bar, flirting and downing drinks. She dressed for him in a pair of tight booty shorts and an even tighter FU tank top. I didn't miss her scowl in my direction before they slipped out of view.

Jealous or pissed?

Both possibilities make my dick twitch.

Rath is DJing, and I get his attention with a snap of my fingers. He lifts one headphone, so I ask, "Where's Cherry?"

"Saw Tris take her down the hall. She was slamming down drinks." He points toward the library. "All good?"

"Yep," I say, clapping him on the back. He loves commanding the music at these parties, lording his eclectic taste over the rest of the frat. I spot Tristian by the pool table, cue in hand, and make my way over. "Where is she?"

"Shit, man." He knows who I'm talking about, nodding over at the stairs. "Our girl was sloppy drunk, so I tried to carry her up to her room. We didn't make it, though. I left her in the library passed out on the couch."

"You left her alone?" I ask, anger shooting through me. "Passed out, in a house filled with frat boy degenerates?"

Tristian rolls his eyes. "Dude, who are you even talking to? After you broke every damn phone in the frat, no one is going to make a move on our Lady. She's safe as houses up there."

Well, he's got a point there.

"You better fucking hope."

"Go check on her if you're so worried." He takes a swallow of his drink, pausing. "Actually, I'll go up with you." For all his bluster about her being safe, I can see I've talked him into worrying a bit. Truth be told, Tristian is better at this than the rest of us. Taking care of what's important. Keeping people happy. Protecting the things he cares about. I'd trust him with her life over anyone else.

Even me.

We head down the hall, past a few closed doors that lead to guest bedrooms. They pretty much only exist as impromptu fuck pads, and during parties like this, they're first come, first served. I hear giggles behind one and assume Tucker is showing the girls a good time. The section of the house with the library is off limits during frat events, a rule established after Ms. Crane had to dedicate a whole-ass weekend to cleaning piss out of desk drawers. It's not worth listening to her bitching about it, and honestly, it's nice to have one room in the house not covered in bodily fluids and beer.

The library doors are open, and Story is lying there on the leather chaise by the window. She's on her back, hair brushed haphazardly out of her face. Her shorts are wedged between her thighs and one of her legs is hanging off the edge of the cushion. From the doorway, I have a perfect view of the milky white skin between her legs, a hint of black lace panties peeking out.

She doesn't just look like she's sleeping.

She looks like she's dead to the goddamn world.

My cock fills up instantly.

"Jesus Christ." I look over my shoulder, pinning Tristian with a glare. "We'd have to fucking blind someone if they saw our Lady like this," I hiss.

He peers over my shoulder, wincing. Throwing a hand out, he insists, "She was covered up when I left. She must have kicked the blanket off."

I see it now, all pooled on the floor. That's what he gets for buying all those ridiculous get-ups for her to wear. Fucking booty shorts and miniskirts. At least Rath got her some jeans.

"I'll take it from here," I say, going to shut the door.

Tristian shoots out a hand, palm landing on the wood. "Yeah, I don't think so."

I narrow my eyes at him. "Excuse me?"

He pushes past me, into the room. "Do you think I'm stupid? I know why you're up here. You told me yourself you'd be adding her to your pregame ritual if you won before." He spreads his arms, daring me to argue. "Well, you won."

My jaw aches with how hard I grind my teeth. "That's my fucking right. You don't get to tell me what I can and can't do with my own goddamn Lady."

He holds up a hand, voice even. "I know. But I also know she slapped you yesterday and you're pissed off about Cartwright. You can't control yourself, Killer." He glances at Story, something dangerous flashing in his eyes. "I'm not going to let you hurt her. If you want to fuck her, then you're right. I can't stop you. But I'm also not leaving."

I roll my eyes so hard, I see spots. "You're going to watch?" Jesus, we haven't done that shit since freshman year. "That's not a part of the ritual."

He scoffs. "Please. One time does not a ritual make." He moves behind me to close the door, locking it. "Plus, you did it in the hallway last time. It wasn't exactly private."

I reach down to squeeze my hard-on, muttering a curse. "Fine, but you're the one who needs to control yourself. Your cock isn't the priority here. This is *my* ritual and shit has to go down a certain way." When he opens his mouth, I shove his shoulder. "I fucking mean it. You get my dick soft tonight and you're going to find out what it's like to have *your* car torched."

"It's okay to feel insecure, Killer." He gives me a slimy grin, reaching down to squeeze his own cock. "I know it looks intimidating when you compare them."

"Hardly," I sneer, turning to Story. I take a minute to watch her. For once the lights are on and there's little threat she'll wake. Her chest rises and falls with even breaths. I stand over her, eyes roaming over that tight little body. She looks so delicate and vulnerable like this, but I know better. She's a fighter. An opportunist. A manipulator. She fooled all those sugar daddies, my father, Tristian. But now, all passed out on the chaise, I'm the one in control.

Completely and wholly.

"You know, seeing her like this," Tristian says, head tilting, "I think I might get the appeal."

He and Rath have never understood my preference for sleepers. They used to give me shit for it in high school every time I'd tell them about watching her, whipping my dick out and leaving a little part of myself with her. Pathological, Tristian had called it.

Now, he's staring at her like he wants to climb between her legs.

I step in front of him before he has a chance.

This is *mine*.

Story isn't asleep. She's drunk. Barely conscious and completely pliable. My dick gets harder the longer I watch her. Looking as though he's testing the waters, Tristian reaches out to brush a strand of hair off her face. She sighs gently, but doesn't wake. Emboldened, I run my finger up her bare leg, up to the softness of her open thighs. Her tongue darts out, pink and warm, but her eyes never open.

I don't care that Tristian is here. I could fuck Story six ways to Sunday with her passed out like this, and it'd be the best fuck I ever had. No having to worry about her waking, no concern about what she'll remember. This is complete dominion.

"No," Tristian suddenly says, voice quiet. "You've got to give her some time to heal, Killer."

I throw him a look, weirded-out that he can read me so well. "I'm not here to fuck her," I say, even though I would if I wanted to. But I've got a ritual to perform, so I jerk my chin at her. "She knew I'd be coming for her tonight. Maybe that's why she drank this much." Looking at the rise and fall of her chest, flushed from the alcohol, I idly muse, "Maybe it's an olive branch or something. She knew I'd like it."

"Or," Tristian offers, petting her forehead, "maybe it's the only way she could stomach it."

I toss him a threatening glare. "Maybe you can keep your opinions to yourself."

He doesn't know her as well as he thinks he does.

Her breasts are pressing against the cotton of her tank, braless like she's been instructed. I push down the straps, sliding them over her shoulders, revealing her supple tits. The cool air makes her nipples tighten and peak, and I graze a thumb over one to feel it stiffen even harder. Story is a beautiful woman. Prettier than she was when we met. That awkward, gangly teenager is long-gone, replaced with womanly curves and an understated grace.

"What was it like?" Tristian asks, and looking up, I realize his eyes are just as dark and hooded as mine. His hand is in his pocket, but I can tell he's rubbing his dick. He elaborates. "Fucking her, taking her virginity."

I look back down at her rosy nipples, thumbing the button on my jeans. "Tight," is my answer, not even bordering on sufficient. "Soft. Wet. She fought a little at first, but I knew she was into it. Scratched my back up a bit when she came."

He makes an indistinct sound. "So it was good?"

"It was good." Lower, I tell him, "She was good for me."

He hums, not looking bothered when I push my jeans down, removing my shirt. My cock weighs heavily between my legs, the ache deep in my balls. The desire I feel for her, the all-consuming want…

It never abates. It just gets worse. The guys call me obsessed. Addicted. *Pathological.* They're probably right. Nothing this girl can give me will ever be enough. I should stop.

I can't.

I place my hands under Story's armpits and haul her up. Tristian moves behind her to cradle her neck. I snap my teeth and open my mouth to tell him to get the fuck away from what's *mine.*

Our eyes lock over her head and he says, "I know you want to piss on her, Killer, but she's not your territory to mark. She's *ours.* She belongs to all of us."

We stare at one another for a long moment, Tristian determined to hold his ground, me trying to reconcile sharing her. I know he's right. The bitch of it is that it's not even about the contract, or tradition, or the structure of the Lords. It's not even about how far we go back, how entwined we've always been. Tristian's the one who finally cornered her in the laundry room that night, setting this ball into motion. Rath manipulated her into feeling somewhat comfortable in the house. All three of us helped create this. Take even one of us away, and the whole thing would crumble.

She's *our* Lady.

He nods, watching me process this, and repeats, "Ours."

"Hold on to her neck," I say as a way of agreement. We position her so that she's reclining on the chaise, no longer slouching. My nose is inches from hers and her eyelashes flutter open. I go still as her hand clumsily touches my stomach. She mumbles something incoherent, and a second later, her eyes close again.

Exhaling slowly, I ask, "What was it like for you?" I watch her lips, parted and so, so red. "When she sucked you off—when she wanted it—what was it like?" It stings to ask for this knowledge that only he and Rath have access to. For me, that day down in the basement, it hadn't been what I really wanted.

Tristian gathers her hair to the side, his voice low and sympathetic. "Trust me, Killer. You don't want to know."

He doesn't meet my eyes.

"I do, or I wouldn't have asked."

He pauses for a moment, like he's choosing his words carefully. "There's a wild side to this girl, Killer. Sure, she fights a lot, but deep down, she's hungry for it. If you could take the leash off of her for a minute, you'd get to see it, too. When she chooses to give in, she's so eager and responsive." He traces her bottom lip, looking lost in thought. "All it takes is giving her a little control— even if it's flimsy—and she just...blooms like a fucking flower." Sighing, he gives me a significant look. "So yeah, I gave back a little of her control and she rewarded me with the best goddamn road head of my life."

"That's why you gave her the car," I realize. It wasn't a quick fix to buying her forgiveness, which I should have known. That's not Tristian's style. It was just another brick in the foundation.

Shrugging, he answers, "Of course. Why do you think she was willing to get so hammered with me tonight?" He looks down at Story, who currently is susceptible to our every whim. "Relationships require a little give and take,

Killer. Even in a situation like this. Sometimes you have to lose a little to win a little."

I snort at his logic. "Well, tonight I'm going to take from our Lady and give a little in return. Since I'm feeling generous, you can stay and watch." I climb over her, knees on each side of her chest, cock aligned with the valley between her tits. I stroke up and down the shaft, knowing it's too dry. I lean forward and thumb her lips.

Tristian crouches down beside her, smoothing her hair back. "Open up for Killer, sweetheart."

"Hmmm?" she asks groggily, eyes staying closed.

"Open your mouth," he whispers as I force my thumb inside. "Let him in."

She hums against the intrusion, sucking my finger. Tristian cups her jaw and wiggles it loose until it slacks. Then I test her by bracing forward, pushing the tip of my cock through her lips. Her tongue flicks out and she sighs. When I'm sure she's truly out and not going to take a bite out of me, I slide the length of my cock past her soft lips and over her warm tongue.

"That's our good girl," Tristian breathes into her ear, and I just barely stop myself from rolling my eyes. I don't know where he gets off calling me pathological with his hard-on for showing off.

Thankfully, he backs off before I get territorial again, propping himself up against the wall as he watches.

The urge to fuck her face is so strong that I'm almost grateful for Tristian's presence. That's not what this is about. But fuck, it's good—good and so damn wet that I have to force myself to pull out, sliding my cock slick from her red mouth. Easing back, I grab her tits and squeeze them together, rocking up into the valley between them. The sweet friction is exactly what I've been looking for, made all the better by the responding, sleepy twitch of her body.

Story's got nice tits, and that's a fact. But they're a little too small for this, forcing me to crush them tighter and closer as my dick glides between them. I graze my thumbnails over her nipples as I do it, and she lets out this tiny little breath of a whimper that shoots straight to my balls.

"Fuck," I grunt, the soft skin combined with the warm pressure already making me crazy. She feels good—so fucking good—and I hold on to her as I thrust upward again and again, my balls slapping against the underside of her tits.

"Not so hard," Tristian says, but there's no threat in his words. I can tell by the low octave, along with the sound of his zipper lowering, that he's jerking off behind me. Somehow, that just makes it hotter, knowing that he's witnessing me take her like this, understanding just how badly he wants her, too. He certainly doesn't stop me, not when I squeeze her breasts again or when I touch her nipples and she makes those fucking *sounds*, like maybe she'd regret not being cognizant for this.

For a while, all there is are the sounds of our harsh breaths and slapping flesh. The sight of my dick pumping between her tits is hypnotizing. It's not like last time, lacking all the lava-hot hatred from her. I've got plenty of my own, though, easily imagining her talking to that fucking pervert the other day. Not just a pervert, but a King.

A Count.

My body draws tight at the reminder, and it isn't until Tristian says, "Ease the fuck off, Killer," that I realize how hard I'm squeezing her. Bruising her, probably.

That just makes it better. Even with Tristian jacking off six feet away. Even with her eyebrows knitting together like she's not sure what's happening, but is too deep under the surface of consciousness to do anything about it. I think about her sleeping in one of their beds, them peeling off her top and seeing my fingerprints pressed into her flesh. I think about them—all these fucking vultures, just dying to have her—unwrapping her like a present, only to find that she's already been used and marked. The Counts. Cartwright. My own goddamn father…

I still with a low grunt, my dick pulsing between her tits. Thick ribbons of my come paint her chest, one shooting all the way to the soft peak of her delicate chin. My shoulders jerk with my release, and I do let go of her tits.

But only to run my finger through that glob of spunk on her chin, rubbing it along her lips before pushing it in her mouth.

Tristian spits a low curse from his spot in the corner. "Can't believe I had to jizz in my pants like some goddamn mongrel. And look at that." He tosses a hand out toward her tits. "Now she's going to know tomorrow. You were too rough. *Again.*"

Pulling a wrist across my mouth, I sit back, committing the sight of her, absolutely covered with me, to memory. "She's fine," I argue, stepping unsteadily to my feet. "She's always bruised easy."

I *want* her to know.

I want everyone to know.

She may be ours, but tonight she was mine.

"Jesus, I need to change." Tristian buttons his pants, grimacing. "Can I trust you to get her to bed? I'm no bitch, but hauling her up the stairs was hard enough, and she still had some of her legs then."

Nodding, I pull up my pants. "Leave it to me."

I wait until he leaves to carry her out of the library, cradling her limp body in my arms, and there's a moment in the hallway, standing between my door and hers, that makes me pause. I should put her in my bed. That's where she belongs. But then Tristian's words come back to me.

...lose a little to win a little.

I go right, kicking her door open and carrying her inside. Carefully, I lay her on her bed, arranging her top just-so. Tristian would clean her up. He'd go into her bathroom and wet a rag and gently take away all the evidence.

I don't.

I want her to know what I did to her, leave her a reminder of who's in charge. Before I go, I look over my shoulder, making sure we're really alone. Then I tilt her face to the side and push a gentle kiss into her clammy temple.

Her only response is a lazy, half-asleep sigh. Deep in my chest, I shove aside the knowledge of why I do this. Tristian can give her control and reap the rewards, but that's him. I want her incapacitated like this because it's the only time she can't reject me. She can't pick someone else over me. Not Tristian or Rath. Not the sugar daddies.

Not my father.

Only me.

STORY

13

DAUGHTERS

I have this dream about the basement.

There's the taste of Killian, bitter on the back of my tongue, the penetrating heat of watching eyes, voices. But there's also the sense of stinging needles, of being held down and made still, of being helpless and hopeless, just like that day with Ray and the tracker. It's strange to think about—places with a sinister nature.

Like that laundry room, which has always lurked in the depths of my brain, this menacing throb of memory. Although I think if I could go back, being the person I've become, it'd be a lot different. I think I'd get on my own knees and swallow Tristian down until his face collapsed in agony. I'd arch back into Rath and revel in his surprise. I'd look my stepbrother in the eye while I did it and show him he can't touch me. Not like they can.

No, the laundry room isn't so scary anymore. But the basement sticks with me. Some days, it's unbearable just knowing it's below my feet, a dead stack of bricks that I can still hear breathing. That's what I dream about. The heavy breath of it below me, bellowing my name, dragging me down.

Let him in…

I wake like that, trembling and cold and far too vigilant, considering the way my head feels. "Shut up. Shut up. Shut up." I reach out and slam my hand down on the phone alarm, accomplishing nothing but knocking it to the ground. "Oh god."

The raspy sound of my own voice stabs in my ears like an ice pick. My eyes are crusted over, head pounding that heavy-breathed basement rhythm, and *Jesus Christ*, why is it so bright in here? I roll over and bury my head under my pillow, trying to hide from it.

What the hell happened last night?

I burp, and the taste of cherry rolls up my throat. Oh. Right. I got fucking hammered with Tristian. The last thing I remember is sitting with him downstairs, cheek resting on his shoulder as I complained about Killian and his pregame bimbos. Someone must have brought me up to my room.

Not Killian's, not Rath's, not Tristian's. Mine.

Well.

For a given value.

I hang off the bed, fumbling a few more times before I finally turn off the alarm. Sitting up, I look down and see my clothes are still on, and it's really saying about the state of my life that my first reaction is surprise. But the neck of my top is stretched out, and when I touch my itchy chest, I go eerily still.

I don't even have to look to know what the dried crusty, sticky substance is. This is definitely a fat load of semen. Maybe it should, but *this* doesn't surprise me. If anything, it's a bit of a relief. It's part of the reason I'd gotten so hammered last night, sick of wondering if he was going to go for the bimbos or come for me, a shiny new pregame ritual.

I'm getting better at anticipating their moves.

In front of the dresser mirror, I take in the way I look. 'Rode hard and put away wet' seems an apt descriptor. My hair is a tangled mess, eyes red, skin splotchy and clammy-pale. The top is a lost cause, stretched beyond repair. Sighing, I pull it over my head and toss it aside.

And then I freeze, an aborted inhale lodged painfully in my lungs.

My breasts are a cream canvas of blue and purple.

It's not as bad as last time, but only just, and if I weren't busy feeling nauseous and violated, I might be able to appreciate Killian's consistency with this. Apparently, leaving his fingerprints in the soft parts of my flesh is part of the ritual. How did I not see *this* coming?

I can't decide if it's better or worse that I can't remember it.

The water to the shower spits to life and I crank the heat, stomach roiling at the thought of what's happened. Where did he do it? Was it here, in my bed? Were the lights out? Did he kiss me the way he does when I'm sleeping?

I'm standing under the steamy spray, palms pressed to the tile, water battering the top of my head, when something penetrates the surface. A memory, murky and indistinct. Hands on my head, pushing my hair away. Fingers on my jaw. A voice, gentle and coaxing in my ear.

Open up for Killer, sweetheart…

Let him in…

That's our good girl…

I start shaking again, hands curling into fists against the wall. Tristian had been there—probably Rath, too—watching and touching and *taking*.

Every time I think I make some progress, get back a little control of my own, it's made perfectly clear that I have none. Each kind gesture one of them makes is negated by the next. The hard truth is that the basement isn't a scary place. It, just like every other room in this house, is just dead bricks and empty space.

Until one of *them* walks into it.

I scrub the semen from my chest mechanically, uncaring of the ache of my breasts, the bruises sore and tender. It's been days since I contacted Ted. He was supposed to be here by now. He was supposed to stop this. He was supposed to blow everything up and make it new. But maybe I'm the fool, always running and waiting and leaving my fate in the hands of small, awful men.

For the first time in a long while, I realize that I'm sick of waiting.

After all, if you want something done right, then do it yourself.

THE SCENT OF bacon and eggs makes my stomach flip almost as miserably as the thought of facing them, but I walk into the dining room, anyway.

Rath glances up from his food, mouth frozen mid-chew at the sight of me. The shower likely has done very little. I still look like hell warmed over. Killian doesn't meet my eyes whatsoever, the avoidance so skilled and effective that it's as if I never walked in.

Tristian is the only one who speaks. "There's our soggy Lady," he says, pushing a smoothie in my direction. "Best hangover cure you ever had. Give it a try."

I eye the foamy green drink, and my stomach gurgles in revolt. Ignoring the glass, I emotionlessly announce, "I need to go see Daniel this afternoon."

Killian's eyes finally jump to mine, eyes flashing dangerously. "Excuse me?"

I don't bother sitting, arms hanging limp at my sides. "It's on my list of duties for the homecoming carnival. I need to ask him for permission to use the property, and then get the permits."

"I can do it," is Killian's flippant reply. He looks back down at his phone, discussion over.

"No, you can't."

Again, he looks up. This time his nostrils flare, a warning clear in his response. "Did you just tell me no?"

"Yes."

He puts his phone down, never breaking my gaze. "Tell me again that I can't speak to my own father. I dare you."

I wait for the swell of indignation and hatred. Instead, all I can hear is Tristian's voice, asking me to open up for Killian. The only thing I feel is cheap. "You guys are the ones who told me this is my job, as your Lady. It's my responsibility to take care of this."

"She's right," Tristian says, giving the smoothie another small nudge in my direction. "If the Royal women let their men handle everything, the fundraiser would just turn into another pissing match. Things are done this way for a reason." Lower, he tells Killian, "Don't make this into a thing. We're all tired."

"Well, you can't go alone," Killian says to me. "And I'm too busy to drive you this week, so it'll have to wait."

"I already called and made an appointment at his office for late this afternoon." I look over at Tristian, unable to directly meet his eyes. I wonder what he did to me. Was that Killian's spunk, or his, too? "Can you take me later?"

"Sorry, Cherry, but the twins have a dance recital this afternoon." He shakes his head, insisting, "I can't miss it."

"I can go with her," Rath says. "All of my studio hours are in the morning this week, and since she has a car now—" I don't miss the snide tone, nor the look he stabs at Tristian. "—I can just ride along. We'll go after classes are over today."

Now I wonder what Rath did to me last night. Tristian and Killian both get off on control—I expect it out of them. But it doesn't seem like Rath's style. "That would be great. Thank you."

"Now that that's settled," Tristian says, pushing the glass back in front of me, "drink."

Stiffly, I lift the glass, taking a tentative sip. It tastes like someone dug up grass and dirt in the backyard and blended it together with the very essence of sadness. I choke it down, willing myself to be strong. If I'm going to take their game into my own hands, then I'll need to start collecting all the favor I can get.

As soon as we get into Killian's truck for the ride to campus, Rath draws me into his side, massaging the back of my neck with a firm hand. I find myself unable to fight it, melting into his deceptively gentle warmth.

"You okay?" he asks. It surprises me, because he's been far kinder ever since I got the tracker and we spent the night together, but quiet and still a bit distant. At my silent nod, he just tucks me closer, smelling like laundry detergent and the vague hint of an early morning cigarette. He presses his mouth to my ear to whisper, "I can smoke you up after we go see Daniel." His hand is wandering up my side, knuckles skating across my breast. When I stiffen in response, he releases a low, dark chuckle. "I've been hard as fuck ever since you laid that kiss on me last night."

There's a loaded pause, like he's waiting for me to offer something up. A hand job on the way to school, in front of the others. A quickie after we see Daniel, stoned and sloppy. A blowjob during lunch.

I sit still and say nothing.

He shrugs, moving his hand back down to my hip. "Yeah, hangovers suck." He sounds disappointed.

From the expression on Tristian's face when he opens the back door and helps me out, he knows Rath was looking for something. Tristian throws his arm over my shoulder and says, "Why don't you give the Lady a break?"

"*Me*? Why don't the two of you?" Rath lobs back, eyes dark and cutting. Halfway to my building, he stops and mutters a curse. "Shit."

"What?" Tristian asks.

"I forgot I need to take my biography write up to my professor's office. It's due today by three." He looks at me, pulling a face. "Actually, I wanted to see if you'd read it over. I meant to ask last night, but…"

He lets the words fall where they may.

"Of course," I say, feeling some of the life seep back into my bones. I use it to square my shoulders. "What is it?"

He pulls his phone from his pocket, giving it a few taps while explaining, "It's the bio for the programs—the ones handed out at the homecoming performance. Nothing important." It doesn't sound *un*important. My phone chimes with a notification—a shared file. "Fuck, but I'll be in the studio until three. Then you and I are going to Daniel's office." He runs his fingers through his hair, looking away, face sulky and pensive.

I give it a quick skim on my phone. "You can't email it or submit it online?" I remember Lockwood well enough. That day in the studio, the Counts and their Countess—Lockwood's TA—had offered to get Rath a pass in exchange for Ms. Crane. I suppose Lockwood is handling the programs for homecoming, too.

Tough luck.

He scoffs. "Lockwood is some hipster fuck who hates anything sent with a signal or a wire. Emails, texts, flash drives—all are a no-go. I still need to find a printer."

I consider this, noting how crudely written the text is, and try on a smile. "Okay, how about I look it over in my first class, retype it in my second, print it out in the student center, and then drop it off at Lockwood's office? We can meet at the parking lot right after that."

"Yeah?" He gives me a rare, genuine grin. "You'd really do all that?"

I hope my smile looks authentic. "Well, I'm your Lady, aren't I?"

He hooks two fingers in my waistband, pulling me in. "Hell yes, you are." The kiss he gives me is slow, sweet, and sensuous enough that I can tell he's still hoping for something to happen.

And something definitely fucking will.

RATH'S WRITING IS bad.

It's not completely unreadable or anything, just rough and riddled with phonetics. Punctuation is nonexistent. There are some sentences that make me see how he's gotten by for so long, because the errors could easily be waved away as someone in a rush. But there are other sentences that barely scrape the surface of coherent. I spend my second class typing up a fresh and improved version, and each new word pressed into my phone's keyboard is like manna from gods, invigorating something I hadn't even realized was lost.

I see her in the student center, while I'm printing the biography out.

She walks into the administration lobby holding a stack of folders, eyes scanning the space. She zeroes on the pair of scanners beside me and marches right over to them, setting her bag and purse between us.

I watch her for a long moment, not believing my own eyes.

What are the chances?

She meets my gaze for only a split second, giving me the kind of bland smile that's meant for strangers who are staring at you, before opening the lid to the scanner and getting to work.

"Excuse me," I say, plucking my printout from the tray. "Aren't you...uh, Genevieve?"

She gives me a longer look. "Have we met?" Genevieve Carter is even more gorgeous than I remember, with her long blonde hair and sharp blue eyes.

Sliding the paper into my bag, I explain, "We actually went to high school together." After a beat, I add, "I mean, not that you'd have ever given me the light of day. I was a grade lower, plus a total nobody."

She looks me up and down, gaze flat and disinterested. I'd dressed more for Rath today than Tristian, which is probably why he was hoping for something on the way to school. Even the tiniest thing can be read as a gesture when their dicks are involved.

Genevieve hums, looking away. "No, I don't think you would have been in my circles." The words have a hint of snottiness to them, which seems in-character for the popular girl I remember.

She and Tristian were a vision back then, but it was also a little creepy. With their matching fair hair and blue eyes, they could have been related. Their features and mannerisms are even similar—the firm jaws, straight postures, and obsessive diets. To most people, it probably looked like the perfect match, but I had an entirely different, and given how well I know the man, much more accurate read on it.

She's *him*, but with long hair, tits, and an extra fuckable hole.

Tristian was basically dating himself.

"I didn't realize you went here." I doubt Tristian does, either.

She looks like she's barely paying attention to me as she scans page after page. "Just transferred down from Vassar. Hence the copious photocopying of my transcripts."

My eyebrows climb my head. "Wow, talk about a downgrade. Sounds like some drama."

She finally pauses then, turning to regard me. "Yeah, it is." Girls like Genevieve are so easy. They walk over the nice girls, the sweet girls, the friendly girls, but the second a bitch walks up, they want in on it. "My dad just got diagnosed with cancer, so he and my mom made me move back."

Well, now I feel shitty.

She rolls her eyes, flicking her hair back. "As if I'm going to be able to do anything about it, right? What do I look like, a cancer doctor?"

"Oncologist," I supply.

She ignores me. "So now I'm stuck in this hellhole, *again*."

"Didn't you used to date Tristian Mercer?" I ask, keeping my voice friendly and curious. "It's so funny to think of all that high school drama."

Her reaction is so fast that I might have missed it if I hadn't been watching so carefully.

She tenses, motions growing more rapid. "Yeah, Tristian." She snorts, glancing over at me. "Oh, my god, that name, right? I can't believe I used to think I'd marry him after college. I'm on to greener pastures, trust me." She gives me this smile that's cracking at the edges, and holy shit, she's lying.

She's *bald face* lying.

"Hm," I twist to leave, "maybe I'll see you around sometime. I can show you around campus, point out the biggest bitches, the hottest guys…"

She gives me a look like she's sizing me up, wondering if I'm someone she wants to bother with, curious about my social standing and if I'll even be useful. She must not come to any conclusion, because she keeps it intentionally vague. "Yeah, we'll see."

If I have my way, one person in particular is going to see.

And I want to be there when he does.

KILLIAN DROPS US off at the brownstone so we can take my car. As we're getting out, he gives Rath a long look and a cryptic nod. "Remember what we talked about."

Rath flips him off and slams the door.

The ride to Daniel's office is quiet, and my heart twists anxiously at the silence. Rath has a way of looking past my façade, to who I really am, like the night in the laundry room when he knew how, despite my terror, what they were doing to me—what *I* was doing—turned me on. We've always had an inexplicable connection, but he can't know the truth about me now. What I know, or what I've done.

"Did everything go okay with turning in my biography?" he asks, touching all the dials on my sound system.

"Yes." I watch him from the corner of my eye, feeling strangely territorial about the way he's fiddling with my car. *It isn't really yours*, I keep reminding myself. "Well, other than having to see Sutton, but she kept her whore mouth shut."

He finally gives up with the stereo, putting his hand on my thigh instead. "Did you have to edit much? I know it was probably a mess."

"No," I lie, remaining still as his hand slides up my thigh. "You did pretty good. You've really made some progress."

"What can I say?" He props his wrist on the headrest behind me as his other hand dips between my legs. "I have an excellent tutor."

I open my thighs, keeping my eyes on the road. "Sometimes you just have to find the right motivation."

"Damn right," he breathes, those dark eyes watching his hand rub me through my tight black jeans. "We can make this meeting quick, you know." He leans in to whisper hot and low into my ear, "Go somewhere and finally fuck."

When his fingers dip lower, pressing hard, I wince.

He pauses, easing his hand back. "Still sore?"

"Yes," I lie, clearing my throat. "Sorry."

He flops back to his seat, face shuttered and stormy. "Jesus Christ, it's been days."

"I know." I give him a quick look that I do my best to fill with dread. "But hey, whatever you want to do."

"Forget it. I can wait." Looking out the window, he mutters, "I think." With nothing more than an outfit and passive rebuffing, I've got him so frustrated that there's a large, obscene bulge pressing at the front of his pants. He puts his hand in his lap and gives it a squeeze, but otherwise doesn't acknowledge it.

The drive to the South Side is familiar, but we go to an unfamiliar area—this one a little nicer. Rath directs me where to park and I peer out at the nondescript building. "Is this Daniel's office?"

"Yeah. You've never been down here?"

"No." I don't tell him that most of my short time living with Daniel was spent avoiding him. Getting caught with him alone, in a hallway or an out-of-the-way space? It just always seemed too dangerous. "I never really understood Daniel's job when I lived with him. All I got was 'real estate', but now I'm thinking that's underselling it."

The building is huge and modern, towering over South Side like a bleak sentry.

"He *is* involved in real estate," Rath says, "but yeah, it's bigger than that. He's kind of got his fingers in everything down here."

"And you think one day Killian will work with him?" I give him a look that shows my skepticism. I just can't see my stepbrother in a suit and tie, sitting at a desk in some nondescript office.

Rath smirks at me. "I think Killian wants to play for the NFL, get a massive paycheck, and tell his dad to fuck off." We exit the car and meet on the sidewalk. "But Daniel isn't going to let something like a professional football career get between him and Killian. I don't see a way out of it for him."

I've always viewed Killian and his father as two sides of the same coin. One quiet. One cruel. Both dangerous. I've sensed the tension in them before. There were fights I'd make it a point to ignore, holed up in my room as the sounds of banging and cussing penetrated the walls. Shouting over dinner. Long weeks of chilly silence. But I'd never known a father and a son before, so I just figured that was natural machismo bullshit.

The grim look on Rath's face makes me wonder, though.

"Their relationship is complicated, huh?"

He grabs the handle to the large glass door, hauling it open. "Fucking understatement of the year," he mutters, guiding me in with a hand on the small of my back. "Only half of it is on account of you." At my startled expression, he snorts. "Please. Like this is news to you." He leads me into an elevator, pressing the button for the top floor.

I sigh, shoulders slumping. "Let me guess, my mom is the other half." Because that's what the Lords are all about. I see that now. They collect territory and lord over it accordingly. My mom had met Daniel, and then she took a piece of that territory and gave a little chunk of it to me. "He hates her, too."

Casually, Rath says, "Only because she's a whore. It's nothing personal."

My head snaps back in shock. "Don't call her that!"

Rath's head snaps back in shock, too. "Why not? She literally is."

"No, she isn't!" Turning to the doors, I will the crawling sense of wrongness to dissipate from my skin. "She's a good mom and a good wife. Whatever she used to do to survive—so *I* could survive—it shouldn't matter."

"It shouldn't," he agrees, his hand heavy on my back. "But it does."

"I can't believe Killian would hold that against her, and then turn around and make me—" My voice clips off into a frustrated growl. It's just so goddamn typical.

Rath lets out this low, slow laugh. "Story, I'm going to tell you something. It's going to be vague and you can't ever fucking mention it, but it might help you out." He curls his hand around my hip. "Consider it me returning a favor for your editing work earlier."

"Okay," I hedge, feeling apprehensive.

"You ever want to get on Killer's good side—you know, like soften him up or whatever?" When he sees my attention's been piqued, he arches an eyebrow. "Just choose him over his dad, for fucking anything. You feel me?"

My forehead scrunches in confusion. "I'm not sure that's an opportunity that'll ever arise, but uh…" Uncertain, I offer, "…sure?"

He shakes his head, looking away. "You're so twisted around about this shit, girl."

Before I can ask what *that* means, the elevator opens to a large, bright lobby. It's empty, and I'm about to sit down when a woman walks into the lobby from a side room. She's pretty, young, and busy straightening her pencil-thin skirt.

She beams when she sees him. "Dimitri! Twice in one week! You boys are going to spoil me silly. Look how handsome you look today."

"Vivienne," he greets, nodding more at her cleavage than anything else. No way those things are real. "I've got a live one for the boss man." He pushes me forward encouragingly.

I give a nervous laugh. "I have an appointment…?"

Vivienne's eyes light up. "Oh gosh, you must be Story!" She heads toward us and before I can react, I'm engulfed in a cloud of perfume and this woman's skinny arms. The press of her ample breasts against mine confirms my earlier suspicions as to their authenticity.

I glance at Rath, and he shrugs.

The woman pulls back to say, "I'm Vivienne, Mr. Payne's secretary. Daniel and your mom have told me so much about you. I already feel like we're practically family! It's so nice to finally meet you in the flesh, instead of just the picture in his office."

It's a lot to take in. Daniel talks about me to this woman? He keeps a picture of me? Fighting down a shiver, I respond, "It's nice to meet you too."

She laughs. "Don't worry, I'm sure he's never mentioned me before, but he's been so worried about you for the last few years. I know he's glad you're back." She nods to the door. "You can go right in. He's expecting you."

Rath moves to come with me, but I shake my head. "Official business, remember? Wait out here." His eyebrow quirks, but he takes a seat on one of the leather chairs and reaches for his ear buds.

I open the office door and there he is. Daniel is sitting at his desk, phone pressed to his ear. He's dressed in an expensive suit and shoes, a perfectly folded handkerchief is tucked in his pocket. If he's any kind of indication of how well Killian will age, then my stepbrother is lucky. The hair near Daniel's temples is going silvery-gray, but the rest is a dark, muted brown. He and Killian share a powerful jaw, but Daniel keeps a short, tidy beard where Killian prefers a 'three days of stubble' look.

I guess I've entered at just the right moment, because he's saying goodbye and hanging up.

I can't help but stare dumbly at the LDZ ring on his finger.

"I thought I saw your name on my calendar." He leans back in his chair—some big, plush, tall, *lordly* thing—and looks me over. Despite all of Vivienne's gushing before, Daniel isn't looking at me like a happy, doting father. His eyes are blank. Almost cold. "What brings you down here? Is something the matter?" His gold watch flashes on his wrist as he rests his cheek on a knuckle and thumb.

"No, um…everything's fine." I dig for the form in my purse and hold it out. "I just need a minor favor."

When I make no move to come closer, he stands, smoothing down his tie as he rounds the desk, taking the form. His gray eyes skim over it. "You need to use the empty lot off Elrod street? Homecoming preparations, I assume?"

"Yes," I reply, feeling a bit off kilter at the cool reception I'm getting. "For the carnival. We'll also need a permit."

Nodding, he pulls a gold pen out of his breast pocket and, without question, signs the papers and folds them back. "Take this down to the city office. They'll approve."

"Thank you."

He holds out the paper, but just as I reach for it, he pulls it back, just out of my reach. He pins me with a long stare. "I can't help but notice that this is typically a job for the Lords' Lady."

Blood rushes to my face so fast it almost makes me dizzy. "Yes," is my answer, barely a breath.

I'm so rigid that I don't even move when he reaches for my wrist, lifting it to inspect the cuff. I catch the hint of Vivienne's perfume on his slow sigh. "To be a Lady is a privilege, indeed. They've been part of the institution long before my tenure at Forsyth. Proper Royal women are the spoils of war."

"I applied for the job," I reply stiffly. "They were just doing me a favor by giving it to me."

"A favor." He gives me a bland smile, clearly unimpressed by my lie. "Of course. You ought to be careful how many of those you're racking up."

My skin crawls, but when I go to pull my wrist back, he holds it, those gray eyes never breaking my gaze. "You know what they tell men about their sons, Story? They tell us they're special, coveted above all else, necessary to carry on one's legacy and lineage and such." He sighs, eying the cuff again. "Personally, I always wanted a daughter. Sons are defiant little creatures from the first step, and then they grow up, just waiting to take everything you've built and make it their own. But daughters…" He tilts his head, thumb rubbing over the skull. "Daughters need their fathers. They're a warm patch of light in a dark and dreary world. If I'd had a daughter, things would be so much simpler." Meeting my stunned gaze, he quietly asks, "Don't you agree?"

The knock on the door makes me flinch. Daniel is the first to break our strange standoff, glancing over my shoulder at the intruder.

"Well, isn't this a surprise!" my mom's voice rings out. "My two favorite people."

I turn to see her standing in the doorway in an elegant suit and soft leather heels. Even though it's been years since Daniel 'saved' her—*us*—I'm still not used to seeing her like this. Her face looks fresh, ten years younger than her age. Her legs are still outstanding. I mean, she paid the rent with that body, after all. But in this outfit, with the gold earrings and fashionable scarf, no one would ever guess she made her living lying on her back.

Her eyes skim over Daniel's hand, still holding my wrist, and skitter to a stop.

"My darling," Daniel says, squeezing my hand before dropping it and crossing the room. He kisses her on the cheek. "What are you doing down here?"

"Thought I'd stop by and let you take me to dinner." She looks at me, her smile beaming. "I saw Dimitri in the lobby. What are you doing here, honey?"

I hold up the slip of paper, hoping my hand won't shake. "Just getting some paperwork taken care of for homecoming."

Daniel nods. "Story's helping the boys with some of the fraternity's charity work. Isn't that so generous of her?" With that smile, you'd never know he just had my wrist trapped in his grip, going off about sons and the daughters they're fucking.

"That is wonderful!" She smiles, clasping her hands together excitedly. "I love that you're helping them out. They do such good in the community."

She says it without a trace of irony or concern, so I suppose my mother doesn't understand the inner workings of the Lords like my stepfather does. "I should get this to the permit office before it closes."

"Oh, no," my mother pouts. "You can't do dinner with us? Please?"

I shake my head. "Sorry, mom. Not today."

She flaps a hand. "Ah well, it was good to see you, anyway." She walks over and gives me a hug. "I just love having you in town like this again."

"You too, Mom." I give Daniel a tight smile. "Thank you, Daniel."

"Any time, Story."

I step back into the lobby, where Vivienne sits at her desk. I study her for a moment, assessing the short skirt, the tight blouse, the obvious lack of a bra. There's a clunky bracelet on her arm with what looks like an initial etched in the gold. She looks up at me and gives me a friendly grin, but I don't feel warmth. I feel an icy shiver running down my spine. I may not be the only one who's being controlled by a Payne, but I just may be the only one with the guts to do something about it.

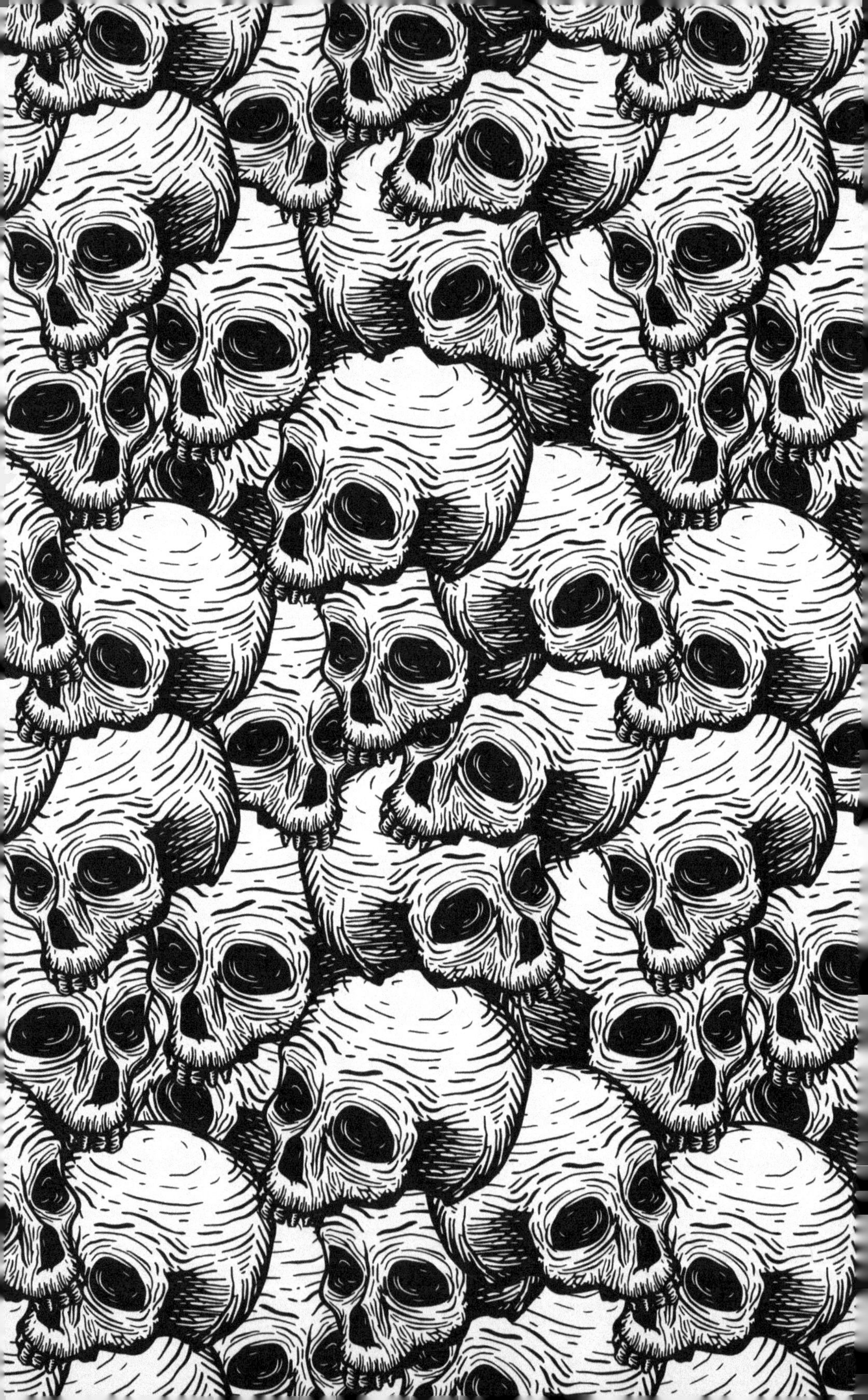

1 4

CLAIMED

I_{T'S OUT OF} habit that I check the mobile tracker app on my phone, confirming that Story is still in class. The implant under her skin is specific, down to the very room, whereas the regular phone GPS was vague, giving only a general area. After the kidnapping, I check more frequently.

Okay, *compulsively*.

Killer must really be rubbing off on me.

Once I confirm that she's where she's supposed to be, I wait on a bench in the hallway outside her classroom. I'm ten minutes early, so I open my ChattySnap account. I scroll through the pictures quickly; bikini models, health and fitness influencers, a few celebrities, and then the people I actually know. I pull up my own photo library and snag a sexy picture of Story from the football game the week before. I'm working on a caption—always willing to show off my Lady—when I notice the heart up in the corner is lit up. I have a private message.

It isn't uncommon for someone to try to slide into my DMs. I'm good looking, rich, and powerful. What woman wouldn't want to get her claws in me? But one woman occupies my thoughts right now, so my intent is to open the message and delete it...until see the picture attached to the message.

It's of Lizzy and Izzy.

What the fuck?

"Such cute, innocent, girls. I wonder what they'd say if they knew the truth about their brother?"

Rage boils under my skin and I click the account. It's private with a generic icon. The screen name is 'executivedaddy10'. I go back again and look at the photo. The girls are in motion, walking out of their dance studio. They have no one idea someone is watching them. My mind calculates, desperately struggling to figure out who would dare send a threat to me like this, when I hear a reluctant, "Tristian?"

My fiery blood turns to frozen steel.

There's only one thing that could temporarily distract me from the thought of someone watching my sisters.

I force myself to look up, eyes climbing a pair of smooth, tanned legs, thighs hidden beneath a little green skirt. She's wearing a white, scoop-necked sweater, her blonde hair flawlessly straight. I don't need to look higher to know it's Genevieve. I've had those warm thighs wrapped around me more times than I could count. I've had those tits in my palms, in my mouth. Those long, red fingernails have left so many notches in my shoulders that it took me months to get used to the sight of my skin there, unblemished by her rapture.

Her blue eyes are wide—slightly panicked—which is smart of her.

It's been three years, but the urge to wrap my fingers around her throat and watch the life fade from her eyes is still all-consuming.

"Oh," she breathes, those red, whore lips of hers pursed in shock. "I can't believe it's really you."

My smile feels colder than ice and sharper than razor blades. "Gen." I'd heard she'd gone to Vassar with no intention of looking back. But here she is, smiling all hopefully, like she's not the biggest deceitful bitch in the whole goddamn world. My phone's case digs painfully into my palm as I squeeze it. "Fancy seeing you here."

In my town.

In my school.

In *my* territory.

This bitch has single-handedly depleted the world of audacity.

She gives a trilling laugh that oozes with nerves. "God, I know. I spent the last two years at Vassar, but my dad got sick and he wanted me back for at least a semester." She looks me up and down. "Wow, look at you. Better looking than ever."

My ex is a lying, cheating, puddle of slut-scum that isn't worth the energy, but somehow it still hurts to look at her. Not because I miss her. Fuck no. It hurts because she's proof of how weak a man can become. Years spent building a future with this piece of garbage. *Jesus*, the plans that were made—Forsyth, complementing careers, an engagement at graduation, a destination wedding, investment property, three children. Looking back at the way I'd greet her everyday like a lapdog, with a coffee and a flower. The sex we'd have, always fast and hard and so intense that it'd leave me sapped but hungry for more. It took me until that night with Story to realize why. Something was always missing with Gen. It wasn't just the lack of eagerness to please me—she would never lower herself to suck my dick—it was also the lack of passion. Need. Devotion.

I was addicted more to the idea of this slut than the reality. She's the only woman I've ever allowed myself to see a future with. The perfect home, the immaculate family, the path laid out before me, clear and expected and proper.

And look what it got me. Her, on that fucker's yacht, those thighs wrapped around his hips as he fucked my future wife like an animal. I can still remember her eyes, gazing up so openly into his. Because Genevieve is the flawless opportunist she was always raised to be, but she's also so disappointingly gullible. She was actually into that guy—her own softball coach—a pathetic loser that couldn't stop reliving his youth. She was into him enough that she allowed him to record the video that would soon after be leaked.

The video that exposed me as a goddamn fool.

The urge to strangle her swells again.

"I'm so glad to run into you," she says, adjusting the hem of her top. It brings her neckline down half an inch, exposing more of her cleavage. "Are you doing anything this afternoon? Maybe we could go grab a coffee. Catch up."

The last time I spoke a single word to this girl was right after I set that yacht on fire. I was getting it from all angles—Killian, Rath, my father, Daniel—and I told her the next time I saw her, I'd be lighting a match to something *she* loved.

I've never meant anything more.

A figure moves next to Genevieve and I jerk my eyes up to find Story has arrived. She and Gen glance at one another, and I see the recognition flicker across my ex's face.

"Hey, sexy," I say, the words cool and easy as I rise from the bench, towering over them both. "Finished already?"

"Yeah, we got out a few minutes early, actually." She pushes a lock of hair behind her ear and gives Gen a bright smile. "Hey, we met before, remember? I'm—"

"Late." I jump in, stepping forward to snake my arm around her waist. The last thing I want is for Genevieve and Story to speak to one another. I'll light that match again before I let my Lady be tainted. "We've got things to do, sweetheart."

Story looks between me and Gen, something small and satisfied sparking in her eyes. She lays her hand on my chest, straining up on her toes to press a kiss to my jaw. "Yes, sir. Just lead the way."

My cock swells so fast that I know my chest hitches.

Holy fuck.

Sir.

Gen stares at Story's hand, at how tightly she's wrapped her body around me, at the way I'm gripping her, loose but undeniably possessive. In a blink, her face goes carefully blank, mouth pressed into a tight line. "Well, Tristian. I see you have your hands full."

I look at Story, gazing up at me so sweetly, and brush her hair from her cheek. "You have no idea."

"Hm." The hum is low and oozing with displeasure. "Maybe some other time."

"Oh," Story says, turning to Gen. "Come and find me sometime if you ever want that campus tour. I'm always around somewhere." She gives this little self-deprecating laugh I might find cute, except I'm too busy imploding at the thought of her and Gen frolicking around campus together. She winces when I wrench her back to me.

"We'll be too busy," I tell her, undeterred by the flash of dread in her eyes as I march her away by the arm.

I can feel her eyes on me as I walk us nowhere in particular—just *away*. "What the fuck do you think you're doing?" I hiss, fingers digging into her muscle. "You don't talk to that whore. I don't even want you looking at her."

Gen randomly shows up at the exact moment I get a private message threatening to tell my sisters the 'truth' about me?

Not buying it.

Story grunts as I haul her along, her short legs struggling to keep up. "The contract only says I can't talk to guys. I already avoid the other Royals. Am I just not allowed to socialize with anyone?"

Her tone is surly and completely fucking out of line, and by the time I find a door, I'm already stiff with rage. I throw it open, only idly recognizing it as a study room. There's a girl in there, hunched over a laptop, head jerking up at the sudden intrusion.

"Get out," I command, voice low and dangerous enough that it spurs her immediately into action. She doesn't even bother shoving her laptop into her bag, sweeping it all off the table and skittering past us, wide-eyed and anxious.

I slam the door behind her and push Story against it, my fingers wrapping around that delicate, slender throat. "What the fuck do you think you're playing at?"

She stares at me, hot and unblinking. "I'm not playing at anything!" I have no idea what's in my eyes, but whatever it is makes her attitude turn on a dime. "Tristian, wait," she says, voice strained as her hand comes up to cup my cheek. "It was just nice to see someone I recognized, because I don't know anyone around here who isn't a Royal. I figured all that high school drama was old news."

My fingers tighten around her neck. "High school *drama?*"

High school drama is Rath fingering Killer's flavor of the week in the backseat of her car. High school drama isn't a video of your girlfriend of three years making love to her fucking softball coach. It isn't a potential arson charge, it isn't the heir to the Mercer fortune being publicly humiliated, and it sure as fuck isn't the one event that led to the girl in front of me on her goddamn knees, crying as I blew my load into that smart little mouth of hers.

She must remember that, too. That and the morning I apologized for it, explaining that I'd just been in a bad place.

"Don't," she breathes, staring up at me with those doe eyes. "If she's really so bad…you shouldn't let her get to you like this, right?"

I give her a humorless smile. "You know it's not that simple."

"I know," she says in a voice that cuts through the feeling in my chest. Just seeing Genevieve's face brought all that old anger to the surface. Now, like then, I want to feel anything else. "Tell me what I can do."

Never fucking talk to her, is on the tip of my tongue, but it's washed away by another request. I reach up to thumb at her bottom lip, thinking about how this mouth is mine. She's nothing like Gen. She loves her new car, but she's not here for my money. She isn't swayed by pretty men or yachts or flowers. Story is my Lady, bound to me in a net of circumstance.

"You can prove it," I tell her, ducking down to press a kiss to her jaw. My teeth scrape against the bone. "Show me who owns you."

I won't force her to her knees—not again—and I won't force her to her back.

I'll let her choose how to demonstrate her loyalty.

Her breath hitches, and there's a long moment where neither of us moves or speaks. "What do you want?" she asks, the tremor in her voice belying the steel in her eyes.

My dick's already hard at any possibility, but I humor her, palm sliding down to her breast. "I want to be inside you, Sweet Cherry. I want to feel what it's like when you come on my dick, quivering around me." I lick her lips, wet and obscene. "I want to feel you swallow me again. That hot mouth around my dick, taking everything I give you. I want to hear you struggling to breathe because you're so full with me." Her eyes look as hooded and captivated as mine feel. "But right now, I want to know that whatever you do, you're doing it because you want to please me. *Only* me." Pressing my thumb into her jugular, I demand, "I want to see your complete devotion. *Show me.*"

She lifts her chin, hand coming up to touch my wrist. Gently, she pries my fingers from her throat. I let her push forward, a hand on my chest, until she has me spun around and up against the door.

And then she sinks to her knees.

I'm disappointed, even though I shouldn't be. I didn't want to fuck her here, anyway. It's too close, too personal, too *raw*. But when her fingers undo my fly, lowering my zipper, I still get a balls-deep shudder at knowing I could, if I really wanted to. I wouldn't even have to order her, I'd just have to ask. I can see it in the way she looks at me.

It's the exact same look Gen had in her eye for the softball coach.

She pulls me from my briefs, her warm palm giving it a couple of slow strokes. "Whatever my Lord wants."

The first touch of her mouth is heaven and hell, all wrapped up into one curl of her tongue. It's so much better than that night in the car—at first, because I can actually see it this time, my hard cock disappearing between those sweet, pink lips. But then she sinks forward and takes me in, a hot-wet glide that makes my toes curl.

And she doesn't stop.

Before I've even wound my fist in her hair, she's letting me hit the back of her throat, lingering there against me, holding me so deep that I know she can't breathe. I feel my jaw go slack, fingers massaging the back of her head. Just when I figure she'll pull back, she goes *deeper*.

I spit a low, "Holy shit," because I would have fucked her throat like this, just like I had that night in the car. It'd been a test to see if she could take it—if she could *like* it—and here she is, giving it away so goddamn freely.

I have to pull her off my dick, fingers fisting tight in her hair. I forget about Genevieve and her lying, cheating, whore face the second my Sweet Cherry looks up at me, eyes wet and wide as she sucks on the tip of my cock.

Humming, I give her hair a pulsing tug. "You're such a good girl for me."

She gives me a long, slow blink. I know Killian and Rath think I'm being a patronizing creep when I tell her she's being good, but the truth is, they've never seen the way her eyes soften and shine at praise. Our Lady likes being good just as much as she likes being bad.

She responds by falling forward once more, so determined to take me deep. But she can only do it when I let her, loosening my grip on her hair. It's the complete opposite from the road head, when I'd pushed her down and made her stay, only to watch her head rise when I allowed it. Now, she sinks down onto me like we're magnetized. She'd suffocate on my dick if I didn't yank her back, almost as eager to see that softness in her eyes again as I am to bust in her pretty mouth.

It feels like it lasts hours, Story stuffing her throat with my cock until I wrench her back to hear her wet gasps. I tell her how good she is, and she holds my gaze before starting all over again. It's messy and overindulgent, and it just might be the hottest thing that's ever happened to me.

I come with a tight, guttural sound, holding her by a fistful of hair so she can't bury me in her throat. I want it shallow enough that she'll be able to taste me on her tongue, and that's exactly what I do, cock jerking my release between her red, abused lips.

She's so good that I half expect her to sink back down to the hilt. Instead, she pulls off, sitting back on her heels, and meets my gaze. I think I could come again when she opens her mouth, letting me see my load sitting there on her red tongue. Holding my stare, she closes her jaw and swallows.

"Fuck," I breathe, thumbing some jizz from the corner of her mouth. I feel like I'm in a trance, hypnotized by the way she instantly sucks my thumb clean, not letting a drop go to waste. Breathlessly, I ramble, "That's so fucking hot. Gen never would have dreamed of getting this nasty." Story sucks my thumb, looking up at me owlishly. "That's why I had to have you like that. So much of high school, listening to Rath and Killer brag about getting head. As soon as I saw your mouth that night, I knew I had to have it."

It isn't until she drops her eyes that I realize what I'm saying, and who I'm saying it to. It's all true. That night had been a crazy whirr of rage, Rath and Killer doing their best to keep me from retaliating. It'd later prove pointless. Only a few days later, I found myself on that dock with the gas can. But that night, I think they knew I needed to see a girl on her knees before me, my dick slamming in and out of her mouth. That's how I know I'd do anything for Killian. Story was his by rights, but there for a few minutes in his old laundry room, he'd given her to me. A little taste of this thing he wanted so badly that it consumed him. And the thing is, it worked. It was an exorcism, proof that being with Genevieve Carter wasn't all it'd been cracked up to be. It'd been lacking. She would sooner cut off her own arm than take me into her mouth, let alone enjoy it.

But as darkly freeing as that night might have been for me, it was something else for Story. A possession instead of an exorcism. A marred moment she might have even wanted if I'd been in a place to put in the effort. What must this have cost her, to get on her knees for me, to look into my eyes again as she swallowed me down, knowing what I've taken?

Suddenly, I see this for what she meant it to be.

To think I felt disappointed she chose this instead of taking me inside that sweet cunt of hers. The sex will be great—I know it will—but it's nothing for us. There's no history or baggage or hurt. Sex will be new and fun, and I can't fucking wait to see that soft, stunned pleasure in her eyes as I rail her.

But getting on her knees for me, after what I did?

There couldn't be a better display of her complete devotion.

I tuck myself back into my pants before crouching down and tugging her into my chest. She goes willingly, even if she still won't meet my gaze. Pressing my nose into her hair, I inhale her sweet scent. I want to say I'm sorry again. I want to thank her. I want to tell her that what's happening inside my head is just as messy as that blow job was, and I'm not sure where this is going, but I know I want to keep it. It's not like it was with Gen. Story isn't an idea. She's terrifyingly tangible.

But that's too much, too confusing.

Instead, I say, "You're more than any of us deserve."

Her fingers curl into the fabric of my shirt.

She doesn't respond.

"Would you like to sleep in my bed tonight?" I ask, stroking her hair from her shoulder. So that she'll understand I'm not her brother, I press a kiss to her jaw, adding, "This isn't an order. You can say no. We don't have to do anything but sleep."

There's a beat of silence, something strained about her breaths. I spend it preparing myself for the likelihood she'll say no. That's okay. I can handle it.

I think.

Instead, she whispers, "Okay."

15

GIVING UP

I'VE GOT TRISTIAN Mercer eating out of the palm of my hand.

Literally.

He opens his mouth, teeth taking the meatball when I hold it to his lips. He gives it a few experimental chews, eyes wary. That's how I know I've got him. I doubt Tristian blindly accepts food from just anyone.

"They're vegan and gluten-free," I assure him. "I used almond meal as the binder, and nutritional yeast as a passable substitute for parmesan."

It's a load of crap, really. Nothing about these could be called meatballs. Ms. Crane was puttering around the kitchen while I was cooking them, and she kept cackling at the ingredients and care I put into them.

"That's a good little fucktoy," she'd say, giving me a wink. I suspect she knows exactly what's going down here, but there's something kindred between the two of us. She'll let me play my games.

He hums, eyes growing wide. "They're *good*."

One could easily be insulted by the shocked tone of his voice. But I'm not. They're not actually that great, and my cooking skills are only a couple notches above Ms. Crane. It's just that Tristian doesn't eat good food very often. The bar here is so low, it's embedded into the floor.

He'd told me about it last night, while we were in his bed. True to his word, he didn't try to push anything. He just talked. Temple propped on a fist, gazing at me as his fingers skated down my chest, he told me about how difficult it is to get good food.

"That's why," he'd said, eyes dark as they traced the neckline of my tank top, "When I find real food—*quality* food—I make sure to stock up. So you can have some, too." In his own twisted way, that's probably a significant declaration. It'd be really sweet, actually.

Except my tits are black and blue, and I can still hear his voice in my ear, commanding me.

Tristian talked for almost two hours last night as we lay in the soft light of his bedside lamp, and the topic was always the same, but weirdly shallow. For a man who loves talking about himself, he really divulged nothing I didn't already know, except for the fact he snores, and much like Rath, he is a cuddler. Unlike Rath, he doesn't mind admitting it, folding me possessively against his chest before finally nodding off.

I also learned that he wakes up at five every morning to work out.

Loudly.

Shrugging, I say. "It's all about the seasonings."

"You really made these for me?" He looks at the tray of meatballs. It'd be funny if this game of mine weren't so serious. I can practically see the cartoon hearts in his eyes. "No one's ever made me food before. I mean, no one who wasn't getting paid to do it." He eats another meatball, bristling when Rath shoves in beside him, snatching one from the plate.

"Fuck off," Tristian says, eyes narrowing as Rath shoves it in his mouth. "These are for me."

Primly, I tell Rath, "They're vegan *and* gluten-free."

He freezes, catching the meatball into a palm when he spits it out. "Gross." When he sees me crack a smile, he throws the meatball away and snakes his arms around my waist, chin resting on my shoulder. "There's so much better stuff you can make. Brownies. Pot roast. Pies. Fried chicken. Cookies."

Tristian rolls his eyes. "You have the palate of a toddler. Aren't you supposed to be getting the surround sound up and working?"

With the weekend comes a slight reprieve. Well, from Killian, at least. His football game is three states away, sending him and the team packing until tomorrow night. I know it's not much—next Saturday is the homecoming game and I'll be expected to be acutely involved. But for now, all I have to do is dress in orange and purple and help set up for the watch-party.

Hence, the meatballs.

I feel Rath's shrug against my back. "Already done."

He's been working on it all morning, holed up in the entertainment room, which I've only recently realized existed. It's equipped with stadium-style seating and a massive, wall-sized screen. It's not big enough for the whole frat, so it seems like the guys have issued an exclusive list of invites. I'm grateful it's not a full-out party, and I hope that if I keep the guys plied with food and drinks, I can sneak up to my room early and get a little homework done. I'd be lying if I said my education came first right now. I'm at Forsyth for protection first and foremost, but if I want to stay, I'm going to have to at least pass my classes.

Ms. Crane left all the snacks and drinks in the kitchen, so I spend the next hour setting up the rec room as my Lords greet their guests. Once the game starts, I pull out my rusty waitressing skills, making sure everyone is happy and fed, especially Rath and Tristian. They're sitting in leather lounge chairs with the best view on the highest riser. From the sound of the game, Killian is playing well, living up to his 'Killer' nickname, slaughtering the other team with pass after pass that I find myself tempted to watch. He's cruel and selfish, but it's interesting to watch the way he moves.

"Are you ready for another beer?" I ask Tristian. It's finally the fourth quarter and, thank god, the end is in sight.

He looks up at the tray of drinks and scowls. "Although I appreciate the service, why are you schlepping all this up back and forth? We have a fucking housekeeper, Cherry."

"It's fine. I offered to help." I shrug, even though my feet really are getting a little sore. I can't imagine poor Ms. Crane having to do it. "Serving you guys is part of my job, isn't it?"

"No," he argues, giving me a look. "Your job is to do what we want you to do, and being a glorified waitress isn't anywhere on the list. Your job on game day is to look pretty, sit on my lap, and make all the other suckers here jealous."

He winds his arm around my waist and pulls me into his lap. He's been needy ever since I saw him outside my class yesterday. Tristian is the most level-headed of the Lords. He's less prone to rage or tantrums. Even when he's abusive or controlling, he does it with sugary words and a pretty smile. He can be kind, in his own ass-backward way. Doting and attentive, so saccharine that it aches. Rath might be a deft hand at manipulating me into caring about him, but Tristian is an expert at manipulating me into thinking he cares. He doesn't—not in any real way. But I knew I was playing with fire by bringing Genevieve into this.

In some ways, Genevieve is the reason I'm here.

Yesterday, when he pushed me against that door in the study room, I saw something dark and familiar flicker behind his eyes. A small crack in his otherwise flawless façade. I'd know it anywhere, because it still haunts my dreams sometimes; those cold blue eyes, so empty yet so full of malice. It's been a long time since I've seen it. All this time living with him, being doted on by him, seeing his sharp grins and feeling his want for me, has made me forget that side of Tristian Mercer is always just below the surface.

That's why I chose to suck him off. Part of me wishes I could go back to that night and do it just like that. Spiteful and calculated. But mostly, whatever happened with Genevieve makes him mean, and if history says anything, he takes it out on me. It was easier to nip that before it started. I need him content and happy—at least with me. For now. Until I can get my revenge.

"Tristian," I cry, holding onto the tray. "You're going to make me spill everything!"

He takes it from me and places it on the floor. I feel the hard press of his cock against my backside and the soft brush of his lips on my neck. Rath looks over and raises an eyebrow.

"You've been walking back and forth in this short little skirt all day, Sweet Cherry." His breath is hot. "It's diving me fucking insane."

I sink into the feel of him, shaking off the insecurity of PDA. At least half the guys in this room were here when Killian forced me to give him a blow job, but Tristian wouldn't make me do that. Whereas Killian gets off on dominance, Tristian thrives on public displays of his affection—exhibitionism. His hand runs up and down my thigh, inching it under the hem of my skirt. I shudder an exhale and the telltale dampness builds between my legs.

He runs his nose along the shell of my ear. "Still sore?"

Releasing a slow breath, I shake my head. I can't pretend forever. Plus, Rath wiggled his way inside my head, and I'm still struggling to push him out. But Tristian? When it comes to our game, he's on the back foot. I have the power here, whether he knows it or not.

It'd be good with Tristian.

Hot, practical, and safe.

I feel him go still at my answer, the cock beneath my ass giving a strained twitch. "Do you trust me?" he asks, voice rushed.

"Yes." It's both the truth and a lie. Tristian wouldn't knowingly harm me— that, I know. But his definition of harm is a lot narrower than my own.

He turns to Rath, pointing to the chair beside him. "Hand me that."

Rath gives him a look, plucking a Forsyth blanket from the vacant seat and handing it over. "Go easy," he whispers, eyes dark.

"Always," Tristian replies, draping the blanket over my lap. His hands disappear beneath it, ducking under my skirt, and when he hooks his thumbs into my panties, tugging them down, I panic.

"What—"

"Shh," he says, sliding the panties down my thighs. "Trust me, sweetheart."

I gulp so loud that my gaze zings around the room, wondering if any of the guys can tell that Tristian is undressing me, bending us both so he can pluck my panties from my feet beneath the blanket.

Rath knows. I can tell by the way he's sprawled, teeth raking over his lip as he watches our laps with a dark expression. "Here," he tells Tristian, holding out a hand.

I watch, stunned as Tristian covertly passes Rath my damp panties. Between one blink and the next, Rath has slid them into his pocket, eyes returning to the screen.

Tristian's voice is a rough whisper in my ear. "Lift up, just a little—that's my girl."

I comply automatically, too full of panic and alarm to do anything but move with the current. It isn't until I feel a hot flash on my backside that I realize he's pushed his pants down. "Wait," I hiss, flinching forward.

But Tristian just drags me back, whispering, "Relax. No one is going to know, and even if they did, they wouldn't look." The sweet, soothing tone of his voice is belied by the words he speaks next. "They wouldn't fucking dare."

On the TV, Forsyth scores another goal, resulting in loud whoops and high-fives.

"Tristian…" I think I'd be angry if I had room for anything but fear inside my chest. So fucking stupid, thinking I could tell him I was ready for sex when we're in a room full of his lessors.

He squeezes my hips, easing me back into his lap. "I'm not Killer," he says into my ear, and for a moment, I wonder what Killian has to do with anything. But then I realize what he's saying. This isn't a punishment. He doesn't want to humiliate me. "I swear to you, no one will realize a thing."

My eyes flick to the screen, a last-ditch effort emerging in a strangled voice. "Shouldn't we be watching the game?"

"Fuck this game. Killer has them up by twenty-eight points." His hand disappears between us, brushing my ass as he takes himself in hand. "But we're still going to watch. Don't worry."

I feel the head of his cock nudging my entrance, sliding through my wetness, a low, barely audible rumble coming from his chest.

Closing my eyes, I sink down.

I try so hard to keep my face neutral as I take Tristian inside me, my fingers digging into the arm of the chair. I can feel the stretch, but it doesn't hurt like it had those first two times with Killian. Tristian's hands guide me by my hips, making me take him slow and easy. The whole time, I'm looking around the room at the backs of everyone's heads, knowing someone could turn at any moment and lock eyes with me as I'm doing this.

By the time I finally settle into his lap, the fine tremors in my thighs have more to do with the feeling of fullness than the anxiety of being caught like this.

I suck in a shallow, desperate breath, knowing that my eyes must be wide and glazed. But Tristian just pulls his arms from the blanket and winds them around my waist in a loose, casual embrace.

"Did you ever go to Killer's games in high school?" he asks, as if his cock isn't currently buried inside me.

My mouth opens and closes on an aborted reply. It takes a long, tense moment before I can answer. "Once." It was early in my mom and Daniel's marriage, back before Killian grew hostile and mean. I went to cheer him on, even though I barely knew him. "He didn't like me being there," I add, breath hitching when Tristian reaches for his beer, hips flexing up into mine with the shift.

I watch from my periphery as he tips the beer back, taking a long pull. "Yeah, he doesn't like us being there, either. I think if he wins, he worries he'll get superstitious about it, and then he has to count on us to be at every game. Killian doesn't like to count on people. Socks, sure. Pregame fucks, absolutely. But people?" He shakes his head. "I love that asshole like a brother, but he's kind of a lunatic."

It's surreal. He's *inside me*, and he's talking about Killian's athletic neurosis like it's any other day—nothing special happening.

And then Killian scores.

The entire room erupts, everyone jumping from their seats, fists in the air.

Tristian doesn't move an inch. "That's right, just settle back," he whispers, tipping the bottle to his mouth again. "No one cares what you're doing."

I realize then he was trying to get me into character. Talking about Killian, the game, it's all just a show. He wants me to know how well he can fake it—that he won't draw attention to this.

Exhaling, I do as he asks, melting back into his broad chest. The motion makes him sink in just a little deeper, and then I *feel* it inside me. His dick jumps with a strong twitch that I'm all too familiar with now. I've felt it in my hand—in my mouth—enough times that I can vividly imagine the sticky pre-cum dribbling from the tip.

For a moment, I'm so overcome with the urge to lift and fall that it's like a physical ache to stay still.

I turn away from Tristian to fight it, cheek rolling on his shoulder.

Rath is staring back at me.

He has his temple propped on a fist, his legs spread lazily in the seat. His eyes are dark and hooded as he watches, and it only takes one glance at his lap to realize the hand buried inside his pocket is playing with those panties.

Or maybe even with himself.

"You good?" he asks, his pocket shifting.

Nodding, I answer, "Yes," even though my fingers are twisting in the blanket.

Tristian hums, pressing a kiss into my neck. "Pay attention to the game, sweetheart. Maybe we'll *score*." He punctuates this with a buck of his hips.

I clamp down hard onto the arms of the chair, biting back a whimper. It's a low-burning torture, forced to sit still as Tristian pretends nothing is happening. Liam, an LDZ member who's sitting in front of us, turns to ask Rath, "These your speakers?" and I clench up at the sudden attention.

Tristian's grunt is nothing but air against my ear. It still makes my heart beat wildly, eyes flying back and forth between Rath and Liam as they discuss the surround sound. We're not watching a movie here. The lights aren't dim.

By the time Liam turns back to the game, my fingernails have pressed divots into the leather.

Tristian's voice is barely a whisper. "Feels so good when you clench up like that."

On the screen, the camera is zeroed in on Killian at the forty-yard line, with only seconds left to go. I know it's just the circumstance, the mindless lust throbbing in every cell of my body, but looking at my stepbrother on the screen, all I can think is that he's fucked me.

Those strong thighs, powerful arms, capable hands, and broad shoulders…

All of them have been used to push Killian inside of me—a lot like Tristian is now. If my brain weren't so fogged with sex-need-wet-hard, I might think to feel a little aggrieved.

These three have completely ruined me.

The least I can do is ruin them back.

With a deep breath, I give my hips a small, tight writhe.

"Jesus," he mutters. "What are you thinking about that's got you so gushing wet all of a sudden, hm?" His arm tightens around my middle, as if he's trying to still me. Nevertheless, I can feel him twitching inside of me, his stilted breath, the way his thighs tense beneath mine. I give him another wiggle. "Cherry," he chides, the word full of warning. He delivers his next words into my ear, quiet and rough and only meant for me. "I will nail you right here in front of everyone. Flip you over, bend you in half, and drill that pussy like I'm looking for oil. Is that what you want?"

Slowly, I shake my head. "No, sir."

His arm flexes around me, and I know his eyes are flashing with that same spark of satisfaction as they had yesterday when I called him 'sir'. "Only a few minutes left to go," he breathes.

They drag on and on, and it feels like the longer it goes, the more electrified every inch of my skin becomes. The blanket is hot—Tristian's *skin* is hot—and I can feel the sweat beading on the small of my back. My face must be glowing red by now. It's almost as bad as that night Rath teased me until I called him Dimitri, and in some ways even worse. All I want to do is squirm and buck and feel him moving inside me. I know I'll be embarrassed about it later, but right now it's all I can think about. Distantly, I wonder why I should even care if he fucks me right here, in front of everyone.

I bear down, clenching around him.

He pulls in a sharp breath, cursing a low, "Fuck me," and I hear more than see his head fall back against the recliner. "Rath? The second this game is over, I'm going to need you to clear this room out."

I don't turn to look at him, but I can hear Rath shifting, sitting forward. "Sure," he says, rising to his feet, and on the screen, Killian is running down the field. The guys in the room are all on the edge of their seats, wondering if he can get them another TD before the clock runs out. Rath goes to pass us but stops.

He looks down at Tristian, jerking his chin. "Hey, let me see."

Tristian doesn't ask. Later, I'll have to remind myself there wasn't any time to talk me into it. Everyone else is so absorbed in the game, the energy in the room reaching a crescendo, that he only has time to gather the blanket in two fists and yank it up, sliding my skirt with it.

For a few heart-stopping moments, my pussy is exposed to the entire room.

Thankfully, Killian chooses that moment to score, effectively capturing everyone's attention.

Rath crouches down to get the tray I'd left on the floor.

Or so it might seem.

In reality, he's getting a nice, long look at Tristian's dick buried inside me. His eyes go heavy and sharp as they zero in on it, a hand coming up to touch my thigh. My pulse is like a freight train in my ear as I watch him slide his hand up, pressing a thumb right into the center of my aching clit.

I slam my jaw closed on a cry.

He's smirking as he retreats, lifting the tray. "Alright fuckers, game's over!"

Tristian has the blanket back over my lap before I can even think to panic, distracting me with a kiss as, one by one, the frat boys file out, looking happy and drunk and ready to cause trouble somewhere else. Rath stands by the door and gives them all blank nods as they leave, his gaze occasionally drifting to us.

When the room is empty, save the three of us, Tristian tells Rath, "Not this time."

It isn't until Rath flips him the bird and leaves the room, shutting the door behind him, that I realize he wanted to watch. The idea makes my stomach twist even more anxiously. What are these guys doing to me?

The second the door clicks shut, Tristian throws the blanket off, bucking into me. I gasp, overwhelmed by the sudden flurry of movement. He lifts me from his lap, and I make a baleful sound at the loss of his cock, sliding out of me. In a whirl of motion, he's got me dumped into the recliner, standing over me with his cock hanging out.

He wrenches my shirt over my head before shucking his own off, tossing it aside. My skirt comes next, yanked over my hips with a sturdy tug that makes the seam strain. His blue eyes take me in as I do the same. Tristian stands before me like the statue of a god, his cock hard and erect, looking down at me greedily. There's no hatred in his eyes—not like with Killian. Tristian wants me, and I need him to think I want him.

I don't even have to fake it.

Tristian Mercer is breathtakingly sexy, cut from marble, leaner and sharper than Killian. A body honed from compulsive self-care and the early morning exercises that woke me up before dawn. His abs are flat, laddered, a sharp V tapering down like an arrow to the strong jut of his flushed cock.

He looks neither surprised nor alarmed at the bruises on my breasts.

"You don't care that I've been with Killian?" I ask, swallowing at the dark look in his eyes. Obviously, it's not a secret, but with the points, the games, the competitiveness...I don't know how this works. "I don't want to get punished for doing something wrong."

He bends to lick under my ear. "Now that your cherry has been popped, you belong to all of us. We don't covet. We're family. Killian had every right to take you that night, and I have every right to take you now."

He demonstrates this by spreading me open for him. His jaw goes tight at the sight, his other hand grabbing the base of his cock, and then he braces himself over me. It's just like he promised before—bending me in half, hooking my legs over his arms. He has spread me wide, and I feel the tip of his cock at my entrance. I'm not a virgin anymore and after the nights with Killian…I know I shouldn't be afraid. At least Tristian has the guts to face me. But this is all new to me. He must sense this because he touches my cheek and says, "Don't worry, Sweet Cherry, don't I always take care of you?"

He pushes inside, filling me with the length of his cock. He's not timid, but he's also not rough. His eyes dart from my eyes to my pussy as he pulls in and out, my body—and tits—lurching with every thrust. The position is strange at first, awkward and too exposed, but the way his body brushes against my clit…

Jesus, it feels good.

"You like that don't you," he says, grinning down at me. I nod, and his eyebrow arches. "You want me to fuck you harder?"

Again, I nod.

"I want to hear it, Cherry, I want to hear you."

"Harder," I say, my voice soft.

He slows his pace, which takes the friction away. "What was that?"

"Harder." This time I'm a little louder, but he stills completely. "Tristian, please."

"Please what?"

"Fuck me," I demand, pushing up on my elbows. "Fuck. Me." It comes out in a growl.

He grins and plunges into me, slow and restrained. "Like that?"

"Harder."

"I can't hear you."

"Jesus Christ. Harder!"

He reacts like a demon possessed, expression turning grave as he slams into me. I yelp and cling to him, calves pressing into his biceps. He's got me pinned to the plush leather, cock thrusting into me, mouth crushed against mine. Over and over again he punches into me, withdrawing before going in deeper than before.

I already know this can't last much longer, both of us too worked up from before, already on the edge of falling. But I can feel him holding on, the knot in the back of his jaw sharp and defined as he fucks me. Tension builds in my lower belly, the force and speed and sheer intensity, creating a desire I didn't know existed.

"You're mine," he mutters against my lips. "Say it."

"I'm yours," I choke out, the words lost as he punches the air out of me.

"Don't fuck with me, Story. Say it. *Mean it*." We're nose to nose. Something dark and fearful is in his eyes. "You're *mine*."

I wrap my hands around his neck and tug at his hair. "I'm yours," I say with ferocity. "I'm your Lady and you're my Lords. I belong to you; body, mind, and soul."

He kisses me, hard and bruising, and the ball of want explodes between my legs, coming out in a deep, shuddering cry. He slams his hips into me twice more, followed by a harsh groan. I can feel him filling me, his cock surging deep inside, but even hotter than that is the look on his face.

Total rapture.

"Goodnight, Sweet Story," Tristian says, kissing me one last time. We're outside my room and my back is pressed against the wall. My bones feel weak from being so thoroughly fucked. To be honest, I didn't know it could be like this. So different with each Lord, so satisfying, especially when it's obvious how much they want—no, *need*—me.

"Say it. Mean it."

I'd said what Tristian wanted. But did I mean it? It's hard to know when my limbs feel like Jell-O and I'm blissed the fuck out.

"You sure you don't want to sleep in my room?" he asks, fingers grazing my neck.

"It's not that I don't want to," I tell him, "but I really could use the sleep and I have a feeling that if I'm in your bed, there's not going to be a lot of sleeping going on."

"Fair enough." He grins and brushes his lips over my neck. "Sleep tight."

I step into my room, kicking off my heels and shimmying out of my skirt. A yawn catches up to me and I let it take over. Juggling three complicated men is exhausting. I wasn't lying about the sleep. With Killian out of town and Tristian satiated, I may actually get a full night's rest for the first time in weeks.

Climbing onto the mattress, I plug my phone into the charger and see that I have a message.

From Ted.

My heart stutters and I freeze, adrenaline sweeping through my veins. I swipe the screen and a video pops up. I already know it's something I don't want to see. It's something that'll keep me awake tonight, staring at my ceiling and flinching at every minor creak. It's probably horrific and grisly, full of things I'll regret laying eyes on.

But I press play anyway.

The footage is in black and white, and the quality isn't great because it's a video recording of a video recording—someone using their phone to capture the image of the computer screen actually playing the video. The video itself is security caliber. Wherever the camera was mounted, it was higher than eye level. It takes me a second, mostly because I'm too full of panic to focus on any one thing, but eventually I recognize the room. It's the entertainment room downstairs.

In it, two bodies are frantically writhing on one of the chairs.

Tristian's fair hair glints from the overhead lighting, and my face—well, it's not hard to recognize yourself, even in the middle of something like this.

Jesus Christ.

I watch the two of us fuck in the TV room, wild and with utter, graceless abandon. It just happened less than an hour ago, and I still feel the weight and impact of Tristian pounding inside me. Feeling nauseous, I turn off the video and throw the phone on the bed.

A moment later it buzzes with a new message.

You think I'm not watching?

Waiting?

Keeping an eye on you?

I've done it for years, and I'm not stopping now just because the parameters have changed. Before, I thought you were a whore. Now I know you are.

Tell me, Sweet Cherry, do you feel anything at all for them? You must not, if you insist on provoking me like this, but nothing about your romp with Mr. Mercer seemed under duress. If anything, you looked just like I expected. One more whore spreading her legs. I guess he did deserve it after buying you that car. He must seem like quite the score to you.

I'll remember that when I kill him.

I stare at the phone for a long moment, wondering if he's watching me right now. Has he really seen everything that goes on in this house? What Killian does to me in his room at night? The private times Rath and I share? Does he know *my* plans?

And when I knock on Tristian's door five minutes later, nervous and dressed in the least provocative pajamas I own, am I seeking refuge beside him because I'm scared for myself?

Or because I'm scared for him?

16

THE HIDEAWAY

HOMECOMING WEEK HAS the kind of energy that jolts through the entire campus. Everywhere I go, there are banners and signs, t-shirts and fundraisers. The spirit is infectious, and I have to admit, it feels nice to 'belong' to a group during the festivities. What isn't nice is the fact I have to spend an hour after classes in meetings with the women from the other frats, planning the layout of the carnival and making sure everyone has their jobs covered.

Bianca starts with, "First things first, we need to choose a charity to represent our houses—"

Marigold steamrolls over her. "I'm donating ten grand to the homeless youth shelter."

"The Counts and I are doing a food drive for the soup kitchen," Sutton chimes in.

"I'm taking the pediatric cancer wing at the hospital." Primly, she adds, "We've already bought a dozen new gaming consoles."

Bianca nods, noting this all down. "Then I guess I'm claiming the animal shelter, which just leaves the Lady."

Everyone turns to look at me. "Oh," I say, startled. "I don't—no one told me we'd be doing individual charities. I figured the carnival's earnings would just be donated to somewhere."

"They will be," Bianca says patiently, even though the others are rolling their eyes. "But each Royal woman has to claim one of the five charities that were voted on over the summer."

I probably would have known if I'd been here last year. Sighing, I ask, "So what's left?"

"That'd be Academic Angels," she answers, thumbs flying over her phone's screen. "It looks like they deliver books to our community's low-income children. I can send you the spreadsheet."

"So I just have to deliver some books and stuff?" I certainly don't have ten grand, or even enough money to spend on a dozen gaming consoles, but I do have a car.

Bianca gives me a look. "You have to purchase *and* deliver the books."

"Oh," I say, deflating.

Sutton raises an eyebrow. "You're going to have to ask Daddy Warbucks, sunshine." I take too long to realize she's talking about Daniel. When I instinctively grimace, she laughs. "What's the problem? He *is* your dad, right?"

Autumn's head springs up, jaw open in shock. "Oh my god, your Lord is *your brother*? Gross!"

"Killian is my *step*brother!" I squawk, face heating. "Our parents married when we were already teenagers. We didn't live together very long, and I don't even know him that well!"

Thankfully, Bianca steps in, turning to me. "Look, the Countess has a point. You should ask Daniel Payne for the money. He's a Lord. He's a *King*. He's bankrolled this before, and I'm sure he'll do it again." Sympathetically, she adds, "It's the Royal women's responsibility, but we usually tap our guys in, at the very least. It's no big deal."

I sink back into my seat as the discussion moves on to logistics, dread swirling in my gut. The last time I saw Daniel was too much. His hand around my wrist. His eyes boring into mine, cold and detached. His voice, dark and cutting. The last thing I want to do is speak to him again.

"I just think the beer stand should be closer to the stage," Autumn says, pen tapping her chin as she inspects the map on the screen. "No one wants to walk all the way around the park for a drink."

"If we put them there," Marigold chimes in, "the lines will run into the crowd. That's a big ol' mess, just waiting to happen."

Sutton nods, agreeing, "The last thing we need is a fight like last year."

"That bad?" I ask, analyzing the blueprint.

"Totally out of control," Bianca says. She's the only one who really lowers herself to speak to me. Not that I'm complaining. "The rule is that—actually, you know what? Everyone needs to hear this, so listen up, bitches." She gets the others' attention, giving us all a long look.

"Tradition dictates we all leave our petty drama outside the carnival. If your houses are having a spat, that's fine. But it stays out of these boundaries." She traces the line of the property Daniel had given us permission to use. "We do this to release some good into this world, and it can't be tainted by your rivalries or battle strategies." She cuts her eyes at Sutton. "Not everyone knows how to play by the rules."

Sutton gives her an innocent look. "It's not the Counts' fault the Princes laced the brownies with pot and get everyone high."

"Yeah, like we're really going to believe that," Bianca replies bitterly. "Only one house has a penchant for drugging people, and it isn't the Princes." There's clearly an old wound there, Bianca's jaw going taut at the topic.

"Well," Sutton says airily, "no one can prove it."

Autumn bristles at the accusation. "You realize some of those were sold to children, right? The Princes would never drug people, especially not kids." She looks at the Baroness and then at me. "Probably the Lords."

"What?" I say, caught off guard. I don't even know who the previous Lords were, but if houses have strategies, then I doubt that's one of theirs. "It doesn't really seem like their style, honestly."

Autumn laughs. "Please. Everyone knows what they *really* are."

"Oh?" I arch an eyebrow. "And what exactly are they?"

"Thugs." She crosses her arms, eying me distastefully. "Payne's well-kept flunkies. The only thing special about this year's Lords is that his son is one of them."

"Excuse me?" I ask, wondering what Daniel has to do with any of this.

Sutton shrugs, looking bored as she inspects her fingernails. "It's like the Duchess said. Daniel Payne is a King. He pulls all their strings."

Marigold jumps in to add, "There's nothing elite about them. Like all the Lords before them, they're just the glorified lackeys who keep South Side at their King's disposal. The whole university thing is just a convenient ruse. Keeps the authorities off their tail."

"That's absurd," I insist. I don't know why I feel compelled to defend them, but my hackles rise regardless. "Killian is an NFL hopeful. Dimitri is a prodigy. And Tristian is a *Mercer*, for Pete's sake. You don't get much more elite than that."

Autumn laughs. "It's kind of funny, actually. Usually, the Lords would go on to bigger and better things, leaving Forsyth and South Side behind. But we all know what's in store for those three, and it's not the NFL, or Julliard, or even the Mercer Corp. penthouse office." At my confused expression, she laces her fingers together beneath her chin, like she's talking to a small child. "Those three are never getting out of here, Lady. Payne would never let them."

Bianca cuts in then, throwing Autumn a sickly sweet grin. "Considering you're not wearing the Princes' ring yet, maybe you should focus more on your house and less on everyone else's."

"I've got that ring in the bag, Duchess." Autumn's eyes narrow, staring her down. "There's still time. Like today, for instance. I'm so fucking fertile that he could—" Her smirk falls when she looks at her watch. "*Shit.* Speaking of, I need to go soon if I want to catch my window." In a flurry of movement, she starts haphazardly shoving her things into her bag, eyes wide and panicked.

"We were done anyway," Bianca says, rolling her eyes as Autumn rushes from the room. "God, can you imagine being a Princess?"

"I don't know," Marigold says, placing her notebook in her bag. "If she pulls it off, she's basically set for life. Being Baroness is awesome, but I'm pretty sure once we graduate, they won't want anything to do with me." She looks glum as she says it, and it makes me wonder what the Barons are like. Are they nice, like the Princes are rumored to be?

There are a few looks as they stand, and I try to figure out what's happening. The Baroness wants to keep her Barons? The Princess is fertile? Daniel is a King? What does that mean? King of what?

Marcus' voice comes floating back to me from the other day.

"Everything."

There's a part of me that's glad to know the other Royals are probably as fucked up as the Lords, but there's no way I'm joining in their little bitch fest. They'd turn it against me in a heartbeat.

I grab my bag and walk out the student center door, looking for Tristian, who's scheduled to pick me up. Instead, I find Killian leaning against the brick wall, hair a shade darker and damp from a recent shower. I know he had practice today—or at least that's what he said on the way to school. He's never the one to pick me up in the afternoons, though. Immediately, I'm set on edge at the sight of him, all looming and still. He looks up as I approach, his expression passive as always.

"Is everything okay?" I ask, shifting uncomfortably. I'd slept in Tristian's bed again last night, even though Killian got home just before midnight. In the back of my mind lurks a worry that I was meant to be waiting for him, naked and unconscious, in his enormous bed. "Where's Tristian?"

Killian's eyes descend my body, taking in the outfit I'd chosen—a short black skirt and a tight red sweater. "Something came up with his sisters. I told him I'd get you."

"Lizzy and Izzy?" I'd met the girls when Tristian took me to their school for lunch. They're sweet and painfully adorable. They both had been struggling with some bullies and Tristian, in a complete lack of irony, asked me to give them some advice. "Are they okay?"

"Of course," he says, like it's not even possible for them to be anything else.

Campus is crowded as we head toward the parking lot. I don't know what I expect—we're rarely alone outside his bedroom—but it's not the possessive feeling of Killian's hand snaking around my waist and pulling me into his side before sliding down to cup my ass.

I look up at him, surprised by such a forward, public move. Aside from my first day back after my run-in with the Counts, Killian only claims me when no one is around.

Unless it's to punish me.

"Don't look so shocked," he says quietly, looking forward expressionlessly. "People have an expectation about a Lord and his Lady." He gives my ass a hard, aching squeeze. "Or would you rather me bend you over the nearest surface and just fuck you in public like Tristian would?"

Well.

I guess someone told him about what happened between us during the watch party yesterday. Swallowing, I wait until a student passes to mutter, "At least he doesn't wait until I'm asleep."

"What was that?" he snaps. I glance up at him in alarm, but it's clear from his questioning eyes that he really didn't hear me.

"Nothing."

The look he gives me is hard, and his fingers dig into the soft flesh of my butt. I don't know why I can't stop pushing him. It only leads to pain and torment, yet I just keep going and going. He's a bear I can't stop poking, even though I know in the end I'll be the one who gets mauled.

"Are you mad?" I blurt. If I'm going to be subjected to his stiff demeanor, then I might as well know why up front.

His eyebrow twitches. "Why would I be mad?"

"Because…" I bite my lip, wondering if I should bring it up. "Because of what happened with me and Tristian yesterday."

Killian flicks me a quick glance, and then a slower one. The confused wrinkle in his forehead smoothes away. "Because you fucked," he guesses. At my nod, he just stares ahead again, jaw ticking. "Did anyone see?"

"Well," I hedge, grimacing. "Rath, maybe. Kind of."

Killian just shrugs. "Then what do I have to be mad about? You're his to fuck, too."

He opens the door for me, but unlike Tristian, Killian doesn't instantly move to help me up into his ridiculously tall truck. He watches me climb in, waiting. It takes me a couple tries in the boots I'm wearing, and I hear his impatient huff of breath before his hands clamp on my waist, effortlessly lifting me inside.

Once he's behind the wheel, he says, "We're not going straight home. I have a few errands to run first, and I'm pressed for time."

"And you want me to go with you?" I ask, not sure I like going off with him alone.

"Yes," is his curt reply.

Being inside the cab, I'm overwhelmed by his clean, soapy scent and the overall nearness of his presence. I haven't seen him since Friday night, except for on that wide-screen while Tristian had me impaled on his lap. That, plus the weekend of respite, must be why I'm suddenly remembering what it's like to wake with Killian inside of me. The way he starts slow and careful—almost tender—lulling me from sleep in a gentle rhythm, the slow drag of his cock pumping in and out. How he gets rougher and more desperate as time goes on. The sound of his whisper in my ear, like he's trying to plant as much seed in my brain as my body.

My body heats at the memory, and I shift in my seat, adjusting the vents to blow in my direction. Killian heads to the campus exit and flicks on a turn signal, but it's not in the brownstone's direction.

I wring my hands in my lap, the tension setting my teeth on edge. I suppose this is as good as a time as any to say, "I'm supposed to ask for Daniel's help."

The funny thing is, I don't realize Killian was maybe—possibly—in something approaching a *good mood* until every trace has seeped from his expression. The line of his jaw tightens, knuckles going white around the steering wheel.

"With?" he asks in a nasty, unnecessarily hostile tone.

Taking a breath, I explain, "I didn't realize the Lady had to organize her own charity drive, but I guess I do. That requires money for supplies, and I have like a hundred dollars to my name." Wincing, I conclude, "So they told me to ask your dad."

The leather around the steering wheel creaks with the way he's strangling it. "Fantastic." It sounds anything *but* fantastic. It actually sounds more like he's saying, 'fuck you', just with different and more interesting letters.

Swallowing, I keep my gaze trained out the windshield when I ask, "Um, can...can you help me instead?"

There's a long pause, one of those hands lifting from the steering wheel to turn off the radio with a quick flick of his fingers. "Why?" he asks, voice full of animosity. "You know he'll give you the money. Just say the word."

"I don't want his money," I insist, but it's kind of hard to throw that out when Daniel is paying my way at Forsyth. Instead, I reason, "This is about us. It's a Lord and Lady thing. It should be you." Softer, I confess, "I'd rather it be you."

Luckily, we're at a stoplight, because Killian looks at me for a long moment, those dark eyes of his taking in every inch of my face.

"Fine," he says, breaking my gaze. The blood returns to his knuckles when he whips out his phone, thumbs tapping something quick.

It's obvious a few minutes later that we're headed to the South Side.

"Where are we going?" I finally ask, recognizing the dilapidated buildings.

Anxiously, I wonder, "Your dad's office?"

"No." He flips on his blinker and turns down a side road. "I told you I have an errand."

"What kind of errand do you have down here?" I stare out the window at the boarded-up businesses and homeless people tucked against buildings. The girls' words from earlier sit heavy in my memory. *Thugs. Flunkies. Lackeys.* "Drugs?"

He throws me an incredulous look. "No, not drugs." After a tense moment, he adds, "Although I certainly could find some down here." In the distance, past the public housing and small rundown bungalows, is a large house. A mansion, really—the same one I'd seen that night with Tristian. The one Gussy-Z had built for his mother.

It's surrounded by an ornate wrought-iron gate with gold accents. Killian pulls up to the intercom and presses the buzzer. A man answers, and after Killian identifies himself, the gates slowly open.

I look around us, a zing of discomfort rolling up my spine. "What is this place?"

The grounds are impressive, green and well-kept. It's like stepping into a different world from the shitty streets just outside the gates.

"You're looking at the new and improved Velvet Hideaway," he says, even though nothing about it looks hidden away. Killian stops the truck in the turnaround and faces me, leveling me with a deadpan look. "It's a whorehouse, Story."

I blink at the mansion and swallow back my apprehension, although I doubt I do a very good job. Visions of my stepbrother forcing me into a threesome— or something worse—flash in my head. "Killian…I know because of my mother…because of everything…you think I'm a whore, but—"

"You are a whore," he says, snorting. "But you're our whore, Sweet Cherry, and my boys and I don't share with anyone but each other." He unlatches his seat belt with a snap. "A patron of this fine, upstanding establishment has something for me, and this is where he told me to meet him."

My heart pounds as he walks around the front of the truck, and I can't bring myself to open the door. With a look of irritation, he wrenches it open and glares at me. "Come on, he's waiting."

I stare up at the house, but I'm frozen.

"What the fuck, Story?"

"I, um," I look up at the bedrooms on the second floor with their soft light filtering through the curtains. There are no similarities between this place and the hotels, but I feel an uneasy prickle of apprehension–one I haven't felt in years. "I…"

He makes an annoyed rolling motion with his hand. "Spit it out, woman."

I take a deep breath. "I haven't been somewhere like this since I was a kid, back when my mother was…uh, you know."

He stares at me for a long, hard moment. "A hooker." He's well aware of my mother's profession before she leveled up and married his dad. It's one of the primary reasons he hates us. Now, he's giving me a long, pinched look. "Your mother took you with her when she worked?"

"Sometimes," I say, back ramrod straight at the memories. "She mostly worked at hotels. If it was a nice place, I'd wait in the hotel restaurant or lobby. If it wasn't, I'd hide in the bathroom while—"

His low growl cuts me off. "You waited in the goddamn bathroom while your mom fucked a John?" He looks at me like he's waiting for an answer, even though one isn't necessary. Looking away, he rakes his fingers through his hair. "Jesus Christ."

"I had headphones." I defend my mother. I've been at the mercy of men—wealthy men, powerful men, cruel men—for survival, so in many ways, I understand it. She worked hard to get us on our feet. Into what she thought was a safe home. "I watched movies on the iPad and kept quiet. I didn't really understand what she was doing. Not until later." I look down at my hands—these fingers and palms that have brought men pleasure. Men I never intended to do such things with. There must be something redeeming in what my mother's done. Else, I'm hopeless. "And then she started seeing Daniel, and everything changed."

The irony doesn't escape me that I was in the company of sleazy men for a lot of my childhood, but it wasn't until Daniel—a nice, generous savior—that anything untoward ever happened to me.

"Well, unless things have drastically changed at home, your mother isn't in there." He reaches out and takes my hand, the gesture so startlingly gentle that it takes me aback. "And you're walking through those doors as someone who already belongs to *me*—not a scared little girl hiding in the bathroom." His eyebrow raises. "Got it?"

I don't expect Killian to show empathy here. I'm not even sure he possesses any, but I don't think he'll do me harm. If he wanted to trap me in a brothel, he'd throw me over his shoulder and drag me in, kicking and screaming. He wouldn't soothingly ease me out of the front seat.

That's not his style.

Once I relent, Killian leads us up the front steps and approaches the door. It's grand, made of rich, dark wood and leaded glass. My stepbrother doesn't knock. He pushes the door right open, like he's been here a thousand times. The elegant foyer is a sight to behold. I take in the marble floors and crystal chandelier, knowing that it may look nice, but a whorehouse is a whorehouse.

"Don't act so nervous," he says, striding down the hall. When I'm still staring at the foyer, he turns to snap his fingers. "And keep up."

I follow him into a large sitting room that's set up like a lounge. There's a bar tucked in one corner and comfortable seating all around. Through the wide glass doors at the back of the house, I see a massive stone patio and fireplace, along with a crystal blue swimming pool.

The room isn't empty.

It's filled with exotic women, each dressed provocatively. I know the look. I can perfectly imagine pressing my nose into the silk and smelling my mother's perfume. I thought it was so glamorous. The slick fabric and lacy edges, the spicy perfume and lotions. It wasn't until after the men left and the costumes were removed that the truth was revealed. Bruises and red, swelling welts, smeared mascara and the scent of liquor.

There are men in the room, too, full of smiles and charm. *For now.* I edge myself closer to Killian, curling a hand around his thick, tattooed arm.

Killian knows the young woman in charge. I can tell because her eyes alight when she sees him, instantly clacking over in her stilettos. "My, my. Killian Payne," she greets, giving him a kiss on both cheeks.

"Augustine." He nods.

"I was wondering what happened to three of you." Her eyes go expressively interested when she asks. "Is Rath with you?"

"Nah, they couldn't make it." She does a good job of keeping the disappointment from her face. But not perfect. He adds, "They send their love," and assesses the mansion, face just as impassive with her as it had been with me. "You seem to be whipping this place into shape."

"Well," she puts a hand to her chest, blushing, "I'm not his first choice. I'm sure you know." At Killian's non-committal hum, some of the seductive artifice melts away. Quietly, she asks, "How is she? The girls still ask about her."

"She's fine," is his stiff response, and I glance between, wondering who they're talking about. "I've already told your girls they can write to her, but she's not coming back. She's happy where she is." In a low mutter, he adds, "For once."

I'm startled by the protectiveness in his voice, left grappling with the curiosity about who it is, this woman whose happiness Killian cares about. Is she a hooker? The thought makes something churn unhappily in my stomach.

It's fascinating to watch her mask click back in place, her apple-pink cheeks blossoming with a sexy smile. The thought comes to me in a flash of appreciation. I could learn something from her. "Well, you came by at the perfect time. I have a new girl who needs breaking in—"

He holds up his hands and cuts her off. "I'm just looking for Nick. He told me to meet him here."

She tilts her head. "Ugly Nick or Pretty Nick?"

"Don't." Killian pulls a face. "You know he doesn't like being called that."

Her mouth slants into a sarcastic smirk. "The less physically appealing *Nick* is in the first room off the main hall. Word on the streets is that Pretty Nick is still out west." For the first time since we got here, her eyes flick over to me, expression shifting a fraction. She offers her hand. "Forgive me, sugar. I don't think we've met."

"I'm St—"

"She's our Lady," Killian says, pushing my hand down. "She's with me."

Augustine nods. "It was good to see you, Killer. Come back when you're here for pleasure instead of business. And tell Rath," her eyes flash hopefully, "there's always an open invitation, would you?"

"I will."

No, I think, teeth clenching, *he won't.*

I feel her eyes on my back as we walk down the hall. When we're out of sight, I note, "You two seem close."

"She's a friend of my father's," he replies, approaching a door. "I've known her since high school."

I suppose it's no great surprise that Daniel's been with whores before. He married my mother, after all. But maybe that means Killian grew up around prostitution, too. I suspect not the same side of it I was on. Distantly, I wonder if Daniel's ever bought girls for Killian—although, I don't see why he'd need to. But if he did, was Augustine one of them? She seems far more interested in Rath, but I'm not stupid enough to think that matters here. Girls like her don't get to choose.

Unable to ask, I shoot for something else. "Your mother was okay with you knowing a…er, madam?"

He cuts his eyes at me, the glare hard and cold. "Don't talk about my mother. Ever."

The tone is chilling and scares me enough that I do nothing but nod, gaze dropping as he raps on the door. A moment later, it opens to reveal a thin woman dressed in nothing but a silk floral robe, tied loosely around the waist.

"I'm looking for Nick," he says, all business despite the fact the woman's breast is fully exposed.

Without a word, she steps back and opens the door wider.

Again, I hold back. I can't just…walk in there. These people were just having sex. It's so invasive, and honestly kind of gross. But it seems I don't have a choice, because Killian grabs my hand and pulls me in with him.

The room is a large, spacious master suite. The bed is messy and features two sleeping women, both stark naked. The third woman goes back to the bed and curls up in the middle, right between them. There's an older, salt and pepper-haired man sitting on the couch in his boxer shorts. His hairy paunch sticks out over it, a cigar tucked between two fingers.

"Killer," he says, standing briefly to shake his hand. "Thought maybe you got lost."

"Sorry. There was a hold up." He doesn't have to look at me to get his point across. This is my fault. First, my meeting ran over, and then I was hesitant to come in here. "Thank you for your patience."

This Nick guy doesn't seem too worried about it, though, gesturing loosely to a metal case propped up against the wall. Killian goes to it and crouches down, flicking the locks and lifting the top. It opens to reveal five large handguns. I watch nervously as he plucks them from the case, one by one, inspecting each.

"This a .22?" he asks, turning a shiny pistol over in his hand.

"Yep," Nick answers, using his cigar to point at another gun. "But that .40 cal is a beast. Might not want to pass it up. Got a good deal."

"Too big," Killian says, not even glancing at it. "The .22 shoots softer."

Nick shrugs, looking unbothered. "Whatever tugs your pecker, boy." Killian grows quiet, continuing his inspection, and Nick turns his focus on me.

He gives his cigar two puffs before saying, "Look at you, sweet little thing. You one of Auggy's girls?" He pats his thigh. "Why don't you come sit on daddy's lap. We can talk about the first thing that *pops up*."

My instinct is to shrink back, but Killian was right before. I'm not some scared little girl, huddled in a hotel bathtub. Maybe the Lords are just like the Royal women said: thugs and lackeys. But they're powerful and far more intimidating than the old man sitting before me. Raising my chin, I level him with a sour smile. "No thanks, mister. I don't like *small talk*."

Nick's eyebrows climb his forehead, and that might be amusement on his face, but the sound of a trigger cocking echoes through the room. My eyes snap to the gun in Killian's hand, pointed directly at Nick's temple.

"Talk to my Lady like that again, and I'll blow your fucking brains out." His voice is low and steady, but there's no doubt about his sincerity.

Nick's gaze slides slowly to Killian, who's holding that gun with the same ease he holds a football, like it's something he does every day. The old man releases a low, rusty laugh. "Didn't realize she was your piece, Baby Payne. No worries." He takes another puff of that cigar. "Just thought she looked familiar, is all."

Killian holds it there for one beat longer, his jaw rigid. Then, in a blink, he's released the trigger and has it back in the case. He reaches into the inside pocket of his jacket and removes an envelope, tossing it at Nick.

"That should cover it."

The old man peeks into the envelope and seems satisfied. "Always a pleasure doing business with you," he says, standing up and walking across the room to the bed. The women shift around, making room. Killian's hand is on the small of my back, ushering me out the door. "Oh, and make sure you tell your father I said hello."

Killian nods and pushes me into the hall, slamming the door behind him. I open my mouth to say something—a 'thank you' or a 'sorry'—but he doesn't let me get a word out. Instead, he pushes me against the wall, his wide palm planted into my sternum. His face is stony, and I'd know that wild, unhinged look in his eyes anywhere.

"Killian," I say, fearing his retribution—a punishment for talking back to Nick. For talking to him at all.

Instead, he crushes his lips against mine. The kiss is so hard, our teeth clash together painfully. I make a small, wounded sound into his mouth, but I can sense the rage pulsing under his skin, and I know he's lost to his senses. His hand grips my jaw, my breast, and then my hip, wrenching my pelvis to his. It's a crazed, possessive series of gestures, like he can't decide how to best claim me.

In a desperate attempt, I wind my arms around his neck, rubbing the hair above his nape in a soothing motion.

And then I buck forward into his hardness.

His breath stutters.

The kiss doesn't stop, but I feel the edge of mania fading away as he licks at my tongue, tilting his head to deepen it. Slowly, his kisses ease, the anger dissipating until his hand snakes around my waist, landing on the swell of my ass.

He pulls back and looks down at me, voice quiet and sluggish. "He shouldn't have disrespected you like that."

Tucking my sore lips into my mouth, I let my arms slide away. "I could have handled myself." It's not said defensively or bitterly. It's more of a revelation to myself than it's meant to be for him.

"You belong to us, Story." He reaches up to thumb at my chin, eyes fixed to my abused mouth. "Everyone needs to understand that."

You need to understand that, he doesn't say.

It's still there in his words, anyway.

"They do," I assure him. "I do."

His eyes go shuttered, like he's coming out of a trance. Stiffening, he jerks away, snatching the gun case from the floor. "Come on. We have other things to do."

When I reach for his hand, lacing our fingers together, he doesn't pull away. He curls his fingers around my knuckles and leads me out.

229

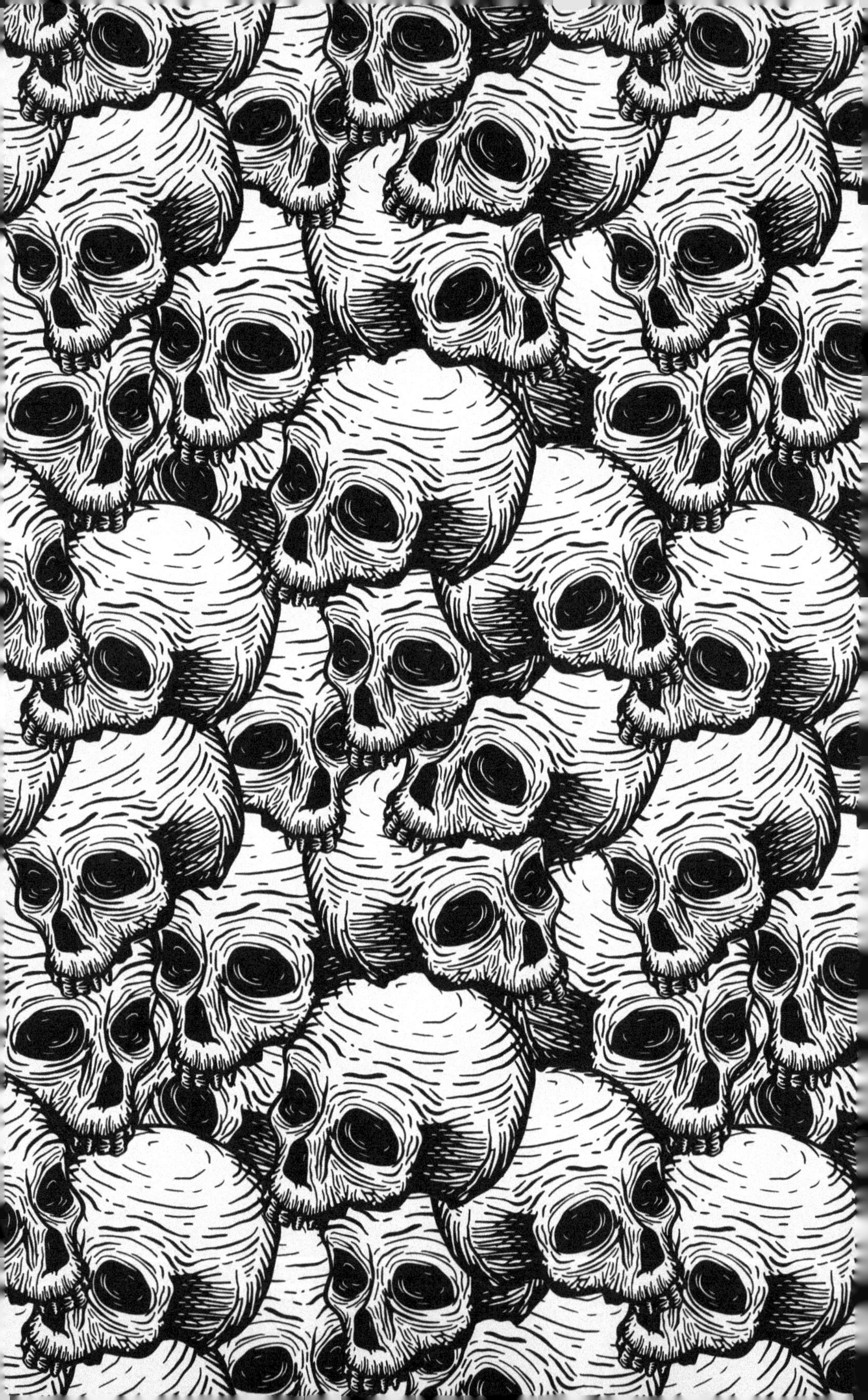

1 7

AUDIENCE

"I'm going to need you to handle this book thing," Tristian says when I answer the phone. He and Killian are two of the only people who call me instead of texting, so dealing with this 'book thing' is going to be a pain in the ass, because the rest of the frat doesn't give a shit. Luckily, Tristian adds, "I just told everyone to swing by." After a pause, he explains, "Actually, I might not make it back tonight."

"What's going on?" It's not like Tristian to just bail on us, especially when our Lady is finally in need of his obnoxiously giving nature.

"It's nothing," he says, but I know instantly he's bullshitting. "Honestly, nothing to bother you two about. I sent some money to the LDZ account, alright? Give our Lady a kiss for me."

I hang up, still sprawled on the couch in my room. I'd just been getting into this sweet Zeppelin vinyl when I got Killian's mass text about Story needing some books or something. After a quick text-to-voice pass, I realized it was that stupid charity thing the Royal women like to do every year. I had to jump through a few hoops to get access to the spreadsheet, and then send it off to Tristian to pass around to the others.

Jesus.

Mondays.

The guys start rolling in twenty minutes later, lugging boxes of books and supplies with them. I stand at the entrance, drinking a beer, and direct them all to the basement, giving each member a nod in greeting. It's only been about three hours since Killian set this ball into motion, and I have to admit, I'm a little impressed at the response.

He and Story arrive amid the commotion.

Killian jerks his chin at me. "How many?"

I scratch my head, thinking, "About twenty, so far."

Killian nods, watching Grant Patel, a neurotically harried sophomore, haul his second box of books down the hall. "Good. We'll have to make a note of who comes last." He gives me an evil grin that I'd usually be all about sharing, but it's weird. For the last few weeks, Killer's been such an insufferable shit. Always sulky and sharp-tongued, too tense for his own good.

Right now, he actually looks like he's in a good mood.

Covertly, I look Story over, searching for any signs of violence or harm.

All I see are two pink cheeks and a very confused expression. "What's going on?" she asks, watching another LDZ member trudge in with a stack of books.

He directs another guy to the basement and casually says, "I said I'd take care of it, didn't I?"

She looks between us, forehead creased in a frown. "Take care of what?"

"The books and supplies you need for that charity bullshit." I tip my bottle back, taking a nice, long swig. "If I were you, I'd have the guys deliver them, too. There's like a thousand on that list. Nobody's got time for that."

Her mouth freezes into a shocked little 'o'. "These are all for me?"

I point the neck of my beer bottle toward her. "Technically, they're for underprivileged kids."

She slides her wide eyes to Killian. "That was so fast!"

Oof.

That hint of a sparkle in his eyes at the way she looks at him?

Killer Payne's got it *bad.*

I don't know how she doesn't see it. She thinks he just hates her and wants to see her suffer, but she never sees the other shit. Months of him pining over her while she was living under his own damn roof. An entire year of high school spent following her with his eyes. Months of him drowning his sorrows in pussy and fistfights after seeing her with his dad. Then, after she left, *years* of wallowing in his own bitterness over it, knowing full well she got the best of him.

This fucker would walk over hot coals if she just came out and asked him to.

Maybe she's getting the idea.

Can't hurt to talk him up a bit. Shrugging, I say, "Killer told everyone to drop what they were doing and get it done, ASAP."

She gapes at him, even though I can see that flash of surprised delight in her eyes. "You didn't have to do that. I still have a few days."

Killian's staring straight at her mouth. For the first time, I feel that crackling tension between them, like maybe they just made out or something. He looks away, that patented Killer Payne mask of indifference sliding into place. "It's a busy week. Might as well get it over with."

I glower at him, bottle swinging lazily from my grip. Dumb as a box of rocks. All the pleased delight gets sapped right out of her eyes.

"Ah. Well, thank you," she says, ducking her head.

Jesus fucking wept.

"Why don't we go down and check them out?" I don't know why, but seeing that dejected curve of her shoulders is suddenly like a knife to my chest. "We can mark off what we get."

She gives me a small smile, tucking her hair behind her ear. "Okay. Where are they taking them?"

I use my bottle to point down the hall. "The basement."

The color drains from her face instantly, voice emerging in a cracked whisper. "The basement?"

Killian flicks his eyes to her, and then to me, and here's the thing. He can be a sort of hard guy to read. Killer's all about this whole stoic façade, like nothing can faze him beyond anger and hatred and a general distaste for things being out of order. But Tristian and I aren't just anybody, and I'm fluent in almost every Killianism.

He's *wincing*. "There's more space down there."

It doesn't matter. Our Sweet Cherry takes two steps back, like someone just threatened her with a machete. "I'm not going down there. You can't—you can't make me." Her jaw is set, and I might not know Story as well as I know her stepbrother, but I know her well enough to see when she's digging her heels in.

I give Killian a meaningful look, tossing a hand in her direction.

See? You're the reason we can't have nice things.

At Killian's glare, I approach her, undeterred at her flinch. She loosens a bit when I just nudge her chin, forcing her gaze to mine. "Baby, it's just a room."

Her lip wobbles. "Please don't make me. Please?" She says the last to Killian, with a lightning-quick glance, like maybe he's too much to look at right now. I wonder which night she's even remembering—Killian forcing her to her knees in front of forty men, or him and Tristian having that doctor shoot a tracker into her flesh—and *wow*. Now that I think about it, yeah.

Fuck that basement.

"Well," I sigh, tossing the last of my beer back. "There's only one thing to do." I call for Marcus, who's just now walking in the door with a group of juniors. "Change of plans. The Lady wants everything upstairs, which means we need some people to lug everything back up from the basement. That's on me for not asking her first. Now," I say at their irked expressions, "she seems to think this might be an inconvenience, but like I told her, LDZ will do whatever it takes to please their Lady. Isn't that right?"

Instantly, they all snap to, nodding.

"Sure thing," Marcus says, giving Story a grin. "Where would you like them?"

It's Killian who answers, "Put them in the back of my truck," but after a moment of their skeptical looks, he turns to Story. "If that would please the Lady."

Fuck me.

He doesn't even say it all snotty-like.

What the fuck happened after they left campus?

Story gives Marcus and the others a rapid nod. "I think—yeah, that'd be good. Thank you. I'm sorry." Quieter, she repeats, "Thanks."

That warms them up a bit, so it's not long before they have all the books stacked in the back of Killer's truck.

"I've got a meeting with the team," Killian says, but he shoves his hand in his pocket and tosses the truck keys to me. "You guys okay delivering them by yourself or do you need the pledges to help?"

"Oh," Story says, pulling out her phone. "Bianca told me the drop off is at the South Side Community Center." She looks up from the screen, meeting my gaze. "You know where that is, right?"

I groan, throwing Killer a glare. "Don't make me go to that place. I can't handle kids today." Always asking questions, with their sticky hands and shrewd little eyes, and they just don't care. They'll tell or ask you anything, and they're such dogged, toxic little shits about it. I should know, I used to be one. "Man, kids are dicks."

Story bites her bottom lip, looking up at me with those big doe eyes. "Please?"

And that's how I spend the next hour perched on the roof of Killer's truck, legs folded, the hood of my jacket raised as the rest of LDZ rolls in, three or four deep. I prop my elbows on my knees and rub my temples, hoping like hell I'm not about to take a ride to migraine town.

I get to look at my Lady in between deliveries, though, which doesn't make it so bad. She sits on the lowered gate, her feet swinging as she tips her face up to the sky, basking in whatever thought is running through that pretty little head. She's looking hot as fuck today in that little skirt and tight sweater, but I already know she's not down to fuck.

She still hasn't called me Dimitri.

I watch with the barest amount of tolerance as each member presents their books to our Lady like they're jewels or something.

"It's not on the list," Jordan Hashford is telling her, pulling a book from his stack. "But this was one of my kid brother's favorites. Look, it's pop-up and everything." Jordan's sending these looks to me, as if he wants me to see how much of a fucking suck-up he is.

Shit's hilarious.

Liam Poole is even worse of an ass-kisser. "I found some Spanish versions for these five books. You never know, right?" He gives Story a winning smile I'm sure has dropped panties at some point.

Story won't meet his eyes. "Thank you, that was very thoughtful."

It's just past four when the last fucker arrives, and I should probably make *him* take Story to the Community Center, but I don't. She pulled out those eyes and that goddamn 'please', and I pray to fucking god she never realizes how much of a sucker the three of us are for it, because suddenly, here I am, driving us to South Side.

When I pull into the Community Center parking lot, Story looks out the window at the square building, eyes curious. "This isn't so bad."

Taking the key from the ignition, I give myself a moment to lament my lack of buzz. "You should have seen it five years ago," I say, following her gaze. "It was in this shitty old brick building out near the avenue, surviving on scraps of funding from the county. The building inspector gave notice it was going to be demolished, so they had to find new digs."

"What happened?" Her gaze moves to mine, full of interest.

"The Lords happened." Shrugging, I tiredly explain, "Daniel grew up going there, and the three of us spent a few summers doing volunteer work—coaching camps and stuff." I give her a long, significant look. "Hence, the kid trauma. But the frat adopted it as our cause, and two years ago we raised enough money to build a new center." I gesture to the building in front of us. "And there it is."

"Wow," she says, her stunned eyes taking in the playground in the distance. "I can't believe the Lords did all that." The impressed, soft expression on her face shouldn't matter, but it does.

Gaining Story's approval is an uphill battle. Sure, I can make her gasp my name while she's coming on my hand, but actual, genuine admiration? Fuck, maybe I should tone down my hatred of children.

Shit.

Maybe I've got it bad, too.

It only increases when we step inside and Clara, the director of the program, comes out to greet us. "I hope this isn't a bad time," Story says, cheeks pulled back in a grimace, "but it all kind of came together in the blink of an eye."

"We never say no to gifts," Clara says with a smile. "We've got a group of kids here for the after-school program. I know they'll be excited to see what you brought!"

Story follows her while I head back to the truck with two members of the staff. One of them must be new because he keeps sending me these wary, suspicious looks, like he's never seen someone walk into this place with his hood up and metal in his face. Good. The less approachable I look here, the better.

It takes seven trips to unload it all, and by the time we're done, Story and Clara have already rounded up all the kids and gathered them in the main room. The energy of the place explodes when they see all the books.

I fold my arms and try to look scary and above all this fuckery. Not that it works, because kids don't give a shit. One boy walks right up to me, shoulders squared like he owns the place. He's small, maybe in kindergarten, but I can already tell he's got one of those big personalities.

"Can I have one?" he asks, pointing into the box at my feet.

Looking away, I mutter, "Take what you want."

He makes himself comfortable as he sorts through the box. "Why's your face so spiky?"

"What?" I give him my best withering glare. "That question doesn't make any sense."

"Spiky," he repeats, wiggling two fingers from his lips. "Shiny spiky."

Snorting, I tell him, "They're piercings, Hoss. You'll understand when you get older."

He makes this scrunched face, like maybe I just broke his brain a little. "I don't think I'll get a spiky face, even when I'm a hundred years old." He gives a low giggle. "It looks funny."

I glare harder. "*Your* face looks funny."

"Yeeeah." He nods, accepting this as a fair assessment. *Jesus*. Six-year-olds. So soulless, you can't even insult them.

"I want this one!" He raises a book, eyes wide and excited, and he just won't go away until I take it.

I look at the cover. There's a girl on the front, dressed in pink, with fairy wings. "Congratulations. You have a new book."

"Yes!" His eyes light up. "Can you read it to me?"

"No." *Hell* no.

He gives me a long, calculating look. "Yes."

Bristling, I argue, "No."

"Yes."

"*No.*"

"*Yes.*"

I pull myself to my full height. "No."

He pauses, head craning to meet my gaze. "...yes."

"Does this really work for you?" I watch him incredulously, three feet of pure stubborn wickedness. This has to be against the Geneva Convention or something.

"Sometimes." He bats his eyes and butter couldn't fucking melt. "Will you read it now?"

Story and the other workers are handing out books to the rest of the goblins. I turn back to him and growl, "Pound sand, kid."

"Please?" He asks, lip pouting obnoxiously. "Just one time?"

The next time I look up, I realize Story is watching me, frozen as she observes our standoff. I try to let go of some of the aggressive posture, but I feel in between a rock and a hard place here. If I'm a dick to this kid, she's going to hold it against me.

Familiar anxiety fills my chest as I stare at the words on the cover. It takes me five tries to sound it out in my head. *Tinkerella.* Just the thought of opening this thing and reading it aloud makes me want to blow chunks.

I crouch down to reason with this kid. "Look, Hoss, here's the deal, man to man. I'm not actually good at reading, alright?"

Little Hoss gives me a very grave nod. "Me either."

Well, fair enough.

Growling in frustration, I snatch the book up, flipping it open. He responds with a beaming grin, dropping right to the floor, eager and ready.

Pulling my hood a little lower, I sit down and open the first page. The words swim for a minute, but I close my eyes and take a deep breath, just like Story taught me to do. Keeping my voice to a low mutter, I read the first line.

"Tinkerella wasn't an…an…" I feel the word out on my tongue, "*ordinary…* fairy. She was an…extra…ordinary fairy…" I go rigid, waiting for Little Hoss to make a shitty comment.

He gives a firm nod.

Glancing up, I spot Story across the room. She's watching me, a small smile on her pretty mouth. A *proud* smile.

Okay.

Guess I'm doing this.

Fuck my dick.

"Unfor....unfortun...unfortunately," I continue, taking my time with each word, "no one knew how...spec...special she was…" I put my finger below the words, following them with my tongue. I go tense every time I know I sound stupid. My stomach twists uneasily, and I can practically feel my old teacher standing over my shoulder, ready to whack me with that fucking yardstick.

"You're stupid. Idiot. It's a five letter word. Get it out, Rathbone. We don't have all day."

It's cowardly, but I don't allow myself to look up. I turn the page and start on the next word, so focused on sounding them out that I've completely lost the thread of what this fairy bitch is up to. Page after page, mangled word after mangled word, curled over the book like it's something illicit and hostile, until suddenly, there are no more pages to turn.

When I finally look up, I realize a few things. First, that I'm sweating bullets, so wearing a leather jacket over my hoodie was an awful idea. Second, that my reading has drawn a whole group of children. Third, that Story is right behind them, listening to me. Watching me. Judging me.

I slam the book shut and leap to my feet, grabbing her wrist. "Let's go."

"Hey," she says, curling her hand around my arm. From the way she's looking at me—being *nice* to me—I'm guessing she can see the wild, hunted thing in my expression. "What's wrong? You did good."

"No, I didn't. I sounded like a fucking moron." There's a ten-year-old watching me, and I get the feeling she's thinking about how much better at reading she is than me. I throw her a dark glower and she flinches away. "Who writes kids' books with such hard words in them, anyway?"

"Adults," she says, tugging me back to my spot in front of the box. "You made that kid's day, and you absolutely *did not* sound like an idiot."

She looks all sincere and earnest, but she's lying. She has to be. I look down at him. He's already started over at the beginning, finger skimming beneath the words, just like mine had. Bitterly, I muse, "Maybe if someone had taken the time with me when I was his age, I wouldn't be such an idiot now."

"You're not an idiot," she says, eyes just as full of steel as her voice. "You shouldn't be so hard on yourself! You've got enough people doing that for you."

"The fuck is that supposed to mean?"

She looks away, jaw set. "It means you've got people like the Princess calling you a thug. A flunkie. Someone with no future, who's destined to always be a South Side lackey. Are you ever going to try to prove them all wrong?"

The words hit me like an anvil, snapping my head back in stunned fury. The Princess might be a mouthy, gossiping bitch, but the thing is, she's *not* wrong. I think that's what pisses me off the most. The Princess is right, and Story can't handle it—can't handle being tied to someone seen as 'less'.

Stepping up to Story, I hiss, "Fuck you," flinging the double doors wide as I storm out. I know she's behind me, can hear those heels of her clacking in double time as she struggles to keep up with my strides.

"Let me guess," she says, managing to sound both winded and bored. "This is the part where you lash out and throw a tantrum because someone possibly had an expectation—"

I whirl on her, jabbing a finger into her shoulder. "This is the part where you open your goddamn eyes!" We're in the parking lot, right in front of Killian's truck, but I still feel like I'm huddled over that stupid children's book. "Look around, Story! Maybe we've fucked you up so much that you can't accept reality, but here it is. I *am* a flunkie with no future. Killian is a neurotic meathead who's never getting out from under Daniel's thumb. Tristian is driving down a one-way street to nowheresville. And you?" I give a grim, breathless laugh. "Jesus Christ. We give you free room and board. We feed you. We clothe you. We shelter you. We give you expensive gifts to butter you up. And then we fuck you. You're our *whore*, Story!" If I thought the look on her face would be satisfying, then I'm sorely mistaken. It doesn't make it any less true. "If it makes you feel better to dress that up, then be my guest. Some of us don't give a flying fuck what the Princess has to say about any of it. If that embarrasses you, then tough fucking shit." I hold the passenger door open for her, waiting. When all I get is her blank, empty stare, I command, "Get in the truck."

She does as she's told, but not before tossing me one last grain of salt for the wound. "As you wish. *Rath*."

I don't let it get to me anymore than it already has. Being Dimitri—to the world, to *her*—was never anything more than a pipe dream, anyway.

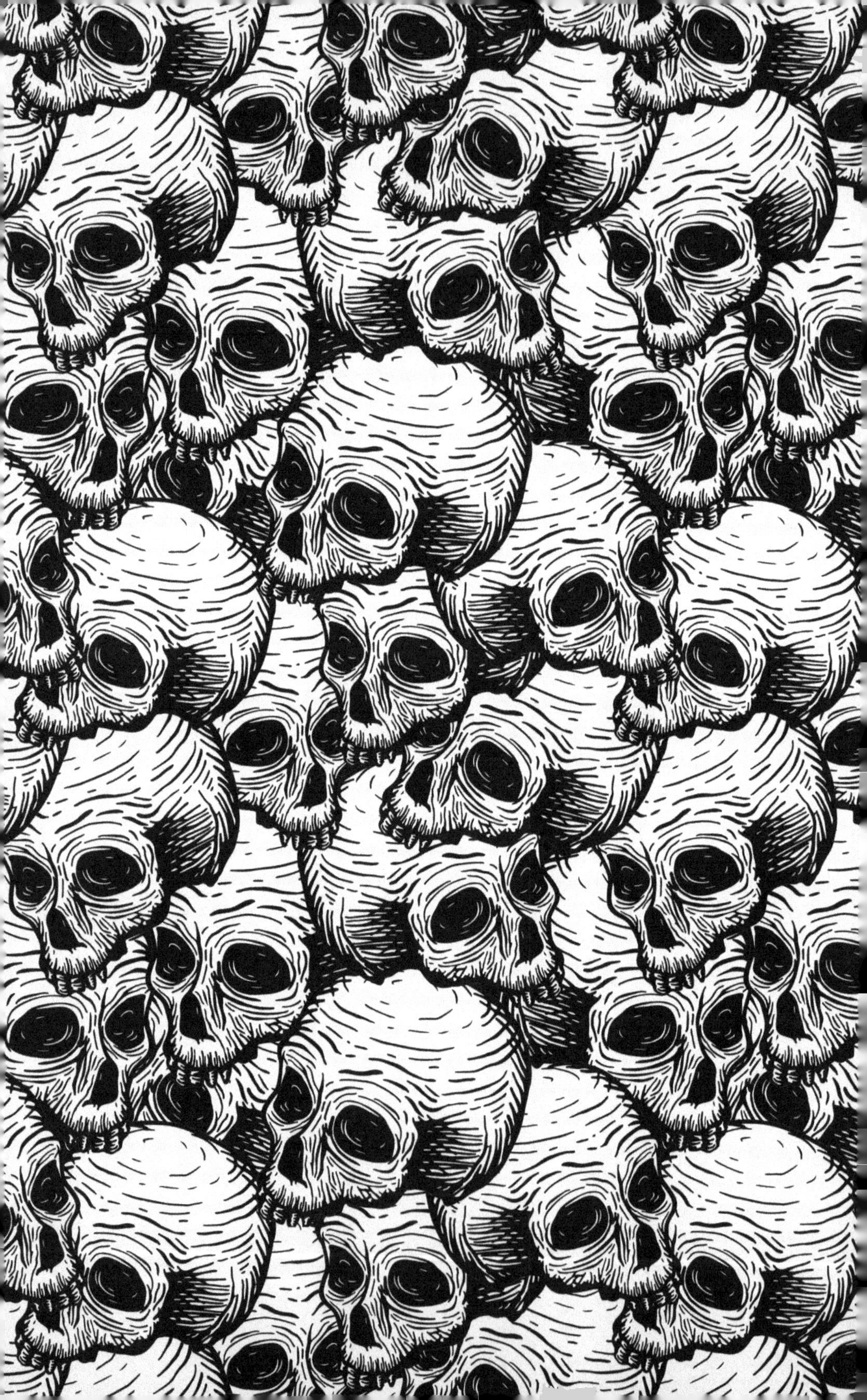

1 8

LESSONS

I WAKE UP feeling like dog shit.

The entire night was spent tossing and turning, too aware of Story, right across the hall. *Sleeping.* It doesn't feel natural or right that I spent all those hours over here when she was over there. But she'd given me a look last night—something weary and earnest—and asked if she could sleep alone.

"For just one night?"

So I disappeared behind my door and left her be, but only because she asked so politely. Maybe it's a bad idea to let her think she has that power. That she can just put those eyes on me and say 'please' and get whatever she wants. For some reason, the thought of sneaking into her room and taking her sat heavy in my gut.

So I lay here. Alone. Restless. *Hard.*

It puts me in a foul mood from the start, too pressed for time to even jerk it in the shower. It doesn't help that Tristian still hasn't come home or told us what the hell is keeping him away. To top it off, his gun isn't in his room, so I know he's taken it with him. He'd only do that if he was on edge about something—not that he's told us. Tristian is just like that sometimes, especially when it comes to his sisters. Always wanting to handle things himself, be the hero.

I try to be understanding about this shit, but the truth is, I can't actually understand. When it comes to Rath and me, we just have each other and Tristian. Rath has his mom, but he's always been distant with his actual brother, and my dad has never been Ward Cleaver. But Tristian has this completely separate sense of family—people he cares about and feels responsible for. People he has blood ties with. People more important to him than *us*.

Back when they were babies, I fucking hated them. We were only eleven at the time, but I knew they were ugly, wrinkly little things. Loud and needy. Always taking up his time and attention. He'd ditch us to take care of them, even though they paid people to do it. It never made sense to me. Worse was when we got older and I realized the twins were actually two little humans comprising all these fucking *reasons*.

They were reasons for him to leave us.

But one day, our senior year in high school, we were over at his house. It was after all that shit with Genevieve went down—after Story had left—and he might have pulled himself together and clicked that mask back into place, but Tristian was still a fucking mess about it. I wasn't in the best place myself, knowing the room next to mine was empty all of a sudden, every trace of Story wiped away.

We'd been in his kitchen when Lizzy walked in, a phone clutched to her chest. Chin wobbling, she explained to Tristian that she couldn't get it to work, and Izzy wanted to watch some kid show, but now the phone was broken, and their dad was going to be mad because it was still new, and I got the sense Tristian wanted them to have the phone, but their dad? Not so much.

So he'd put his big hand on her shoulder and pointed her in my direction. "Go ask Brother Killian to take a look. He's good with those things."

She'd presented it to me with those big, wet eyes, and it hit me like a bolt of lightning. The twins aren't competition for Tristian's loyalty. They're just a new part of this thing we've been building since grade school.

Family.

His family, but ours, too.

I'd probably maim and kill for them.

By the time I get downstairs, Rath is already there, looking grumpy and a little hungover. I'd heard him playing into all hours, so he must be on some kind of creative binge. At least, that's what I think.

And then Story walks in.

I freeze with my glass of orange juice halfway to my mouth, eyes taking in the outfit she'd chosen for the day. I'm used to seeing Tristian's Sluts-R-Us wardrobe on her, and occasionally she'll throw in something that's clearly meant to appeal to Rath. But she never dresses for me anymore. Not since that day down in the basement.

Not until right now.

She's wearing a pale yellow dress, the fabric soft and comfortable looking, skimming right above her knees in a gentle sway as she walks to her seat. Something that's probably meant for summer, even though it's getting cooler now. Her hair is pulled to the side in a loose, thick braid, locks of hair framing her face in a way that looks messy, even though girls probably spend forever getting it the perfect amount of tousled.

"Morning," she says, perching on the edge of her chair.

I look at Rath, but his eyes are glued to his phone. When Ms. Crane walks in with Story's Tristian-approved meal of something gross with way too much granola, I stop her. "Bring the Lady something edible. Tristian's still out."

Ms. Crane heaves this gigantic sigh and walks out, muttering, "…not a goddamn meal service…"

I only meet Story's gaze for a second, but when I do, she's giving me a small grin. That's how we eat breakfast—the tension and animosity between her and Rath palpable. No skin off my back. Story eats sausage with syrup and hash browns, looking so goddamn cute in that dress that I think I'd probably just whip it out and jack off right here, if time permitted.

I know this thing between her and Rath is serious when he takes shotgun instead of sliding in the back with her. If there's one thing he loves, it's teasing her on the way to school, skating his fingertips up her bare thighs, always acting like he's trying to get something going even though he knows damn well we don't have time. They spend the entire drive silent and avoidant. If Tristian were here, it'd be bearable. He'd be giving Story orders for the day and telling Rath to cool it with the booze at night. But me?

I tighten my fingers around the wheel and keep my mouth shut.

FORSYTH'S JOSEPH M. Hale New Media building gets evacuated just after class starts on account of a busted water main. There's a good ten minutes where they have us all waiting out front, the sky above us overcast and threatening rain, before some harried professor steps out and tells us classes are cancelled for the day.

The other students are buzzing about it, acting all annoyed and inconvenienced even though we're all secretly rejoicing over the day off. For me, this would usually mean an extra two hours spent in the gym. But when I see a flash of yellow lingering around the fringe of faux-grumpy co-eds, I realize Sweet Cherry had a class in the same building.

The idea comes to me like some dirty, forbidden thing.

She and Rath are on the outs, and Tristian isn't here. She's dressed for *me*. I organized the thing with the books, and I left her alone last night, and I let her eat a disgusting breakfast. At this exact moment, she doesn't hate me, because somehow, I've pulled ahead.

And I plan to keep it.

Her face doesn't light up when she sees me, but her eyes also don't fill with the hardened coldness I'm used to.

Well, that's something.

We stare at each other for a long moment, my eyes dropping to that tantalizing patch of skin above her neckline. The fabric of the dress is almost—but not quite—sheer. I can perfectly envision my fingers pushing those straps down her shoulders, the way the fabric would catch on the swell of her tits, how I'd have to slowly peel it down to reveal those pretty little nipples of her.

I raise my gaze to hers. "Want to learn how to shoot a gun?"

When her face *does* light up, I know I'm in trouble.

Fuck, maybe we all are.

I TAKE HER past the city, past the suburbs, farther north than I've been in years. It's wilder out here, a little patch of rural fuck-all before the county limits shift over into another territory. This one is ours, though.

My dad used to take me out here, back when I was barely eleven, and then when we were a little older, Rath and Tristian, too. I remember the first time he mentioned maybe marrying a woman who also had a kid if he planned to bring her out here, too, and I remember feeling pissed off about it. Fucking ridiculous notion, my dad treating her like one of his kids instead of one of his whores.

Story spends the drive quiet and coy, but I can tell she's excited. She keeps fidgeting with the hem of her dress, the tail of her braid, the straps over her shoulders, her bright eyes taking in the scenery as I turn down a back road.

The truck jostles with the bumps in the dirt road, rough and uneven, and from the corner of my eye I can see her tits bouncing along, perky and free beneath that fabric as she grips the roof handle. It's about half a mile to the clearing in the trees, revealing a field of tall weeds and not much else. I park near the tree line, peering up at the sky and wondering if the weather will hold for an hour or so.

Story is already out of the truck.

Rolling my eyes, I jump out with her. If I'd known she'd get this easy for a little target practice, I could have been making headway a hell of a lot sooner. She watches silently as I reach back into the truck, hand shoved beneath the driver's seat, and fish out the gun and some ammo. Then I reach into the back for the bottles of water I keep back here for after practice.

I jerk my head toward the field. "It's over here."

There's a makeshift log shelf about fifteen yards out, a little rotted and worse for wear, but still sturdy enough to balance five bottles of water on. Once I have them all in place, I stride back to where Story's waiting, an arm curled around her middle, hand grasping her elbow.

"They aren't very far." She squints into the distance, mouth pursed dubiously.

Snorting, I unload the clip with a flick of my fingers. "Let's learn to crawl before we learn to walk." When I've got the clip loaded, I slide it in. "First rule of gun safety: Never point a gun at something you aren't looking to kill. It doesn't matter if your finger's not on the trigger. It doesn't matter if the safety is on. It doesn't matter if it not's loaded. It doesn't matter if god him-fucking-self comes down to say nothing bad will happen. You understand?"

Unblinkingly, she nods. "I understand."

I hold her gaze for a moment, just to make sure she's taking me seriously before I slide in behind her. "I didn't bring ear protection, but it's loud. *Really fucking loud.* Be prepared for it so you don't freak out."

Again, she nods. "Okay."

I pull her against me, her back to my chest, and lift the gun in front of us. "You see this?" I ask, thumbing the little lever. "This is the safety. There's no red dot, so—"

"It means the safety is on," she guesses.

"Right. And this is the hammer. You cock it right before you shoot. Hold it like this." I arrange her soft hands around the grip, pleased to see that she rests her finger against the trigger guard. I give it a light tap, murmuring, "That's called trigger discipline. Never put your finger on the trigger unless you're ready for it to discharge." I raise the gun toward the bottles of water on the log. "Look down the sight, get a feel for it."

I see her cheek scrunch when she closes an eye. "I can see them."

"Good." Reluctantly, I let go of her hand, skimming my palms up her smooth arms. Resting them on her shoulders, I continue. "It's going to have some recoil, so you have to brace your arms and shoulders. Hips too." I move my hands down to her waist, giving it a squeeze. "Don't hunch. Make sure your footing is solid."

She nods, adjusting her stance a bit. "Okay."

I fix my eyes to the creamy patch of neck below my chin. "You think you can handle it? The loudness and the recoil?"

Her chin rises and falls. "I can handle it."

I duck my head, brushing my lips against her ear. "Then release the safety." Her throat bobs with a swallow, but her stance remains firm and steady as she thumbs the lever. "Cock the hammer." Her thumb comes up and pushes it down. "Now put your finger on the trigger." She slides her finger onto the trigger, back going tense, because she knows what the next instruction will be. "Shoot."

The pop is loud, and this might just be a .22 cal, but the kickback is real. She flinches, but holds her stance, exhaling a slow breath and taking her finger off the trigger.

She lowers the gun. "I *missed*."

I hide my grin behind her head, because she just sounds so fucking incredulous, like she was expecting to pick up a gun and be an instant sharpshooter. "Of course you missed. It was your first time. Try it again."

Sighing, she lifts the gun, remaining still even when I lean in close, explaining, "Don't duck behind it like that—it's not a shield. Focus on the front sight, not the back sight. Align the top of that notch with the middle of your target." When I feel like she's aimed it, I instruct, "Now inhale. Exhale. Hold it…and shoot."

She's more prepared for the recoil this time, only her eyebrow flinching. "Missed."

"Again."

She gets it on her third try, the water bottle in the distance flying off the log. She yelps a laugh, but doesn't lose her posture. "Again?"

She sounds so breezily delighted that I have to fight back my own chuckle. "Again," I agree.

She hits the second bottle, but the third takes her two tries. "It's sprinkling," she says, frowning as her eyes flick up toward the sky.

"Keep your focus," I command, giving her hips another squeeze. "You're not always going to be in ideal conditions when you're defending yourself."

Nodding, she aims for the fourth bottle. That's when I step back, letting her brace her own body, watching with heavy-lidded eyes as she effortlessly takes it out. The sprinkle has turned into a steady shower and the weight of her dress' fabric is sitting heavier on her tits. She's an exercise in contrasts. All that smooth, delicate skin inside that pretty little dress as she cocks the hammer of the pistol.

I'm pretty sure I've been harder at some point, but for the life of me, I can't remember it.

Without asking for direction, she aims at the last bottle and buries a bullet right into the middle. Just like I taught her, she slides her finger off the trigger before thumbing the safety, turning to me with a breathless grin.

"How'd I do?"

I want to tell her she did really fucking good, but before I can deal with the conflict of giving this girl a compliment, the sky opens up and begins fucking hammering us. I get the gun out of her hand before grabbing her wrist and sprinting back to the truck. She slips halfway there, the ground soft and muddy, and almost falls.

Except I catch her.

She looks up at me and laughs in a way that's so carefree and buoyant, for a moment it stuns me. I'm shocked back into motion at the sudden crack of lightning, hauling her to the passenger side and giving her a boost to the seat. I slam her door and get to the driver's side, wrenching it open and flinging myself into the cab.

The inside is almost as loud as the outside, the rain beating into the roof and our harsh breaths filling the silence. I empty the chamber of the gun before bending to tuck it back beneath the floorboard under my seat.

When I rest back in my seat, I can feel her eyes on me.

"Thank you." Her voice is so gentle that it almost gets lost in the cacophony of rain and thunder. "Not just for—I mean, thank you for last night. For letting me sleep."

Looking at her, I drag a wrist over my mouth, catching a drop of rain before it meets my lips. It kind of seems counter-intuitive to say, 'you're welcome', and it's not like I'm going to sit here and pretend it was no problem. Instead, I respond, "Whatever," and act like my eyes aren't as glued to her tits as that dress is.

When I see her chest hitch with an inhale, I look up, just catching the rake of her teeth against her bottom lip. I still remember with perfect clarity the way those lips had looked around my cock a few nights ago. The way they felt on my fingers when I pushed my sticky come between them, leaving myself on her pink tongue.

As soon as our eyes meet, lightning cracks in the distance.

We meet over the distance between us in a confusing flurry of mouths and hands, my fist grabbing her hair as our lips crash together. She makes a small, desperate sound that I swallow with my own grunt, surging over the console to deepen the kiss.

I know I can be too aggressive, and I know she hates that about me, and I know that I could have her over this console and in my lap so easily that it wouldn't even faze me. But I don't have to.

She's the one to climb over the distance, and if I help her along by yanking her across it, then for once, she doesn't mind. She fucking *burrows* into my lap—there's no other word for it—and then it's all just weight and teeth and the sweet, crazed way she's rocking into me.

What I'm getting at is this:

It's not my fault.

There's another crack of lightning and my hands are shaking with restraint, because that's what it takes to shove those straps down her shoulders instead of ripping them right the fuck off. Her skin is damp and warm, and if she were sleeping, I'd take this slow, really soak in the soft give of her tits, but she's so awake that it *hurts*, her teeth clashing painfully with my own.

She can blame it on the way I'm fisting her hair, lip curling up at the energy coursing through my veins. But it wouldn't be honest. She kisses me like it's a punishment and a reward, all wrapped up into one delve of her tongue. It doesn't let up.

Not even when I fumble between us to get my pants unbuttoned.

She rocks into me, these small, gnarled breaths creeping from her throat, and when I frantically shove my jeans down my hips, she just bounces up to give me space.

"Knew you fucking wanted this." I'm not proud of the way I touch her, fingers fisting the crotch of her panties. I grind my knuckles into her slick clit and revel in the groan she makes. "Tell me," I demand.

She gives a short, distracted nod, chanting, "I want it, I want it, I want it…"

The way I jerk her panties to the side is bordering on violent, but I can't stop it now. It takes one twist of my hips and a hard shove of her shoulders to impale her on my dick. She makes this shocked, bitten-off cry, right into the cavern of my mouth, and I capture it like an animal.

I fuck her like one, too.

Punching my hips up in short bucks, forearms pressing hard into her shoulders, I make her take me deep and hard. She responds by gasping the same air being knocked from my lungs in low, angry grunts.

"You get it now," I growl, and there isn't enough space between me and this steering wheel to fuck her the way I want, but I don't think it matters. At her frantic nod, I demand, "Tell me you get it."

There's nothing soft here—nothing but her. Her tits and dripping cunt, the damp expanse of her skin as I drive her down onto my dick. Something about her softness just makes me want to crush it. Not out of hate or anger, but this raging impulse to use it all up before it gets snatched away.

"I understand now." She opens her glazed eyes, answering, "I belong to you, Killian Payne."

I barely even recognize the sound being ripped from my chest—a vicious, guttural, inhuman sound—and I know I'm hurting her. I'm pulling her hair and our noses are crushed together, and Tristian is going to dress my ass the fuck down when he sees the bruises I'm pressing into her delicate shoulders, but it's unstoppable.

She comes with a strangled cry. I can feel it, her walls clenching around me, the rush of her slick, hot pussy trying to keep me. I push her head into my neck, teeth gnashed as I jostle her closer, arms crushing her to my chest.

I drill up into her once, twice, three more times before going rigid, filling her pussy up with my release. The whole time I'm pumping into her, I just hear her voice, over and over.

I belong to you, Killian Payne.

The urge to say something back is strange and new. I feel it in my chest, not in my head, and I guess that's why I can't get the words to form on my tongue, too foreign and mystifying to give shape to. She lifts her head, and our faces are so close, her breath fanning over me, that I can see every speck of color in her eyes. Brushing a piece of wet hair off her cheek, I find that I don't even need to try. The words come unbidden, without effort or thought.

"God, you're so fucking beautiful."

Her breath stalls and maybe mine does, too. But even though I should take the words back, shove them deep inside and never let them see the light of day, I find I don't want to. I've made her declare herself to me, give me her everything, and I've taken every piece for my own. But if there's one person in the cab of the truck who *owns* the other, it's her.

I belong to Story Austin.

And I'm pretty sure I always have.

STORY

1 9

SANGUINE

ONE OF THE pluses about fucking Killian yesterday is that there was very little pressure about the sleeping arrangements for the night. Killian didn't seem to expect anything, and from the way he avoided my eyes when we arrived back at the brownstone, it seems like he didn't want to call attention to what happened in the truck.

He called me *beautiful.*

It wasn't just the words, and I think we're both too smart to pretend otherwise. It was the way he said them. It was in the weight of his stare and the sweep of his thumb on my cheek. It was the tone of it, all soft and gentle and full of awe. We might have had a hard, rough fuck, but the moment after was contrastingly and confusingly tender.

It's not a look I'm used to seeing on Killian.

The sex was almost too intense. If I had to use only two words to describe it, they'd be 'dulcet brutality'. Much like sex always is with Killian, it'd been slightly terrifying. *Unlike* sex with Killian, my terror had nothing to do with the man inside of me. It was that captivating build of energy, like the lightning outside had struck right inside my veins, turning my blood to chaotic lava. It was mindless, driven by something stronger and far more complicated than mere need. I'm not sure I liked it.

Possibly, I'll have to try it again.

Just to make sure.

Now, I'm standing in front of my mirror, turning from side to side to make sure the sleek black dress I'm wearing hides any marks. My hair is a thick, tousled cascade of unruly curls. The dress is tight, with a deep, loose, plunging neckline. My eyes are ringed in a soft charcoal black, lids fading from a vivid purple to a smoky gray. The lipstick I chose is called 'decayed orchid', and it makes me look two shades paler in contrast.

I'm Rath's perfect date.

His performance at Forsyth's annual homecoming alumni banquet necessitates a bit of arm candy, which is a role I've been expected to fill since the moment I set pen to paper. I know very well that he's been preparing. I've heard him up there every night, the familiar notes floating down to me from a floor away. At least I've stopped imagining myself in his bed at the sound of it, his arms wrapped around me, his even breaths tickling my ear.

The truth is, I don't feel much of anything but a low thrum of nervousness about what's to come. I'll be Rath's arm candy. I'll kiss him on the cheek and wish him luck. I'll pretend the things he said to me in the parking lot meant very little.

And then I'll watch him fall.

I walk down the stairs carefully in my heels, so focused on my footsteps that it isn't until I reach the landing that I realize Killian isn't alone. Tristian's blue eyes have followed my approach, eyebrow cocked as he lets out a low whistle.

"Sweet black Cherry," he greets, head askew as he inspects me. Tristian has been gone for two days, and aside from a couple texts and photos with him and his sisters, I haven't heard much from him.

"You're back!"

"Miss me?" His eyes flash with pleasure when I throw my arms around his neck. He lifts me from my feet and gives me a spin. "Couldn't miss seeing our Lady all dressed up, could I?"

But when I pull back, I realize I'm not the only one who's dressed up. Tristian is in a crisp, white suit, his blond hair styled impeccably, and Killian is dressed in dark navy, tattoos all but hidden beneath the neat drape of menswear. My stepbrother is lazily gnawing on a piece of gum, eyes fixed to my cleavage. Idly, I wonder when I'll be expected to be this for him: a date who's been tailored to his tastes, someone to show off instead of someone to hide behind doors and bed sheets. I wonder if I'll be ready when it happens.

Rath's transformation is the most noteworthy.

I turn when I hear him coming down the stairs, struck speechless at the sight of him. He's taken his piercings out for the occasion, and he's dressed in all black. His hair has been pushed out of his face, but is still messy enough that I can recognize the troubled man underneath. *Barely.*

When our eyes meet, he pauses, his dark gaze leaving mine only to take in my black dress. His long fingers fasten the button on his jacket, a quick and skilled motion, and then he clears his throat. "Ready?"

I leave Tristian to go to him, smoothing my palm up his crisp lapel. "You clean up nice." I catch his gaze, giving him a soft smile. It's an olive branch that I desperately need him to take.

The crack in his exterior comes in the form of a slow exhale as he watches me, unblinking. Finally, his arm winds around my waist, pulling me close. He bends down to whisper into my ear, "How am I supposed to focus up there when I know you'll be in the audience, looking so fucking obscene?"

I try not to shiver at the feel of his fingertip skating down my cleavage, sending him a slow smirk. "I'm sure you'll manage." I strain up to glance a kiss off the corner of his mouth.

If he hears anything suspicious in the words, he doesn't let on. Instead, he just takes my hand and tucks it into the crook of his arm, leading me toward the door. It's strange to imagine the way I look, covered in Rath's darkness and flanked by Tristian's light, Killian's hardness. I wonder if I'm finally learning what it means to be a Royal woman. To be both ruthless and smiling. Rigid and yielding. Sincere and synthetic.

THERE ARE A lot more alumni than I'm expecting lingering in the lobby of the auditorium. For a quick moment, I have second thoughts about going through with it, but then I look down at the cuff on my wrist and find my resolve. Over near a bronze bust of the program founder, I can see some of the other Royals. The Baroness plays violin, and I can see her Barons in the front row, stoic and still. The Counts, including Perez, are dressed in all black, presumably here to support the Countess, Sutton.

The Princess is alongside two other upperclassmen at the entrance, handing out the programs. Tristian cranes his neck to get a good look at her, and then leans forward to smirk at Killian.

"Did you see the Princess?" he asks.

"Yeah, I saw. No ring."

Tristian shakes his head. "What's it been now? Three years?"

Killian agrees, "Three years, three failures."

Frowning, I ask, "What do you mean?"

"The princess can't get knocked up." Tristian's lip curls in an amused smirk. "No baby, no heir."

"I'm sorry, what?"

Killian snorts. "They're fucking obsessed with it. The Princess has three months to get pregnant or they start all over again with a new girl. Autumn, or whatever her name is, is probably on her last month if she's not knocked up yet. The pressure is intense because of all their traditions and legacies."

I think back to the conversations at the homecoming meeting and it all makes a little more sense. Well, sort of. Not that creating an heir to a bunch of stupid frat boys makes any sense, but more and more I'm learning Forsyth isn't like most places.

"And she knew this when she applied to be their Princess?"

"Definitely," Tristian says. "The application to be Princess is more than just an interview. There's a whole masquerade ball and selection process. Apparently, it's an honor to carry around a prissy prince bastard."

"Idiots," Killian mutters. Our eyes meet for a brief, hot moment before he quickly looks away.

"Well, don't you boys look handsome." The three of us turn. My mom, dressed in a gold shimmering gown, grins widely at us, while Daniel finishes up a conversation with another patron and walks over to join her. "Don't they clean up, well, Daniel?"

"Son," he says, clapping Killian on the back. Then thrusts his hand out. "Tristian."

Tristian shakes his hand, and I sense a ripple of tension between the two. My mother, as always, is oblivious. "My little novel," she says, pulling me in for a hug. "You look so pretty, although the makeup's a tad heavy, don't you think?"

I roll my eyes. "You look nice, too, Mom."

She releases me, leaving me in the awkward position of needing to greet Daniel. I give him a tight smile and prepare myself for a hug. Before I can, Tristian's arm slips around my waist, pulling me close. "Mrs. Payne, you look outstanding. I was about to extend an invitation to the frat party this week. You look like a sorority girl."

Mom *giggles*, tittering like a schoolgirl, before tossing Tristian an admonishing look. "Tristian, how many times have I told you to call me Posey?"

"Thought you couldn't come tonight?" Killian says to his dad, mouth pressed into an unhappy line. "Didn't you have a business meeting?"

"He did," my mom says, cutting in, "but I told him we needed to be here to support Dimitri on his big night. He's worked so hard to get here. All those long days and nights practicing." She gives me a look. "Shows how successful you can be if you put your mind to it."

My mother isn't shy about her disappointment in my running away from boarding school. She felt like it was disrespectful to Daniel, who spent so much money to send me there. You'd think a woman with my mother's life experience would have better self-awareness, but I suppose I can't blame her for living in the land of denial. It's only one letter off from 'Daniel', after all.

A woman dressed in black comes out and announces the program is about to begin. Tristian rests his hand on my lower back, ushering me toward the door. Neither my mother nor Daniel miss the gesture, taking in Tristian's claim with varying degrees of curiosity. I take my program from Autumn and try not to look at her ring finger or her stomach. I fail at both.

Nerves tickle my spine as we enter the auditorium and locate the seats reserved for us by Rath. Again, I wonder if I should do something, like pull the fire alarm, turn off the lights, but it's too late. The deed is done.

The seats fill around us and I'm hyper-aware of the cream paper programs in the hands of every person in the room, including the other frats. It's as if there are two hundred ticking bombs and I'm the only one who knows they're about to detonate.

"You okay, sweetheart?" Tristian asks, always watching. "You look a little pale."

I cast my gaze at him, pushing my hair back off my neck and giving him a sweet smile. "Just a little warm."

Thankfully, there's movement on the stage, drawing everyone's attention. Tristian rests his hand on my leg, and I'm all at once relieved and nervous about him making such public gestures in front of my mother. From the gleam in her eye, I'm betting the prospect of me landing a Mercer has her brimming with excitement.

Once again, I think about the Princess and her attempt to willingly get pregnant. Jesus. That's definitely a no-no with the Lords. It's in the contract that I'm required to take birth control. Although, with the way Killian obsesses over filling me with his come, I have to wonder what would happen if I actually got pregnant.

They'd probably strap me to a different sort of table and take care of it.

That's what I think about as the lights dim; how these people—these *men*—want absolute control, particularly with me. I have no autonomy over my own body, even down to the clothes I'm wearing right now. Sure, I picked it out for Rath, but only because he'd chosen it first. The small things I do to take back my control are growing consequential in the greater scheme of things.

At least until tonight.

My heart pounds anxiously as the room falls into a soft hush, focusing on the stage. I open my program, skimming the list of performers for one name: Dimitri Rathbone. My heart skips a beat when I read his biography.

It's exactly as I'd turned it in.

Tonight everything changes. I'm not just going to fuck with the little things anymore. After tonight, I'm going to destroy the big things, too.

WE SIT THROUGH each performance, the cello solo, the trio of violinists, the acappella groups. From what Rath told me beforehand, it's a presentation for the alumni and other esteemed guests—the people who provide the financial donations to keep the music school flush with new instruments, equipment, and the best instructors. But it's more than that. There are important people in the audience. The conductor of the New York Symphony, my mother tells me, plus the various organizers of art & performance grants. There's big money in this room, and even though Rath told me he's trapped in this godforsaken world of Daniel's, I know he wants out. He wants options.

Too bad he's a manipulative asshole who doesn't deserve any of it.

I barely hear the musicians as they're introduced and trotted out to perform.

The hammering of my heart is louder than the deep bass that fills the room. Nausea rolls in my belly, pushing bile into the back of my throat. I've been a sugar baby, a thief, a getaway driver, but this is the most dangerous thing I've ever done. And I'm doing it all while wearing an expensive gown and spike-heeled shoes.

There's no going back. Every person in the audience has a copy of my deceit in their hands. My revenge. Rath's comeuppance.

I'm focused on those slips of paper, watching as people in the audience check their programs right before each performer is announced. I pause on the cellist who appears before Rath, reading his biography.

David Grayson: A junior from Winston-Salem, North Carolina. He's played the cello since he was twelve-years old. The winner of the National Orchestra Award and the Guthman Scholarship.

The whispering starts the moment David leaves the stage, carrying his cello with him. A few chuckles teeter through the quiet room, and then the woman next to me gasps and thrusts the program at the man with her, whispering furiously. I glance slyly at Killian and Tristian. Killian is dozing next to me, eyes shut. Tristian is not-so-discreetly playing on his phone with one hand and stroking my thigh with his other.

There's no going back. It's showtime.

I straighten in my seat, which instantly draws Tristian's attention. Staring at my program, I fake a surprised breath, saying, "Oh my god."

"What?" he whispers, slipping his phone in his jacket pocket and pulling out the program. "Is Rath next?"

I nod. The panicked expression on my face isn't fake in the least. "There's something...*fuck*. Tristian, his biography." I place a trembling hand over my mouth. "Please tell me it's just my copy."

Tristian reads it over, his features going eerily still. "Is this the biography you turned in?"

"No, of course not," I blurt. Killian shifts next to me, rousing. "I mean, I turned it in, but it didn't look like this. This is *not* what I gave them."

"What's wrong?" Killian asks, rubbing his fingers into his eyes. "What are you freaking out about?"

"Rath's bio," Tristian hisses, leaning forward to look at Killian beside me. "Someone fucked with it."

I push my folded program in Killian's face and watch as he reads the words I know by heart.

Dimitri Rathbone: A junior, majoring in classical piano. Dimitri is the winner of the prestigious Forsyth Music Award. Although an accomplished student with a four hundred on the SAT, he's a barely functioning illiterate who graduated high school by threatening and bribing his peers, teachers, and administrators into overlooking his crippling learning disability.

"Holy shit," Killian breathes, looking suddenly more alert. Although he and Tristian exchange a panicked glare, I can't help but notice that neither says a word about it not being true. Every word of it is a fact.

"I'd like to present our next performer," the announcer says from the corner of the stage. "Dimitri Rathbone is a junior, majoring in classical piano. Dimitri is the winner of the prestigious Forsyth Music Award. An accomplished student with a four hundred on the SAT, he's a barely functioning illiterate who graduated high school by bribing—" Her voice cuts off sharply, mouth snapping shut as her eyes read the program. For a long moment, she seems unsure what to do. Ultimately, she gives the audience a flawless grin and introduces, "Dimitri will be performing an original solo piece, titled *Triste Historia in C Minor*."

Rigidly, Rath emerges from behind the curtain and a loud burst of laughter rumbles from the front row. Sutton glances back with a smirk, and I feel both guys tense beside me. I can tell from the pale, stormy look on his face that Rath heard the introduction—or what little of it she read before catching on.

His body goes tight and coiled the instant he hears the laughter, and I remember him so clearly telling me about those times in grade school, how the mocking laughter of his classmates still haunts him. At first, he tries to keep his reaction from his face, eyes blank and emotionless, but I see the tick of his jaw, the anxiousness in the tense curve of his shoulder. He perches on the bench and reaches for the sheet music, but his trembling hands fumble with the pages, sending one skittering to the floor.

The audience erupts with a renewed wave of laughter.

When he curls over to pluck it from the floor, the tendon in his neck is stiff and bulging and his face is already shimmering with sweat.

I'm surprised to feel relieved when the first notes ring out. The truth is that, even knowing how badly he's hurt me, it's hard to watch this. The way his mouth purses into a jagged grimace. How his fingers stumble over notes I know he's practiced for weeks. This is something he could probably play in his sleep, but now his fingers lurch over the keys—the same fingers that have brought me such rapture and such misery—and his shoulders grow stiffer with each error.

I wonder if it feels like it felt for me, that night down in the basement. Is he trying to ignore us? Is he on the verge of crying? Does he imagine he's somewhere else—somewhere softer and kinder?

Does he want to fucking *die*?

He finishes the piece, but only barely, fingers stilling on the final discordant note. The audience waits a long, awkward beat, until Tristian begins aggressively clapping, filling the silence. It's too little, too late, and when Rath rises, picking up his sheet music and bowing before the crowd, I get a good glimpse of his dark, empty eyes.

That's when I know.

This thing I'm doing with the Lords is dangerous. One day, I'm going to slip up and get caught, and Rath isn't going to forgive me. He's going to do his best to rend away all the satisfaction that's swelling in my chest at the sight of him up there, sweaty and defeated.

So I'd better hold it tight.

• • • 💀 • • •

I stir, knowing that Killian is watching me from the foot of my bed.

I can feel the weight of his stare like a palpable thing. It doesn't scare me like it used to. It's actually a bit of relief to know he's come for me, to know that little knot of anticipation inside my belly can finally loosen and ease. He'll make it feel good, and if I can pretend I'm still asleep, he'll even make it soft and slow.

I keep my breaths even, waiting. There's a small rustle of movement from the foot of the bed, but nothing more. No fingertip skating up my bare legs or mattress dips to signal his approach. I wait for so long that my body responds like one of Pavlov's dogs, a rush of slickness building between my legs.

I inhale deep, pushing my breasts out, hoping to spur him into action. A slide of my heel against the mattress as my thighs rub together. A breathy little whimper, as if I'm dreaming of his touch. A hitch of breath when I touch my belly. The rush of air on my skin when I spread my legs invitingly…

There's a low scoff, and then, "Christ, does he really buy that?"

My eyes fly open.

Rath is tipping a bottle of something amber to his lips, his dark eyes slashing over me like razor blades as his throat jumps with three hard swallows. "Has he ever *really* seen you sleep? Because I know how still you get when you hit that REM. You're like a goddamn corpse."

The words seize my lungs as much as the deadness in his eyes does. My heart kicks into overdrive, because I thought I'd seen Rath at his worst, but clearly, I was wrong. He looks like a shadow of a person, his glazed eyes rimmed red with the poison he's pouring down his throat. He's drunk and pissed off, and I'm the reason for all of it.

Maybe he knows it was me…

Swallowing, I arch my back, brushing my fingers over my inner thigh. I can turn this around if I just use the tools at my disposal. I let my legs fall open, eyes sliding shut as I push my fingers into my panties, bucking into the pressure.

If he thinks I'm nothing but their whore, then that's exactly what he's going to get.

"What are you doing?" It's barely phrased as a question, lacking in inflection and anything approaching curiosity. He sounds *bored*. "I'm not here to fuck you, girl." He waits for my eyes to open—for my fingers to slide away from my center—to tell me, "Wake up and get dressed."

My chest rises and falls with panicked breaths. "Why?"

Despite his disinterest, he still *looks*, those dead eyes of his fixed right to my damp crotch. When he finally looks away, he takes another swig of the booze and then caps it, twisting away to slam it onto my dresser. "I need a ride."

"A ride?" I finally sit up, blinking the sleep from my eyes. At least my secret seems safe. "Where?"

"You'll see," is all he says, opening one of my dresser drawers. He begins pulling out clothes, tossing some on the floor and others on the bed. It isn't until he hunts down a pair of black pants that I realize it's the same outfit I'd worn that night with Tristian and the fire.

Of course.

He wants revenge.

"Rath, wait." I stumble out of bed, stalling him with my hand on his arm. "What are you going to do? Because last time, there were consequences, and Tristian was sober enough to actually plan it through. This?" I gesture to the whiskey, the pile of black clothes. "This isn't going off half-cocked. It's going off *a quarter* cocked."

He stares down at me, and I realize he's put his piercings back in. They glint in the light of my lamp, and I know if I touched one, it'd be warm from his skin. "If you don't get dressed and drive me where I need to go, I'll do it myself."

It's as much of an empty threat as it is an empty promise. He knows I wouldn't let him drive in this condition. Sighing, I rip my tank top over my head and reach for the clothes.

That's how I find myself behind the wheel of my car—*Tristian's* car—well, *my* car—Rath slouched low in my passenger seat as I drive toward campus. I hadn't been able to pry the bottle of whiskey from his hand on the way out of the house, so he's got it tucked snugly between his thighs.

The only words he utters are slightly slurred commands. "Turn left at the next light."

Tense and uncertain, I ask, "Are you going to tell me where we're going?"

Coming out like this was a bad idea. Tristian could find us in a heartbeat if he wanted to. I could call, and Killian would answer. But drunk or not, Rath is my Lord, too, and I have no idea how to tell him no.

"We're going to the Purple Palace," is his answer, head tipped back against the seat. His voice hardens, the chill within it making a shiver roll up my spine. "It's where the Princes and their little cunt cow live."

"Jesus," I groan, turning left. "What are you going to do?"

"You don't need to worry," is all he says, head lolling to the side to look out the window. "This is something I've had planned for a while already. Everything is set."

"Okay," I say slowly, not feeling the least bit put at ease. Before we'd left the brownstone, he'd heaved a bucket into the trunk of my car. It's sealed with a lid, so I don't know what it's inside. Maybe it's gasoline? "But I'm guessing all that whiskey wasn't a part of the plan, so maybe you should save it for tomorrow."

He doesn't answer.

It's not that I don't think the Princess deserves whatever he's got planned for her. Because she does. Full stop. She helped Perez kidnap me. She's been nothing but a petty bitch afterward, as if I'm the one in the wrong here. No, I'd love to see that bitch go down.

But not at our expense.

"It doesn't need to be all bad, you know." Shifting my grip on the steering wheel, I try to make my words come breezy. "Now it's out there. People know.

You don't have to have it hanging over your head all the time. You can get help now—*real* help, because I'm not—"

He cuts me off, voice rusty and harsh. "Do you have any idea who was in that audience?" I can only spare him a quick flick of my eyes, but when I do, I wish I hadn't. He's still that same shadow person I'd found at the foot of my bed, only now I realize why it's so unnerving.

It's the look of a man who has very little to lose.

Exhaling slowly, I hedge, "Your family?"

There's a long pause, and then a raspy laugh. "Good one." He shakes his head, lifting the bottle of whiskey. "Talent scouts. The three biggest Forsyth has ever seen. Not only do they think I'm a fucking idiot who can't read—"

"You're not—"

"But I also bombed the fucking performance because of it." He tips the bottle back before adding, "So yes, it needs to be all bad."

I hadn't known about the scouts. My stomach twists in something like regret, but I shove it down. I can't say I was doing Rath a favor, because it'd be a lie. I did it because I've been humiliated at the hands of the Lords time and time again. I did it because of that smirk to the camera he had set up in his bedroom. I did it because he thinks I'm his whore. Someone to toy with and manipulate and use.

I did it because he fucking deserved it.

And I refuse to feel guilty about it.

IT'S FOGGY, AND the visibility is shit, but I can still see the Prince's palace beyond the gate. It's a large house that takes up a full square block of the street. It's not actually a palace, but I can see where it gets its name. It's old— Victorian, maybe—and an enormous stone wall surrounds the building. There are turrets on either side, and I'm guessing when one stands in those rooms, they have an almost complete view of campus.

"How are we supposed to break into that?" I ask, eyeing it skeptically. "Where are they?"

He stands beside me, following my gaze, and sets the bucket down. "What do you mean, where are they?" Flippantly, he tosses a hand in the house's direction. "Sleeping in their great big communal bed. Fucking, maybe. Filling that cunt up to the brim so they can keep her."

I whirl on him, jaw dropping. "They're home?!" He barely wobbles when I shove his arm. "We can't break in while they're *there*! Are you insane?"

Wordlessly, he takes the knife from his pocket, flipping it open with a *snick*. I flinch back, but he just crouches down to a little gray box below a number pad. "We won't be going in that side of the house. That's the Princes' weakness." He speaks as he uses the tip of the knife to work a screw. "The Barons, too. They're given these big, shitty-rich-people houses, and they stick to one room like they're a pack of wolves." He looks up to cock an eyebrow at me. "Could you imagine sleeping with all three of us every night?"

I wrap my arms around my middle, eyes anxiously scanning the street. "Yes."

There's a pause before he asks, "...you can?"

I look down to watch him open the front of the gray box, revealing a nest of wires. Shifting from foot to foot, I babble, "You'd be wrapped around me like a greedy, pot-scented monkey. Tristian would be completely naked and flexing his pecs, even in his sleep. And Killian would probably spend two hours pacing around the bed, trying to find the most subtle way to jerk off into my mouth with the two of you blocking his usual runway." Sighing, I meet his gaze, concluding, "It'd be insufferable."

He gives me a slow, glazed blink. "Tristian flexes in his sleep?"

"Rath, this is stupid." I nod at the box of wires. "We're going to get caught. Can we please just—"

I'm going to ask if we can come back tomorrow night, but at that word—

'*stupid*'—something in his eyes catches the light and hardens. He reaches into the box and curls his fist around all those wires, yanking it back with a silent grunt.

The keypad goes black.

Getting onto the grounds involves Rath prying the gate open enough for me to squeeze through, then pulling the bucket through, and then watching with my heart in my throat as he squishes himself between the iron, arms trembling with the strain of keeping the gap open.

From there, things are easier than expected. We walk around the exterior and Rath checks door after door. The side door leading out onto a veranda. The French doors in the back. A utility door off the main garage.

Infuriatingly, it's the front door that's unlocked.

When the knob gives, Rath sends me a look, rolling his eyes. "And you think *we're* arrogant."

The easy mode of entry doesn't make my heart pound any less as we quietly enter the foyer. Rath carefully closes the door behind us and then lifts a finger to his lips, as if I'm the one who needs to be told to be quiet. He ignores the panicked glare I send him, picking up the bucket and stalking noiselessly for the stairs.

I'm seriously rethinking that whole idea of calling Killian as we climb to the second floor, pausing on each step to assess any creaks. I have a fistful of the back of Rath's black hoodie, the fabric soft and worn against my palm as we creep slowly down the hall. I'm running scenarios over and over in my head. When—not if, *when*—we get caught, what will happen? Will they call the police? Or are they like Perez and my Lords, happy to take things like revenge and justice into their own hands. And if so, what will they do to us?

Sickeningly, the tracker implanted beneath my skin is bringing me *comfort* right now.

I'm still feeling disgusted at the notion when Rath stops, turning to a door. It's open only a crack, and I watch tensely as he reaches out to gently push it open.

My blood runs cold at what I see.

There's a gigantic bed—larger even than Killian's—and only a single slash of light, perhaps from an en suite bathroom. But there's no mistaking three Princes and their Princess, all sound asleep as we watch. The four of them are stark naked, the Princes' cocks and balls on full display as the Princess rests between two of them, back rising and falling with her even breaths.

It's a surreal moment, the realization that I'm watching these people at their most vulnerable. Rath—my Lord—could go in there right now and sink that knife of his into soft flesh, and there'd be nothing I could do to stop him. There's fear and dread, yes—so thick that it makes my stomach turn. But there's also a sense of power in looking up at my Lord and seeing that violent glint in his eyes.

I give his hoodie a furious tug.

Soundlessly, he leads me away.

Whatever he's looking for really is on the other end of the house. We go through one hall, and then another, north to south. The light is dimmer over here, but there are rooms that still look used. One with a vanity and clothes strewn about—dresses, skirts, tops—clearly Autumn's. There's another room with more masculine décor, probably belonging to one of her Princes.

And then there's the room I follow Rath into.

"What *is* this?" I breathe, taking in the room with a stunned apprehension.

After setting down the bucket, Rath carefully shuts the door behind him, hand easing the knob flush. His answer comes on an exhale, carried tonelessly by the same indifference on his face. "The nursery, of course."

It's like something out of an advertisement. The entire room carries the faint scent of baby powder. There's a crib against the wall made of intricately carved, dark wood. It looks old, like maybe it was made with the house itself. The bedding inside is a soft, pristine yellow, with little twinkle lights hanging from the mobile like a constellation of stars. On the wall above it is a finely embroidered tapestry that looks just as antique as the crib itself—a large-bellied woman with flowing golden locks and a crown perched on her head.

A Princess.

I stare at it all with a building sense of awe. "These people are all fucking crazy." I thought the Lords were unbelievable with their thuggishness and rules, but this is another level entirely. Recruiting some random girl to carry their Royal spawn is so ridiculous that this is seriously approaching LARPing territory.

When I turn to mention this to Rath, I find him bent over, wedging the tip of his knife below the lid of the bucket.

Wringing my hands, I ask, "What is that?" As much as I hate the Princess, I can't get on board with burning their house down—especially not with them still in it. I'll wake them up myself before I let that happen.

He acts like he doesn't even hear me, wedging the knife in deep and giving it a twist. The lid pops up, and he peels it back, tossing it aside carelessly.

I peer reluctantly at the contents, forehead creased with a confused frown. "Is it…paint?"

"No." He throws me a look, closing the knife with a flick of his thumb. "It's five gallons of blood."

"What?!" It's all I can do to keep my voice to a whispered yell. "Where did you get five gallons of blood?"

"Baby," he says, pausing to hold my gaze. "Is that really something you want to know?"

After thinking about it for a moment, I decide, "No."

I watch in a mystified silence as he unzips his hoodie and shrugs out of it. He reaches up to grab the neck of his shirt next, tugging it up over his head. It rustles his hair, making it fall over his eyes, but I can still see his gaze through the fringe, dark and challenging. Chin raised, he tosses his shirt away, the cords of his muscles shifting with the movement. I know instinctively what he's asking me to do.

I hold his stare as I copy him, peeling off my sweater, and then my tank top, standing in nothing but my bra and jeans. "What are we going to do?" I ask, voice cracking in uncertainty.

He bends down to sink one long, bare arm into the bucket of blood. When he looks up to smirk at me, he's transformed into the same man I'd seen that night in the tub. A demon, black-eyed, piercings glinting like fangs. Only now he rises and brings a red-soaked arm with him, blood cascading down his fingers in thick rivulets.

With a whip of his arm, it splashes gruesomely against the wall. The crib. The tapestry.

Me.

I flinch at the spray of blood, slashed in a fine line across my torso.

"They won't suspect us," he says, grabbing another handful of blood. He flings this one against the crib, the blood staining the yellow bedding like a crime scene. Then, he starts walking around, flinging more. "Blood is a Baron trademark. They use it in their weird, fucked up rituals. Some say they even drink it, although, to be fair," he turns to look at me over his shoulder, "people around here do tend to exaggerate their gossip." He punctuates this with a *splat* of blood against the window, using his palm to smear it around. "Which is something I'm sure they'll all be doing tomorrow. Talking shit, spreading it across campus, having themselves a real good laugh."

There's a basin in the corner, one of those old-fashioned porcelain things that used to have a purpose but are mostly for decoration now. He snatches it from the table and dunks it into the bucket, wrenching it up in one quick motion. The blood splashes sickeningly across the wall, dripping down like something out of a horror movie.

"Well?" He's watching me, waiting, his chest heaving with angry breaths.

Swallowing, I walk forward, staring into the surface of the thick blood. It's so dark that it's nearly black, and it feels gooey and cool against my hand when I dunk it inside, grimacing. I choose the door, splattering a sloppy 'x'. It's strangely mesmerizing, a bit like a paint project I had in second grade art class. While I'm admiring my work, blood dribbling sluggishly from my hand, Rath is behind me dousing the crib in the stuff. The blood pours in a waterfall over the little mattress, and at some point, he's gotten blood smeared across his side.

He looks like something out of a post-apocalyptic film. Eyes both empty and crazed, covered in blood, jaw set in grim determination. The blood he throws splashes like an explosion of crimson on the rocking chair in the corner. The changing table gets a coat of red, and then the lampshade and all its crystal tassels. I splatter it over the walls, feeling the wildness grow inside of me as I desecrate this place meant for innocence and birth. If the Lords' house is full of dead things, then the Purple Palace is full of things that shouldn't be created. The potential is there, but it'll never be right. There is nothing nurturing about this house or the people within it.

I shudder to think of anyone bringing a child into this place.

I dip a throw pillow into the bucket and slap it against the closet door, creating a bursting flower of grisly red. When I turn to do it again, I find Rath in front of the cleanest patch of wall, the muscles in his arm shifting as he paints a design with his fingers.

A pentagram.

Getting an idea, I cover my palms and curl my fingers into them, pressing the pinky-sides of my fists to the wall. Five dots above each and they look just like little baby footprints. When I look over, Rath is watching me, the corner of his mouth pulled up into a loose, wicked grin that I can't help but return. He copies me, and for a few minutes, we make a little path around the pentagram, tapering them off to the blood-soaked corner. I finish it off by scrawling two words over the textured wallpaper:

The Barreness

Maybe Rath thinks it can't get any better, because suddenly, he's lifting the bucket, walking to the crib, and dumping the rest of the blood into it. It streams from between the bars in rivulets, gushing to the floor in thick ribbons.

I can only imagine the looks on their faces when they open the door to find this.

I wish we could plant a camera.

When it's done, Rath stares into the crib like he's hypnotized by the sight of it. I watch him drag a wrist across his forehead, leaving a gruesome smear of blood in its wake. Reaching into the crib, he pulls out a blood-soaked teddy bear. It was yellow when we first arrived, joyful and bright and kind of creepy.

He shoves it up against the wall, takes his knife from his pocket, and stabs it right through the heart. When he pulls his hands away, the teddy bear remains, nailed there like a crucifixion.

The second our eyes meet, I'm the one who's hypnotized. He stalks toward me like a malevolent entity, blood spattered and black-eyed, and when he pushes me against the wall, I go willingly, feeling a bone deep awareness that he can never find out the truth.

Because Dimitri Rathbone will destroy me.

I can feel it in the way his eyes search mine, fingers feathering down my face. They leave a cool, sticky, wet path from my forehead to my chin. This is Rath, dressing me in his war paint. He's saying, *This is how you belong to me.*

I feel the kiss all the way down to my curling toes as his slick body surges into mine. His hands are slippery, gliding over my ribs and breasts as if I'm his new canvas. I clutch at his hips when he wedges a thigh between my legs, calling up that same dark magic that had gripped me when I found him at the foot of my bed. My body flares to life in a whirr of harsh breaths and firing nerves, desperate for his expanse of skin and heat and taut muscles.

It'd be so easy to give into it—just like with Killian and Tristian—so easy to open myself to him, to let him pull and push and take.

And then I'd have nothing left.

He grabs my face between two strong palms when I try to pull away, his forehead grinding painfully into mine.

"Why won't you fuck me?" he asks, so close that his eyes are nothing but a vague obsidian blur.

Swallowing, I answer, "If we stay here much longer, we'll get caught."

He pushes my head against the wall with a barely controlled jolt. "Don't fucking lie to me, Story. I know you want it." He punctuates this by raising his knee, grinding it into my center. When my jaw goes slack, he takes the opportunity, licking hotly into the seam of my mouth. "You want it, but you're pushing me away. Tell me why." His voice is a low growl, daring me to lie again.

I don't bother.

Looking into his empty eyes, I tell the truth, chewing out the words like they're gristle. "Because you're cruel and heartless, and the thought of letting something so dead into my body makes me want to heave."

There's a long pause, his chest brushing my own with every breath passed between us. "You think I called you a whore to be *mean*? You think I did it to hurt you?" He tips my head back, thumbs digging into my cheekbones. "I know you, girl. It's the lowest you can possibly think of yourself. And I accept it. Don't you get that?" He looks frustrated and pinched, the divot between his eyebrows begging me for something I can't comprehend. "Because even if it's true, I don't fucking care. That's enough for me—*you're* enough for me. I didn't say that to hurt you. I said it to *free* you." The smile that comes over his face is sharp and bitter and full of viciousness. "But I'm not enough for you, am I? That's the real rub. Tristian has money and Killer has glory, but I'm just the stupid fucker who hangs off their coattails. Is that it?"

"You think I don't want you because you're not rich or elite enough?" Shaking my head, I reach up to touch his jaw. "Everything you hate about yourself could be loved. They're the best part about you. Your mind is beautiful, Dimitri." It almost hurts to see the flash of hope in his eyes, all that fury melting away. "But your heart is ugly and twisted."

That flash of hope is extinguished by his falling eyelids. "What does that—"

He doesn't get a chance to finish.

Our phones go off at the same time, wrenching us from the moment. It's almost as painful to leave it as it is to remain within, but I know the second I see Tristian's name on my screen that our time is up.

Rath is silent and somber as he gathers our clothes, stuffing them into the bucket. I follow wordlessly when he slips from the room, fingers tucked into his waistband as leads me back through the halls. I hold my breath as we pass their bedroom, knowing that they're all lying there wrapped around one another, these arrogant people playing their hands at creation when they're not even smart enough to know they're hosting two intruders.

Drunk or not, if push came to shove and they woke up, I'm betting Rath could beat them, because they might not realize it yet, but he *is* enough.

I wonder if it was like this for the other Royal women. Did Sutton find herself feeling like this, that day in the parking lot, when she led me to Perez's van? Did she look at her Count and think to herself, *Mine is better than yours*? Is that where all her fucking audacity comes from?

If so, it's feeble.

I know where I want my strength to come from, and I refuse to draw any of it from these cold, empty boys.

STORY

2 0

P O W E R   P L A Y

TRISTIAN IS STARTLINGLY ungentle when he pushes Rath and me under the spray of his shower, stepping in behind us. "What the fuck…" he keeps muttering through gnashed teeth, palms frantically scrubbing the blood from my skin. My flesh is raw, pink from the abrasive sponge he lathered with soap. At least the water is warm. "Fucking diseased, toxic, hepatitis-ridden, Baron-bleeding bullshit."

"Glad to see you're not overreacting or anything," Rath says from the other side of the shower, naked and loose-looking. At some point, he reclaimed his bottle of whiskey and didn't look willing to let it go, even when he stripped off his clothes. He tips it up to his mouth as Tristian lathers up the sponge for a second time.

He was waiting for us in the garage, standing in the dark, worried and annoyed. He'd forced us to strip there, grumbling about trailing blood across the house and Ms. Crane. The mention of her was why I'd agreed immediately to strip down completely. I didn't want to experience her wrath.

Tristian led us to his shower, turning on the showerheads and ordering us inside. Rath took one side, and I took the other. Tristian stripped down and stepped inside with us, armed with top end bath products, including brushes that look like torture devices.

"I can't believe you'd be so fucking reckless and—" Pausing, Tristian's jaw hardens. "Actually, I can believe that. But *you*." The look Tristian gives me makes me turn away, unwilling to deal with it. He responds by fisting my hair and scrubbing the sponge down my side. "You should have woken me up. Called me. Done *something*. You don't just fucking go off into the night like—"

"Like she did with you?" Rath asks, watching lazily as Tristian washes the blood away.

"That was different," Tristian argues, spinning me roughly around. His glare follows the motions of the sponge, eyes pinched tight at the corners. "I wasn't drunk and pissed off. I did it the right way."

"You hadn't just had your entire future sabotaged in front of the gatekeepers of an industry!" The rage swells under his skin. "And I wouldn't count Daniel catching you on tape as 'doing it the right way'."

"He what?" I ask. It's the first time I've heard of this. "He knew we were there?"

"It's resolved," Tristian says. He removes one of the two shower heads and directs the spray across my backside.

"Whatever." Rath pushes a long 'pssssh' through his teeth. "She was fine. Weren't you fine, little Cherry? Didn't big daddy Rath get you home in one piece?" I don't like the way he says it, all biting and caustic.

Tristian cuts him off. "Things were different then. There weren't people trying to…" He trails off, pushing me under the water. Pinkish blood washes down my belly and pools at our feet. He sneers, "This is revolting. Covering yourselves in someone else's blood, god only fucking knows who or what."

The bottle of whiskey sloshes as Rath raises it in a clumsy gesture. "It's some kind of cattle blood, you fucking lunatic. There's no hepatitis."

I stand obediently as Tristian lathers up my hair—fingers catching in the knots a little too pointedly—because this is what it means to be a Lady. Breaking into a frat house. Coming when called. Letting Tristian fuss over me like his wily dog. But the truth is, there's a cold, detached edge to his gaze and motions that makes my stomach flip anxiously.

My eyes catch Rath's and he's watching me, head lolled back onto the tile. The jut of his chin looks altogether indolent and defiant.

So does the jut of his cock.

Autumn said it. These men are thugs. They get off on this lifestyle. Revenge, chaos, pain, and torture. For once we're on the same side of it, and I won't deny it ignites something under my own skin. I'm staring at his arousal when it really hits me that I'm in a shower with two men. I don't need to drop my eyes to know that Tristian's cock is just as hard and demanding. I can feel it every time he jostles my head, fingers digging painfully into my scalp. The tip of his dick keeps grazing my hip like a silent threat.

"Head back," he commands, voice low and full of warning. I know better than to fight, letting him wash the shampoo from my hair. "Remember that talk we had about you calling us out on our bullshit sometimes?" He flings a hand at Rath, stressing, "*This* is that bullshit. Something like that happens again, you wake me or Killian! Do you understand?"

Rath snorts. "You're such a drama queen."

"*I'm* a drama queen?" Tristian whirls on him, eyes flashing. "I'm not the one who snuck out at two in the morning to decorate a nursery in cow's blood! No one's a bigger drama queen than you, Rath."

Rath rolls his eyes, reaching out to spin a finger in Tristian's direction. "Don't point your boner at me."

The sponge Tristian throws smacks Rath right in the middle of his chest. "Wash yourself!"

The shower is big, but not big enough that our shoulders don't touch when Rath moves beneath the spray. I go where Tristian leads me, almost slipping as he wrenches me to the side. His hand clamps hard on my waist to steady me, but something thick and worried lodges itself in my throat. I can't handle Tristian when he's like this.

Or can I?

Swallowing, I reach down and wrap my fingers around his hardness, staring up into his fiery glare. "I'm sorry," I assure him, giving him a long, wet stroke. The knot in the back of his jaw ticks and I strain up to press my lips to it, lying, "We were careful."

For a long moment, he's unresponsive, his fingers digging into the soft flesh of my hips. Then suddenly he has me slammed up against the tiled wall of the shower, his mouth crushed to mine. It's a deep, demanding kiss, his breath hissing frantically from his nose as he bucks into me. He reaches down to grab my thigh, jerking it upward to hook around his hip, and it's like I'm right back against that blood-stained wall, buzzing with anticipation. It's just a different man meeting my needs.

He grabs my ass and roughly hefts me up, grunting with the effort. Unthinkingly, I wind my legs around him and prepare myself for what I know is coming.

He enters me in a hard thrust, swallowing my cry.

Beside us, Rath's still under the spray. He waves the bottle of whiskey and says, "Oh, don't mind me. I know that nut of yours couldn't wait the twenty steps to your bed."

I doubt Tristian even hears him. He's too busy fucking into me, his teeth grazing my shoulder as his hips shove me against the wall, over and over. I wind my fingers into the back of his hair and hold on, aware there's nothing I need to do here—I'm just along for the ride. I lock my ankles together and throw my head back with wild, gasping breaths. The steam is thick in my lungs, filling it with Tristian's myriad of scents, and I might be powerless, but it doesn't feel like it.

I doubt even Genevieve could have reduced Tristian to such a mindless, vicious mess of punching hips and nipping teeth.

My mouth is falling agape on a gasp when my eyes open and catch Rath looking back at me. He's leaning against the wall beside me, body a long line of pale skin and corded muscle. The mouth of the bottle hangs precariously from two fingers, but that's not what has my attention. The wiry tendons in his forearm shift and pull as he strokes his cock, his abs taut and sharp. He looks almost as hot and evil as he had when he was covered in blood, his wet locks of hair plastered to his face as he watches his friend fuck me.

I used to watch my mom sometimes when she was with her men—the way she'd touch them, look at them, smile at them. It was all fake, that much I knew. But I also knew it worked. I well remember calling it up in my sugar baby days, trying so hard to conjure up a sultry presence that didn't suit me at all. Those men didn't want sultry, anyway. They wanted shy, naïve, stupid girls who didn't realize the value of what they were giving up. Vultures circling overhead, hungry to scavenge the last remains of our youth.

I press my head to the wall and give Rath a look. It's neither sultry nor shy, because these men don't want either of those things. I know that now. They want to feel that I'm desperate for them—so desperate that I can't bring myself to fight back. They don't scavenge. They conquer.

In a blink, he's pushed off the wall, and we meet over the distance, straining, our tongues curling together like old friends. Tristian drives himself deep inside of me, jostling my body, but Rath follows gracefully with the jolts that are tearing whimpers from my throat, his arm bobbing in a more pointed rhythm.

It's nothing like I expected it to be. There's no greed here among them. When Tristian lifts his head, Rath lets me go so Tristian can take my mouth. When Tristian tears away, he buries his face in my throat and sends me back to Rath's waiting tongue. It's sweltering and slippery and too crowded, and I can barely breathe with the way they're passing my gasps back and forth. It's almost too much to feel—to give—to take.

My orgasm disagrees.

I don't even realize I've let go of Tristian and latched one arm around Rath's neck until the stars fade from my vision. He's panting these short, whiskey-scented breaths into my mouth, his shoulder jumping as he strips his cock, and I don't even know which of them comes first. I just know that Tristian is slamming me hard into the wall, cock surging hot and thick inside of me, and then Rath is exhaling choppily, the motions of his shoulder going suddenly still.

Tristian doesn't let me go, even when my feet hit the floor, which is a good thing. I'm not convinced my legs would hold me. He gives me to Rath instead, wraps my arms around his neck and lets my cheek rest heavy and weary against Rath's slick chest. Then Tristian turns me to the spray and cleans his spunk from my thighs, fingers dipping between my legs to rub it away into the hot water. I make a sound into Rath's neck when Tristian's fingers push inside me, and Rath responds by cupping the back of my head in his wide palm.

"Don't want to drip all night, do you?" Rath asks, adding, "Seems like a good plan."

I give my head a weak shake, spreading my feet for Tristian, letting him wash away the physical evidence of what we'd just done. But no matter how hot the shower is, how hard they scrub, what I did to Rath today is scorched into my bones.

And what I've got planned for tomorrow will burn down the whole damn house.

THE WEEKLY PREGAME party is in full swing. LDZ members have been rolling in with sorority girls on their arms for the last hour, and the bar is already packed. Killian is across the room, surrounded by his blondes, each of them hoping to be the one he picks tonight. I suppose the word hasn't gotten around yet that my stepbrother has a new target for his pregame ritual.

These parties are getting old—same people, same booze, same tired games. The only things missing are Rath and his music.

Tristian stands by the sound system, trying to figure out how to get everything hooked up. "This thing is so complicated," he mutters, looking annoyed. "I have no idea how to even get it synced to my phone."

"He may still be up in his room." I skim the crowd, even though I know I won't find Rath. He hasn't made an appearance since disappearing through his door after our shower. "Do you want me to go get him?"

"Unless someone wants me to smash this with a hammer," he says with a serene grin, "I think that's a good idea."

I squeeze his fingers. "Got it. No smashing until I get back, okay?"

We're all tired and frayed, but I know without having to be told that appearances should be kept up. I'm not sure if it's gotten out yet, what we did to the Princes and their Princess, but I can still feel a strange building energy all around us.

The storm is coming.

I swing by the kitchen first to grab a drink for Killian—the special lager I know he likes. Like always, I've set aside drinks just for the guys, hidden inside the fridge. I'd set it up special earlier in the afternoon. Weaving between the guests, I approach him and his little playmates. "I'm going to look for Rath," I tell him, strategically positioning myself in front of a blonde, "but I thought you may need another drink."

He takes it from me, his dark eyes boring into mine. "Thank you, Lady." I try to act normal as he takes a sip, licking his lip after he swallows. "Are you going to meet me later, or do I need to come find you?"

Instinctively, I realize it's less of a threat than it sounds coming from his wet lips. He's wondering if I'd like to fight, or if I'm down to honor what I'd said in the truck the other day. That I belong to him. Wholly.

I edge in closer, putting my hand on his taut stomach as I ask, "Ten o'clock?" Surprise flickers in his eyes, which descend to my cleavage. I'd worn something loose and provocative, and the valley between my tits is on perfect display for him. He undoubtedly thought I'd try to get out of it.

He hooks a finger into my cleavage, his knuckle grazing the skin. "My room."

"Aw." One of the blonde girls attaches herself to his side, putting on a fake pout. "Didn't you want to join me and Heather in the hot tub?"

Killer shoots her an irate look, and I almost have to admire her ambition.

Almost.

But not quite.

"Killian won't be joining you in the hot tub," I inform her, and even though I'm smiling, I can tell from the way her face tenses that she understands I'm not playing around. Although, just to be sure... "And maybe the next time you see a Lord with his Lady, you should know your fucking place."

The energy around us snaps, the blonde pushing away from Killian. I know how it works around here with the LDZ guys. They wouldn't dare to even look at me unless one of the Lords sanctioned it. The girls, though? I don't know the policy, and frankly, I don't care. I'm not scared of starting shit with them.

She clearly isn't up to the task. "My mistake," she says, not sparing Killian another look as she leaves. "Enjoy your night, Lady." The other girls look like they want to follow her, but they wouldn't dream of leaving Killian alone at his own pregame party. Nevertheless, I can tell from their expressions that they understand the rule of law I'm putting down.

Flirt all you want, but he's ending the night with me.

Turning back to my stepbrother, I promise, "I'll see you then." Killian's still got the bottle frozen halfway to his mouth, so I give it a little tap. "Drink up."

His shocked eyes follow me all the way to the stairs.

"Rath?" I call, knocking on his bedroom door. "Are you coming down? Tristian's music has super weird vibes. Are you sure you don't want to DJ?"

I still have my fist raised when the door swings open and a hand reaches out to snatch my wrist, stopping it in mid-air. Rath stands before me, shirtless and rumpled, and from the looks of it, still drunk. A new, half-empty bottle of whisky hangs between the fingers on his other hand. From the scent of him, I'm not sure the shower we took last night did him much good. He reeks of booze and smoke, red-eyed and too pale.

He looks like hell.

"If you bang on this door one more time, I'll snap your wrist."

I swallow, trying to carefully pry it away. "Sorry. I just wanted to check on you."

He holds my wrist a moment longer—just to let me know he could hurt me if he wanted—and then drops it. "I'm the same as I was yesterday. Pathetic. Stupid. Humiliated."

"You're none of those things," I tell him. "You're an amazing pianist and musician. That's what matters."

He snorts. "Really? Because that's not what everyone else is focused on."

I'd like to assure him that's not true, but by now, I've seen the video posted all over social media. Rath is right. No one cares about his music. It takes everything in me not to come back with something smart, like, *How does it feel to be humiliated in front of a crowd? To have no one help you?"* But I don't. I can't.

"Those people are just jea—"

The look he gives me is lethal. "Don't you fucking say everyone is jealous, Cherry, or I'll rip your tongue out." He walks over to a pile of papers on the desk, plucking one from the stack. "This came today. My application to the summer program with the New York Orchestra has been denied."

Whatever rush he got from trashing the nursery or from our time in the shower is gone. I take a tentative step into the room, waving the weed smoke from my face, and reach for the letter. There's no mention of the event but… "I'm sure it's a coincidence," I lie.

He snatches the letter back and tears it in half, tossing the pieces on the floor. "Whatever. Fuck it. I know who did this." He swallows another thick throatful of whiskey, collapsing into a heap on his couch. "The Princess and The Cuntess. They screwed me over, and I'm going to make them pay."

"You really think it was them?" Well-founded paranoia keeps me from assuming he's not playing me right now. That's exactly something I'd expect out of Rath. They should *never* be underestimated.

The curve of his bare shoulders is saggy and defeated. "Of course they did it." His eyes are shiny and hollow when he looks up at me. "The Princess was handing out the programs, and the Cuntess is Lockwood's TA. Rub two brain cells together, Cherry." He takes another swig of his drink. "Until I can come up with a plan, I'm going to sit here and get fucked up." He jerks his chin toward the door. "Go downstairs and do your job. There's nothing you can do to fix this."

My primary goal in coming up here is to keep up appearances—play the doting Lady—and keep him from knowing that I'm the one that turned in the false bio. Now that I've done that, he's right. I have a job to do. People to meet and promises to keep.

And miles to go before I sleep.

I WAIT IN Killian's room, dressed in nothing but his jersey. Admittedly, it's a bit on the nose, but I doubt he'll see past it to wonder why. While I wait, I walk around, inspecting everything, preparing. There's a plate on his desk he always empties his pockets onto. There's forty-nine cents in change, sorted by coin, the keys to his truck, his wallet, and a charging cord, carefully wrapped into a neat coil. It's all lined up, orderly and snug.

His laptop is closed, and I don't bother trying to sift through it. Maybe I'd find a video of myself getting nailed in Tristian's shower.

Idly, I wonder how many points that's gotten him. Did Rath get some points, too? This whole game of Spin The Story must be getting interesting. I'm betting that Killian is in the lead, and poor little Rath has fallen so far behind…

I hear him coming long before he reaches the door, the sound of a palm sliding against the wall, footsteps heavy on the hardwood. It's a relief. I'm not quite fluent in chemistry, so this entire plan was a calculated risk.

Honestly, though, what here isn't?

On his dresser sits a row of seemingly random odds and ends that I know are anything but. His lucky socks. A baseball card with the same date as his birth year. A single piece of orange Chicklet gum. A scrap of worn pink ribbon, no more than five inches long. A piece of strange looking wire.

So these are his superstitions.

All of his precious game day confidence, collected over more than a decade.

I sprawl on the bed to wait for him as if it's my own—and I suppose, in a way, that's true. Killian enjoys seeing me in his bed. If it were up to him, I'd probably always be like this, sleepy and pliant, wrapped in his jersey, cheek pressed to his pillow, ready to be taken in whatever way strikes him at that particular moment.

It takes him three tries to open the door.

I watch the knob jiggle and jostle, and when he finally pushes it open, he stumbles through, head shaking. "Fuck," he mutters, clumsily closing the door behind him.

Then he stares at me.

His eyes give a series of heavy, squinting blinks. "You came."

Pretending I don't hear the slur in his voice, I give him my sweetest smile and then arrange my thighs just-so, giving him a peek of my white panties. "I said I would, didn't I?" When he doesn't move, I slide from the bed, approaching him coyly. "I've been waiting."

His lips part when I reach for the top button of his shirt. "Me, too," he says, watching dumbly as I push the buttons through the holes, exposing his chest, inch by inch. He sways but corrects himself, torso jerking to the side. His eyes are glazed and heavy-lidded, and I watch from my periphery as he touches a lock of my hair, bringing it up to his mouth. "…so pretty…"

"What's that?" I ask, as if I didn't hear his mumble.

He drops my hair, clearing his throat. "Nothing, just—didn't think you'd be waiting."

"Why?" I ask, head tilted curiously as I push the shirt from his shoulders. "Because I might be sick of you sexually assaulting me?"

He gives another series of slow blinks, forehead wrinkling. "What?"

I brush my hand over the bulge in his pants, effectively derailing his thoughts. "Tell me about your tattoos," I demand, pitching forward to graze my lips against the ink on his chest.

"My tattoos," he repeats, tongue sounding heavy and thick. "That—uh, got it two years ago. It's a lion. King of the jungle…" He's slurring harder now, head looking heavy on his neck. It's a bit disappointing, actually. I'd hoped to have him a little more coherent for what comes next.

"Why did you get it?" I ask, rubbing his dick through his pants. "What does it mean?"

His answer comes in the form of three hard breaths, like he wants to speak, but keeps forgetting to. "First championship for Forsyth."

I hum, moving to his other shoulder. "And this one?"

"Griffons guard treasures," he answers, swaying into me. I reach out to steady him, but his nose remains planted into my hair, inhaling. Mumbling, he adds, "And they mate for life."

That makes my eyebrow arch. "Do you think that's who you are, big brother? Someone who mates for life?"

A deep rumble comes from his chest, one of his hands grasping my hip. "I like when you call me that." It comes out rough but hungry. A confession he'd probably regret if he could remember it tomorrow.

"Big brother?" I ask, pushing him toward the bed. "I guess you would like that, wouldn't you? A sweet little sister, sleeping right next door. I bet you think that's sexy, huh?"

He groans, pushing his hardness into me. "Fuck yes." When his knees hit the bed, he tumbles back, shirtless and startled-looking. The surprised, confused look slips right off his face when I get to my knees, unbuttoning his pants. I tug them off, revealing his hard dick and tight balls. He goes easily when I push him back, arranging him with the press of my smaller body.

"You know what I think would be sexy?" His hips flex into me when I drag his earlobe through my teeth.

"…fuck your tits…" he mumbles, eyes still on the prize, even this far out of it.

I tangle our fingers together, resting them above his head. "No," I sigh, reaching for the cords I'd prepared earlier. "Tying you up."

"Whuh?"

If my heart weren't hammering with the possibility of being caught, I might think to laugh at the purity of his response, so full of distaste and confusion. Oh yes, Killer Payne doesn't get tied up by anyone or anything. He's the king of the fucking jungle, guarding all the treasures.

He'd be so embarrassed to know how easy it is to bind his wrists.

His bicep shifts with a small, ineffectual tug. "The fuck?" I leave him there, fingers twitching, shoulders squirming, as I descend the bed to bind his feet. "What are you doing?"

"Don't you like it, big brother?" I wrap the cord around his left ankle, securing the knot tightly. "I know how much you're into the freaky, kinky stuff." His eyes follow me like they're lagged behind, catching me a second too late. "Sneaking into my room," I muse, securing his other ankle. "Sliding into my bed. Making me eat your come." I cinch the cord in a sharp, vicious motion. "Forcing your dick into me while I'm sleeping."

His legs pull inward feebly, but it's too late. I've got him spread out on his bed, naked and incapacitated. It should be enough, but the truth is that it isn't.

That's why I reach under the bed and slide out the gun.

His head jerks up at the sound of the hammer cocking. Just the way he taught me. "What the hell?" He tries to squirm up the bed, eyes looking a little more coherent. *Good.* "What the fuck are you doing?"

Shrugging, I say, "Just having a little fun," and walk around the bed, dragging the barrel of the gun up his bare leg. "Seeing what all the fuss is about. I've been wondering what it's like, you know? Having someone all defenseless and compliant to use like a cheap toy. Someone I can hurt." I give him a wicked grin, walking closer. "I could kill you, big brother. So easily, I could kill you. I could blame it on the Counts, or one of your daddy's lackeys, like that Ugly Nick, or someone else who wants revenge. I'm sure you have quite the list of enemies."

His eyes follow the barrel of the gun, but I can tell he's still fighting the fog of the drugs. "Put that gun away or you'll regret it." The attempt at being stern is ruined by the way words come out, lazy and thick-tongued.

"Will I?" I ask, dragging the gun over that sharp cut of muscle beside his hip. "I drugged you, you fucking psycho. I've got you all tied up." I toss a glance at his bookshelf. "I even turned off your cameras." At his expression, eyebrows knitted together, I add, "Yeah, I know all about those. And apparently, I'm not the only one. You've got really shit security for a guy who claims to *be* security."

His nostrils flare, and he gives the cords another tug. "Story," he says, trying so obviously to inject some firmness into his voice. "If you untie me right fucking now, I won't hurt you."

I pause, watching him, and then I throw my head back and laugh. "You really aren't getting it." To prove my point, I jump on the bed, straddling his hips. I point the gun at his forehead, right between his eyes. "I've got the power right now. I know this is new for you, so let me give you a little rundown of how it works." Swallowing, I adjust my grip on the gun, enjoying the way his gaze never leaves it. "You spend every minute wondering if you're doing something wrong. Something bad. You learn to become flexible and agreeable. You start thinking maybe you're crazy, because you can see yourself getting close to this person—this person who hurts you—but every time you try, you're reminded of what you are to them. A thing. A possession. A *toy*." Jaw clenching, I fight down the wave of emotion, struggling to remain just as passive as Killian always is. "And even when things feel good, you can't enjoy them. Not really. You're too busy hating yourself for it."

"I don't," he tries, throat bobbing with a hard swallow. "I didn't—"

"Yes, you fucking did."

I can practically tell how difficult it is for him to peel his gaze away from the barrel of the gun, but he does it, eyes finally meeting mine. "Yeah, I did." He's still now—the prey frozen beneath the gaze of the predator. "But I can't help it."

My grip tightens. "Bullshit."

His head lolls side to side. "I can't. I can't stop. I knew you were mine since the first time I saw you. I tried to let it go. That night I saw you with him…" I watch from the corner of my vision as his fingers strain toward the cord. "…sitting in his lap, letting him touch you like you were another one of his cheap whores. It should have made it easy…fucking disgusting…you trying to fuck my own goddamn dad…"

My blood runs cold. "*What?*"

But he just keeps babbling. "…wanted to let it go. Even tried giving you to Tristian. Thought seeing you like that would make it go away, but it didn't… just made it worse."

"You think I *wanted* him?" The anger rises again. "You saw your father molesting me and thought I was seducing him? *What is wrong with you?!*"

I think he tries to flinch at my hissed sneer, but all he manages is a weak little twitch. "I wondered for a while…then the sugar baby bullshit…knew you wanted him."

"You were wrong!" I lower the gun, placing it on the nightstand, safety on. "You know what your problem is, Killian? You've never had someone take from you. You've never been beneath them, helpless and afraid and confused because you're feeling all these new, horrible things." Grabbing a thick fistful of his hair, I wrench his head up, growling into his face. "But you're about to."

He's only half hard beneath me, his cock pressing into my center, but all it takes is a couple rocks against it before it begins stiffening. His eyes are heavier now, going unfocused, so I give his hair another rough pull.

"Let's see how you like someone using you," I say, shimmying my panties down my thighs. I keep the jersey on. No tits for him tonight. "Because here's the truth, big brother: I like it when you fuck me. It feels good, even when it hurts. Even when I'm hating you for it, there's always that little spark inside of me that hopes you'll do it again."

It's a confession made more to myself than him. Last night when Rath came into my room, I'd been anticipating something that never happened. In those scant seconds before he'd made himself known, I'd built it up in my head. The way Killian would touch me. How he'd feel sliding inside of me. His lips brushing my skin. The odd tenderness of the way he'd fuck me.

I'd been, however briefly, *disappointed.*

Now, he feels hard and ready beneath me, my slickness covering him as I work him against his cock, sliding it between my folds. Killian blinks up at me, and it's a different look from before—lost, as if he's forgotten the plot of this whole thing.

The second I begin sinking down onto his cock, he lets out a soft groan, head rolling to the side. I watch his mouth go slack in time with my own, my body taking him in the way *I* want for once. He feels just as good like this, all soft and pliable, and the long drag of his cock as I lift and drop is enough to make me shudder.

"That's the injustice of it, you know." Gasping, I plant a palm into the center of his chest, rocking into him. "All of you feel so good. You've got these perfect fucking bodies, and you know just how to work mine. It's so unfair."

I can feel him trying to thrust up into me, these mindless little twitches of his hips, but he can't do anything except swell and contract with his deep, sluggish breaths.

"Are you listening to me, big brother?" I grab his chin, nails digging into his jaw, and wrench his face forward. Teeth gnashed, I give him the same steely order he'd given me once. "Look at me while I'm fucking you."

His dark eyes fix on mine, but I'm not sure they're connecting.

Not until he murmurs, "God, I love you."

My hips stutter, fingers sliding from his face. Disbelief surges inside of me, and then an anger so fierce that I can perfectly see myself using that gun. "You don't know how to *love*," I spit, riding him in earnest now. I came here to *take*, and that's exactly what I plan to do. I lay both palms on his chest and roll my hips, keeping him deep inside. It doesn't take long to figure out what feels good here—the right way to move, the best way to rock—without someone directing and using me.

He's hard and hot inside of me, but I'm not so sure Killian even understands what's happening anymore. His eyelids keep rising and falling in time with the buck of my hips, gaze unfocused as his body jostles. I close my own eyes to really lose myself in the feel of him beneath me. Like this, I can almost understand the appeal. There's no shame here. No sense of fear or judgment. When I grind down, a low sound ripping from my chest, I don't have to worry about giving someone the wrong message.

I don't have to worry about them knowing how much I like it.

I ride and rock and *take*, and when I feel the pressure building so close to the surface that I swear I can taste him on the back of my tongue, I allow myself to open my eyes and look at him. This person who's been nothing but a threat to me. This boy I could have belonged to willingly, if only he wasn't so intent on hurting me. This man who claims he'd kill for me.

This man who claims to love me.

My orgasm shatters me into pieces, right on top of him. I throw my head back and bask in it, trembling and breathless as I come apart so sweetly. I dig my nails into his chest and let myself fall away. It's the oddest sensation when I resurface, to still feel like myself in my own skin. It's as if those pieces came back together with shards I'd long ago lost, clicking back into place as tidy as the row on Killian's dresser. I can feel his cock swelling as I clench around it, the telltale stiffness that I know all too well.

"I don't think so," I puff, luxuriating in the slow slide of his dick as I lift myself from it. It slaps onto his belly, slick and flushed and angry looking.

But Killian himself is asleep.

I acknowledge the backwardness of this as I pull my panties back up my thighs, admiring the sight of him. I reach under the bed for the container I'd put there earlier, prying the lid off. The red surface shines back at me, reminding me of last night. But this isn't blood—just paint. I climb on the bed, straddling him one last time. Dipping a forefinger into the paint, I trace a jagged-looking crown onto the middle of his chest.

"There," I say, tilting my head as I inspect it critically. Sliding to my feet, I cap the paint and leave it by the door.

Just one more thing left to do before I go.

2 1

I N V A S I O N

"Dude," I hear, just before I'm punched in the arm, "get the fuck up."

I rouse, blinking at the bright light coming in the living room window. My head feels like someone cracked it open with a sledgehammer, scooped it out with a melon baller, and then filled it with nothing but gauze. "Jesus Christ," I mumble, rolling over to the sight of Rath standing above me. "What time is it?"

"Past time to get up," he says, eyebrows all knitted up. "The fuck happened to you?"

I scrub my face and sit up. It takes me two attempts, temples throbbing. "Hell if I know. One minute I was partying like usual, and the next," I squint up at him, grimacing, "you're standing over me and I feel like I licked sandpaper."

Rath scratches at his bare chest. "What, you blacked out?"

"Maybe," I hedge, but I already know something is up. I don't get blackout drunk. Sure, I drink and use the occasional recreational drug, but my body is a temple. Too much of that shit will screw me up. Also? I don't lose control. Ever. "Where's Killer? Story?"

He ruffles the back of his hair, face scrunching up. "I don't know. Just got down here."

Rath doesn't look much better than I feel, but that's no surprise. He's not like me. Rath is just fine with getting blackout drunk, and that's pretty much what Killer and I expected him to do last night. The only signal he was still alive at all had been the bass-pound of his rage-filled music blaring all night.

Ms. Crane walks in and pauses, scowling at the room. "The three of you are going to turn my crusty ass into a goddamn murderer."

"You know we'll give you a hand." Rath rubs his temple. "And you already are a murderer."

She has a point, though. The living room is completely wrecked and I doubt the other rooms look much better. This isn't necessarily unusual; I just don't fucking remember much past playing DJ and talking to some of the guys. I remember Story handing me a drink and going to look for Rath, but that's about it.

Ms. Crane just shakes her head. "Breakfast is ready, you unstable ballsacks."

"Is Killian already in the dining room?" I ask, leaning forward to get my bearings. The room is a little wobbly, but eventually rights itself.

She sniffs over a mess on the table. "If he were, I'd put my foot up his ass. Weren't none of you looking over those trust fund rodents last night. About had my fucking fill of it."

Rath and I exchange a look. Not only is someone always around to watch over the party, but Killian is always the first one down. I figured with his new pregame ritual, Story would be shacking up with him last night, but god only knows what that looks like. I struggle to my feet. The floor sways beneath me and I grab onto the chair.

"Hey," Rath rasps, reaching for me. I wave him off. "You okay?"

I swallow, my tongue feeling swollen and too dry. "No, I'm not fucking okay."

Rath must be finally putting some pieces together here because his eyes blink wide before narrowing to a squint. "Since when do you drink enough to wake up like this?"

I don't need to answer. The look we share says it all.

Some shit went down here last night.

It's a testimony of how concerned I am that I manage to keep up with Rath as he jogs up the stairs. The difficult thing about having so many hustles is that I don't even know what to worry about on any given day. When we reach Killer's door, I don't even let myself think up possible scenarios—too many possibilities.

When I push it open, I sort of wish I had. It might have prepared me for the sight of my friend, sprawled out naked and bound to his bed.

"Holy shit," Rath blurts, eyes widening. "Holy fucking shit."

The only thing that makes the hot surge of fury in my chest abate is the fact that he's breathing. Obviously, he's passed out just like I had been. Fuck, maybe even like Rath had been.

"Story," I say, shoving past Rath into the hall. Her door is closed just like his was, and I pause for a moment before turning the knob, not sure I'm ready to see what's on the other side. A million visions pass through my mind, each worse than the other. Story, tied up like Killian is, naked but also violated. Someone else's come dripping down her thighs. Her pussy all torn up, tear tracks dried on her cheeks. The longer I wait, the worse it gets, so I don't need Rath's shove to spur me into motion. I push the door open, lungs aching with the possibilities.

What we find is enough to make me black out again.

Story's curled up in the middle of her bed, wearing Killian's jersey, sound asleep. Breathing. Whole. I want nothing more than to climb in behind her and clutch her to me, bury my nose into her hair and fall back asleep, knowing everything is fine.

Only it isn't.

Sighing, I push past Rath again, back across the hall. It's a jarring sight, the blood red crown painted into the middle of my friend's chest. The first thing I do is begin untying his wrists, my fingers yanking too hard at the cords. It isn't until I go to round the bed for the second wrist that I realize Rath is getting his ankles. We share a brief look, Rath muttering, "…fucked up shit, Jesus Christ," and Killian doesn't stir for any of it.

"Hey man, wake up," I say, shaking his shoulder. He moans but doesn't open his eyes. "Killer!" I give him a harder shake, relieved when his eyelids raise and lower in a long blink. I know when he pulls a face, lips smacking, exactly what he's feeling right now. The sandpaper tongue. The head full of gauze.

Killian grumbles, "…the hell?" and starts looking a little more coherent, glassy eyes opening in fits and starts. "What's going on?" I know when he realizes he's naked—that something is *wrong*—because he goes rigid. He looks like he instantly regrets it.

"Easy," I tell him when he starts sitting up. There's a bottle of water on his nightstand, so I uncap it and hand it over, watching as he clumsily raises it to his lips. He downs the whole thing in four hard gulps.

"You good?" Rath asks, pacing nervously around the foot of the bed.

Killian's nod is heavy. "What happened?"

I ask him, "You don't remember?" and he shakes his head.

"Last thing I remember is drinking a beer in the den. Coming up the stairs." When he reaches for his chest, I grab his wrist, stopping him from smearing the paint. Killian reaches for his junk instead, giving his balls a slow, curious scratch. "Fuck, my balls ache." He pauses to blink down at his dick, forehead screwing up in confusion. "Did I get some pussy last night?"

"You know what this is," I say, shooting Rath a glare. I don't bother hiding the contempt from my voice, and Rath doesn't bother pretending he doesn't hear it.

"Yeah," he says, dark eyes taking in the scene, "I sure fucking do."

I spell it out, anyway. "You fucked with the Princes, and this is retaliation." Frustrated, I rake my fingers through my hair. "They had us drugged, in our own house." I should have seen that coming. If the Princes are working with the Counts, and possibly even the Barons still, then we're fucked. Prince tactics are one thing, but…

Oh, shit.

I stare wide-eyed at Rath. "Prince tactics."

The Princes were here last night. Killian's obviously got some bitch's pussy juices dried on his dick. Story is next door, passed out. Alone.

I can see when it clicks for him, his jaw going slack at the implication, but I'm already rushing back across the hall.

Story's in the same position she was in before, which makes it easy. I press a knee into the bed at her side, rucking that jersey up to see what's underneath. The white cotton panties provide a little relief, but not enough. I hook my fingers into the elastic and begin shimmying them down her thighs.

Rath's right on my heels, so when Story starts squirming, slowly rousing, he carefully wedges himself in behind her. Pulling her upper body into his lap. "Shh," he says, grabbing her wrists when she tries to groggily push me away. "Relax, baby."

I get the panties down her ankles, hearing Killian shuffling in behind us. Wedging a hand between her warm thighs, I gently pry them apart, trying to make her open up for me.

"Whuh?" she asks, eyes blinking open. She clamps her knees together, eyes flashing in alarm. "What are you doing?"

"Hey, hey, calm down," Rath commands, smoothing her hair back from her forehead. "Tristian just needs to check you over for a second. Nothing to worry about."

"Check me over…?" Her eyes ping between me and Killian, then behind her shoulder to Rath. Her heels slide against the bed as she backs into his embrace. "Why?"

Glancing behind me, I see Killian running a wet cloth over his junk. We exchange a dark look. "Don't be difficult," is my answer, grabbing her knees and giving them a little tug. "It'll just be a second." It's the truth. None of us are in a fit state to fuck her right now. Maybe she senses that, because with a bob of her throat, she reluctantly lets her knees part, exposing her pussy to me and Killer. "That's our good girl," I say, giving her thighs a soothing stroke before pushing them apart, wide and obscene.

My dick instantly begins filling at the sight of her, all pink and pretty and *ours*—only I have to be sure. I touch her sweet little lips, fingertips spreading them open to reveal her hole. I can't see anything—no blood or spunk or swelling. Keeping her open with the fingers from one hand, I use my index finger from the other to check. She clenches when I sink it inside her, feeling around for anything sticky and wet. My shoulders collapse in relief when I realize it's not there. I shake my head, looking at Rath, and then Killian. "Nothing."

Killian jerks his chin, eyes fixed to where my finger is disappearing inside her. "Check her ass," he mutters, voice low.

Story tenses, yelping, "What?" but I'm already sliding my finger from her pussy, wetting it in my mouth, and then prodding into that tight ring of muscle.

"Just for a second," Rath says when she bucks, wrestling her closer. "Come on, relax."

She doesn't, but I still manage to force my finger past the resistance, effectively stilling her. Her wide, pretty eyes gape back at me in shock. It isn't until her breath hitches that I realize what that shock is actually about.

Arching an eyebrow, I can't help but give my finger a testing thrust, sliding it back a little just to sink it back inside.

From my periphery, I can see her toes curl. She breathes out a stunned little, "Oh," and when my knuckle brushes against her pussy, I'm the one thinking, '*oh*', because it looks like our Lady is learning something new about herself this morning.

She fucking likes it, the little freak.

Suddenly I'm rethinking my position on being fit to fuck her.

But before I can play around some more, Killian is saying, "*Tris.*"

Right.

I pull back, clearing my throat. "She's fine. They haven't had her."

Rath lets go of her arms, but starts shucking up the jersey, baring her tits to us. They're flawless, the pale skin unmarred by bruises or sticky residue. Whatever happened occurred before Killer could get his pregame load off, that much is certain.

I climb off of the bed, trying to ignore the sight of her, all spread out and bare for us. "What do you remember about last night?"

She snaps her knees closed, shoulders shuffling against Rath as she lowers the jersey to cover herself. "I-I don't know. I came up here to get ready for..." Her gaze flicks to Killian, and then down at his exposed junk. She swallows, glancing away. "I came to get ready, and I...I don't know what happened. I only had one drink." She clutches at her head, wincing.

"Doesn't make sense," Rath says, hand steady on her back as she sits up. "Why would they drug all of us and do that to Killian? What's the endgame?"

"They did it because it's the only way those pricks could get one over on me." He rubs at the red marks on his wrists, scowling. "They had to drug me and tie me down. And they had to drug the three of you to make sure you didn't stop them." His face darkens, eyes drinking Story in. "This was about me. About fucking with me before the game. Messing with my process and rituals and—" His expression changes, chin snapping up to meet my gaze. "My superstitions."

He bolts from the room.

I watch him go, wondering what that's supposed to mean, and for a long moment there's nothing. I could hear a fucking pin drop with the sudden hush of silence that falls over the house.

And then from across the hall comes a pained, furious roar. "Motherfucker!" His shout is followed by the sound of something heavy hitting the floor, followed by a cacophony of destruction. Shattering, pounding, crashing.

By the time I cross the hall to see what the hell is going on, the room has already been transformed from his usual tidy space to utter chaos. The dresser drawers have been pulled out and tossed on the floor. Piles of clothing are strewn everywhere. His closet is flung open, and he's on his knees, rummaging through a box on the floor. "They took my shit," he's barking, face all hard and red. "My socks. My baseball card. The guitar string, the gum, the—" he pauses, jaw going tight.

Lurching up, he rushes to his desk, opening the laptop. I snap my fingers encouragingly, knowing what he's looking for. "Good idea." Footage of what took place in the room.

"Anything?" Rath asks, coming in behind us, Story shifting from foot to foot over his shoulder.

Killian clicks around, eyes narrowed, but I know when his shoulders sag that it's hopeless. "The cameras were turned off." A few more clicks and his teeth are clenching. "Worse, fucking *everything* is wiped. Goddamn it!"

Rath and I see it coming a mile away, but Story visibly flinches when the laptop crashes against the wall, clunking onto the floor in an injured heap.

There's a long stretch of tense silence.

I'm the one to break it. "So they knew about the cameras." That's huge. If they control the footage, then they've infiltrated the entire house. They had intel.

Killian stalks over to the shelf and picks up the helmet that's been there since the day we moved in. Beneath it is a camera—small, black, unobtrusive. He yanks it off the shelf and throws it with the laptop. "Son of a bitch."

"Oh, my god." Story's staring between the three of us, her cheeks flushed a vivid pink. "There was a camera, that whole time? Does that mean they have videos of us...*you know*?"

I throw my arm around her shoulder and pull her tight, pressing a kiss to her head. "Don't worry, sweetheart. We'll find who did this before anything gets out." I look over to watch Killian pulling on his clothes, his motions jerky and mechanical. "We can have Pretty Nick monitor security. Right, Killer?"

"Sure," he snaps, stomping his feet into a pair of jeans. "I'll just pull South Side's biggest up-and-comer out of whatever project he's doing and ask him to keep an eye out for our sex tape leak. I'm sure my dad will fucking love that." Snatching his keys and wallet from the floor, he shoves them into his pocket. "Or maybe have him patrol campus. I doubt anyone's going to be suspicious of the six-five South Sider with *face tattoos*. He'll go right under the radar!"

I roll my eyes, rubbing Story's back soothingly. "You don't need to be a smart ass about it."

"I restrained myself the other night," Rath is saying, standing tensely by the doorway. I already don't like the look in his eyes—that spark of grim determination. "Next time, I'm not stopping at a little blood. Nothing is off limits."

His threat rings in my ear and fear pounds in my chest. I fumble for my phone in my back pocket, checking it for the first time since waking up. I immediately go to my ChattySnap account where I see a slew of notifications— not unusual for the pregame party. I click on the direct messages, fearing another threat, but there's nothing new.

Whoever sent that first one had me running around for two days, keeping the twins in sight while my father was on a business trip to New York. Nothing happened other than carpool and dance practice and the twins constantly begging me for ice cream, but the initial message was enough to set me on edge. Someone is out there, trying to fuck with me. And how many of them can there be?

The answer isn't good.

"I need to make a call," I say, stepping away.

"Now?" Killian says, flinging a hand at the scene of the crime.

"I need to check on my sisters." My thumbs are already on the screen.

"If there's something you need to tell us, now's the time," Killian says, jaw tight. "Like why you disappeared for two days, and took your gun with you?"

I pause, holding his gaze. I know I should tell them about the message, but the last thing either of them needs on their plate is my family drama.

"Look," I say, willing him to understand. "Whoever is fucking with us? They already destroyed Rath's music career, and they obviously want to fuck with your football performance. Everyone knows the most important things in my life are the twins. If someone wants to get to me, that's how they're going to do it."

Story goes to follow me out of the room, asserting, "I'm sure everything's going to be fine, big brother. No one's going to hurt those girls. They wouldn't dare, right?"

Rath passes us in the hall, muttering, "I'm going to go double check the rest of the house. See if Ms. Crane noticed anything."

As the phone rings, I glance back in Killian's room. He's standing there motionless, gaze fixed to the destruction, a confused expression frozen on his face. I'm about to ask what's wrong when Izzy answers, shifting my attention. My sister gives a boisterous greeting, immediately jumping into a story about what happened at the school play the night before. Relief washes through me at the easy joy in her voice. Smiling down at Story, I point to the phone, mouthing, "She's okay."

"See?" she whispers, nudging me. "I told you everything would be fine."

I look at Killian once again and the confusion on his face has shifted into something deadlier. Cold, calculated rage. Story's wrong. Everything is *not* okay. Someone violated our home. Someone fucked with Rath and Killian, and someone is threatening my sisters. Whoever did this didn't just get revenge, they've signed their death warrant.

AFTER CATALOGUING THE house, it seems that Killian was right. It's looking more and more like he was the primary target. *Last night*, at least. It's obvious the Lords are under attack and we have no choice but to handle it. Princes,

Counts, Barons…

It's getting to the point where it doesn't matter who's behind it. I can tell as we eat a quick, cold breakfast that all of us are strained, the dark glances we share making it obvious that each of us is itching for retaliation. It can't be like the last two times, the three of us divided and pecking away at it on our own. A silent agreement passes over us.

Whatever happens next, we have to do it together.

Killian and I are the first to get into the truck, Rath and Story lagging behind. We're all late enough for our first classes that we aren't bothering to rush now. Killer's been silent ever since that scene in his room, face unreadable.

I watch him stare out the windshield, eerily still. "What's up? You worried about them having all those videos?" Truthfully, I sort of am. The older they get, the more I realize how difficult it's going to be to hide who I really am from my sisters. Videos of me nailing Story aren't exactly going to help matters.

His gaze slides to me slowly, as if he's busy thinking. "I'm not worried about that." At my questioning look, his gaze goes back toward the door, where Story and Rath are just now bounding down the steps. She's got Rath loaded down with a box of carnival prep materials and he doesn't look happy about it. Roughly, Killian says, "But we need to figure out what we're going to do."

"About the Princes?" I ask.

He shakes his head, eyes following Story as she approaches the truck. His voice is quiet but sharp—just as lethal as his eyes. "About the fact our Lady has been playing us."

STORY

2 2

S P I D E R W E B S

I HAVE TO give it to them; the Royals know how to put on a hell of a homecoming carnival. From the brightly lit rides, to the sweet scent of kettle corn in the air, to the long line of students paying double at the beer truck, everyone seems to be having a great time. This, shockingly, includes the Royals, who—as Bianca not-so-kindly suggested—seem to have taken the night off to pointedly ignore one another.

Admittedly, I've been worried for a couple of days now. Killian lost the Homecoming game last night, and he's been absolutely *seething*. My Lords have been tense, clearly itching for a way to get back at 'the Princes'. I'd be lying if I said I haven't been tense as well. I have to strike the perfect balance here—shock at being drugged, fear of what could happen next, horror at someone having videos of these three men using me like a pocket pussy with a heartbeat. Luckily, they're so focused on the Princes that they barely give me a second glance.

Being little more than a fucktoy has its uses, it'd seem.

Today, everything is shiny and bright, like the plushies over at the ring toss, or the clown's face grinning over the funhouse. It's a little slice of good out of an otherwise shit pie, and I enjoy it to the fullest, laughing with Bianca as we shake our hips to Rath's energetic DJing.

Even Killian seems to have taken a break from simmering in rage over the lost football game to make an effort. I watch from a distance as he pushes his sleeves up to his elbows, passing a massive hammer from fist to fist. The lights around the strong man game flash and he gets into position, feet shuffling. He raises it over his head and brings it down in a hard swing, crashing violently into the pressure plate. It sends a ball soaring toward the bell at the top. Loudly, it rings and a group of kids, some wearing Forsyth football jerseys and tiny cheer outfits, shriek in excitement. Izzy and Lizzy are among the fray, and Tristian monitors them while occasionally checking his phone.

"Again!" the kids keep saying, looking bright and delighted.

Shockingly, Killian does.

Well, at least he's found an outlet for his rage.

My phone vibrates against my hip and I pull it out, thinking I may have caught Tristian texting me. But what I find is a message from my mother instead.

Mom: *Sorry we couldn't make it to your carnival! Daniel had something come up. Miss you-XX*

I just barely stop myself from pulling a face. Seeing her and Daniel at Rath's performance was awkward enough. The last thing this evening needs is the two of them hovering around.

Story: *That's okay. I'm too busy to mingle much, anyway.*

I glance back over at Tristian, whose eyes are darting around anxiously. It's a lot more complicated to figure out how to strike back at him. I watch as he pulls the girls close. Like he said before, the way to get to him is through his sisters. But there's no way I'd mess with them. Besides, I know him better than that. Rath and Killian were easy. One defined moment of humiliation and revenge is enough to shake their foundations. Tristian requires a longer con. To make him think I'm falling for him. That I'm his, and only his. Then I'll betray him, just like Gen did.

God, the irony is thick and delicious.

As a bonus, he's paranoid enough that just the thought of someone coming after him sets him on edge. He's so caught up in himself, so vain and narcissistic that he'll never even see me coming.

"Hey," Bianca says, nudging me. Judging by the blue-zippered pouch she's carrying, it's looking like she wants to make an honest liar out of me. "The beer truck is out of ones. We need to call Mr. Payne's guys and have them send someone over with change."

I'm learning that my stepfather has his fingers in almost everything that goes on in this town. Apparently, he provides the upfront cash needed to fund the booths, particularly the beer truck. As twenties and higher bills come in, the change decreases and we swap it out with Daniel's money guy, 'Ugly' Nick.

The same Nick from the brothel. I haven't met the Pretty Nick yet, but if his name is as fitting as Ugly Nick's, he must be some kind of supermodel.

If I have questions as to why a man who frequents a brothel and sells firearms is somehow participating in the organization of a university-adjacent charity, then no one is willing to give me an answer. Killian had just shrugged and said, "It's business, and none of it is yours."

But I know just whose business it is. I'm catching on that Daniel Payne is more than a real estate guy. He's maybe even more than a real estate guy who employs shady people, like arms dealers and thugs with facial tattoos who are 'up-and-comers' on the avenue. Just how deep does this go? More importantly, is it in my interest to find out?

Probably not.

We were each given a walkie-talkie to communicate during the event. I lift it to my ear and press the button. "Eagle Four, this is Lady. I need someone to meet me at the gate." I release the button and a response comes crackling back.

"Ten-Four, Lady."

Bianca hands me a zippered bag filled with cash. "Do you want me to walk with you?" she asks, just as Autumn's voice comes across the walkie-talkie.

"We're out of cotton candy," she says, her voice mingled with static. "Can someone grab a bag of mix out of the storage truck?"

The most disappointing thing by far has been the complete lack of reaction from Autumn regarding what Rath and I did to her little nursery. The most I was gifted was a chilly look between her and the Baroness right after we arrived. It's sowed some discord among them, but it's hard to say exactly how much.

Bianca raises her eyebrows and I say, "Go help her. I'll try to grab one of the Lords to walk over with me to meet Ugly Nick." I fight down a shudder as I say his name.

"Be careful," she says, nodding at the bag. "There's, like, two grand in there."

I push the bag under my arm, hiding it between my sweater and shirt. "I will."

Starting across the carnival grounds, I look over to where I'd just seen Killian playing the game, but he's no longer there. Tristian and his sisters are gone as well. I keep looking, but I don't see Tristian's blonde hair, nor Killian's enormous frame, and I'm reaching the gate before either of them makes themselves known.

Ugly Nick is already waiting for me. He looks a lot different from the last time we met, although that *had* been a brothel. Today, he's wearing clothes, his hair combed back tidily, and it doesn't matter that there's a cigar hanging from forefinger and thumb. He looks like any other man—shirt buttoned down, khakis crisp and pressed. A second guy lurks a few feet behind him, clearly acting as a guard. His hand is on his hip, revealing a gun tucked into the waist of his pants.

I slide the pouch through the gate and watch as he takes it, opening it to inspect the cash inside. There's a moment where he fans through it, eyes jumping up to observe me in quick flicks. Eventually, he zips it up and nods at the other guy, who hands him a red pouch in response.

"Now, don't go spending this in one place," Ugly Nick says, giving me that slimy grin as he passes the pouch back through. But the moment I reach for it, he snatches it back. "Ah, ah. *Manners,* young lady. What do you say?"

Narrowing my eyes, I clutch the walkie-talkie. "I have to get that back, ASAP."

He gives me a tsk. "That's not the magic word."

Biting down my frustration, I move closer to the gate, fingers curling around the iron bars. His expression changes on a dime when I give him a shy, nervous smile. "I actually don't really know how this all works. Maybe you can give me some pointers. Or maybe you'd like me to do something for you?"

Coming closer, he rests a forearm on the bars, his posture loose and careless. He licks his lips. "You can do whatever you like, princess."

His eyes are fixed to my mouth, giving me the perfect opportunity to shoot my hand out, lightning quick, snatching the pouch from him. "I'm not a fucking princess," I say, smiling at his peeved expression. As I walk away, I add, "I'm a lady."

I take the money over to the beer truck and leave it with the Barons, who are in charge of that. Halfway to the ring-toss to check their money, my walkie-talkie crackles, Tristian's voice coming through. "Lady?"

Fumbling for the button, I assure, "I'm here."

After another crackle, he says, "Your presence is needed at the Funhouse."

"Is something wrong?" I glance up at the stage and notice Rath isn't DJing at the moment. He must be taking a break.

"Nothing's wrong," says Tristian's voice, "other than my Lady asking *questions* in defiance of my direct order."

I hold back a sigh. *Great.* Tristian is in one of his bossy and most likely horny moods. Clicking the button, I assure him, "I'll be there in a minute."

The funhouse was rolled in on the back of a truck and unloaded like the rest of the rides. The entrance has a funky giant clown hanging over the oversized door that secretly gives me the creeps. It had a long line all evening, but now it's suddenly deserted, a piece of caution tape adhered across the steps. Marcus stands under the mouth of the clown, nodding at me as I approach.

"Is he inside?" I ask.

"Yeah," he answers, gesturing inside. "Just follow the path."

I step inside, taking a wary look around. The sound of the door closing and latching behind me isn't making me feel any less creeped out, either. I'm in a room of optical illusions, the walls slanted to make it seem like a long narrow hallway. The floor is titled to keep me off balance and I shoot my hands out to steady myself as I navigate it. When I reach the next room, designed to seem like the floor is up and the ceiling is down, I call out, "Tristian? Are you in here?"

"Back here, Cherry," he calls, and I head in the direction of his voice. I step into a room of mirrors—or rather, the illusion of mirrors. Against one wall, Tristian's reflection spirals out into a twisted presence.

"Hey," I say, feeling a little off balance. "What's going on?"

"We wanted to have a little talk," he answers, the image disappearing.

"About what?" I ask, distracted by a movement in one mirror. I look behind me, but there's nothing there but my own reflection. "Come on, guys. Stop messing with me."

"Why would we do that?" comes Killian's voice, low and dull-sounding. "Turnabout is fair play. Isn't that right?"

I whirl at another flash of movement, turning to face my own reflection again. "What are you talking about?"

"I'm talking about the messages," Tristian says.

"About you drugging us," Killian adds. "Sabotaging us."

Rath's voice comes deadlier than the others. "About you turning in that bio."

My breath stutters in my chest, stomach dropping. I turn, but can't see anything except the panicked lines around my mouth. "I don't know what you're—"

"Sour Cherry." Tristian's voice cuts me off. "Insulting our intelligence is only going to make this worse for you. Do you really want to go there?"

My limbs feel like lead, heavy enough that I stumble back. But then Tristian's reflection appears in the mirror, just over my shoulder, and all I can see is that night he pushed me to my knees. All I can hear is the night he told me to open up for Killian. All I can taste is my stepbrother, salty on my tongue. All I can feel is the stab of loss and betrayal when I saw Rath on that video, mocking me for wanting a scrap of their kindness.

Beyond the wild static of dread is something hard as steel. Two images appear in the mirror, flanking him, their faces all clear. This time I don't bother looking behind me. I know they're really there. I can feel the pitch-black hatred rolling off them just as tangibly as I can feel their heat.

If they really know, there's no point in lying.

Raising my chin, I ask, "What gave me away?"

"Oh, you were plenty sloppy," Killian says, his menacing gaze boring into my reflection. "But in the end, it was something small—something you said to Tristian yesterday. You were out in the hall, talking, and you called him—"

"Big brother." I remember the way it'd felt coming from my lips, something illicit and sacred, and I'd instantly regretted it. "So that's it? That's your big discovery? You just sort of *remembered*?"

"It was easy, after that," Rath says, eyes hooded and black. "You're the one who wrote my bio. You brought us all our drinks. You were away the day before, for two whole hours. But Tristian wasn't around to compulsively track you, because you sent him a message that would get him out of your hair, didn't you?"

Frowning, I ask, "What message?"

"We know it's not the Princes." Ignoring me, Killian asks, "Only one house is really into drugging people. What is it the Counts offered you exactly? We're all curious. I mean," he glances at Tristian, "Jesus Christ, he bought you a fucking car. It must be more valuable than that."

I narrow my eyes, feeling affronted at the mere idea. "If you want me to stop insulting your intelligence, maybe try showing some. I was never working with the Counts." Laughing, I spread my arms, refusing to back down at their glares. "The truth is, I was working with the Lords the entire time. The three of you taught me everything I needed to know." Nodding at Rath, I say, "Framing another house for your retaliation was your idea. And it wasn't half bad, honestly. I thought the red crown was a nice touch."

Killian doesn't look convinced. "Then where did you get the drugs?"

Grinning, I say, "From you, *big brother*." His eyes flash, but there's too many emotions there to pin down what's sparking in them. "Don't you remember? The day you took me to the whorehouse, I asked if you were heading down that road for drugs. You told me that's where I could find them." Tristian's absence had been the only reason I took the chance, riding down to the avenue. In a nice car like mine, it wasn't long before I was approached by someone looking for a customer. "That's not all I've learned from the Lords, though. For instance, Killian taught me how horrible it feels to be publicly humiliated, so I used it on Rath." I turn my gaze to Rath, looking him in the eye. "You taught me what it means to feel deceived into thinking someone cares about you, so I used it on Tristian." To Tristian, I say, "And you taught me how it feels to have someone take all of your control away, which helped me take Killian's." I end with a glare at my stepbrother, spinning my finger in a loose gesture. "You built the wheel, boys. I just gave it a nice little spin."

I don't flinch when a hand comes up to grab my hair in a fist. Killian holds my gaze and asks, "How long have you been playing us, *little sister*?"

"Me?" I ask, hoping he can see the spite in my smirk. "Since the first second you let them touch me, three years ago." His fingers tighten in my hair, but I keep my expression completely blank. He doesn't know it yet, but Tristian taught me that, too. "Or maybe since you saw your father molesting a child in your own house and were spoiled and ignorant enough to think I wanted it, you piece of shit." I cry out when my head snaps back, scalp straining against his grip.

"You're a liar," he growls, nostrils flared wide. "I told them this would happen. That you're nothing but a whore, just like your mother. I fucking told them you'd play us. I fucking told them!"

"What if I did?" I yell, throat straining. "You think you didn't deserve it? For everything you've done to me?"

"You signed up for this," Killian says, his voice noxious in my ear. He shoves me forward, letting my hair go, and I stumble, catching myself on the mirror. "*You* asked to be our Lady!"

Finally, I turn to them, chest heaving. "I did. And you know what's messed up? I was willing to do anything you asked—be anything you wanted—but that wasn't enough for you, was it? You just had to take more." Squaring my shoulders, I tell them, "I know about the game you played. I know about the scores you kept to see who could hurt me the most. I know about how you earned them. I know about the fucking *prize*." I spit the word like it's poison on my tongue, seeing the awareness hit their expressions in a wave. Killian's eyes are cold and aloof, as though he expected nothing less. Why should he? We've been at one another's throats for years. Voice dripping with disdain, I add, "You're all weak, pathetic hypocrites. You can dish it out, but you can't take it."

Rath lunges forward, his palm shooting out to grasp my throat. He shoves me so hard against the glass that I can't tell what's rattling—the mirror or my skull. He crushes his forehead to mine, voice emerging in a venomous hiss. "You made me trust you. You made me think you wanted to help me. And then you turned around and used it to destroy me. My whole fucking future!" He's shaking with his roar, trembling with rage, which would be a good signal for me to back off.

I don't.

I dig my fingernails into his wrist and roar back. "You ruined me first!" The crush of his fingers doesn't faze me—not tight enough to cut off my air supply. *Not yet.* I stare at the bulging tendons in his neck, breathless. "You're the worst. Did you know that, Rath? I know you're the one who really won that game, and I know how you did it, too. Every second with you was a joke." It doesn't matter that the lump in my throat makes my voice crack, or that my eyes begin swimming with unshed tears. It feels so goddamn good to finally say this. "I expected Killian to be an abusive asshole. He's never pretended to be anything better. And Tristian?" I give a watery laugh. "Tristian has the depth of a sadistic robot. He's too emotionally inept to even understand what he's doing is wrong most of the time. But you? Oh, *you* know," I breathe, crushing his wrists between my fingers. "You knew just how to handle me. By scamming me into letting my guard down. Making me feel pity for you. Making me feel safe with you. By making me think someone as empty as you could ever—" My nails are embedded in his skin, and now I'm the one shaking. I must be drawing blood by now. "My one regret is that I only ruined you a fraction of the amount you ruined me."

His fingers finally clamp down, squeezing hard around the column of my throat. "I should fucking kill you," Rath sneers, his fingers digging into the soft flesh. White spots fill my vision, body seizing as I fight for air. His lips pull back, exposing his teeth. "I should watch the life fade right out of your eyes for what you've done to me."

"Rath," Killian says, his voice quiet and hard. A moment later the hand is gone, and I bend over, gasping for air.

"You know what Lords do to Ladies who betray them, Story?" Rath asks, slamming his hand into the mirror beside my head. He hems me in, dark and looming. "You should. Killian gave you a little taste of it once. Do you remember that? Down on your knees for everyone to see? The way they all laughed? Some of them were hard as nails walking out of that basement. Probably went back home and jacked off thinking of the way it *should* have gone down."

Tristian's voice cuts in, closer than I'm expecting. "A proper Lord would have had you turned toward them in offering. He would have had each of those forty men—one by one—jack off until they covered you with their come."

"We saw it once," Killian adds, and from over Rath's shoulder, I can see him pulling that knife from his waist. He gives the blade a little flick. "freshman year. I can't even remember her name, but I remember what she looked like when I shot my load down her tits."

"Cassandra." Rath hums, scratching a fingernail down my cheek. "Oh, she was so much like you. Sweet on the outside, but scratch the surface?" His smirk is empty and brittle. "Fake. All you bitches are fake."

I shake my head, saying, "You're not going to do that to me." It's a testament to what I've come to know about these men that I say it with an unshakable confidence.

Rath's mouth curls up into a vicious grin. "Oh, Cherry. What makes you think we wouldn't?"

"The same reason Killian didn't do it before," I answer, tipping my shoulders back against the glass. "You wouldn't want them marking what's yours."

Tristian's low, malicious laugh rings out. "You're calling yourself ours now, are you?"

"Am I wrong?"

I'm not theirs in any way that really matters. Not by choice. But they've never cared about that, and I can see in their eyes how little they care about it now.

Rath moves aside when Tristian shoulders in, both of them pinning me against the glass.

Tristian grabs my chin, wrenching my gaze to his. Weeks ago, the look in his eyes would have been enough to make my knees weak. It's just like before—just like that night in high school. The man who's seen me as someone to coddle and care for is gone. All that remains is a chilling cruelty.

This time, I'm ready for it.

"You're right," he says. "You don't belong to LDZ, Story."

Killian stalks toward me with the knife. "You only belong to us."

Rath's words are a stream of venomous air. "And we keep what's ours."

When Killian brings the knife down, I close my eyes and hope for an oblivion I know they'd never be kind enough to give.

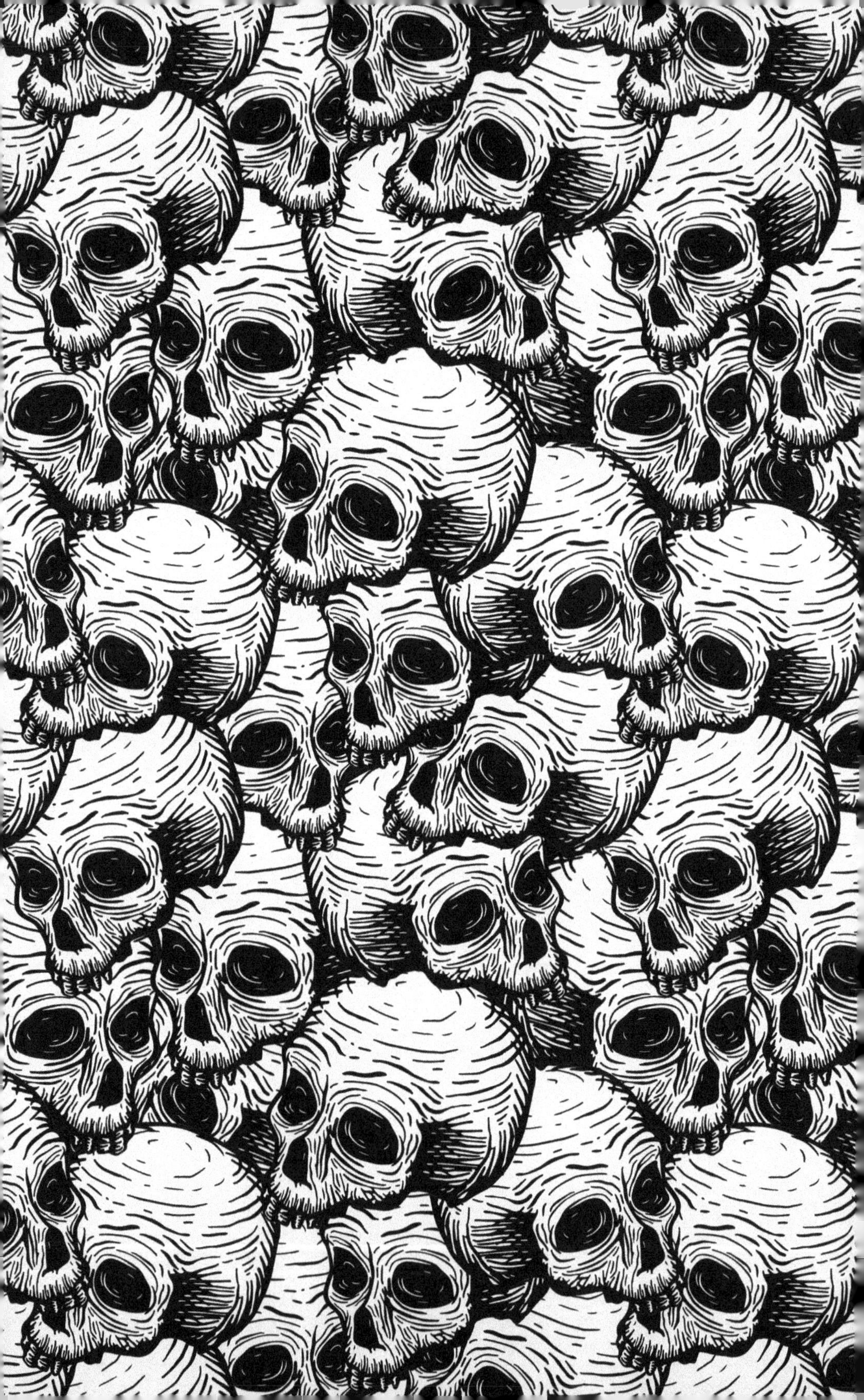

2 3

W R A T H

PEOPLE CALL KILLIAN unhinged and impulsive for his rage issues, but actually, he spends more time keeping them in check than not. People don't see that. They see a bottle of beer flying across the room and smashing into a wall and think he's such a loose cannon. They couldn't be more wrong. When he finally lets it out, that's not impulse. That shit is finely calculated. The rage is always there inside him, but he knows when he can get away with it and when the time isn't quite right.

It wasn't always like that, though.

The first time I met Killer, he was gunning for me—really amping up into a nuclear explosion that was destined to end with my teeth on the pavement. All these years later, I can't even remember what set him off, the fucking psycho. He was bigger, even then. We were barely eight years old, and both little shits to boot. I knew right away this kid could chew me up and spit me out.

I still fought back.

I think that's why he came back the next day, striding up to the corner store my mom worked at, shiner and all, to ask if I wanted to go play a game of HORSE on the court by his house. Killian and Tristian are both North

Side blood. Killer likes to bicker about that—fucker thinks there's something worthwhile in the cred—but I don't give a shit where his dad came from. He can tattoo himself all to hell and act just as hard as he wants, but deep down, the guy's all North. He's never gone to bed hungry and mad at the world because of it.

He and Tristian have never been dicks about it. Hell, Killer bought me my first keyboard, sick of always waiting for me to finish lessons at old man Kinley's house. Tristian got me my first piece of proper recording equipment, demanding I put down a sick track for his twelfth birthday party. If they had something, then one of made damn sure I had it, too.

But they don't know what it means to feel like trash because their shoes have holes. They've never needed to carry their jacket close because it's the only one they've got for the whole winter, and every other kid you've met has had sticky fucking fingers. They've both seen hard times, don't get me wrong—plenty of rough to go around in the North Side, too—but they can never really know *this* kind.

Story could, though.

I saw it in her the first time we met. Those wide doe eyes of hers took in Killian's house, and I could tell it'd never really be home to her. Too nice, too clean. Impossible to be comfortable there. I got it, though. It should have made me want to get close to her—to show her it wasn't all bad for people like us. To show her that Killian and Tristian didn't care about that shit, because they had that privilege. But for some reason, it just made me fucking hate her. Having her there was proof that I could never exactly fit, either. She made me feel humiliated. Inferior.

It was just my own bullshit. It took some time, but standing here, watching Killer cut her shirt down the middle, ripping it open wide, I get that now.

Now that she's humiliated me intentionally.

It's a different kind of hatred, because it's not hatred at all. It's the one person who could understand, who could really *know* what it's like to struggle, to walk in the company of wealth and feel like scum, stabbing me in the fucking back. It's knowing that I stood there that night, weeks ago, and told her about my old teacher—the one who used to mock and taunt me—only to have her use it against me. It's that I handed her something small and fragile, only to watch her smash it in my face.

This shit is worse than betrayal.

I may not have the rage issues that plague Killian, but something deep inside feels wounded enough to make it feel like I do. White-hot anger boils my blood, and if Killian hadn't spoken up earlier, I may have strangled the life out of her.

All the work I've done for the past few weeks, the kindness and attention and patience—fucking mind-numbing, ball-aching patience—had been for nothing. She never wanted my approval. She was just playing a game of her own.

Sweet Cherry is about to learn a very difficult lesson.

Lords always win.

And we keep what's ours.

"You know how the Dukes mark their Duchess?" Killian asks, gently running the tip of the knife between her tits. "They brand her. Tie her up, hold her down, and burn their icon into her skin—wherever she wants it." I see a shudder roll through her body, and so does Killian. It makes his eyes harden. "The Barons make the Baroness get a tattoo of their pentagram. I like that. It's got everything; style, permanence." He snatches up her wrist, sneering at the cuff. "The Lords just have *this*. Leather and metal. You can take it off whenever you want. It's against the rules, but you don't actually care about those, do you?" With a sharp yank, he has it off her wrist in a second flat. "It doesn't matter. Since you can't seem to understand your fucking place, we're going to carve three letters into your skin." He leans in until he's nose to nose with her, lips pulled back in a snarl. "And they won't be LDZ."

Story *laughs*, not even struggling against mine and Tristian's hold. "That's your big punishment? You're going to cut me up?" She strains forward, mouth pressed into a crooked twist. "Here's a secret, Big Killer. *I don't care.* I stopped caring about what you did to my body somewhere between the tracker and being in your bed of nails."

He plants a hand in the middle of her chest, driving her back. "You drugged me, tied me up, and then fucked me. You know what that's called right?"

This makes her eyes go tight, smile sharpening. "A taste of your own medicine."

He puts the blade to her sternum, right between her tits, and gazes pensively as it presses into the flesh. "Here's a secret for *you*, Story. It didn't work." Voice lowering to a hiss, he tells her, "Your pussy felt good, little sister. Best fuck I've had all year, really. You should reconsider your lifestyle if that's your idea of revenge." To me and Tristian, he says, "Hold her."

As soon as the words are out of his mouth, she goes stiff, me and Tristian clamping hard on her shoulders, pinning her to the wall. From the bloodless expression on her face, I'm thinking she's going to scream.

But she doesn't.

The moment Killian drags the knife down her chest, blood bubbling up around the metal of the blade, she throws her head back and looks like she wants to. Her throat swells with it, like it's a living thing clawing up from her lungs, but she won't let it free. She won't give us the satisfaction. Killian connects the lines of the 'K' slowly, making it just as neat and tidy as he always is.

And then he hands the knife to Tristian.

Tristian takes it, letting Killian take his place at her shoulder. "The next time you pull something like this," he says to her, caressing her breast with the tip of the blade. "You can imagine me sinking this knife into your chest, because that's exactly what I'll do. Are you listening?" He grabs her chin and roughly wrenches her gaze to his. I thought I'd seen the worst of Tristian that night on the docks when he torched the yacht, but I was wrong. He's never looked as scarily inhuman as he does now, nose to nose with Story. "You threaten my sisters again, and I'll kill you."

Her face goes slack, right before screwing up in confusion. "What the hell are you talking about? I would never—" Her voice garbles off, jaw clenching shut as Tristian carves the 'T' below the 'K'.

When he hands me the knife, my fingers fist it hard enough to ache. We switch places, which gives me a perfect view of their handiwork. The cuts are too shallow for my taste, two lines of blood crawling slowly toward her navel, and I have to wipe it away to see the skin that's about to bear my mark.

I reach up with my bloodied fingers, smearing a messy smudge over her cheek. I'm expecting her to grimace and turn away, but she disappoints me, turning into it instead. There's a crazed mania flickering in her eyes that's almost fascinating to see. It's what makes me speak next. "You know I actually started to feel bad about what happened that night? I was thinking to myself," I press the tip of the knife into her skin, "maybe if we'd taken our time, been nicer, we probably could have had you without all the fuss. We could have…" I dig the tip in, following her wince with a surge of my body. "…*wooed* you. Truthfully, I have no fucking idea what that would have looked like. But I found myself thinking about it. Isn't that funny?"

She gasps at the line I make, no doubt deeper than the others.

"But like you said, I do know how to handle you. I knew how horny you were that night, remember? I whispered it in your ear. I felt how wet you were. You've always been easy for me to read." But I pause, lifting the knife. "Which letter should I choose, Cherry? 'R'?" I follow her gaze, waiting for her eyes to blink open to sneer, "Or 'D'?"

I can see her pulling that steely defiance around her like a comforting blanket, and it doesn't waver. Not even when she parts her lips to say, "Go ahead. It'll be the only 'D' you'll ever give me."

My knuckles go white around the hilt of the knife, and for a moment, I want nothing more than to raise it over my head and slam it into her cheek. Jaw clenching hard, I swipe the blood away and finish my initial, undeterred by her full-bodied wince.

When it's done—all our initials carved into her flesh—I step back and look at it. I'm not like Killian, who's probably going to get off at the sight of it. It doesn't make me happy to see it. It doesn't make her feel any closer to being mine. It doesn't make this gaping maw in my chest any better. Looking at Story, she might be a little stiff and pale, but her eyes are pure steel.

In the end, it's kind of underwhelming.

Sharing a glance with the others, it's clear they feel the same way. It's not like we talked about it, but we all know what we wanted out of this. Tears. Sobbing. Begging. Promises that she'll be better. We wanted this bitch to throw herself at our feet, or at the very least, fight back.

Instead, we get the defiant jut of her chin, and it doesn't matter that she's acting.

She looks *bored*.

Tristian, all the fine details of his carefully composed mask cracking, pushes her to her knees. She goes down easily, as if she's been expecting and preparing for this all along. Fuck, maybe she has. Maybe this whole thing was part of her plan. Maybe she's right and we've created something unbreakable.

Doesn't mean we won't try.

Killian's there to grab her wrists, wrestling her arms behind her back. "Let's see how you like being tied up," he spits, using her wrist cuff to bind her hands.

She doesn't look surprised when she sees Killian unzip his pants. But when Tristian does the same—and then when I reach for mine—she laughs again. "Wow, you almost had me with the knife punishment, but this? Come on." She shakes her head. "So predictable."

I allow my jeans to sag down my hips, taking my cock in hand. I coax it to hardness, watching from my periphery as the others do the same. "That wasn't the punishment, Story."

Tristian works his palm over the head of his cock, scuffing closer. "That was a deed."

She arches an eyebrow, all that steely challenge still sparking in her eyes. "A deed?"

"A deed of ownership." Killian gives his cock a few firm tugs, eyes boring down into hers. "And now we're going to enjoy our property."

"We're going to cover you in our come, Sweet Cherry." I grab the front of her hair, forcing her eyes to mine. "We're going to force you to eat it. Swallow it. Take it."

Tristian adds, "And then you're going to walk out of here with your head held high like nothing happened, and do you want to know why?"

Killian is the one who answers. "Because that's what whores do."

2 4

CARVED

THEY LOOK LIKE animals. They sound like animals. They *feel* like animals.

I know my chest should hurt where they carved their initials, but I can't even feel it beyond the background throb of a shout that never escaped. No one is coming to save me, and even if they were, would I want them to? Would I want anyone to see me like this? To know what I am?

No, this is just for the four of us.

This punishment was as written in the stars as the rising tides, and who knows? Maybe I'm a fool. Maybe I was arrogant to think I could get one over on them. To think I could take control and keep it for more than the space between one moment and another. To think I could change it.

Maybe I'm naïve to believe they no longer have the power to hurt me.

Maybe I don't care anymore.

The shame is easy to push away as I watch their fists strip their cocks. I know them well enough to understand how different they are in this. Killian doesn't allow himself anything approaching gentleness. He's who the term 'self-abuse' was meant for, beating his dick like it's both the transgressor and the weapon.

Tristian, on the other hand, barely seems to pay attention to the motions of his hand at all. His eyes—that icy, laser-sharp focus—see nothing but me. He's the hardest to look at like this, on my knees for him with my blood-stained cheeks, feeling the creep of something black and gnarled twisting in the pit of my throat. But I always knew the day would come I'd meet this side of him again, ugly and cruel, unable to drive it back with my quick tongue and empty promises of devotion. I'm ready to face it.

Rath, though.

Rath is stunning.

He looks like malevolence personified—*true* royalty—and perhaps the worst part is that he wears it so well. The veins in his forearm bulge as he fists himself, and he's not like the others. This isn't a means to an end for him. Rath wants to savor it, collecting the moisture building on the tip of his cock and using it to slick the way as his black eyes burn into mine.

I know then that these men were built for this. There was never anything that made them this way—it was nature, not nurture. I'm convinced they sprang from the universe fully formed into the nightmares looming above me.

The more I think about it, the less I can imagine them any other way.

Beneath it all is an old friend. I've known it for so long that I don't even bother shrinking away from it anymore. It's my hatred, burning hot and bitter, and turned so far inward that it stings worse than the letters cut into my flesh.

Because despite it all—the debasement and humiliation and hurt—I look at them standing there like vengeful sentries, and I still *feel* something.

Killian was right before, that night in the hallway weeks ago.

I really am broken.

It's the only way to explain how my belly clenches with want. It's the only reason my pussy could ache like this, gone slick at the sight of their hooded gazes and rigid cocks. Something within me is defective. It must be, else I'd never want to tip forward and take the taste of them on my tongue, or crave the sound they make when they erupt, knowing that I'm the reason for it. And here, in the dark, surrounded by mirrors and heat and panted breaths I can't escape from, I allow myself to admit that it's not just about the power it gives me.

Maybe I'm just as fucked up as they are.

It's impossible to know who to watch as they surround me, cocks hard and erect, taut abs flexing with need. Rath's eyes are zeroed in on my tits, while Killian stares straight at my mouth. My eyes meet Tristian's in the mirror just as he drags his attention away from his own reflection. The blue of his eyes is as cold as ice, but the hint of pleasure streaking through them is unmistakable. They act like it's the end of the world, but they love this. He fondles his balls like he's loading a gun, his chest heaving with every tug. Killian thumbs the soft flesh of his head, pulling and pushing against the ridge. Rath rocks in a steady rhythm, and I know them all. I know these slacked jaws and pinched noses. I know that when they're like this, Rath's shoulders curl lazily inward, but Tristian's go rigid.

I know that when Killian approaches me, grabbing roughly at my chin, he's seconds from exploding.

"Open your fucking mouth," he commands, his voice a barely unrecognizable rumble when he rubs his thumb over my bottom lip.

I don't make it easy, clamping my lips shut. He stabs his thumb between them, laughing darkly. "You open up, Sweet Cherry, or you're going to be cleaning spunk out of crevices you didn't even know you had." He squeezes the back of my jaw and I relent. "That's right. Know your fucking place." He rocks back on his heels, cheeks red, hand fumbling as he reaches his peak. The growl from his chest lets me know it's coming, that *he's* coming, but I still flinch at the first burst of his release, surging warm and thick over my lips and tongue.

"Jesus," Tristian grunts, standing just to my side. "*Jesus Christ.*" Killian's cock continues to spurt, while Tristian erupts, painting the side of my face and hair with his ribbons of come. It's less thick than Killian's, clinging to my ear and dripping messily down my shoulder.

It's no surprise that Rath takes his precious time, edging himself closer and closer, but making us all wait for him. The sound of hot, ragged breath fills the room, and Tristian's voice rings out.

"Get her, Rath. Mark that pretty little body up."

"Yeah, Rath," I taunt, raising my face to him, "Mark me up."

He stands before me, cock as red and angry as his own face. "Shut your fucking mouth," he growls, in such a complete opposition to Killian's previous order that it pulls a crazed, mangled laugh from my chest.

Sneering, I reply, "Whatever pleases you, my Lord."

The flash of deranged wretchedness in his eyes does give me pause. I wouldn't call what I feel guilt—he doesn't deserve that. But there is a weight to what I've done. A mark just as permanent as their initials sliced into my flesh. I fucked with Killian and messed with Tristian's head. But Rath?

It was my finest work, spun out of a viperous hurt. A wound that was meant to scar. If it hadn't been him on the receiving end of it, I'm betting he would have appreciated it for the art it clearly was. Instead, his hand hooks roughly under my chin, jerking my gaze upward.

"You look at me when I come on you." he spits, voice rusty and harsh. "Watch me the way you watched me up on that stage."

Looking up, I recall the tittering laughter of the crowd, the humiliation on his face, the rigid slant of his spine as he played for them all. The instant my gaze meets his black eyes, he lurches forward, jerking his cock up and down. He coats me in his spunk with this look on his face, like maybe he wishes he had more. He doesn't need it—I can feel him all over me. In my hair, clinging heavily to my eyelashes, slashed across my cheek, and yes. Inside, too. The vestiges of those sleepy, safe mornings in his bed. The way his hair would curl so softly against the pillow. The weight of his arm around me. How gentle and content he'd look after his orgasm, as if he'd felt the same way I did.

If I'd never felt that warmth, maybe the cold wouldn't have seemed so devastating.

So when I fall forward to take the tip of his cock into my mouth, it's not to bring him pleasure. I hold his stare while I do it, knowing he can see the rebellion in the way I suck him clean.

"What the fuck?" he chokes, face screwed up in outrage. "What the fuck is *wrong* with you?"

"I told you she was a whore," Killian says, tucking himself into his jeans. His stormy face watches as Rath shoves me back, sending me sprawling on my backside. "Even after all that, she's probably wet for it."

"Fuck you," I spit.

If saying those words to Tristian yesterday had been my first mistake, then this is my second. It's a flash of weakness—the knowledge that something can bother me.

I can see Rath's expression shift when he hears it, adjusting the knife he's still clutching in a hand. My eyes follow as he raises the hilt to my face, the leather and metal smooth against my skin as he runs it over the globs of semen, pressing so hard I can feel it in my teeth. "You want to know what I think, Cherry?" he asks me, eyes empty and hard. "I think he's right."

I catch the look he shares with Tristian a second too late. He's behind me, holding me tightly to his chest before I realize what they're planning to do. I still kick out with my leg, though, catching Rath in the ankle.

Beyond the tightening of his jaw, it doesn't faze him. He crouches to his knees, wrenching my knees apart, and says to Killian, "Hold her open."

I fight against Tristian's hold, and then Killian's powerful arms, splaying my thighs wide. "I'll scream!"

Rath sends me a cold smirk. "Promise?"

Then he lifts my skirt, grabs the crotch of my panties, and cuts them away in one swift yank across the blade. The air hits my overheated center in a sudden burst of exposure. I know when Rath and Killian realize how turned on I am because they each send Tristian this *look*.

Before I can translate it, Rath is wrapping my discarded shirt around the blade of the knife, and then turning it in his palm.

The spunk-covered hilt of the knife enters me in a hard, unforgiving thrust.

I cry out, less from the shock and pain than the relief. I didn't realize just how badly I needed to be touched until I finally am. Killian's fingers dig into the soft flesh of my thigh as he spreads me farther, chewing out an order to Rath.

"Fuck her with it."

Rath watches as he slides the hilt back, only to shove it back inside of me. I twist against Tristian, trying to scramble away, but it's like meeting a brick wall.

"Wait," I gasp, digging my fingernails into Tristian's arm. "Wait, hold on. I can't—"

Rath looks me in the eye as he gives the knife another thrust. "What's wrong, Cherry? We all know how much you like it." The corded muscles in his shoulder jump as he pushes it back inside, the cold metal of the blade guard meeting my slick lips. My hips flex up instinctively—involuntarily—and his mouth tips up into a mean grin. "Yeah, your cunt's hungry, isn't it? Because you're a fucking freak. Look at you, bleeding and covered in our come, and all you want is to get off."

"No!" But it's a pointless protest. They've all seen it now. They know how to touch me—how to hurt me—and Rath isn't about to let it go.

He drives the handle of the knife into me as if it were his own dick, hard and fast. "That's why you keep coming back," he says, voice low and full of venom. "It's because you're broken inside. You wouldn't last a week with someone else. You need a man who'd hold you down and own you, because you're just like your whore of a mother. You're *defective*, Story."

I shake my head, but a tear is already rolling down my cheek. "I don't—I'm *not*." But even as I say the words, my hips are bucking into it, chasing the tight promise that's coiling deep within my belly.

Rath gives a breathless laugh, and then Tristian grunts, "Show her what else she wants. Remember yesterday morning?"

I don't know what he's talking about. Not at first. But Killian gets this dark gleam in his eye, and suddenly Tristian shifts behind me, flattening his arm across my chest while his other hand disappears. His palm slides over my ass and he spreads my cheeks. Then, he pushes a finger in—

I suck in a shocked inhale. "Tristian!"

With a wiggle and a push, his finger slots right into my ass, causing me to seize in alarm. Tristian wrestles me closer, breath hot and fast in my ear.

"Relax, or it'll just hurt more." It's almost like the version of Tristian I've come to know. The soft cadence, the sweet words. But it's completely void of the caring warmth, mechanical and aloof.

The thrust of the knife slows while Rath watches Tristian pushes his finger inside of me, but he blinks and starts again, giving the knife a couple slow, shallow thrusts. The dual pleasure ripples through me, and I bite down on a cry of desire. Tristian slides in another finger, increasing the sensation.

"Your pussy is gushing for this." Rath says it matter-of-factly, gaze fixed to mine. "That's how wrong you are, Cherry. You could never be a normal girl. You know that, right?"

I thrash against Tristian and Killian's hold, but deep inside, I know he's right. It's not even long before my hips begin following the rhythm, the sting and stretch so far gone that now nothing is left but the fiery building *need*.

I don't even realize I'm speaking, the voice coming from my throat foreign and garbled with desperation. "Please, please, please…"

"Please what?" Rath's voice is practically disembodied as he slowly removes the knife. Tristian continues to finger my ass, slowly pumping them in and out. It still feels good, but now that I know what I'm missing, I can't help but want more. "You want me to stop? I will, you know. All you need to do is ask." Tilting his head, he presses the end of the knife against my clit, applying sweet, delicious pressure. Just as fast, he pulls it away. He wonders, "Or do you want me to make you come?"

I writhe, seeking a friction that doesn't exist. "Please!"

His eyes narrow. "Please *what*? Use your fucking words!"

"Let me come!" The words escape unwelcome, like a demon clawing its way up my throat. I lean my head back and meet Tristian's eyes. "Please, Tristian."

If anyone will give me what I want—what I *need*—it's this man. The one who dotes on and babies me. But that man isn't here right now. His eyes are cold, and he yanks his fingers away, leaving me sore and stretched and crying out with the loss. But then Rath shoves the handle back into my pussy, hard and jarring. He builds a glorious rhythm, and my body chases the thrusts.

"You think you deserve to come?" Rath asks, and even though he's looking at me, I know he's speaking to the others.

It's Killian who answers. "No."

The hard finality of his voice is like a second knife, this one sunk right into my aching center, blade-side first.

Rath pulls the handle out and leaves me there, bucking into thin air. "Seems like a waste of a nice begging cunt, but fair is fair," he says, using my shirt to clean the slick from the hilt. He looks down at me, at the way I'm writhing and aching. He's sweating, too, wayward locks of hair plastered to his pale forehead. "I prefer you like this, anyway."

Killian lets my thighs go, and when he stands up, I can see he's already hard again, bulge pressing against his zipper. "You remember this," he says, throwing my soiled top at me, "the next time you think you can win."

Tristian is the last to slide away, not bothering to unbind my wrists as he carelessly dumps me on the ground, ignoring the fraught way I'm rubbing my thighs together. At this moment, I think I'd probably sacrifice anything—including the last shreds of my dignity and pride—in order to relieve the pressure and finally fall over that precipice.

"Someone will come for you," Killian says, and they're *leaving*. My eyes track their casual retreat from the room, and I want to call them back, to tell them they can't just *leave me here*, all used up and bloodied. But I don't.

When I open my mouth, the only thing that escapes is a sob.

I DON'T KNOW how long I wait. Maybe it's an hour. Maybe it's ten minutes. But I spend it staring at myself in the mirror, a plethora of reflections beaming back at me, broken and eerily motionless. I don't look pretty like this. I don't look like a Lady. I don't look like anyone. I look like a lump of flesh and fluid, and I spend too long thinking that this is in some way profound.

Aren't we all?

Not for the first time in the last month, I wonder where Ted is. My ace in the hole. My win condition. My perfect, twisted weapon.

I once thought this man was the worst of the worst. Someone so terrifying that it made being here worth it. But now?

Now I doubt myself, remembering Rath's words.

"That's why you keep coming back. It's because you're broken inside. You wouldn't last a week with someone else. You need a man who'd hold you down and own you, because you're just like your whore of a mother. You're defective, Story."

Oh, and it's bad then. Because suddenly I'm wondering how right he is. I'm wondering who Ted even is, and if I built him up inside my mind as this ominous, unconquerable boogey man for nothing more than the convenience of having a *reason*.

Was Ted just my excuse to come back to them?

The more I think about it, the more it begins making a horrific sort of sense. Jack was murdered, but as nice as he was to me, he was a hustler. He had enemies. My roommates had access to my mail. Someone could have seen the letters, the photos, and riffed off them for the sake of misdirection. It would have been fucking brilliant. The 'whore' smeared over the wall in Jack's blood. The way I left, so panicked and harried and afraid.

Now, I can't even think of Ted ever mentioning Jack being killed, and that doesn't seem right. He should have bragged about it. He should have sent me proof to scare me. He should have been *all over me* about it.

It's as if everything I've known to be true—the very foundations of my being—begins crumbling around me, brick by brick. Maybe the problem isn't Ted, or the Royals, or the daddies, or Daniel. Maybe the problem is *me*.

I'm the only common denominator.

I'm spiraling down this black hole of uncertainty—curled on the floor, slumped and silent, sticky and soiled—when I hear distant footsteps approaching from the entrance. It should scare me, the thought of someone coming in and seeing me like this.

I just can't seem to care anymore.

Let them see the flesh and fluid. If I can't be a person, then I can at least be that.

Seeing Tristian appear in the doorway doesn't bring much comfort. I can't help but wonder if he has more abuse in mind, and somewhere in the back of my brain, I wonder if I'd care if he did.

Rationally, I know it could get worse.

But right now, I just can't see it.

"What do you want?" I ask, knowing the question comes out bland and emotionless. I don't have an ounce of feeling left in me, let alone generosity.

Apparently, to my shock, he does. "Here," he says, pulling his sweater over his head. He doesn't hand it to me, though, instead stepping aside to reveal another person.

Another Lady.

Charlene's blonde hair reflects in the mirrors, an expression of stunned pity frozen on her face. He gives her the sweater and softly says, "Don't let anyone see. Clean her up and get her back to the house."

She dips her chin in a solemn nod. "I will."

Tristian's eyes fall on me again, probably gaining some satisfaction from the fact I haven't moved an inch since he dumped me here like discarded trash. "Don't," he says, turning to the doorway. "*You* did this, Cherry. Don't forget that."

Charlene doesn't move until he leaves, the door clicking shut down the hall. Even then, it's only a long, deep sigh. "Oh, girl, you look like hell."

Oh, no.

Hell would be an upgrade from this.

Hell only has *one* devil.

"You can untie me and go," I tell her, rolling to my back and pushing myself into a sitting position.

"A Lord gave me an order, so I don't really have a choice. Neither do you." She reaches into her large square purse and pulls out a package of wipes. "But I'm happy to help. Trust me, Story, no one understands what you're going through more than me."

I'm not prepared for her kind words—or any kindness at all, actually. The last time I saw this woman, she was telling me to fight back, probably while knowing the consequences I'd be facing. She'd been cold and unsympathetic. An ally to the Lords alone.

Now she approaches me slowly, crouching down to gently unfasten the wrist cuff. Once it's gone, she doesn't move away, even though she should. I'm disgusting. Sweaty and covered with body fluids. Broken.

She just looks sad. "Here, take these." The wipes are wet and cold between my fingertips, and she watches as I stare at the flimsy cloth, wondering what it's supposed to do. Wipe it away? How can you wipe away something that's embedded into the fabric of your being? I don't know what my expression is reflecting, but it makes her explain, "We just need to be able to walk you out of here without people asking questions."

Robotically, I lift the wad of wipes to my cheek and begin rubbing the skin.

"There you go," she says, her smile looking more like a tight grimace. It falls completely when her eyes drop to my chest. "That's a really brutal punishment."

It should be uncomfortable having her help me like this—like I'm a child or invalid—but I can't seem to feel anything. "Did your Lords do this to you?"

She shakes her head, making her earrings clink. "God, no. My Lords picked me because I'm docile and hate *real* confrontation." She plucks out a strand of hair, wrinkling her nose as she tries to strip the semen out of it with another wipe. "Last year, when I submitted to *your* Lords, mine were mad. But it wasn't..." Sighing, she pushes my hair over my shoulder, starting on the skin there. "They cared more about losing their dumb inside game than about losing *me*. But they also respected it. Killian, Tristian, and Rath had a lot of guts taking a run at me last year. Plus, let's face it." She gives me a weighty look. "Those three were Royals the second they set foot on this campus. I think maybe it was easier for my Lords to step aside than to butt heads with real sons of South Side."

"Yeah," I answer, voice rusty. "I bet it was."

We spend a lot of time cleaning my face and hair, the length of my arms, the curves of my shoulders, but when Charlene's gaze falls to my chest, she locks up, shifting back. I just give it an apathetic look and scrub a wipe over the wounds.

She sucks in a sympathetic hiss. "Doesn't that hurt?"

I meet her gaze, my voice strangely curious. "You'd think it would." It just doesn't penetrate. It's like that shield I pulled around myself got stuck and nothing can get through. But nothing can get out, either. I can feel it all roiling around inside me, this knowledge that I'm not quite right and never will be. This certainty that I'm broken. What's the word Rath had used?

Defective.

We both stare at the bloodied wipe for a suspended moment, the air thick with tension around us. Charlene starts, "Look, Story…" I know the instant she meets my gaze what she's going to say. It's not just the pity that's been shining in her eyes since she stepped foot in here. It's the brief flash of fear that joins it. "I'm loyal to LDZ, and I know this probably isn't my place. But this isn't *right*. Couldn't you…I don't know? Go to someone? The police?"

It's nice of her, really. Until this moment, I wouldn't have thought it possible for me to laugh again. When I do, it's nothing like it should be. It's a dark and sad and hopeless thing, and I can tell from her wince that it's a touch too caustic. "Could I?"

It's a genuine question.

Charlene's face screws up, and the way she averts her gaze is a better answer to my question than words. "Okay, maybe not."

Yeah, maybe *not*.

Daniel Payne probably has them in his pocket, just like everyone else.

But I was raised on a prostitute's ethos, anyway. My mom used to tell me who to reach out for if she ever had a bad trick, and the list was long—at least ten names. The police didn't even make that cut. Because she knew then, like I know now, that people like them don't save people like us. They're just another foot on our backs. And the cleaner I get, Charlene eventually helping me to stand, pulling Tristian's sweater over me, I feel the truth of it in my bones.

No one is going to save me. Not the police. Not family or friends.

Not Ted.

There's no one to run to and beg for mercy, and there's no such thing as heroes. There's only me, walking out into the misty night, with a better Lady at my side. She cups my elbow to lead me away, but I look out over the lot at all the dwindling carnival goers and freeze at the sight. The lights that had seemed so bright and fun before. The sounds of laughter and music. The scents of warm, sugary food. The unavoidable presence of vibrant life.

Now it all feels dull and fake. Everything is less shiny, flimsy looking. I'm exhausted just looking at it, thinking of all the energy I'd need to prop myself up as someone who's not withered inside, because I'm tired.

I'm so fucking tired of fighting.

I KNOW THEY'RE in the house when I arrive, trudging mechanically up the steps toward my room. I don't see them or hear them, but I don't need to. I can feel them like a weight of awareness, settled heavy on my shoulders, as if they're psychically pushing me to my knees. It's so palpable that my knees nearly buckle when I reach the landing, knowing that Killian will be right across the hall.

My bedroom is untouched from earlier in the morning, and it's such a bizarre thing to see. How can something so close to me remain so unchanged when I feel *this*?

I enter the bathroom because it's expected of me, and that's why I undress, too. It'd make sense to clean myself up, hide all of this away and plaster on an unaffected smile. That's what I should do—make them think I'm unbothered. It would drive them fucking crazy. But I just can't muster the strength. I feel hollowed out and empty, my organs replaced with cold and sharp things, and the second I turn to the mirror, I shrivel at the sight of myself.

I don't realize what I'm doing until there's glass everywhere. One second I'm thinking *no more*—no more mirrors, please, just *no more*—and the next, I'm hurling something hard and heavy into the glass.

It barely takes any force to send it shattering to the counter and the floor in a cascade of silver. Stunned, I look at it all, reaching down to pluck a shard from the sink. A slice of my reflection stares back at me, her eyes wide and full of dead things, and suddenly it all makes sense.

I can escape everything. There's relief here, deep within the knowledge that I hold the strings tethering me to this world. It'd be so easy. I flip the shard curiously between my fingers, inspecting the sharp edges. The light reflects off the glass and throws a beam of light against my skin, shimmering and brash. It'll hurt for a little while, but then it'll never hurt again. I'll just be another cautionary tale, like that Lady their freshman year. A few years down the line, some future Lord is going to tell their Lady about me. He's going to say, "Story Austin. She was weak and pathetic. Slit her wrists upstairs in the bathroom because she couldn't hack it. They drove her too far. So be a good girl, and maybe you can get out of this unscathed." The Lady will be sad for me, even as she disparages me in her own thoughts. Foolishly, she'll think herself stronger.

"Put it down." The voice comes so quietly that I'm certain I'm imagining it. I'm too entranced by the sight of the shard against my wrist to bother glancing up to make sure. I'm thinking that it'll only take a few seconds if I do it right, and I allow myself to feel a moment of guilt for old Ms. Crane, thinking of her on her hands and knees in here, mopping up my blood. I hope she can forgive me for causing one last mess.

When the blood bubbles up around the glass, dark and wet, everything seems very clear.

This is how I free myself.

Once and for all.

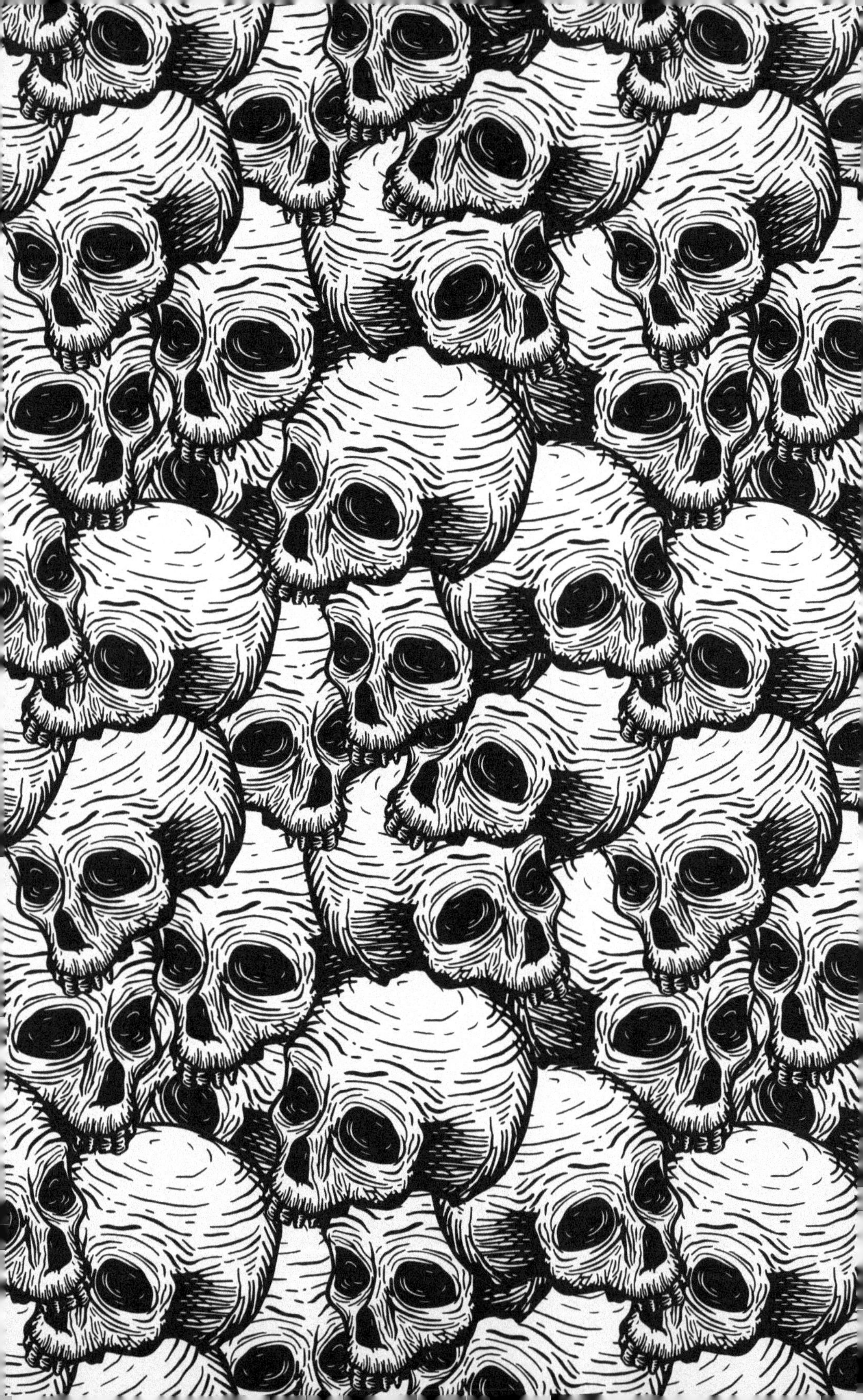

2 5

A M B U S H

 I step out from the shower and dry off. It's been a long day—a whole-ass week, really. The carnival ended an hour ago, the guys and I doing our share of the cleanup after leaving Story in the funhouse. I still have the sight of her on her knees, bound and covered in spunk, my initial carved into her chest, burned into my brain like the brand I'd threatened her with.

The lying whore had it coming for what she did to me and the others. I knew bringing her in here was a risk, but I thought she was too weak to make a move. Turns out, Story has a backbone. She'd be an excellent asset to the Lords, but to what end? So she can betray us? Sell our secrets and souls to the highest bidder?

Jesus Christ.

I taught her to use a gun.

So why is it when I flop down onto my bed, inhaling the vestiges of her scent on my pillow, I don't feel anything but defeated?

I lie on my back, well aware of the hollow cavern in my chest, and try to draw the memories of what she did to me from my brain like a syringe. The marks on my wrists are a physical reminder and everything else is a hazy blur, but if I struggle through the fog, I can make out these little snatches of memory. The caress of her hair against my face. The weight of her body on my hips. A sound she made, breathy and keening. Her words in my ear, low and vexed.

"Don't you like it, big brother?"

My cock swells at the memory of her words, at the sensation of her pussy sinking down onto me. But it's not enough. The sex wasn't the problem. It was the loss of control—just like she said. And the fucked-up thing is, looking back, I can see exactly what she was doing and how she was such a deft hand at playing us.

In another universe, I might have found it in me to feel proud. She fucked Rath over *so good*. Got into Tristian's head so deeply. Brought me to my knees so efficiently. I should be enraged, but while the fury is still there—the impulse to strike and wound and damage—there's also something lurking beneath it.

When I was a kid, Ms. Crane used to say that every life is a patchwork quilt assembled from our hurts and joys, and it always stuck with me—a square on my very own blanket of bullshit. I used to think of it like that, as if every person had their squares, all fused together to form the fabric of who they'd become, and no two could ever look alike. I know mine is ugly and tattered and frayed, not fit for covering anything except my own fucked up insides.

How much of Story's was constructed on account of us for her to have played us so expertly?

And why does the answer to that make my fucking heart sing?

I pause then, hearing someone coming up the stairs. Tristian's in the basement handling LDZ business, and I can hear Rath right above me, listening to something fast and depressing through his speakers, so I know it's not them. Ms. Crane went to bed long ago.

Story's footsteps are light but obvious, crossing the distance to our doors. She doesn't even pause in front of mine, the sound of her bedroom door closing ringing with a grim finality. Briefly, I wonder what she looks like. Has our come dried in her hair? Are her cheeks still stained with blood and tears? Would it make me satisfied to see it?

Now that my immediate aggression has been spent, unloaded on her like a stack of dynamite, I feel depleted and weary. Keeping Story is a full-time job that's making my muscles ache.

I'm in the middle of deciding whether I want to rub one out when I hear a crash from across the hall. I pull on a pair of boxers as I cross the room, striding over the distance between our doors and giving her knob a try.

It's locked.

My jaw goes rigid because it's barely an inconvenience, but it's getting old. Everything is a fight. Even when things started to get easy, it was just a trick. I see that now. That day in the truck when she climbed into my lap and we fucked, fast and hard and so desperate that sometimes I can still feel the imprint of her fingernails in my shoulders. It was fake. It had to be, because it was too easy.

Now I'm stomping across the hall and digging that key from my desk drawer, and the weariness is still there, but some of that aggression is creeping back in, salivating at the prospect of having another go at her. It comes out when I jam the key into the lock and thrust it open, revealing a dark, empty room. There's a slant of light slashing across the bed from the bathroom, door cracked a few scant inches, and I don't think twice about storming into it.

I freeze at what I find inside, all that tight hostility zapped away in the span of a single blink.

The mirror is shattered, glass scattered everywhere, and among the debris is Story, naked and pale.

Holding a shard of glass to her wrist.

My bones turn to ice, and for a long time, I can't move. I try to speak, but my jaw won't unclench, tongue fused to the roof of my mouth. The come *is* still dried in her hair, and her chest…

It's gruesome and inflamed, our initials difficult to make out beneath the swollen, scabbing skin around it. The tracks of tears are gone, but in their place are empty eyes and a dead expression, as if she left her body back in that funhouse and now it's just walking around without a driver. Her gaze is fixed to her wrist, so slender and flawless, and I have no idea what she's seeing, but it can't be the same image I'm taking in, because she looks so…

Relieved.

My voice emerges in a ragged whisper. "Put it down."

I don't think she even hears me, because she doesn't blink. Doesn't flinch. Doesn't move at all, except to shift a delicate finger over the jagged shard of glass. It looks wrong there, pressed to the vibrant blue of her veins, and my chest goes tight in a way I'm not expecting. It isn't until I realize she's already cutting into the skin that my body begins to move.

I take three steps into the bathroom, barely noticing the sting of the glass beneath my feet and wrench her wrists apart. "Drop it!" I snap, nicking my fingertips as I angrily pry it away. She makes a small, wounded sound, forehead furling in confusion. She's a wraith, contained inside nothing but what her hand is doing. Her forehead furls in confusion, gaze climbing my hand to meet my eyes. I can practically see her snapping to awareness, surfacing from whatever hypnosis she'd been under.

"What?"

I hurl the shard of glass into the sink and grab her by her arms, giving her a jarring shake. "Don't you fucking dare," I growl, watching the moisture build in her eyes. "You don't get to take what's mine!"

"Why do you care?" she asks, chest hitching. "Haven't you hurt me enough? Isn't it enough?" Her palms come up to shove at me ineffectually. "Isn't it fucking enough?!"

The sob that wracks her body is a shocking thing, full of shuddering agony. And it should make me feel something other than relief, but *fucking Christ.* Agony is something.

Agony isn't dead.

I don't know what compels me to drag her into my chest. The truth is that

I'm always on a knife's edge with this girl. I either want to fuck her or kill her. Kiss her or kick her. Caress her cheek or yank her hair. It's never made any sense to me, but it's never had to. Until a few days ago, I'd always leaned to the easier side of the blade. Hurt, strike, yank, wound. Since she drugged me, I've found myself wondering if she feels it, too—how addictively intimate it can be to hurt someone. Maybe hugs and kisses are nice. Fuck if I know. But I know the look in her eyes when I say something mean—when I yank her hair and grab her too rough and call her a whore—and I don't care what other people think. That's a certain kind of closeness.

God fucking knows, it's a lot less confusing than *this*.

She cries into my shoulder, her little body heaving with sobs. She doesn't touch me back, but she doesn't pull away, either. Her skin is colder than mine, tits pressed up against my bare chest, and when I run a hand down her back, I don't know what the hell I'm doing.

Only a couple hours ago, I was pushing a blade into her skin.

I was bitterly shooting my nut into her mouth.

I was helping Rath fuck her ruthlessly with the handle of that knife.

I was seeing her puckered asshole taking it and feeling so hard and excited about it that I almost forgot to hate her for what she did to us.

Now, I'm saying, "Shh," and, "Calm down," and, "That's not happening. I won't let you."

It's not often I find myself on this side of those feelings, but I think about hurting her some more, and I just…somehow know.

I know it won't bring me any pleasure.

I press her closer, my hand curled protectively against her head as she cries, and some of that chest-clenching pressure eases, melting away at the feel of her in my arms.

I can't say that I'm sorry, because I'm not sure I am. She fucked us over. She tied me up and used me. She took away my rituals, knowing how much I needed them. She made me think I had her—that she belonged to me, willingly, *wholly.* These weren't betrayals that could go unpunished. Surely she had to know that. This woman broke the one thing I can't look past. The one thing that makes us Lords. *Trust.*

But deep down, beneath the tattered squares that define my fabric, is the knowledge that she's probably right about one thing.

We struck first.

Wrapping my arms around her waist, I lift her just enough to spare her feet as I walk her to the shower, sliding the glass door open and lowering her to the clean tiles. She goes easily when I peel our skin apart, because even after all these years, Story doesn't cling.

I wonder who made that square in her quilt.

I wonder if it was me.

Gently, I command, "Turn the shower on," prying one of her hands from her face. "Get it warm, the way you like it." She obeys perfunctorily, her little shoulders jolting with a restrained sob. I watch her test the spray, adjusting the knobs automatically, hands shaking each time she reaches out to feel the water. "Is that good?" At her shaky nod, I order, "Get under the water, clean yourself up. Wash your hair."

The longer I watch, the more I *want* to say the words. They wouldn't be welcome—they *shouldn't* be welcome—but I feel them in the pit of my chest, hard like a boulder, and seeing her tears mingle with the water makes them so goddamn difficult to ignore.

I'm sorry.

It had to be done.

I'm sorry.

SHE DOESN'T FLINCH when I run the cotton over the cuts on her chest, even though I know the antiseptic hurts like a bitch. I'll be finding that out myself here in a few minutes, since my feet are cut all to hell. I'll probably spend all night getting the glass out.

For now, I've got her on the bed. Her gaze is fixed dispassionately over my shoulder as I pick up her wrist, running the cotton over the cut she made. It isn't very deep—won't need stitches. Rath's initial had been cut deeper than this, but for some reason, I'm more careful with this one. It's fucking stupid, sitting here cleaning up the mess I made myself. The mess I refuse to even apologize for. It doesn't make sense.

And yet, I reach for the ointment I'd found in the first aid kit and get to slathering all the cuts with it. The contrast of the letters tattooed on my knuckles—KILL—with the gentle way I'm dabbing the pads of my fingers onto her wounds, angry and vivid-red, is almost laughable. I don't patch wounds; I make them. That's made obvious by how sloppy the bandages look when I clumsily press them to her skin.

Rubbing my nose, I inspect my handiwork, her full tits perky and perfect on either side of the initials. I'd be lying if I said my dick isn't hard, and it isn't just because of the way her robe is opened, teasing the sight of her tits. It's the letter between them, the 'K' that's scabbing and still swollen. She's going to wear that for the rest of her life. The thought makes my blood run lava-hot, something in my chest unwinding at the knowledge I'll always be a part of her.

I'm not completely senseless. I know it's abominable.

"Remember that one Easter?" I ask, sweeping the fold of her robe back to reveal her pebbled nipple. "It was right after you moved in. Dinner was fucking terrible. My dad was riding my ass about being nicer to your mom, and you—" Fuck, she was wearing this dress that killed me. It was a pale pink I could see right through when she stood in front of the dying sun. My balls were aching all day. She was different then—awkward, but with a carefree naivete about her. She was sweet and cute, and I still thought she was mine. "We spent hours that night in my room, playing games. You got so frustrated that I actually let you beat me."

She sat between my legs as I taught her the controls, and I thought about claiming her then. There's no way she couldn't feel how hard I was. She'd send me these smirking little grins every time I let her win, and the more I think about it, the more I suspect that night was the happiest I've ever been.

In the end, I chickened out, too young and dumb and fucked up to risk ruining that square in my quilt.

But I saw her later, when she was sleeping in her bed. It was the first night I really watched her—the first night I allowed myself to stand over her and stoke myself to the sight of her soft body and wet mouth.

"Story," I say, touching her chin. "Look at me."

She obeys, just like she had in the shower, and I understand now, like I understood then. She's turned off, shut down, reduced to following orders because she's been taught that not doing so means suffering of one sort or another. She's nothing like that girl anymore. She's all rough edges, that light in her eyes so dimmed that I can't even see it anymore, but she's still enough. The sight of my thumb pressing into her bottom lip still makes my spine feel electrified.

And I could have her.

All I'd need to do is tell her to lie back and open up for me, and she'd part her thighs. She'd lay there impassively as I pushed into her, still flush with the memory of that knife. She'd fix her eyes to the ceiling as I fucked her, trying to cling onto whatever scraps of that girl are left so I can weave them into my quilt and imagine it bringing me warmth.

I draw her robe closed, sighing. "Let's get some sleep."

I'm DRAG-ASS ALL day, tired and annoyed at every little thing. Two hours cleaning up glass, another hour picking it out of my feet, and five more hours spent laying stiffly at Story's side hasn't made me inclined to take Neil Takac's bullshit.

"You don't have to pay," I tell him, not bothering to keep my voice professional. "You entered into this agreement, no one forced you."

Every first Sunday of the month, my dad has us go around collecting the dues. It's tedious, and more often than not, someone has to cause a ruckus about it, as if it's some big surprise. It's a waste of our skills and talents. Either one of the Nicks could easily be doing this bullshit. As always, I suspect it's my father's way of punishing me for getting all these tattoos.

"You want to look big and bad, son?" he'd say, giving me a nod. "Then that's what you're useful for."

Rath is just as crabby as me. "If you want to give up Mr. Payne's protection, it's no skin off our noses."

Tristian is the only one who plasters on a smile and level with the guy. "Mr. Takac, you didn't pay last month. I'm sure a fine businessman such as yourself can understand how that puts us in an awkward position. If we let it slide for you, then we'll have to let it slide for someone else, and then someone else. You don't give your services away on credit, do you? Why should we?"

Neil glares around his body shop, swiping an oily rag over his sweaty neck. "It's a bad quarter, fellas. I just don't have the money today. If you need to pull the protection, then I understand."

But he doesn't like it. A body shop in South Side? This place is practically screaming 'steal something', which is pretty ironic given the three jacked cars he's got sitting on the back of the property.

My dad doesn't generally like us to blackmail people unless it's warranted, so I don't bother. Instead, I ask, "You insured, Neil?"

Eyes narrowing, he answers, "Yes."

Nodding, I wonder, "For two hundred? Because you got some nice cars in here."

Tristian offers, "I'm thinking he'd need more like three."

"Well, you're the car guy." I shrug, gesturing to Tristian. "You insured for three?"

We leave ten minutes later, the bag in my pocket a couple grand heavier, and walk shoulder to shoulder toward the avenue. The thick clouds in the sky decide to finally break, moistening the air with a fine, misting rain. Shoulders curled against the chill of it, I finally bring up what's been on my mind.

"We need to talk about Story."

Tristian huffs. "I'm fucking sick of talking about Story. She's hot, she's cold. She wants to be ours, she stabs us in the backs." Scowling into the distance, he shakes his head. "She can't be trusted."

"I know," I say, my feet still aching as I trudge along the damp sidewalk. "Which is why we need to let her go." I'm three paces away when I realize they've both stopped. I turn to look at them, setting my jaw. "She's a liability," I say, hoping to reason with them. "And right now, liabilities are dangerous."

"Even more reason to keep her close," Tristian says, eyes flashing in challenge.

I knew this would happen. Tristian can talk all he wants about being sick of her shit, but at the end of the day, she's his little plaything. And he's not like me and Rath. Random one-offs will get him by, but just barely. He needs someone he can really sink his claws into.

"We're not keeping her. That much is certain." I jerk my head, waiting for them to follow. "Like you said, she can never be trusted."

Tristian scoffs. "Well, how exactly do you plan on doing that without making us look like a bunch of weak pussies?"

There's little precedent for this. Sure, there have been other Ladies who didn't fulfill their mission. Back in '63, the Lady slept with a Baron, immediately violating the contract. She was stripped of her duties and her Lords-purchased belongings and forced to walk to the Baron's mansion in nothing but her bra and panties. She was theirs to deal with after that.

Then there was Jacqueline Wilkins, Lady for the class of '81. She developed a coke habit so massive that she started stealing valuables from the house. The

Lords at the time set her and her dealers—the Counts—up with friendly police. She got three years for the drugs, and then later, a nice little charge for an assault while she was inside, adding a cool decade onto her sentence.

"The problem," I say, scoping out each alley we pass, "is that regardless of what we do with her, it'll go public and the Kings will ask questions. Especially *ours*."

Rath toys with the ring on his lip, scanning the street. "Yeah, that's not a conversation I want to have with Daniel."

Tristian grabs my arm, pulling me to a stop. "So let's not. We can push harder, crack down."

I throw my arms out. "With what resources, Tristian? We don't have the time to chain her to us!" I can see he doesn't care—fucker calls *me* stubborn—so I finally release a hard breath, shoving my hand through my hair. "She's going to kill herself."

Rath kicks a foot out, looking bored. "Don't be dramatic. She's just—"

"I walked in on her last night with a blade to her wrist," I snap, satisfied to at least his head jerk back in surprise. "This wasn't acting," I say before either of them can try. "I looked into her eyes, and you know what I saw? Nothing."

Rath watches me with a skeptical expression. "What happened? When was this?"

I look around, not wanting to have this discussion on the avenue, of all places. "After she got home. She was in her bathroom. She fucking shattered her mirror, and then tried to use one of the shards to—" I press my lips together, not liking the way it feels to remember it. Looking at Tristian, I will him to understand. "We can't push her any harder, and if I'm being honest, I don't want to. It shouldn't have to be this goddamn difficult. I don't care about my dad, or about fucking LDZ or the Royals or the other Kings. What good is having a Lady—having *her*—if she'd rather be dead?" I ignore the stunned looks on their faces, averting my gaze. "I had to have Ms. Crane keep an eye on her today. I think we've taken this thing as far as it'll go. We're all fucking miserable. What's the point?" Irritated, I jerk a hard shrug. "What's the fucking point?"

There's a long moment where the world moves on around us. Cars creep by, music blaring, and people pass like we're invisible. The avenue isn't like anywhere else I've ever known. No matter what, it just keeps on chugging, the biggest cog in the South Side machine, keeping everything running in a perfect cycle.

Tristian is the first to speak, voice thoughtful. "Maybe being upfront with Daniel is the best thing to do. Maybe he'll have an idea about how to fix this."

"It's not a bad idea," Rath says, crossing his arms as the rain begins falling harder. "Plus, if he thinks we've been hiding it from him? It'll only make shit worse, Killer."

"You know what'll happen if we take this to my father," I say, voice low and full of dread. "You're right. He'll have plenty of ideas, and the first one will be taking her from us, and keeping her for…" I think of her sitting on his lap, his hand snaked around her waist and resting on her belly. I think of her words last night in the funhouse, and the thing is, I can't trust them. She could be lying about her never wanting it. But there's a chance she isn't, and if it's true?

Then I'm the one who deserves that knife.

Shaking my head, I insist, "Fuck that. I'm not letting that happen."

We start walking again, and I can tell they're as lost in thought as I am, struggling for a solution to a problem that only we can really be blamed for. It's not like the other houses don't sometimes lose a girl. Shit, for three years running, the Princess has cycled out in her fourth month. The Countess sometimes gets busted. The Duchess has a tendency to just…fucking disappear. Of all the houses, LDZ probably has the second-best track record with these things.

Kind of hard to beat the Barons.

We arrive at the last location just as the sun begins fading. It's a warehouse that's more often than not illegally operating as a nightclub. As always, we dip into the alley to knock for access to the back door. It reeks of piss, booze, and stale cigarettes, and my feet are killing me, raw like ground meat from the glass last night.

"Shit," Rath mutters, patting his pockets. "Left my piece at the house."

Tristian and I both roll our eyes. He fucking would. It's not the end of the world. My gun is tucked into my waistband, and I can tell that Tristian's got his.

"We'll just do this and dip," I say, not feeling great about how much money I'm carrying. Aside from old Neil, the avenue's been looking flush, businesses happy to fork over their dues in whatever form they please. There must be some serious tax crunching happening, because almost everyone preferred paying with paper. I'm basically a walking target.

I bang at the door again, annoyed and quickly losing my patience, when headlights swing into the alley, bearing down on us from the other end. Tristian looks casual as he tucks a hand beneath his shirt, resting it on his gun. But Rath and I share a look and I know he's feeling what I feel.

Unease prickles at the back of my neck.

I bang at the door again, reaching for my own gun. We're so focused on the headlights that we don't even notice—don't even *hear*—who's approaching us from the other mouth of the alley.

Not until Tristian grunts.

2 6

CORROSION

THE EMAILS COME in just after five.

The first one is curt, lacking in any of Ted's usual flowery tone.

I tried to warn you.

I stare at it, unable to muster much in the way of alarm. Ever since what happened in the funhouse, I can't seem to feel much of anything. Not even last night, when Killian found me in the bathroom with the glass pressed to my wrist. Not even when he gently placed me in the shower or carefully cleaned my wounds.

Wounds that he had made.

Not even when he asked me, voice so quiet and soft, if I remembered that blink of time when things had been good. Of course, I remember. Despite feeling out of place in their home, it was the first time everything had seemed full of promise and possibility—a new future laid out before me. I remember going to bed that night and wondering what it might have been like to kiss him, and then feeling stricken by the impropriety of it. He was supposed to be my new brother.

Sometime after, Ms. Crane brings a plate right to my room. It's schlocky macaroni and cheese with ground beef stirred in, and she doesn't even cuss me a warning against telling that 'big blond fuckface', so I'm assuming Tristian has all but written me off.

The second email comes as I'm staring impassively at the dinner, unhungry and uncaring.

I've been wondering, Ted has written, *should I make it slow? Or should I just put a bullet in their heads and be done with it?*

I look at my phone screen, feeling nothing but mild disappointment. All talk.

Ted is all talk.

Which means I came here for nothing. It means all the pain and torment and useless heartache had no point. It means I'm worse than a fool, because a fool doesn't know any better, but me? I knew exactly what they were.

I get the third email ten minutes later. There's no text, only an attachment.

It's a photo of the Lords.

They're outside somewhere, strolling down a street. Rath is wearing his leather jacket, but Killian is in short sleeves, looking thuggish and intimidating as his eyes fix to something in the distance, out of frame. Tristian is there, too, the sharp angles of his face turned away.

They look alert, like they're in the middle of doing something they know is wrong. There are buildings behind them, places I've seen before. I realize they're on the avenue, close to where I'd bought the drugs the other day. I've driven by that bench, have looked into the large, barred window of the pawnshop, have stopped at that traffic light.

They're out there right now; Killian, Tristian, Rath.

Ted.

The email that comes after is to the point.

Either you come and watch them die, or I come to you, in that big, empty house.

The bowl of macaroni crashes to the ground as I lurch from my bed, frantically pulling on the first pair of pants and shirt I can find. I'm flying down the hall when I stop short, almost teetering on the edge of the stairs. I don't know who Ted is, and I can't be certain what he's capable of, but if there's one thing the Lords have taught me, it's this:

No one's going to protect me unless I protect myself.

I burst into Killian's room first, dropping hard to my knees to search beneath his bed. I yank out the box he keeps it in—it was there the night I tied him up—but when I unlatch and open it, it's empty.

I rifle through his closet next, which is easy. Everything is carefully organized, from his jeans to his belts. Most people would keep odds and ends in their closest. Mementos. Things they know they should throw away, but they don't. Equipment, old electronics, just about anything.

Killian's closet is pristine.

It has clothes, shoes, jackets, baseball caps, but little else. The shelf above his shirts holds nothing but five shoeboxes, and in a display of unutterable absurdity, each of them contains actual shoes.

His nightstand and desk are equally unhelpful, so I leave, pounding up the stairs to the third floor. There's no way Killian is the only one with a gun. I search Tristian's room next, which is almost as tidy as Killian's but not nearly as sparse, and the instant I open the closet, I know there's no way I have time to sift through it. It's such a perfect metaphor for Tristian. The room is bright and open, clean and sleek, but hidden within it is a jumbled mess of designer clothing and discarded things. It's all been packed in there haphazardly, as if he doesn't like acknowledging the clutter long enough to do something about it.

I slam the closet and check under the bed, the nightstand, the dresser.

There's a safe beneath his desk.

Of course Tristian would take safety more carefully than Killian, who just closes it up in a box beneath his bed.

My phone buzzes with another notification, and I frantically pull it from my pocket, thumbing the email open. To my bafflement, it contains only a number:

One.

I blink at it, unable to decipher what that means. Does he know I'm here, looking at Tristian's safe? Does he know the combination? I might know Tristian pretty well now, but not nearly enough to guess a combination. Izzy and Lizzy's birthday? Who even knows.

Growling in frustration, I leave the room.

Rath's room is the most difficult, and not only because it hurts to walk inside. There's nothing tidy or organized about it, and the second I step over the threshold, the sour scent of smoke and booze slaps me in the face. There are clothes strewn over the floor, record covers, sheet music, a guitar propped up precariously against his couch. Rath has always been messier than the others, but I've never seen it this bad. I step over an old takeout container and, ignoring the bed, go right to the nightstand. There's plenty inside—condoms, lube, guitar picks, loose change, a tube of acrylic paint, lighters and matches, a crumbled cigarette—but no gun.

His dresser is next, and then his closet, and Rath might be messier than both of the other two combined, but at least he isn't obsessed with clothes.

His closet is the jackpot.

I find a shoebox that's tucked out of the way, but still easily accessible— well worn, as if he goes into it often. Inside is a crumpled pack of cigarettes, a bottle of prescription pills, and three IDs that look and feel fake. The only orderly thing inside is a tightly rolled wad of money. It's thick and bound with a rubber band and even rolled together, it's obvious how much time he put into flattening each bill. I can only assume this is his piano fund. Finally, and most important, is a gun. I feel my lips curve up into a smirk at how alike we can be, but it falls instantly away, stolen by the memory of what happened in the funhouse.

Just then, I get another buzz from my phone.

Two.

I freeze, realizing what this is.

A countdown.

His worn black hoodie is beneath my foot, so I pick it up and shove my arms inside. I snatch the gun from the box, so clumsy and rushed that the crumbled pack of cigarettes comes with it as I cram it into Rath's hoodie pocket.

It's hard to understand—I can't follow the threads, and I'm not sure I want to—but something happened to me while I was on the floor that night, surrounded by mirrors. It wasn't the punishment. Not exactly. Although that had been excruciating, it was the self-doubt that cut the deepest.

Because the thing is, I've always been a coward.

I've always counted on someone else to do what needed to be done. Before Rath's performance, Killian's pregame party, and the way I've been with Tristian, I've been largely hands off in the making of my fate.

Rushing out the door into the sprinkle of chilly rain, I'm eased by the certainty that once and for all, for better or for worse, everything ends tonight. Pointing my two enemies at one another, never getting my hands dirty…that's not bravery. That's not survival. It's just weak.

Tonight, someone is going to be on the other side of this gun.

Maybe it'll be a Lord.

Maybe it'll be Ted.

And if all else fails, maybe it'll even be me.

Despite the steady strum of rain, the avenue is as bright and alive as the carnival had been, and just as harsh to be in the presence of. My mom didn't work down here for very long. Originally, we were from a couple counties over. That city had been smaller, and a lot more dangerous to be visible in. The day she decided to give South Side a stroll, that's what she said to me.

"It's easier to be invisible in a place like that." I remember with perfect clarity the way she looked, sitting at her vanity and putting on lipstick. At my skeptical expression, she sent me a small grin, tapping

me on the nose. *"Hopefully, you never need to be invisible, my sweet little novel."*

If she only fucking knew.

She met Daniel not long after, and I think I always suspected he'd been a client. Now that I'm a little older and a lot wiser, I wonder if maybe it wasn't worse.

A man like Daniel doesn't need to buy sex.

When my phone pings with another notification, I don't need to check it. The last number had been '*six*'. They seem to come at random intervals, and I'm not sure what the final number is meant to be, since we're going up and instead of down, making it difficult to calculate how long I have before…

Before whatever happens when the time is up.

I drive straight to that little strip I'd seen in the photo, but they're long gone. I'm not deterred, eyes scanning the distance as I roll down the avenue. I pass shops and street corners, the men I'd bought the drugs from, the girls in mini-skirts, the boys in their skintight pants, the customers, the happy people, the sad people—all of them converge into a writhing rainbow of humanity. Places like this aren't scary to me. They're more like home than Daniel's house ever was.

Being invisible sounds nice.

I get two more buzzed notifications, so I search harder, down to the warehouse Tristian had taken me that one time, and then toward the Velvet Hideaway—the brothel Killian had taken me to.

Still, I don't see them anywhere. The sun is fading fast, and I get stuck behind an old Chevy that can't decide which lane it wants to be in. When my phone dings with another notification, I finally stop to check them, hoping for another picture.

Nine, it says.

There are no more photos.

"Shit," I hiss, banging the heel of my palm on my horn. The windshield wipers thump to the rhythm of my pulse, and it's as I'm craning my neck around that I catch sight of a street name.

No.

Not a name.

A *number*.

I make an ill-advised U-turn, causing a silver car to swerve and lay on their horn. Ignoring it, I speed toward 13th Avenue, and then 12th. I'm halfway to 11th when my phone chimes again.

Ten.

10th Avenue, I find, isn't much of anything compared to the main strip. Down here, it's all vacant lots and old manufacturing businesses. There's a grouping of tents and makeshift shelters in the first alley I pass, but few cars. The second alley I pass is dark and deserted and much too narrow to get my car through for a proper search.

I'm considering looking on foot when I reach the last alley.

The buildings that bracket it are tall, constructed from old brick that looks like it's crying. Tracks of oxidation trail down from the roof like crooked fingers reaching for the dark pavement below.

I know before I even swing my car into the mouth of the alley that they're there.

I can feel them.

My headlights fall on their three forms and I hold my foot on the brakes, frozen at the sight of them, warbled and distorted through the rain on my windshield. They're all squinting into the light, Tristian's hand disappearing beneath the hem of his shirt. Killian looks uneasy, the broad line of his shoulders tense. Rath takes a couple steps to the side, like he's calculating that the three of them being all clustered together might not be the best idea right now.

I'm so focused on them I miss the figure approaching from the other side of the alley.

Everything happens so fast that I can barely parse it through the rhythm of the wipers. One moment, they're all standing around looking nervous, and the next, Tristian's head is snapping back. There's a flurry of movement, Killian's hand thrusting out with the gun as Rath flies forward to jump the guy.

But then it all comes to a screeching halt, because the attacker has something around Tristian's throat—a rope or a wire—and Tristian's fingers are clawing at it, but he's right in front of the guy and Killian can't take his shot.

I watch, heart hammering wildly against my ribs as they stall, Killian's back shifting, bellowing, twitching. I realize he's yelling, but I can't hear it in here—not over the beat of the rain.

The second I open my door, I do.

"I'll fucking shoot!" Killian's snapping, arms rigid as he aims the gun. If I can see it as the empty threat it is, then chances are the other guy can, too. Tristian's pinned against the attacker, shielding him from anything.

"Drop it," the voice shouts, yanking Tristian's neck back, "or I'll strangle your boy."

My breath seizes as I watch Tristian struggle to breathe, face red and contorted as his fingers scrabble at his neck.

Rath says something low and panicked to Killian, but I can't make it out.

Killian's furious, "Motherfucker!" is perfectly clear, however. He lowers his hand and in a series of swift movements has the clip out of it, chamber emptied, and is chucking the empty gun across the distance. "If you want the money, you'd better let him go first."

I blink the rain from my eyes as the attacker reaches around Tristian, yanking his shirt up. I see the gun in his waistband, silver and gleaming in the beam of my headlights, for only a brief moment before the attacker is plucking it out.

The gasp Tristian makes when the man shoves him forward makes my stomach turn. It's a wet, desperate, painful-sounding thing, and he lands on his hand and knees immediately after sucking it in, back heaving.

The attacker himself is a disappointment.

He's just a man with a ski mask pulled over his face, leather gloves covering his hands. If this is Ted, then he's nothing special. He's not eight feet tall, or four feet wide. He's not carrying an Uzi or being flanked by henchmen. He's simply one lone man.

"Nothing personal, boys," the guy says, landing a hard kick into Tristian's side. "Got a job to do." Tristian curls against the blow, and even this far away, I can tell that awful wheezing sound is still being drawn from his throat.

Rath says, "Hey!" and charges at him, but the guy has Tristian's gun pulled on him so fast that Rath almost tips over in his haste to pull back.

"I'll be taking that money now."

Without question, Killian pulls a pouch from his pants and lobs it at the man, hitting him square in the chest. "Take it and go fuck yourself," he spits, edging closer to Tristian, who's only now pushing himself to his knees.

He tucks the pouch into his waist, leaving the gun trained on Killian. "Oh, the money isn't the job, Little Killer." Cocking the hammer on the gun, he explains, "It's the payment."

The sound of the shot ringing out makes me yelp in shock. If any of them hear it, there's no way to tell over the panicked flurry of motion that happens next. Rath flies at the man, clutching his arm and giving it a hard twist. Tristian scrabbles against the wet ground toward Killian, who's bending over, almost like he's looking for something on the ground.

I don't realize why he's actually folded over like that until he collapses to his knees.

Rath is struggling with the attacker, but all I can see is my stepbrother, as crumpled as the pack of cigarettes in my pocket, fists mashed into his stomach.

I know then that I'm not crazy.

The maelstrom inside my head is a chaotic swirl of relief, despair, and confusion. I've imagined this moment for so long, it feels surreal to watch it unfold. To see that desperate terror in Rath's eyes as he tries to wrestle the gun away. To know that Tristian's sputtering breaths are caving his chest with every frantic inhale. To watch the bowed curve of Killian's shoulders as he curls there in the wet alley, bleeding and so alone.

Because that's what they'll be.

Suffering and hopeless.

No one to help.

I don't need to ask how it feels. I think of them cutting those letters into me. I think of their vicious expressions as they covered me in their come, fucked me with that knife, and left me there on the floor, bloody and crying. I think of the basement, of Killian's hard eyes, and the frat's jeering taunts. I think of the library, Tristian forcing his fingers into me. I think of the video and Rath's scheming grin. The sting of the tracker being pushed beneath my skin. Tristian's voice in my ear, coaxing me to open up for my brother. Killian's hands on me in the night, taking and using. I think, most of all, of that night in the laundry room. It was the bedrock of what we've become, and now it's all stacked up into a crooked tower of their sins that's finally toppling over.

I should throw my head back and laugh into the rain, because it's perfect.

This is the perfect place for them to die.

But the reality isn't so simple, because yes—there was the laundry room and the basement and the mirrors. But there was also last night, Killian's eyes blank but soft as he talked about that Easter, years ago. There's the way Tristian had looked at me when he said he didn't like me being mad at him. There was Rath in that bathtub, telling me how he'd made plans—not for him, but for me.

It should be so clear to me, watching Rath lose his grip on the attacker's arm. I should feel good as I watch Tristian cover Killian, pushing a hand into his gut. I should feel free and so fucking alive right now. But when the attacker raises the gun at Rath, all I feel is grief, because I can see the awareness on his face—the dull, pale flash of acceptance that he's about to die—and all I can think about are those soft mornings.

Nothing about it is simple or easy.

I'm pulling the gun from my pocket before I really have a chance to think about what I'm doing. I blame the rain for Killian's voice coming to me, unbidden.

"First rule of gun safety. Never point a gun at something you aren't looking to kill."

Pointing my gun at the man is the first easy thing about all of this. Clicking off the safety is the second. Aiming through the sights is the third.

But pulling the trigger?

That's the easiest of all.

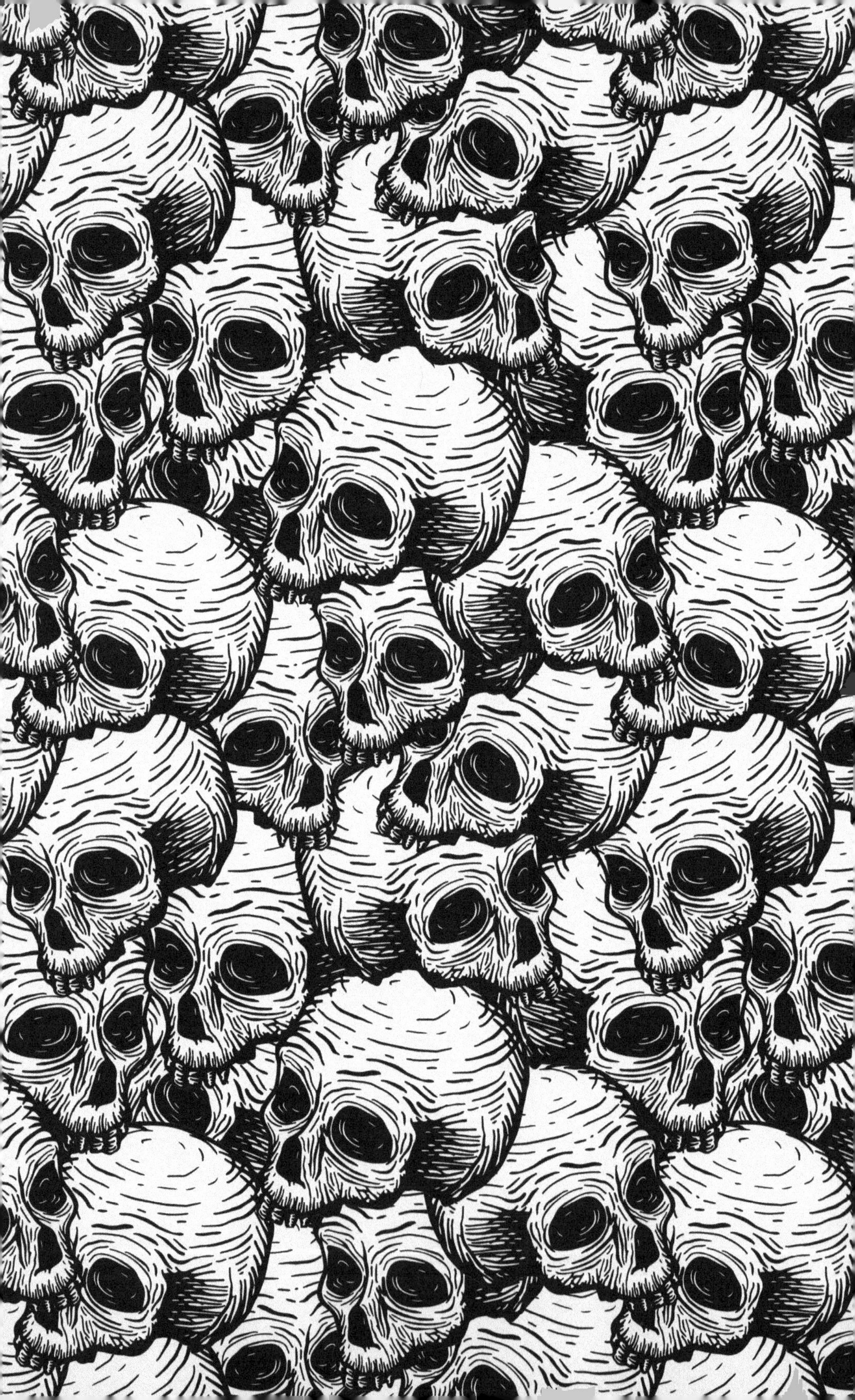

2 7

SECRETS & LIES

MY EARS RING painfully. For a long moment, all I can hear is that, mingled with the throb of my own pulse. Rath's tight, dreadful expression is still frozen in the backs of my eyes, and the first inhale I take goes on so long that my chest feels like it could float away without me.

The man's collapse to the ground is an afterthought, something I only notice when I realize the deafening pops have stopped. I'm still squeezing the trigger, but all it does is 'click' ineffectually.

I can't seem to get my finger to stop trying.

The sobbed breath that tears from my throat is the only thing that shocks me back to awareness, to Rath's black eyes gazing back at me, to Tristian's stunned face, to Killian's harsh profile as he glances over his shoulder.

Rath is the first to burst into motion, diving for the gun that's fallen on the slick pavement. I hold my breath as I watch, half expecting the attacker to jump back up. Isn't that how it goes in horror movies?

When Rath comes charging at me next, I shrink away, terror growing heavy in the pit of my stomach. Despite that, I can't seem to lower the gun from the exact spot where I was aiming. I know it's over—that the man must have half a dozen bullets buried in him—but my finger keeps clicking the trigger, over and over.

He pauses at my flinch, but not for long. His fingers are icy and wet when they slowly reach up to grab my wrist. The gentle touch is a shock against the taut tendon there, jumping with every useless pull of the trigger.

"Story," he says, breathless and coaxing as his other hand gently covers the gun. "Come on, baby. Let it go."

"I-I can't." The adrenaline has me in its clutches, and I'm not sure if I'm shivering or if the world is just trembling around me, but I think I'd have better luck lifting the car behind me than uncurling my fingers from this gun.

Rath wedges his fingertips beneath my palm, forcefully prying it away, and for a long moment, I watch the rain drip from the fringe of his dark hair, fat drops splashing on the leather of his jack.

Over the distant shriek of sirens, I ask, "Is he dead?" and I'm gasping as hard as Tristian. "Did I kill him?"

Rath rips the gun from my hand and shoves it into his jacket, hands coming up to frame my face. "You did a good thing," he demands, the rushed intensity of his voice snapping my gaze from the rumpled mass of black on the ground. "I need you to get in the car. Right now, Story."

He doesn't give me a chance to obey, running to Tristian and Killian and crouching there on the wet pavement. "We need to get out of here, like ten fucking minutes ago," he's saying, slinging Killian's arm over his neck. In the distance, the sirens are drawing nearer, piercing through the dusk.

But I find myself walking toward the body, feet heavy and splashing as I pass them, approaching it—because that's what it is now, an *it*—with an unnecessary caution. The chest isn't moving. The fingers are still. The water running down the pavement is dark with his blood.

I just have to know.

I have to know what Ted looks like.

I pause three times before finally pinching the mask between my fingers and yanking it up. When I do, I bury a scream into my palm, because one of my shots hit right in the cheek. It's gruesome and mortal and so fucking ugly.

Ugly Nick.

"Oh my god," I gasp, flinging myself away.

My brain isn't firing on cylinders, because my first thought is that Ted is Ugly Nick, even though that makes no sense. Then I remember what he said to them before, about this being a job.

I didn't kill Ted.

I just killed his fucking *lackey.*

"Story!" Rath is hissing, yanking me back by the hood of the sweater I'm wearing. "We have to fucking go!"

"But that's—!"

"I know!" he snaps, wrenching me away from it. "The cops are coming, we have to run!"

Run.

It's like everything snaps into place with that one word, and suddenly I'm hearing how close the sirens are and knowing that we won't be able to leave the scene in time. I whirl around, taking a hard run toward the car and Rath is right on my heels, our feet pounding the pavement. As soon as we approach the car, I notice Tristian is two steps ahead of me, tearing my temporary license plate from the back before diving into the back, where's he left Killian. Rath goes to take the driver's seat, but I lurch in front of him.

"Get in!" I demand, ignoring his protest when I close my door.

The second his ass is in the passenger seat, I'm mashing down on the gas, reversing out of the alley just as the blue and red lights appear on the other end of it.

"Go, go, go!" Rath chants, but it's unnecessary. I'm already peeling out, flying down 10th Avenue and away from the main drag. He looks into the backseat, twisted around to get a look at Killian. "How bad is it?" I'm too busy looking in the rearview and panicking at the swirl of blue lights to pay attention to what Tristian is doing back there, but whatever Rath sees drags a miserable sound out of him. "What do we do? Killer, what do we do?!"

"Drive." Killian's voice is strong—not the sound of someone who's on the precipice of dying—so I do exactly as he asks.

Evenly, I advise, "Hold on to something."

No one listens to me. I can tell, because the second I pull the e-brake and jerk the wheel, whipping the car through another alley, Killian *keens*. It'd be an awful sound coming from anyone, but coming from him, it's even more startling.

"Jesus fuck!" Tristian hoarsely barks, sounding both shocked and pained.

"Hold on," I snap, and this time, they all do. I jerk the wheel again, careening onto 14th Avenue and only narrowly missing a parked tractor trailer. The gear shift is solid in my hand, and I'm not good at much— I've always sucked at math and history—but *this* is like slipping back into a comfortable pair of long-lost jeans that miraculously still fit. For a moment, it's like I can feel Jack and his big sister in the back seat, anxious but still wearing big, toothy grins. It helps that the car handles like a dream, allowing me to weave between cars as I fly right through a stoplight.

Rath sucks in a sharp breath, palm coming up to brace against the roof of the car. "You're going to get us killed!"

Roughly, I switch gears. "Shut up." And since I know he's glaring, I add, "I'm not saying it to be a bitch, I just really need to focus." I punctuate this by zipping between two cars, the blue lights still in the distance behind me. They're not close enough that it feels futile, but they're not far enough for any comfort. There's gridlock up ahead, so I pull sharply to the left, into oncoming traffic.

"Look out!" Rath shouts, flinging a hand toward the dash, but I'm already swerving around the car barreling toward us. Another screeches to an abrupt stop, fishtailing for a few yards and just barely missing us. "What the *fuck*!"

Unbothered, I take us back over the median, sliding smoothly into the right lane. A couple more veers to the left, the right, and I've got wide open road ahead of me.

Rath is breathing hard, body coiled tight. "Should have taken my chances with the cops. Jesus Christ, Story. Where the hell did you learn to drive like that?"

Jerking my hand, I shift gears and stomp on the gas pedal. "Jack taught me," I answer, and if we weren't running from the cops with my stepbrother bleeding out in my backseat, I might even have it in me to grin at the memory.

"Jack," Rath parrots, his eyes boring into me. "Who's that? Some sugar daddy you were fucking?"

"What? No." I flick him a dark look before merging into the zip of highway traffic. "Jack was one of my roommates back in Colorado. He was a very skilled thief and also incredibly *gay*."

"What does a thief have to do with driving like that?" Rath asks, rifling through my glove compartment.

"He had this crew," I nervously babble, thinking of his sister and the other two guys who lived with us. I know how it sounds, but they were all the most innocuous people—easy to be around. They were very good at not asking questions. "They would case out different places. Nothing you'd think of, though. Auto repair stores, small restaurants, mom and pop stores. Places with shitty security and cash left in the drawer."

"You were the getaway driver?" Killian guesses, and I shiver at the sound of his voice.

I nod. "The first time was by mistake. I didn't even know what they were doing, but they came running out, yelling at me to go… and well, I went." The adrenaline is still in full force, causing me to babble. "I drove so fast I almost wrecked the car. When they asked me to do it again, I said yes, because…I don't know. It was money, and I was good at it, and it was kind of nice." Darkly, I add, "I'm not used to guys wanting something from me that doesn't include opening my legs for them." The tense and very pointed silence that follows doesn't last long.

Tristian's voice comes, panicked and gritty-sounding from the back seat. "We need to call Daniel."

"No!" Rath and I bark in a flawless unison. The quick, aborted look we share is full of nervous energy. "We can't call Daniel."

"Why the fuck not?!" Tristian's words are edged in a belligerent panic, and I wonder how bad it is.

"Because we just killed Ugly Nick," Rath answers, eyes hard. "And I'm not walking into South Side again until I know why."

"We have a fucking bullet wound here, Rath!"

He whirls around, snapping, "And we might have more if we go back there!"

"Goddamn it." It's growled so low that it sputters off into a wracking cough. It hurts just hearing Tristian speak in that gravelly rasp. "So what do we do?"

It's Killian who answers. "Find a place to hunker down for a minute. Call Ray. Buy us some time."

"Time for what?" Tristian asks. When no one answers, he heaves this big, grainy exhale and shoves himself between the front seats. "Okay," he says, pointing out the windshield. His hand is bloody. "Take the exit up here and go west. The faster, the better."

I don't ask where we're going. Wherever it is will be the place I finally come clean about Ted.

About everything.

THE CABIN IS tucked away in the pitch-black woods, only illuminated by the headlights of the Charger. Rath and Tristian squeeze out of the backseat, hurrying to help Killian out of the car.

"Seven six two five," Tristian barks, nodding at the cabin. Killian can stand, but he needs help and his enormous frame weighs heavily on his friend. "The lockbox on the door. That's the code."

I run up and punch in the numbers, getting a red light the first try. My hands are shaking and I can smell the sulphur on them, because I shot a man. I killed him.

I'm a killer.

I get the code right on the second try and the lock unlatches, allowing me to open the solid wood door and swing it wide enough for the guys to get Killian in. I instantly spot the long plank wood table in the middle of the room and command, "Get him on the table." I look at Tristian. "Is there a first aid kit or something? Supplies?"

"Hall closet. Tool kit on the floor," he grunts, jaw clenching as he and Rath leverage Killian's massive weight on the edge of the table.

I dart to the hallway, noting how small the cabin is. The Mercer family is loaded, with homes all over the country. I've seen pictures on Tristian's social media of a beach house made almost entirely of glass, overlooking crystal blue water, and a mountaintop home that seems more like a lodge than a single-family dwelling. I've heard there's a penthouse in New York, an estate in Rome, but this…

It's a small, rustic cabin that smells musty and has furniture half a century old.

One thing is for certain; no one will suspect a Mercer owned this place.

Anyone who witnessed us running from a murder wouldn't find us. Downside? There's also no one to help Killian if he's seriously injured.

And he doesn't look *not* seriously injured. He's two shades paler, and he's shivering, all of us still soaking wet from the rain.

Tristian darts around the room turning on lamps. "Welcome to my dad's bug-out cabin." He points distractedly around the room. "Kitchen, two bedrooms, a small bath off the hall. The windows are reinforced, with bars on the outside, there's no other egress but the one we just came through."

"Bug out?" Rath asks, lifting Killian's shirt to reveal the bullet wound. It's not like I'm expecting. It's not some enormous gaping wound that's spraying blood. It's just a small pierce, blood sluggishly draining from it. I know nothing about gut wounds, but it must be a good sign that this one is located right by his side.

Right?

"Yeah, this place has belonged to the Mercer men for over a hundred years. No one knows about this place, not even the wives." He stoops by the fire and starts to load in logs, and I realize for the first time that we're *all* shivering, but Killian could be in shock. "It's strictly a hideout. Doesn't exist on tax records. Fully stocked with food, booze, ammunition," he nods at the toolbox in my hands, "and medical supplies, just in case."

"Who is your father hiding from?" I ask, carrying the box to the table and unlatching the lid. Inside are medicines, medical instruments, gauze and bandages. A small pamphlet is taped to the top. I rip it off.

"Wives. The mob. The IRS. Zombies." He shoves rolled up newspaper under the logs. "Who the hell knows. Don't ask, don't tell. That's the Mercer philosophy." Tristian strikes a match, staring at the flickering flame for a beat before setting the newspaper on fire. He pokes a few small sticks into the fire and dusts his hands off on his thighs. "It'll heat up fast. Let's take a look."

We all stand over my stepbrother and look at the wound, and I respect Tristian for being driven and calm, but none of us knows what the fuck to do.

Killian raises his eyebrows. "Now might be a good time to call Ray!"

Rath jumps into action first, pulling his phone from his pocket. He pauses, glancing at Tristian. "What are the chances Mercer paranoia accounts for use of burner phones?"

Tristian grins.

A few minutes later, Rath has Ray on the phone. The only thing I know about the man is that he put that fucking tracker beneath my skin. It doesn't endear me to him at all, but I'm still relieved at Rath's pensive expression as he sits near Killian, giving Ray the rundown with a bowed head. Ray must give him a list of instructions, because eventually, Rath goes quiet, and then stands, inspecting the wound.

"It's still bleeding, but not—oh. Right." He nods at Tristian, gesturing to Killian. "We need to look at his back."

Killian rolls his eyes, muttering, "I'm right here," and twists to give Rath a view.

Rath's eyes go wide at what he sees. "Oh, fuck! Yes, it's—yeah, you're right, it went right through." To me, he snaps his fingers. "Gauze, gauze, fucktons of gauze!"

I rush to his side, getting a good look at the exit wound, and my pulse hammers as I push a wad of gauze into it. I get another handful of the cloth and do the same to the front, applying pressure on both sides, and that's when Killian meets my gaze.

"Thanks," he says, voice low and full of something I don't have the bravery to face.

He won't be thanking me later.

We spend the next thirty minutes trying to heat him up and stem the bleeding, Killian wincing as Rath goes through the motions of determining if anything vital was hit. The longer he speaks to and listens to Ray, the less panicked and hopeless he looks. His expression transforms into a stony sort of determination when he finally hangs up.

Rath shrugs out of his jacket, explaining, "We need to cut him out of these wet clothes, keep applying pressure, and then…" He pushes his wet hair away from his face. "We have to wait for the blood to coagulate and hope it just caught muscle." To me, he asks, "Any antibiotics in that thing?"

I rifle around, reading the various labels. "Yes!" I give a bottle a rattle, tossing it to Rath, who catches it deftly. "There're painkillers, too?"

Killian rolls his head to the side, gaze searching for Tristian as he shivers. "Did I hear you say something about booze before?" At Tristian's nod, Killian decides, "Load me the fuck up."

Before we do, Tristian runs around the house, dragging a mattress into the main room and placing it on the floor. He has it set up with clean bedding right in front of the fireplace, which is where they carefully drag Killian to.

When Tristian pulls out his knife to cut away his shirt, I flinch so hard that I knock over a lamp, gasping as I fumble to catch it. He only stalls for a moment, his blue eyes piercing mine just as surely as that bullet had punctured Killian.

Looking away, he cuts the shirt as Rath tears it away.

Eventually, Killian is naked and warming in front of the fire, tipping his head up to take a long swig of the vodka Tristian had found in the freezer. "We need to figure out what to do about Nick," he ultimately says.

Rath shoves his fingers into his hair, giving it a nervous tug. "I can't believe he tried to fucking rob us."

"That's not like him," Tristian agrees, eyes wild but pensive. "Daniel will understand, won't he? He'll get that we were just defending ourselves. It's not like he was in on it. Killer's his own son, for fuck's sake."

Rath lifts his shirt over his head and begins pacing. "We need to make sure he was doing this alone. Just because Daniel didn't orchestrate it doesn't mean someone else didn't. Has Ugly Nick ever struck you as the self-driven type?"

"He wasn't." My voice emerges, small but certain, and I struggle not to shrink against the weight of their gazes swinging to mine. "He wasn't working alone."

Killian's eyes are already glazed, but they still look sharp and alert when they narrow. "What we're you even doing there, Story?"

Swallowing, I perch on the table they'd just lifted Killian from, hugging my middle against the chill of my wet clothes. "There's something I need to tell you."

Rath's eyes are a blazing inferno and he's standing stiffly, fists curling, like he already knows what I'm going to say. "If you're about to tell us you had something to do with this, you'd better walk out that fucking door and run for your goddamn life."

My voice gets lodged somewhere in my throat, because I want to tell them I wasn't involved—not intentionally—but I'm not sure if it'd be true.

Tristian's voice comes, quiet and thoughtful. "No," he says, head shaking. "She fucked us over. She stabbed us in the back. But this isn't her style. Right?" He says the last part to me and I almost have to laugh.

Oh, if he only knew how much this *was* my style.

Running away. Making other people do my dirty work for me. Being ultimately unable to follow through. Realizing that I've messed everything up.

It's signature Story Austin.

Shoulders curling in on myself, I begin.

"I ran away from boarding school because someone was stalking me." I look them all in the eye, bracing myself for the worst. "He calls himself Ted."

TEN MINUTES LATER, Killian only looks half lucid, but Rath and Tristian look fully, terrifyingly alert.

"That's why you really left," Tristian guesses, looking away to take a pull out of the bottle of vodka. "It wasn't about us."

"It *was* about you," I argue. But after a moment of silence, I'm forced to concede, "Not just about you, though. And it wasn't about Ted, either." I rub my forehead, wondering if this is something I even need to go into.

Fuck it.

Might as well.

"I became a sugar baby *because* I wanted to run away. I needed the money, and it was…" I give a heavy shrug, unable to even be embarrassed. "It was what I knew. When my mom needed money, that's what she did. I was young and stupid, and all these old perverts were champing at the bit to throw money at me just for showing a little skin. It was quick and easy, and it was going to help me get away from Daniel."

Rath's head snaps back in surprise. "Why were you trying to get away from Daniel? The only person more loaded than him in this town is Tristian's dad."

"I didn't care about that!" I insist, and it's true. "My mom always wanted the nice life. The lavish life. The life with nice houses and fancy cars and elegant parties. I just wanted to be *safe*. And Daniel?" I shake my head, saying in no uncertain terms. "He wasn't safe. Not for me."

Killian turns to look at me, and even through the painkillers and booze, his eyes are still brash and livid. "What are you talking about?"

"You know what I'm talking about!" I burst, lurching to my feet. "You saw it with your own two eyes, Killian! Daniel…he'd get tipsy and close me up in his office, and go on and on about me being so pure and sexy. He'd—" I chew the next words out with a sneer, "He'd *touch* me. He'd make me sit in his lap and then put his hands up my shirt. He'd tell me I had to keep myself chaste, and then he'd talk about how well I was developing. It was disgusting!" Pulling in a long breath, I add, "I knew every day I stayed in that house was one day closer to him following through. And I refused to do that. I refused to *be* that."

My bark of laughter is a dark, brittle thing. "I spent years around my mom and her Johns, but no one ever did anything like that to me. Not until she married him. So I wanted to get away, before anyone could…" I make sure Tristian is looking me in the eye when I say, "But then there was you. You really just bulldozed over all those hopes, didn't you?"

He clenches his jaw, looking away. "I already told you about that."

"You apologized," I acknowledge, ignoring Rath's confused glances between us. "But it didn't take it away, Tristian. What happened that night… it changed me. So I shut down all my sugar baby accounts and begged Daniel for the money to leave. Can you imagine what that was like? Begging the man who's had his hands on you—a child—for money to go away?"

Killian's eyes are on me, unblinking. "What did he make you do?" It's a question that makes a shiver roll up my spine, because I can hear the revulsion and fury in his voice, and for once—Jesus Christ, for *once*—it's in defense of *me*.

"Nothing," I assure, sniffling against the chill. "My mom was there the whole time. I guess he didn't have it in him to make a proposition." Weirdly, he seemed agreeable to the prospect of boarding school. It hadn't really taken much in the way of persuading him.

"Can we go back to this Ted fucker?" Rath asks, spreading his arms. "So what, he followed you around the country, apparently murdered your gay roommate, and you just decided…'*hey, might as well go see those three guys who done me wrong and hope he fucking kills them*'?" He pushes a fingertip into his temple. "Are you fucking crazy?!"

"That's not how it happened," I say, but it's only half true. I shift uncomfortably under their accusing stares. "Because there was a chance the three of you could beat him, too. And I thought…I don't know…"

It's Killian who finishes for me. "You thought at least one would get taken out."

I guess it sounds pretty bad when it's said like that. "I felt safer with you," is my reply, and that at least isn't a lie. "You hurt me, but I knew—I *thought* I could handle the three of you. I thought I could be your Lady, and you'd protect me."

Rath's tongue swipes out, running absently at his piercings. "You thought?"

With a heavy nod, I confess, "There came a point where I was just…so fucking mad at all of you. So tired of the things you did to me. I was impatient, and I acted impulsively by sending that picture—"

"You think!" Rath thrusts a hand at Killian, to the wound in his stomach. "Fucking hell, Story! You set this guy on us without even saying anything. How the *fuck* were we supposed to protect you from something we never knew existed?!"

"Stop," Killian says, rubbing the dampness from his hair. "She couldn't go through with it. Could you?" Biting nervously on my lip, I give him a nod. He nods back. "You don't want to see us dead."

It pains me to admit it. Maybe even more than all that stuff about Daniel, or Colorado, or Ted. "You've done a lot of really horrible things to me. You've hurt me, manipulated me, controlled me, pushed me to my knees time and time again. But I think…" I sink heavily onto the table, my eyes filling with unshed tears. "I see the bad in all of you, and it's so ugly. But there might be some good there, too. I don't know—there *might* be, right? Do I want to see it snuffed out?" When a tear falls, I swipe it away, looking at all the muddy tracks our shoes have made over the floor. "No. I don't want to see you dead. I want to see you *sorry*. I want to see those good parts of you and know they're the reason I keep coming back. I want to know I'm not broken—that I'm here because of…" I roll my watery eyes, rushing out, "Easters, and comfortable mornings, and car rides, and lunches. I need to know that, because otherwise?" Shaking my head, I decide, "Otherwise I'm nothing."

They don't realize this, but it's as much a revelation to me as it is to anyone else. The truth is, I'm tired of pain. Tired of feeling it, and tired of inflicting it. I just want to fucking *breathe*. I want to be a good person—a *whole* person—the kind of person who doesn't lay awake at night thinking about how to make other people suffer.

Even when those people maybe deserve to.

I think it starts with being better than them. Being stronger not because I can strike back, but because I choose to move forward. Being a survivor not because I step on someone's back, but because I take what's coming and handle it myself.

And I think it starts with saying this:

"I'm sorry." They don't deserve it—not for my own revenge, and not even for this. But it's not about them. Not really. It's about the way I've been feeling since leaving Colorado behind. It's about the black, roiling sickness that's infected my soul and the way it's been driving me around like a parasite to a host. "I'm sorry for not telling you about Ted. For using you to get back at him. For using him to get back at you. I'm just…I'm sorry."

It's about freedom.

"Don't." Killian reaches up to rub his fingers into his eyes, the gesture slow and lazy but still somehow full of agony. "None of this would have happened if I'd—" His hand falls and he looks away, jaw flexing with a swallow that sounds as pained as it looks. "I was such a fucking idiot. Thinking you wanted him. That he wasn't just taking anything he thought he could own. All those fucking things I did because I thought…" He doesn't need to say it. It hangs heavy in the air between all of us. Everything he's done, every injury he's inflicted because he thought the worst of me. He lays his hand over his wound, eyes pinched. "Tomorrow, we're going to work out what to tell my dad. We'll explain about Nick, try to get a line on this Ted motherfucker and show him what it means to come at us. Story's going to tell us everything she knows about this guy. Documents, emails, phone calls, texts—all of it." Sliding his heavy eyes to mine, he finishes, "And then you're going to leave." It isn't said ungently, but it still makes me pull in a long, steeling sniffle.

"I understand."

"No, you don't." Killian doesn't smile often, and though it's hard to consider the sad curve of his lips anywhere in the ballpark, that's what it is—an anemic, bitter-looking thing. "Tristian and I will give you money if you need it. I don't know what it'll look like for you to start a new life. Go to another school, if you want. Go back to Colorado to your band of thieves. Join the French Foreign Legion—I don't fucking care. But whatever you do, you won't belong to us while you're doing it."

Rath folds his arms, head bowed as he watches his feet. "We talked about it earlier. Before you found us, we were trying to figure out how to do it."

Tristian, his blue eyes boring into mine, elaborates, "How to let you go."

For a long moment, I'm speechless, unable to digest what they're saying. "Why?" I eventually choke out.

It's Killian who answers, the lines of his face worn and weary. "You don't want us, Story. You never did. You came here because you wanted someone standing between you and some sicko creep. I might not have known that at the time, but…I could feel it."

"Me, too," Rath says, looking first at me, and then at Tristian.

Tristian's head hangs heavy on his neck as he gazes into the crackling fire, lifting his palms to the warmth. "They say if you care about something, you should let it go." There's a long beat of charged silence, and then he finally lifts his eyes to mine. "For the record, that's the stupidest fucking thing I've ever heard. If you really cared about something, you'd put that shit behind lock and key and never let it out of your sight. I voted to make you stay." He takes a long swig of the vodka, throat jumping with his swallow. "But none of us really feel like scraping your corpse up off your bathroom floor, so I guess Killer has a point. You can't make someone want to be with you. Can't say I haven't tried." Bitterly, he notes, "Once or twice."

No one seems to have anything to add, and I'm too busy fighting back useless tears to bother thanking them—not that I should.

Rath heaves a hard breath. "This place got some dry clothes, or what?"

Tristian puts the bottle down, pushing to his feet. "Follow me." He doesn't look at me as they leave the room, and I get the sense that, buried in his insistence that he didn't want to let me go, was a very significant declaration.

I don't allow myself to see it.

Instead, I edge around Killian to approach the fire, desperate for a morsel of warmth as I crouch, shivering and coming down from the adrenaline high. As far as confessions go, that could have gone worse. But now I'm sitting here trembling in front of the fire and remembering that I killed someone. It doesn't matter that he was a bad guy intent on killing other people for nothing but money. I took a life out of this world. There was a time the thought might have empowered me.

Instead, I just feel cold.

Something tickles my hip and I almost jump, except a glance reveals it's just Killian's knuckle, arm splayed out at his side to reach me. When I look over my shoulder, though, he's staring into the fire, eyelids heavy.

"Remember that time I made you a sandwich?" he asks, sweeping his knuckle back and forth.

I take a moment to decipher what he's talking about. But then this is how Killian works. He takes the best part of an otherwise shitty memory and uses it to define the moment. *Easter*. A truly terrible day, despite the night we spent in his room. *The sandwich*. The time he fed me after a particularly brutal mid-sleep fuck.

"Yeah," I answer, remembering the peanut butter and jelly. The glass of milk. Eating it in his bed as he clicked around on his computer. The way I was with him after, making myself soft and cuddly and oh so grateful.

There's a long stretch where he says nothing else and I find my attention returning to the flames, even though I feel his knuckle against me like a brand.

His voice is heavy and slurred when he suggests, "We could do that again."

I give the fire three fast blinks, because he can't be talking about the sex. He can barely sit up without looking like he's in some serious pain. Chances are he isn't asking to make me a sandwich, either. Since there isn't any come dripping down my thighs for him to wash away, I can only assume he's talking about the other thing.

"You mean…?" I chance a look over my shoulder, catching the way he's worrying his lip between his teeth. "Now?"

His knuckle slides away with his gaze. "It's not an order."

Because they aren't giving those to me anymore. They're giving me away, letting me go. And tonight is the last night Killian Payne will ever watch me sleep again. Unbidden, I think of the words he spoke a few nights ago, too drugged up to realize he was telling me he loved me. I'm thinking of how I told him such a thing was impossible. Killian can't possibly know how to love anything.

But he believes he does.

I know what I'm going to do, but it still takes me a long moment in front of the fire to work up the nerve. In the end, it's laughably easy. I take off my shoes first, setting them close to dry. Then, I peel off my wet socks. I shrug out of the hoodie I'd stolen from Rath's closet and then tug my damp shirt over my head. I stand up to shimmy my pants down my legs, leaving my panties on, but nothing else. It's such an odd feeling now, undressing in front of these men. There was a time the thought would have made me shudder and curl in on myself. But nothing of my body hasn't been seen, tested, or explored by them. I turn to my stepbrother without shame, and the way he's looking at me—soft and surprised—makes an invisible fist clench around my insides.

When his eyes fall to the bandages on my chest, all of that softness falls away.

He's warm when I press my body into his side, carefully resting my cheek on the bold, vivid Griffon inked into his shoulder.

"Griffons guard treasures…and they mate for life."

He makes room for me, swinging his arm wide, and when it slowly comes around my shoulders to touch my bare side, I allow myself a moment of unforgivable self-indulgence. I imagine that we're lovers—the kind who do things like this. Curl up with one another against the cold. Fingertips skating over skin. Warm breath puffed into my hair. I imagine those words he said were true. That he loves me. That he'd kill for me.

I allow myself to pretend.

Apparently, Killian wants to do the same. "What would you have done that night?" he asks, wide palm sweeping along my back. "If I'd kissed you."

I know without asking that he's talking about that night in his room years ago, but it's hard to call up the memory of that girl. "I don't know," I answer honestly, unable to imagine it. Would he have been sweet and gentle, like he's being now? Or would he have forced his way into my mouth, greedy and impatient?

"Would it have been like…with my dad?" His voice is a dull rumble beneath my ear. "Would you have wanted to run?"

This, at least, I can answer with certainty. "No."

His chest dips with a deep exhale, and when his hand leaves my skin, it returns with the edge of the blanket Tristian had brought, lazily covering me with it. "Guess it doesn't matter now."

I listen to the sounds his lungs make—the beating of his twisted heart—and a lot of things have gone unspoken tonight, but none so much as this.

There's no going back.

Some wounds can never be mended.

I WAKE UP before I even realize I've fallen asleep. The fire is still burning and neither me nor Killian have moved an inch, his hand still heavy on my shoulder. I can feel from the deep, even rhythm of his breaths—from the subtle snore beneath my ear—that he's fallen asleep, too.

Tristian is asleep beside him.

I've never seen Tristian truly unkempt and out of sorts before. The closest he ever gets is basketball games and fucking, and even then, his hair remains supernaturally well kept. Now it's flat and limp, only half-dried from the rain and accompanying a shirtless chest and a pair of boxers that look a size too small. He has his arm thrown over his eyes, mouth parted with his measured breaths, and he's clearly brought every blanket the Mercers have ever owned and piled them here on top of us.

I take a second to swim my way out of them, sitting up to peer around the room. I find Rath across the distance in the kitchen. He's sitting on the counter, kicking his feet, fingers clutching his hair in two tight fists. I watch him for a long moment, awkward and unsure.

Killian barely stirs when I extricate myself from his side, careful not to jostle him as I wrap a blanket around my shoulders. Rath must be lost in thought, because when I approach, he jerks in surprise.

"Shit," he breathes.

"We should get some sleep." It goes without saying that there's a lot to do tomorrow. Calls to make. Questions to ask. Ostensibly an appointment with an actual medical professional—Ray, at the very least.

Rath looks so far from being able to sleep that he's practically vibrating as he jumps off the counter. "Then go back to your cuddle pile," he sneers, wrenching open a drawer. "I'm on a mission to find one goddamn cigarette, and if I can't, then I'm stealing your car and driving to the nearest store."

I suppose he's not feeling as forgiving as Killian.

Sighing, I turn and walk back to the mattress. It's a big mattress, but not huge. Maybe a queen. Tristian's fingers twitch when I edge around him to reach for my discarded clothes. But when I shove my hand into the pocket of the hoodie, I'm grateful to find that accidentally pilfered, crumpled pack of cigarettes is still there.

The look on Rath's face when I return with them is probably the closest to forgiveness I'm going to get. "How the hell?"

Shrugging, I pull my arm back into the blanket. "Took them when I stole your gun."

He pauses at this, brows furrowing as he opens the box of cigarettes. Then he snorts. "These aren't cigarettes," he says, pulling one from the pack. "They're blunts."

"Oh." My face falls, although I don't know why. Inexplicably, I really wanted to save the day. "Sorry."

He gives me a confused but distracted look, pulling a box of matches from the drawer. "For what? These are like five times better than a cigarette." Popping the end of the blunt into his mouth, he strikes the match and lights it. The ember glows red-hot as he sucks in a deep inhale and holds it in his lungs. "Fuck *me*," he exhales, shoulders falling as the smoke streams from his mouth. He gives the blunt a lingering look. "Ignoring the fact that we're only here because you killed a guy, you're a goddamn angel, Sweet Cherry."

The words are like a knife to my chest.

And I should know.

"Did he…" My voice cracks and I clear my throat, wondering. "Did he have a family?"

Rath slides back onto the counter, puffing at the blunt. "Ugly Nick? Not fucking likely." When he sees my relieved reaction, he pauses, taking a slow hit of the blunt before extending over the distance between us. He gives it a little inviting bob and I hesitantly take it. "Don't beat yourself up over that shit. One less Nick isn't going to hurt anything. It was getting confusing anyway."

The weed is smooth and harsh all at once, and my cheeks flush when I cough. "That doesn't make me feel any better," I say, mouth slanted unhappily.

Rath takes back the blunt, and he's not like Tristian. Rath wears the half-drowned rat look very well, hair falling into his dark eyes as they hold mine. "Okay, how about this? You see those guys over there?" He uses the blunt to point to the mattress. "They'd kill for you. No questions asked. Full stop." Rath shakes his head, some of that manic energy disappearing from the line of his back. "Think what you want about us, Story. Think we're twisted and cruel and heartless and controlling and *empty*. Maybe you're right. But that's real shit. How many people can say someone would kill for them?" He lazily flicks the ashes into the sink. "Maybe it's less that you killed a man, and more like you saved three."

I nod, ducking my chin into the blanket. "Maybe."

He tips his head back against a cabinet, looking down his nose at me. "Did you get what you needed, Sour Cherry? Setting us up, getting your revenge?"

Since I'm too weary for the pretense he's offering me, I open the blanket, asking, "Did you?"

The blunt halts halfway to his lips, and then his hand slowly falls. It takes everything in me not to take a step back when he slides off the counter and steps up to me, those black eyes locked on my chest.

When he reaches up to peel away the bandage, I let him.

Something dark and shuttered passes over his face at the sight of their initials. I haven't looked at them yet and I don't bother to now. I avert my eyes to the window above the sink, wondering how many hours are left with them.

His fingertip is gentle as it brushes the skin. "I know what you think," he says, the words nothing but a gossamer breath. "You found out about the game and figured it was fake. And you're right." Even knowing it's true doesn't stop the way my heart twists at the easy admission. When he touches my chin, forcing my gaze to his, I have to set my jaw to stop it from wobbling. "*Partly*," he amends, pinning me beneath his demon eyes. "The tutoring, the blow jobs… it's true, they were fake. I was just having some fun. I liked having you there, toying with you, knowing you'd go down to your room and touch yourself because of it." He slides his eyes to my mouth, looking unapologetic and yet strangely sad. "But there were some things that were real. I never used those mornings we were together. You can check the spreadsheet yourself if you don't believe me."

I'm not sure I can afford to do that.

It's hitting me now that leaving these men will be hard enough without wondering whether those gentle touches and sweet kisses were perhaps genuine. I know myself well enough to understand the things I'd cling to.

"I regret being caught," he says, eyes unabashed. "If you'd never found out about the game, then maybe you could have trusted me. And god knows I regret pissing you off, because you're apparently really good at being a scheming bitch." The crooked line of his mouth softens the words, even if what he says next shatters the levity. "But this?" His eyes fall to the skin between my breasts, hands coming up to hold the blanket away. He releases a long sigh as he inspects it. "It's the closest I'll ever get to being a part of you. To being inside of you. I want to say I regret it, but I'd be lying."

He doesn't sound happy about it. Not victorious or spiteful. There isn't a hint of triumph in the way his eyebrows go low, as if maybe he's disappointed in himself. For admitting the weakness? For having one at all?

He's perfectly still when I strain up on my toes to push our mouths together. I don't mean it to start anything. It's just that the scraping disquiet inside my chest is desperate for one last taste.

One last taste of the easy mornings.

What I get is vodka and weed, Rath's tongue delving inside the crease of my lips. His hands pushing the blanket from my shoulder. Grazing down my bare sides and landing on my hips. Dragging my body against his, curling his back to surge into me.

When he lifts me to the counter, my blood goes liquid hot at the feel of him between my thighs. I can feel his growing hardness, not just because of the bulge in his pants, but in the way he kisses me. Long, lingering plunges into my mouth, only to retreat and brush his wet lips against mine. It's a tease, but it's also a test.

"You can," I breathe, pressing my heel into the back of his thigh. "You can fuck me." He's always most excited when I beg for it. "Please?"

He cups my jaw then, and the kiss becomes searing. I spread my legs for him, invite him in, twist my fists into the sweater he's wearing and haul him closer. For a moment, things are rough—his fingers tangling into my hair, digging into the soft flesh of my thigh—but then he's shuddering against me and sliding away.

He drags a wrist over his mouth, averting his eyes. "It's going to be hard enough without knowing what I'm missing."

I take the blanket when he extends it to me, sliding from the counter to wrap it back around my shoulders. That twisting disquiet in my chest just worsens at the rejection, and I don't know how much of it is showing in my expression until it's reflected back at me in his.

His shoulders sink. "Goddamn, girl." He jerks me roughly into his chest, folding me into his long arms. I take too long to realize it's a hug. To bring my arms around his waist. To tuck him into the cocoon of the blanket where it's nothing but warmth and mornings and plans that he'll never get to use.

He cups the back of my head in a wide palm, stroking my hair as he quietly speaks. "I'm about to give you some hard truth, Story. You might not want to be part of us, but deep down, that's exactly what you are. Whatever gives that instinct to kill for someone? It's not something you can shake off. If it were, then Killer would have done it years ago." I can hear him swallow beneath my ear, voice dropping to a whisper, soft like a secret. "And I'd be doing it right now."

It's the best thing any of them could have given me—this proof that there may be hurt and misery here, but there's tenderness too. There's something good. Something worth wanting, even if it's too agonizing to cling to it.

"Lay with us?" I ask, voice tight with things I refuse to say. Apologies, promises, and yes. Regrets.

He brushes a kiss into my hair. "No cuddling."

"Never."

I go back to the mattress and carefully reclaim my spot at Killian's side. He hasn't moved since I left and he doesn't move now, the sounds of Rath undressing mingling with the crackling of the fire. Killian's shoulder is still warm beneath my cheek, and I listen to the steady beat of his heart as I wait, refusing to feel conflicted about the gratitude I feel for hearing it—for knowing that he's alive.

The mattress dips when Rath slips beneath the blanket and I already know what to expect. I say nothing when he slots up against my back, all that bare skin meeting mine as he drapes an arm around me.

Nothing but this.

"Goodnight, Dimitri."

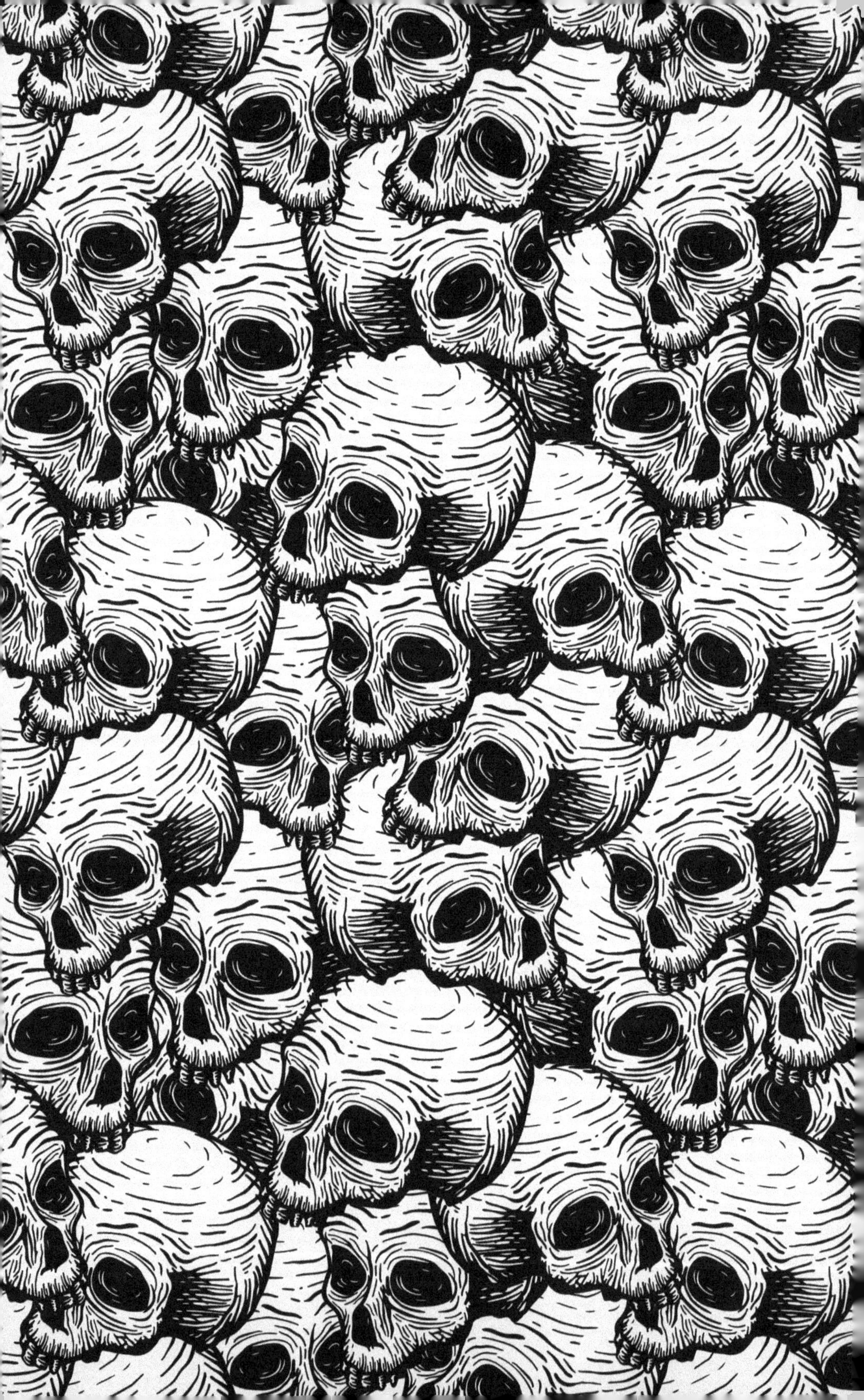

2 8

R E G R E T

OLD HABITS DIE hard.

It turns out that even a night filled with murder, gunshot wounds, a high-speed getaway, home-cooked triage, and loaded confessions aren't enough to make me sleep past five in the morning. I wake up before the sun does, the fire in front of us slowly dying. Killian is still on his back, forehead creased with a frown even in sleep. Story is resting against his shoulder, her hand limp and curled on the center of his chest. Rath is pressed up against her back, his arm tucked around her waist.

Fucking idiots, telling her to leave. To start a new life. A life without the three of us.

I get a pot of coffee started for them—tea for myself—and do my pushups over by the couch. The mornings are always my favorite time of the day. Getting lost in the routine, making plans inside my head, preparing for whatever bullshit is spread out in front of me for the day.

I'm working toward my three hundredth pushup when Story begins stirring. I watch, arms pushing me up and bringing me down, as she turns into Rath, sleepily nuzzling her head in beneath his chin. I can tell when everything comes back to her, because she lets out this long sigh and begins the arduous process of extricating herself from them.

Sitting up, she gives her arm a little shake—must have fallen asleep—before turning to look for me. Her brow furls when she sees my part of the mattress is empty, gaze swinging around the room.

When her eyes land on mine, something in her shoulders eases.

"Morning," I huff out, almost done. "Coffee's in the kitchen."

Usually, I'd try to put her off drinking it, but now I'm not sure if that's my place anymore. Are we still her Lords? If we are, then for how much longer?

Once again, I'm reminded that this whole 'letting her go' plan is bullshit.

She carefully rises from the mattress, bringing a blanket with her. It drags along the floor as she shuffles to the kitchen, following the scent of the brewing coffee. We can't wait much longer to get Killian somewhere, but I don't have it in me to wake them up just yet.

Two ninety eight.

Two ninety nine.

Three hundred.

I hop up, feeling hot and restless, like my skin's too tight. This cabin is far from being my favorite place, even at the best of times. I want a hot shower and something organic to eat.

Story walks back into the main room with a mug in each hand, looking rumpled, face drawn. "I brought your tea," she says, going to set it on the table. She freezes when she remembers what happened on it. The enormous blood stain probably helps remind her. "Uh, I'll just…"

I swoop in and take it from her, perching on the edge of the couch. "Thanks."

She gives a tight-lipped nod, taking a seat. "His pulse is good, and he's warm, but not too warm." Her eyes are fixed to Killian as she says this, raising her mug for a slow sip of the coffee. "How long do you think?"

"Until we call Daniel?" I run my fingers through my hair, struggling through an exhaustion that both makes sense and doesn't. "I don't know. A few hours, maybe."

She hums and her blanket slips a little. Just enough that I catch the edge of a scab.

I put my mug onto the table, not caring about the blood. Lacing my fingers together, I look at my knuckles and gently command, "Let me see."

There's a moment of still silence, and then, "See what?"

I slide her a dark look. "You know what."

Her eyes go shuttered and blank, but with one shrug of her shoulders, she lets the blanket fall away, exposing her bare chest to me. I can really only look at it from the corner of my vision at first, having to take it in incrementally, facing this ugly thing I've helped inflict on her in stages.

Full-on, it makes my stomach turn.

It's scabbed and red around the edges—Irritated. But someone's seen to it. The skin is a little oily, like it's had ointment applied at some point. Heaving a breath, I look away, my eyes landing on the first aid kit at my feet.

I bend over and pop it open. "Come here."

There's ointment inside the kit. Bandages. Antiseptic. I start with a sterile wipe, tearing the paper-lined foil and plucking it out. It still takes a moment to face it again, mouth twisting sourly when I finally do.

Story's turned her body to me, one of her legs curled beneath her. But she won't meet my gaze.

I adjust, scooting closer as I inspect the letters.

K

T

R

She flinches when the wipe touches her skin, which makes me flinch, too.

"Does it…hurt?" I'm pretty sure that's an idiotic question. Nothing about being mutilated like this is painless. But she just shakes her head, remaining still as I gently run the cotton down the marred skin.

"Is it…" She works her jaw, eyes fixed to the floor. "Does it look…bad?"

It sure as fuck doesn't look *good*.

I consider the question before answering, wondering why she can't just take a peek herself. Then it hits me. "You haven't seen it yet." She shakes her head and something inside of me thrashes around, banging painfully against my ribcage. I think it might be whatever sorry excuse is standing in for a soul. I clear my throat, dabbing around the 'T'. "It's scabbed over well, but it's a little irritated. Probably from sleeping with—" My words cut off, because I can't.

I can't pretend this is okay.

"Story."

She presses her lips together, looking everywhere but at me. "I know. You don't believe in regrets or forgiveness. You were in a bad place. I pushed you too far. You're sorry." She finally looks at me then, and even though she has every right to, she doesn't even look bitter when she says, "I remember."

Well, fuck.

Why not just put a bullet in my gut, too?

For a while, I think there's nothing I can say to that. It's an accurate summary of the apology I gave her for that first night, years ago. I'd said all of that. I'd bought her flowers. Clothes. Baked goods. When she was upset about the tracker, I'd bought her a car.

What do you buy someone after carving your initials into their flesh, jacking off onto their cheek, and then fucking them with the hilt of a knife and leaving them on the floor in a puddle of come, blood, and their own tears?

Hallmark doesn't exactly make a fucking card for that.

Since it already feels like she's buried a blade in my chest, I might as well give it a nice twist. "You didn't send those messages about the twins, did you?"

Just as I expected, her brow pulls together, head shaking. "What did they say?"

It came to me last night, right after she told us about this Ted fucker.

Story wouldn't involve my sisters in her shit. It's just that all the videos went missing, and she knows—she fucking knows how badly I never want my sisters to know the truth about me. It would have been the perfect revenge.

But she's too good for that.

She'll hurt us because we deserve it, but she'd never put our beef on two innocent kids. I feel like a goddamn fool for not realizing that sooner.

"Nothing." I clean around the cuts and lie, "Probably just some internet troll."

Obviously, it was Ted.

And if Story knew she'd put them in danger by setting this guy loose on me, she'd never forgive herself.

"But it means I did this for nothing," I add, feeling my jaw go tight. I make a promise to myself then, that whoever this guy is, this crime is partly on him—and he's going to fucking pay for it. "So yes, I owe you an apology."

She looks away, expressionless. "I knew what I was getting into. I knew what might happen if you—"

"No." My voice is hard and firm, and when I wrench her chin forward, forcing her eyes to mine, I make sure she understands. "I made a promise to take care of you, and I bailed at the first sign of doubt without asking any questions." Reaching for the ointment, I add, "I don't know how Killer and Rath feel about it, but it makes me fucking sick."

It's not a lie. The thought of my initials being carved into her skin as proof of ownership makes me want to scoop her up and take her back to that mattress to flex some of it. But the fact it was done in anger, to inflict pain as a goddamn *punishment*, makes me physically ill.

"You're wrong," is what I say, gently applying the ointment. "I do regret it."

I can feel her eyes on me as I work, wishing I could mend this skin and start over. But I can't. The damage, as always, is done.

"You're a good brother," she says.

"Yeah." I give a quiet scoff. "I'm just not good at being anything else."

"You could be." When I raise my eyes to hers, she's wearing a sad expression. "I mean, this is clearly despite all evidence otherwise. But I think you could be. When you care about something…" Her teeth tug at her lip as she thinks her words over. "When you *let* yourself care about something—really care about it—then I bet you could be amazing." That sadness coalesces into a small, somber smile. "I just don't think it could be with me."

"You don't know that," I argue, even though I know she's right.

There's no coming back from what I've done to her.

As if to drive the nail in the coffin, she takes a steeling breath and lowers her eyes, taking in the letters scabbed in her own blood. She reaches up to run a fingertip over them, expression turning contemplative.

"R," she breathes, touching Rath's initial.

Because she looks confused by the choice, I say, "It had to be Rath. You know why, don't you?" When she just gives me a curious look, I explain, "Because Dimitri never would have done that to you."

He never talks about it, but he doesn't need to. He couldn't stomach seeing the 'D' on her chest—not carved in deep and angry like that.

At her silence, I go on, "He didn't use to be like that. Dividing himself up into two versions of himself. The second you started calling him Dimitri…." I give her a look. "Or maybe more accurately, the second you took it back—that's how he began seeing himself."

"Oh," she breathes, glancing over at the man in question.

I don't tell her this, but I tried it, too. Unfortunately, it doesn't work for me. I've never been good at lying to myself like the other two. I can't pretend I didn't do this. I can't act like I was just in a bad place and forgot to give a shit.

Maybe I'm just not that great a person.

Sighing, I pull the blanket back up around her shoulders. "We need to talk about Ted."

She picks up her coffee. "What's there to say?"

"Anything," I press, sliding the first aid kit away. "Everything you know about him."

Looking into her steaming mug, she gives a heavy nod, beginning, "He was nice at first."

Over the next few minutes, she spills it all. How he'd tell her she had a nice smile. How he'd ask about her being a virgin, subtly pressuring her for a meeting here and there, but never seeming put off when she refused. Then, the letters at boarding school. The escalation. The photos he sent to her in Colorado—guys with their eyes crossed out, 'whore' scribbled on the back. She tells me about Jack and his gentle disposition. About the way he looked the last time she saw him, lifeless and dead-eyed.

Then she tells me about the photo she sent after Killian fucked her for the first time.

"I just knew it'd get a rise out of him." She says this without apology or shame, and I don't blame her. "He never wanted anyone else to have me."

We're silent for a long while as I take it all in, making plans to hunt down who owns this email account. Daniel has resources, and failing that, few options are closed to a Mercer.

"It's kind of weird," I muse, taking a sip from my tea. "First Daniel, then Ted, then Killer."

She gives me a confused look. "What do you mean?"

I shrug. "Just all these guys obsessed with your virginity. I mean," I shift, gesturing to the mattress. "With Killer, it makes sense. The way he grew up— the kind of women he grew up *around*—I get that it'd be a big feature for him. But the others?" Shaking my head, I joke, "Just didn't realize it was that big of a deal to so many people."

"Yeah," she says slowly, eyes roaming to Killian. "Daniel and Ted. Weird."

She strangely quiet after that, no longer bothering with her coffee. There are a lot of things I still need to say, but it doesn't feel like I deserve to. I want to tell her to stay. To keep being our Lady. To trust us to keep her safe this time.

From Ted.

From ourselves.

Instead, I rise from the couch and run a hand through my hair. "I'm going to get cleaned up and see if Killer's ready to call his dad."

She nods, eyes following me as I walk to the bathroom.

When I come out ten minutes later, she's gone.

So is the car.

29

PARADOX

THE SUN HAS overtaken the horizon by the time I get to the looming office building overlooking South Side. It's early enough that the city has barely come to life, but the air is buzzing with the promise of a new day, the damp chill receding with the fresh rays of sun. From the front steps of Payne Holdings, Inc., it's easy to imagine last night never happened. I never killed a man in a dark, wet alley. I never ran from the police as my stepbrother bled out into the back of my car. I never opened myself up for them, showed my Lords just what kind of Lady they've been living with these last weeks. It's almost as if I could go back to their brownstone and find them all at the dining room table, doling out orders for the day.

Instead, I'm here.

With a deep breath, I reach out for the handle and give it a pull. It's not locked. I stride through the doors, past the empty security desk and chairs, and mash the button on the elevator. The last time I was here with Dimitri, and I well remember him pressing the button for the top floor. That's what I do now, and it's surprising.

I'm not nervous in the least.

When the elevator dings, I step out into his immaculate lobby. The receptionist I met before, Vivenne, isn't in the lobby. I walk past her tidy desk on the way to my stepfather's office, catching a scent of her perfume. It's an oily, lingering scent that makes my nose itch. I wonder if my mother smells it on him when he gets home. On his suit. On his skin.

Does she turn a blind eye to it the way she did with me?

Daniel's door is cracked, and I pause outside, hearing his voice carry as he speaks on the phone.

"I know it's a mess. Dead bodies tend to leave one. I pay you to handle situations like this." His voice is strained with irritation, and from the ebb and flow of it, it sounds like he's pacing. "Chief, it's not my job to tell you how to deal with something like this. If you happen to 'lose' the bullet and any other evidence, I'm sure everyone will understand. Just," his voice tightens, "fix it."

I push the door open just as he rests the phone on the receiver. His shoulders tense and his eyes dart up, but whatever annoyance he had with the chief slips away into that signature Payne indifference.

"Story," he says, my name falling from his mouth like something that's disappointed him. "Things are a little hectic right now. Maybe you can come back—"

I cut him off, saying the words that I've been holding in for so long. "I know who you are."

It isn't until he's seated in the chair behind the desk that he raises an eyebrow, shrewdly asks, "Who exactly am I?"

He's going to make me say it. Once he does—once it's out in the open, veil lifted—the game is over. I doubt he'd want that. Personally, I'm done playing games.

"You're Ted."

Propping an elbow on the arm of the chair, he slowly swivels side-to-side, pinning me under his fierce gaze. "And you're my Sweet Cherry." My skin crawls hearing the name come from his mouth and it's only half due to the casual confirmation of all my fears and doubts. It's been years since anyone but the guys called me that.

God.

All this time, my own stepfather was stalking me.

"Well," he adds, rubbing two fingers over his mouth, "you *were*. Now you're just…" His eyes sweep over me dismissively, lip curling in distaste. "Used up trash. Just like every other woman. Can't say I didn't warn you."

He sounds bored and repulsed, and the bile I taste in the back of my throat is the only thing that stops me from responding.

Leaning back in his seat, he asks, "What are you doing here?" He raises a hand. "No, let me guess. You're here to ask for more money. Or maybe for my help transferring away from Forsyth. Perhaps you're looking to get away from my son and his friends, which wouldn't surprise me." His mouth curves into a mean smile. "I didn't think you'd last long with them. Good boys, but a bit on the rough side. No finesse, I think you'll agree."

Unable to hear him speak of them, I clench my teeth. "I want you to leave them alone."

"Leave them alone," he listlessly repeats.

"Obviously," I say in a steely voice, "you sent Ugly Nick after them last night. He shot Killian—almost killed him." The bile creeps up again, but it's a different sort. The memory of the gun in my hand, the scent of sulphur, Nick's limp body on the ground, the wound to his cheek…it all makes me want to heave. "And I know you did that because…because I provoked you, but—"

"What is this about Killian?" He jolts from his chair, face gone ashen. "What do you mean he's been shot?"

"Like you don't already know what Ugly Nick did!" I snap.

"Clearly, I do *not*!" he shouts back, swiping his smart phone from the desk and thumbing through it. "Why would Nick shoot Killian?" He seems to ask this more to his phone than to me, and there's a flash where I feel like I've gone mental.

"Because you sent him," I answer, voice dripping with disdain.

His eyes snap up to mine, sparking. "That's ridiculous. You think I want to kill my own son?"

"I—" But I find I can't answer, because I don't know. Maybe Daniel is just a brilliant actor, but the frantic way he's listening for Killian to answer his phone doesn't look fake.

"Where is he?" he asks, trying to call Killian's phone again. "How serious is it?"

I'm thrown off balance by his reaction, stammering out, "He's alive. It's… serious, but probably not fatal if they can get him to someone soon."

"Where is he?" Daniel asks, not looking happy about needing to repeat himself.

I shake my head, laughing darkly. "I'm not telling you where they are. You really expect me to believe you had nothing to do with this when you emailed me the location?"

"What location?" he asks, slamming his phone down. "The only time I've emailed you in the last two years was right after you sent me that disgusting picture."

I thrust an accusing finger at him. "And I remember what it said! *'I take my restitutions in flesh'.*"

An eerie quiet settles over the room, the only sound being the squeak of Daniel's leather shoes as he slowly circles the desk and stands before me. There's something dark brewing under Daniel's skin, something I've never witnessed before. A chill runs up my spine as I realize that I'm not in the presence of my stepfather. I'm standing before The King.

"I didn't send Ugly Nick to hurt my son. When I told you I'm taking my restitution in flesh, I didn't mean from him." He tilts his head, those menacing eyes cutting into me. "Do you realize how valuable those boys are to me? To my enterprise? To my legacy? Killian and I may have our differences, but he's my most prized asset—my *heir*. And *you*." He scoffs, sneering, "You had so much value before you spread those twiggy little legs for my son. Do you have any idea the kind of offers I had for you? The opportunities!"

I flinch back at his roar, almost stumbling over. "Offers?"

"Oh, yes." He bears down on me, driving me back into the wall. "You'd be surprised what you could get for a sweet little sixteen-year-old virgin— provided you can get her parents out of the picture and keep her…intact."

I stare at him in horror. "You wanted to *sell me*?"

He tilts his hand back and forth. "I like to think of it as more of an exchange of assets." He snorts, looking so much like his son that it jars me. "Killian thought I got you for him, you know. I love my son, but he does tend to exaggerate his importance. When you returned, I actually believed I had a second chance. You're older, but a twenty-year-old virgin is still a bit novel. Not that it matters anymore." Flicking at the worn hoodie I'm wearing, he chews out, "You're worthless to me now. A waste of four years providing for you, educating you, hunting you down over states and counties to keep tabs on you." He shakes his head, giving a barbed laugh. "You should have stayed in Colorado and saved everyone the trouble."

"Then why?" I gape at him, utterly lost. "Why did you kill Jack? Why would you send all those letters threatening me, and Ugly Nick—"

He gives me a long, narrow-eyed look. "I don't know who Jack is, but I didn't kill anyone—not on account of you, and certainly not my own legitimate flesh and blood. If that's your measure of your own importance, then it would seem my son has rubbed off on you." Holding my stare, he sleazily adds, "In more ways than one."

"I-I don't understand," I rush out. "*You're* Ted."

His eyes flash in exasperation. "Ted was a fake name I used for all of three months to ensure my investment wasn't letting dirty old men between her thighs. Ted doesn't exist! His account is long gone." He saunters over to the window, irritably musing, "Before your crude email a few weeks ago, I didn't even realize the address was still active."

My mind spins. If he didn't send Ugly Nick, then who did? Who sent me those texts? Once again, I feel off kilter, like there are pieces to the puzzle I'm missing. When I look at Daniel again, this doesn't seem to be one of his worries.

"So," he begins, demeanor shifting to business as usual. "Which of my wayward sons killed Nick? Was it Rath? You'd think someone with that much precision on a piano would have less of a twitchy trigger finger, but you'd be wrong."

I'm stunned that he can talk about it so cavalierly—as if a life hasn't been taken. As if we're not under attack by some mysterious entity he claims to know nothing about.

"It was me." The confession pours out of me lifelessly, quiet and unbidden.

"You." His face remains blank, gaze trained on the streets below. "And where am I to send Ray? Killian needs seen to, I assume."

"I-I can't say." Even if Daniel is telling the truth about not being behind the attack, I get the sense Tristian wouldn't forgive it. "He's going to be in contact soon. Today."

"Then we'll have to settle this among ourselves for now," he says, crossing his arms and turning to me. His eyes, the ones that match his son's, flicker with resolve. "I've got a dead body in the morgue with our figurative fingerprints all over it, bribes to pay, destruction of evidence, and the loss of a seasoned South Side foot soldier. This is, naturally, on top of boarding school, Forsyth tuition, and the considerable depreciation of the investment they were meant to be recouped with." He shakes his head, looking me up and down. "There are many people in my employ, and even more in my debt. But do you want to know what's interesting? No one has cost me nearly as much money as you have."

What I say next makes my stomach turn, but I can't think of any other way. "Maybe Tristian can—"

"I already told you." His shoulders go as tight as his voice. "I take my compensation in *flesh*."

Deflated and full of dread, I ask, "What does that mean?"

"You've been to The Velvet Hideaway." It's not a question. "We're a modern facility, providing more upscale services than what you'd find out on the avenue." He steps forward and runs his finger down my cheek. In a flash, I'm fourteen again and he's got me in his lap. "I already know you're comfortable in front of a camera, and since you're fucking Tristian, I assume you have *some* experience performing in front of a group." He turns on his heel, pacing back to the desk. "I've decided you'll perform for me. I think I'll charge five-hundred for the live audience and two-fifty for virtual."

I try to follow what he's asking me to do. Maybe it's the strain from the last forty-eight hours, or the lack of sleep, or just everything, but I can't. Perform? In person? Virtual? "What are you talking about?"

"It's time for you to make good on your debts." He raises his chin, eyes piercing. "You can't possibly earn enough to truly compensate for what you've lost me, but I'll settle for the tuitions and whatever it takes to make this Nick situation disappear." His mouth purses into something thoughtfully derisive. "I can't bill you as a virgin, but that's okay. We'll put you in something slutty and young. A schoolgirl skirt, perhaps. Knee-highs and pigtails. Set you up with my best guy and really play up that dewy ingenue thing you've got going on." He grips my chin, forcing me to look at him. "Don't worry. The man I have in mind is a professional. He'll make it hurt like it's your first time."

"You're asking me to have sex with someone," I realize, feeling like I might be sick, "in front of other people?!"

"Don't consider it a request," he answers, eyes hard and cold. "Consider it extortion. Because if you don't, then I just might fail to pay off the people investigating Ugly Nick's grisly murder."

My mouth works around a series of aborted replies, brain swimming with disgust. "It was self-defense."

He scoffs. "Sure, you can take your chances with that. Someone with a history of lying, whoring, running away, and increasingly erratic behavior will appear very reputable."

I lurch out of his hold, banging into the wall behind me. "I'll tell my mom."

"Alright." He just shrugs, slinking back over to prop himself against his desk. "But I think we both know what she'd say if she were here. She'd tell you this is just what women need to do sometimes. She'd say it's important—for the family — plus, it's only one time. Are you really going to tell your sweet mother, who's found herself on her back to support you more times than either of us can count, that you refuse to repay that favor because you're *above it*?" When my face twists in outrage, he lifts a hand. "Before you decide, you should know that I'll stop at nothing to protect my son. Killian will be fine. And Tristian? He's a Mercer, and therefore, untouchable. But Rath, well…he's got debts of his own, you see." He tsks, head shaking. "Troubled boy with a long rap sheet. It might be difficult to keep him out of this if I find myself… unnecessarily *aggrieved*."

I find myself lost in a suspended moment of acknowledging how utterly stupid I am. Walking in here and telling him I'm the one who killed Ugly Nick. Telling Daniel to leave them alone was giving him a peek at my hand—at the things I care about.

If there was any doubt about him being a Lord, it's gone.

The wall is solid and cool as I slide down it, knees too weary to hold me upright. There was a time when the thought of doing something like this was unspeakable. Deplorable. The height of impossibility.

Throat clicking with a swallow, I ask, "One time?"

"Yes."

"And you'll leave us alone?" I ask, voice trembling. "After this, you'll let me go. You won't follow me, or let Dimitri get busted. And…" My chest hitches with a sharp breath. "You can't tell them." I can't bear to have them think this is what I am. That maybe this is what I've always been. That everything I said before was a lie.

His reply is perfectly congenial. "Of course."

If I had any left, I think there'd be tears in my eyes. As it is, I just raise my gaze to his and give my dull, lifeless answer.

"Tell me when."

30

TEMPEST

It's been a while since the three of us passed out in the same room, so it takes me a second to realize what's waking me up.

Tristian's frantic voice.

My eyes blink open heavily, taking in the dark fireplace, the pile of blankets. It eventually comes back to me that we're in the cabin, all piled on a mattress on the floor. Last night was so much like a fucked up dream that it barely seems real. I take in the facts, struggling through the fog of sleep. We're on the floor because we were wet and cold, and Killer was shot. Killer was shot because Ugly Nick tried to fucking rob us. Only Story killed him.

A lot of 'kill' happening here.

Bear with me, brain.

There was the gunshot, and then Story's confession, and then an agreement that we were going to let her go and take care of this mysterious Ted motherfucker by ourselves. There was a blunt and a kiss, the feel of Story's hands fisted into my sweater, and then there was this mattress again.

"Goodnight, Dimitri."

I jolt upright, scrubbing a hand over my face. The first thing I see when I turn is Killer, grimacing against the pain in his side. He's clammy and miserable looking, and we need to get this show on the road because I'm no Ray.

Tristian is looming above us, jabbing his foot into my hip. "Wake up! Story left."

"Gone?" I ask, craning my neck to look around the room. That doesn't sound right. We're not done yet. "Story?" I call, rising slowly to my feet.

Tristian rolls his eyes. "You don't think I've tried that? The car's gone, too."

I already know she's gone—can feel it in the coldness of the spot beside me—but I still take a cursory check of the house. The bedroom and the bathroom are both empty, and when I trudge to the window, wincing against the bright sun, my stomach drops.

It really is gone.

"Fuck." That's when I see it. A note on the kitchen table. Killian's blood smears have seeped into the wood, and the paper is right in the middle of it, like a bullseye.

Her wrist cuff is laying on top of it.

"What does it say?" Killian asks, craning his neck to watch.

"Uhhh." I start to read the note too fast, the words jumbling together. "Goddamn it," I growl, taking a deep breath, just like Story taught me, slowly sounding out the words. *"I'm going to fix this. Please don't come for me. I hope you find a new Lady."* There's something scribbled out at the bottom, and then, *"Tell Ms. Crane I said thanks for everything."*

"That's all?" Tristian asks, coming up to read over my shoulder. "There's nothing to fix. We came up with a plan. Story is leaving town and we're taking care of this Ted guy!"

Grunting, Killian tries to lift himself to a sitting position, hand clutching his side. "Story has two M.O.s. She runs away, or she makes shit worse. At least this time she left a note." He gestures for Tristian to come help him off the floor, and Jesus wept. His face crumples into a grimace for the ages and he's panting, even though he's barcly up on his elbows. "She couldn't have left that long ago. We can track her. Find her and stop her before she does anything stupid."

"Let's stop you from doing something stupid first," Tristian says, shaking his head as he eases Killian back down. "We need to get you to a doctor. There's a Jeep in the garage," he explains, standing over him. "Let me get my shoes on and we can all go find—"

"No. You're staying here," I tell him, grabbing my jeans and pulling them on. "Both of you."

"What?" He reaches for his own shirt. "You're not going alone."

"Fucking watch me," I snap, stabbing my arms through my sweater. "We don't know if whoever put that hit out on Killian is still looking for him—or for the two of us. Killian needs to rest and you need to be ready for the go signal."

"Then you should stay here. I'll go," he argues, moving faster. Now we're engaged in this fucking ridiculous rendition of competitive dressing, as if whoever gets there first has dibs.

I shove on my boots and grab his gun, tucking it in the back of my pants. "It makes more sense for me to—"

He shoves my shoulder, face going hard and stormy. "I'm the one who wanted the tracker!"

"She called me Dimitri!" My words bring Tristian up short, that fire in his eyes dimming.

"When?"

Giving my laces a hard yank, I answer, "Last night."

He scrubs a palm roughly down his face, muttering, "Fuck."

It's no secret between the three of us what I've been waiting for. I know they don't actually get it. It's just a name to them. But if nothing else, they both understand that it means something between Story and me—something big.

I know I've won when his shoulders deflate, his fingers yanking his hair back in a tight, frustrated gesture. Tristian stalks over to the kitchen and opens a drawer, pulling out a set of keys. I catch them when he tosses them to me. "You find our girl, and you bring her back to us."

Tristian wasn't lying last night. He's always had issues with letting things go. For Killian and me, this has never been a bad thing. It's hard to find true loyalty, especially in the kinds of situations we find ourselves in. I don't think either of us really expected Tristian to let Story go—not of his own volition. Chances are, she's trading one stalker for another, and this one has the keys to her cage in the form of that tracker. Still.

For her, he'd try.

She doesn't realize it yet, but that's the biggest gesture he could ever make.

I think it's the first I'm realizing it, too, snatching up my jacket and passing him on the way out the door. Because other than his sisters, Tristian has never cared for someone more than himself. Not Genevieve. Maybe not even Killian and me.

The hard truth is that Tristian probably loves her.

The harder truth is that maybe we all do.

It doesn't take long for the tracker to reveal Story's location.

As soon as I drive into town, glancing down at the phone, it becomes obvious she's in South Side. A dozen worries card through my brain. She's turned herself in for Ugly Nick's murder. She's gone back to the scene of the crime to look for clues. She's hunted down this Ted guy and is bargaining herself.

The reality is almost anticlimactic.

Daniel's office.

I swing the Jeep toward the avenue, feeling paranoid at every car that passes. The three of us are used to having enemies, but we usually know who they are. Intimately. This Ted guy is a complete unknown factor. If he can stalk Story across state lines, murder her roommate, and hire a born-and-bred South

Side foot soldier to do his dirty work, then chances are this guy has access to some serious resources.

I've got nothing but a phone, a gun, and a score to settle.

He can fucking try me.

Annoyingly, as I enter South Side, I notice Story's dot on the move, speeding down the surface streets. I shift away from the avenue, following my target. She's got a good ten minutes on me, but it's not long until the dot becomes fixed, a stationary objective.

I know where it's leading me, and the certainty of it sits heavy in the pit of my stomach, but it's not until I find myself parked in front of the Velvet Hideaway that I allow myself to ask the question that's swimming inside my brain.

"What the fuck?"

What the *fuck* is Story doing at Daniel's whorehouse?

The second I climb out of the Jeep, my muscles coil. I've only been here a couple times since the grand opening. Once was with Killian to intimidate a rowdy client, and the other was to collect the nightly take. Daniel's always made it clear that the three of us have credit and are free to take a go at whoever we like, but none of us have bothered with that since the early days. Daniel and credit are two things you don't want to mix.

As soon as I walk in the door, I know something is happening. The Velvet girls are comprised of the avenue's best hustlers, finely curated by none other than Daniel himself. He's got a real hard on for class, considering his roots. Never understood it myself. But there's an energy in the air, a couple girls scurrying past me, in such a hurry that no one even spares me a glance. Usually when one of us walks into this place, someone's all over us, eager to please any one of Daniel's pampered little show dogs.

Now, I have to wander around the first floor searching for Augustine. I find her in a parlor in the back of the estate, pulling boxes from a closet.

"Auggy," I greet, taking in her harried expression.

"Oh, Rath!" She dusts her hands off, and despite being busy, her eyes light up at the sight of me. She goes through the motions of kissing my cheek and rubbing up against me. "What brings you here?" Augustine is a few years older, but you wouldn't know it to look at her. Daniel likes to keep his girls looking young and fresh, and I suspect she landed this gig because she exemplifies the brand he's striving for. Killer and Tristian are dead sure she has a massive, throbbing crush on me, but they're not true South Side. They don't know any better. The truth is, that freshness of hers won't last forever. Auggy's a whore in search of some security. The best way of getting it is to find someone important to cozy up to.

I give her a bland look. "I'm looking for—"

"Daniel," she guesses, dropping the pretense. I don't miss the flash of disappointment in her eyes. "He's out back in the pit."

I do my best to keep my surprise from my face. She doesn't need to know I didn't come here looking for our boss. "Is there a show or something?"

The pit is Daniel's newest pet project—emphasis on 'pet'. He's spent weeks renovating the twelve car garage out back into an amphitheater-style venue. Live sex shows aren't quite what they used to be down on the avenue. People go online for porn these days. But that's not a barrier for him—not anymore.

Daniel has an affinity for properties, but he's also got a fixation with sex work. Always has, for as long as I've known him. It's no secret where Killer gets his obsession for owning a girl. Most dudes who get a new stepsister don't automatically assume she's being given as a gift to welcome him into manhood. But with Killian, it made perfect sense. That's exactly the kind of vibe I'd expect from the Payne household. The first time he called to tell Tristian and me about it, we didn't even bat an eye. Just said congrats and asked about her tits.

When I get out to the large building, I can sense that things are already being put into place. Someone passes me with a ladder and some extension cords. A girl rushes by with a bundle of clothing. Stepping inside, I spot Daniel instantly down in 'the pit', speaking to none other than Pretty Nick.

Although, I guess he's just 'Nick' now.

The reigning Nick is tall and hard-looking, a lot like Killer, but with none of the flair. His tattoos aren't the kind that are well-planned and well-funded. A lot of them are crude, probably done in someone's kitchen over a forty ounce and a blunt. Pretty Nick is another one of Daniel's new pet projects.

Again.

Emphasis on 'pet'.

The look on Daniel's face when I approach them is hard to read, but he definitely doesn't look happy about me being here. "Where's Killian?" is his first question.

I shift uneasily, looking around the building. The pit is meant to be visible, and that's exactly something I don't want to be right now. I also can't miss the enormous iron bed set up in the middle of it. *Disgusting.* "He's taking a minute. Have you seen Story?"

"Taking a minute?" Daniel asks, eyebrows furling in a way that's never been good. He turns to Nick. "Nicholas, go get yourself cleaned up for the show. Remember what we talked about?" Pretty Nick jerks his chin in acknowledgement and leaves. Guy hardly ever talks. Weirds me the fuck out. Daniel levels me with a look, hissing, "I want to know what happened and where my fucking son is. And don't give me some bullshit runaround, Rathbone. I already know Ugly Nick is dead, and I already know Killian was injured in the process."

Whatever I feel at him knowing everything runs second to the certainty that only one person could have told him. "Where is she?"

Daniel shoves his phone into his pocket and folds his arms. "The girl is none of your concern."

"She's my Lady," I argue, feeling brittle and frayed. "She's always my concern!"

"Then consider this about *your* Lady," he sneers, lowering his voice so the passing staff can't hear. "She owes me, and tonight she's going to pay off her debts. *You* are going to tell me where the fuck my son—" I turn on my heel and walk away, his incensed voice calling out to me. "Rath! Get back here!"

I ignore him, my blood thrumming with thick, black vitriol as I storm through the building, throwing open the first door I see. "Story!" I bark, but the room is empty—just a storage closet. I slam it and go to the next, and then the next, but she isn't here.

No one stops me as I march across the distance between buildings, bursting into the mansion. I've got no idea what my face is doing, but the girls give me a wide berth, jumping aside as I climb the stairs and start searching rooms. The first door I open reveals a businessman in his late forties absolutely railing this skinny little redhead. Uncaring, I slam the door and go to the next.

Augustine catches up with me halfway down the hall. "Rath!" she whispers frantically, struggling to keep up with my long strides. "You can't just come in here and disrupt—"

I reach behind me and pull the gun from my waistband, whirling on her to press the barrel into her throat. "Tell me where she is," I snarl.

Her words cut off with a yelp, hands flying up defensively. "Who?! Who are you looking for?"

"Story!" I roar. "The girl doing the show tonight!"

"Upstairs!" It's a testament to Auggy's experience in this industry that she looks more annoyed than scared.

I lower the gun. "Sorry for yelling."

See? I can be fucking polite.

She doesn't look appeased, eyes narrowed as I turn and stomp away toward the staircase. The third floor is all but deserted. I know from the initial tour that it's the girls' living space, bedrooms meant to house three or four at a time, crowding them up into little tornadoes of resentment and designer perfume.

I find Story in the third room I check.

Her head snaps up in alarm when I barge in, those doe eyes going big and round before shifting to a new sort of shock. "Dimitri! What are you—"

I storm inside and grab her arm, hauling her out of the armchair. I know my voice is too hard when I say, "We're leaving," but the sight of her in a plaid skirt and knee-highs has my teeth gnashing.

She doesn't struggle until we reach the door, pulling up short and yanking her wrist back. "Wait! I can't!"

"Is this what you want?" I snap, turning to shove her against the wall. "You want to be a whore, like your mom?"

The click of a gun being cocked is loud in the silence, but it's not as jarring as the feel of a barrel pressing into the back of my head. Story's face pales, but I just roll my eyes, assuring her, "That's just karma coming back to bite me."

It's also sloppy.

With a duck and twist, I've got Pretty Nick up against the door, the barrel of my own gun digging into the space below his chin. "We've already killed one Nick," I bite out, annoyed by the smirk he gives me. "Think that's funny? I've been told once or twice that my trigger finger is twitchy. Might want to watch yourself, *Nicholas*."

"I'm just doing what the bossman says," he says, lifting a shoulder in a loose shrug. "Watch over the girl. Check to make sure she's got a clean, smooth twat. Freak her out a bit so she's resistant during the show."

My trigger finger really does feel twitchy then, jaw clenching as I imagine this motherfucker peeking his way under Story's skirt. Taking her down to the pit. Holding her down and fucking her. Making her *resistant*.

"Dimitri," Story says, voice trembling. "Don't. Please?"

I know she's right. The last thing the three of us need is another dead body is this fucking mess. Still, it isn't until I feel her hand on my shoulder that I shove away from Pretty Nick, spitting, "Get the fuck out of here. Tell Daniel I said he can find another twat."

Nick wiggles the gun in his hand. "He won't like that."

"I don't think I give a shit!" I swing the door open and show it to him, unbothered by the glance he gives me on the way out. "What the fuck are you doing?" I ask her, trying to shove down the furious, injured thing clawing inside my chest. "You want to fuck that caveman in front of everyone?!"

Her gaze turns flinty. "Of course I don't!"

"Then why are you here?"

"For us!" she screams, and the way her eyes go shiny makes me want to pull this trigger on something. *Anything.* "He said if I don't clear my debts, he's not going to cover up what happened with Ugly Nick. He said…" Her chest hitches, and she looks away, eyes welling with unshed tears. "He said he'd let you take the fall with me."

I take in this information in increments, but it all leads to the same place. "Story." She doesn't meet my gaze, even when I push my gun into my pants and frame her face, ducking to search her eyes. "Baby, he's bluffing."

"You don't know that," she replies, voice strained. "You don't know him— not the way I do. This isn't about the money, Dimitri." A tear finally brims over, tracking down her cheek. "I thought—I said Tristian could—because he has money, and he'd…" But she shakes her head. "Daniel just wants to humiliate me. He wants to ruin me."

I give her a gentle shake. "I won't let that happen."

She pulls in a sniffle, squaring her shoulders. "You have to." Before I can argue, she looks me in the eye. "This is all connected, don't you see? Ted, Daniel, Killian, *all of it*. If I do this, he'll let me go. He'll leave us alone. It's only one time, and it's not like—"

"Don't," I growl, unable to hear her rationalize this. I hold her gaze, willing her to see the truth in my next words. "If I have to watch that guy fuck you, then I won't be able to stop myself. I'll kill him."

Her breath stalls in her chest at my words, but before she can respond, the door is flying open.

Daniel's mouth is pressed into an unimpressed line. "You're trying my patience, boy."

I never knew my father. He was supposedly someone my mother loved, but he dipped out before I was old enough to form a memory of him. Daniel was the closest thing I ever had to one. When we were younger, he used to call us that. *His boys*. As if the three of us were brothers. Family. My mom never much liked it, because she knew the kind of shit Daniel had his hands in. But me? Oh, I ate that shit up with a spoon.

I let my hands fall from Story's face, turning to him. "You're really going to whore out your own stepdaughter."

If I thought putting it into the bluntest terms imaginable would elicit even a morsel of shame, then I'm disappointed. Daniel doesn't even blink. "Story's been selling herself since she moved into my house. You know that as well as I do. What do you think she's been doing in that house with you for the last month?"

The question hits me, and the answer isn't as easy as a snappy comeback. Story has changed us since she came back. She's brought out the worst in us, but she's also managed to reveal the best in us.

"She's ours," I tell him. "You have no right to her."

And he *laughs*. "Didn't I teach you anything, Rath?" Raising an eyebrow, he looks around the room. "Possession is nine-tenths of the law. Just because I let the four of you entertain this arrangement of yours doesn't change the fact that she's *my* asset. Always has been."

Clenching my fists, I chew out a terse, "We have money."

"This isn't a debt that can be paid off with Mercer money," he snaps, confirming Story's words. "Tonight, she's going to be down in the pit taking someone's cock. Come to terms with that however you like. I see you've formed some kind of," his lip curls, "attachment. That's not my problem. This is a business. You're going to walk out this fucking door with me and mind your own." To Story, he thrusts out a finger, voice full of threat. "If I see one hair on that cunt tonight, you're going to be taking a second dick in a second hole."

I feel her shudder against my back, fingers curled into my leather jacket.

I have to wade through an ocean of red-hot fury to find the word that jumped out at me in that tirade. Something important.

Something useful.

The idea forms in my head, and it's complete *crap*. There's no dressing it up, otherwise. It doesn't include getting Story out of here before she's forced to give away another part of herself. Daniel wouldn't allow it—I see that now. He's full of shit. This isn't about business. This is something personal, and I know Daniel well enough to understand what that means. I'm not going to be able to stop her from going into that pit.

I press my phone into Story's hands, pitching my voice to a whisper. "You call one of the others if something happens, you understand?"

She looks at the phone owlishly, something dark and haunted swimming in her eyes. "I-I can't—"

"Yes, you can," I assure her, grabbing her chin to wrench her gaze to mine. "We've made you do some really fucked up shit, Cherry, and you've handled it. You're not some trashy avenue skank. You're a *Lady*. Don't you fucking forget that."

I don't give her a chance to argue. I march out of the room, knowing Daniel is right behind me. As soon as I hear him close the door, I set my jaw and turn to him—this man I've seen as a father.

A mentor.

A King.

"I want to make a deal."

3 1

T H E   P I T

THE PRESENCE OF Daniel's thugs and Augustine hovering by my side are the only explanation for why I don't go darting for the door at the sight of all the people streaming into the amphitheater. Hundreds of them. Almost all of them are men. Some of them look drunk. Fat. Old. Sleazy. They're noisy, but I barely hear them over the blood pounding in my ears, and every step I take is focused on settling the contents of my stomach.

I'm pretty sure if I puke, Daniel could find some way to turn this into a snuff film.

I'm still tucked in the shadows waiting for the signal from the video and sound crew, and I refuse to look for the man I'm supposed to sleep with, but I know he's nearby. He's big and mean-looking, a lot like Killian, but with none of the polish. Pretty Nick is the exact kind of South Side guy I don't want to find myself beneath. Did they dress him up like sex doll, too? Doubtful. He'll be the hero in this bizarre show, while I'm nothing but a prize. Just thinking about him makes me sick. I belong to three men. They might be cold and cruel, but even after everything we've been through, this still feels like a betrayal. I made a promise to the Lords—written in ink, but also in blood.

Augustine's been chilly to me all day. Well, almost all day. She seemed perfectly nice until Dimitri showed up. Now, she keeps throwing me these quick, sour glances. She tosses me one of these now, her mouth pursed as she looks me up and down.

"You're going to have to do a money shot. You know what that is, right?" At my lost expression, she sighs. "It means he can't cream pie you. He has to pull out and," she makes a crude gesture, fist pumping, "bust on your face. In your mouth. On your tits. Whatever he's feeling."

I look away, feeling my face pale. "Oh."

Augustine flicks a hand, all the bracelets on her wrists jangling around. "Just keep your eyes closed. Dicks aren't precision instruments."

I press my lips together. "Right." I happen to already know a thing or three about this.

Something in the distance catches her attention and she cranes her neck, face twisted into outraged disbelief. "No fucking way," she says under her breath. "What the hell did he do to—" Her words clip off, and she inhales, jaw setting. "Well, I don't know what he did, but it must have been big."

I frown at her. "Huh?"

"Either he has something on Daniel, or that boy just sold his soul." She rolls her eyes toward the crowd. I don't know what she's referring to, but it looks like she's trying very hard to not seem affected by it. "Either way, he showed up. That's more than anyone's ever done for me. Hell, or half the other girls in this place."

"What are you talking about?"

"It's time," Augustine says, getting a signal from one of the crew. "I'd tell you to pretend like the cameras weren't there, but that'd be terrible advice. You're putting on a show. Give Daniel what he wants, or the payment will be worse than this."

She pushes me with a hard shove, and I stumble through the curtain. The energy of the crowd immediately shifts, going from anticipatory to predatory. Augustine's right. Not only does Daniel have expectations about what's to happen, so does every man in this room.

I haltingly make my way toward the place Daniel had referred to as 'the pit'.

That's exactly what it is, too.

I have to walk down three steps to get into the sunken area that holds only a large bed, three cameras mounted to tripods, and a table with supplies. Condoms, lube, rags, *toys*. Futilely, I try to tug my skirt down.

One of the men shouts, "Yeah! Show us them titties, baby girl!" and I lock up, feeling like I might be sick.

Suddenly, my ears are filled with the sounds of loud, melodic rock music. From the corner of my eye, I see a figure join me on the platform, and I physically recoil. My throat tightens, fight-or-flight impulse kicking in. I can't do this. I can't bare myself in front of this pack of wolves. They'll take me apart, piece by piece, until there's nothing left for myself. I want to run, hide, scream.

But when I finally find it in me to look up, I don't see a wolf.

I see Dimitri.

He's standing by the bed with that impassive expression I now know is just a shield. He left here over twelve hours ago, but he came back. Must have, because I feel the heat of his eyes blazing toward me, and I can't do anything but stare back at him, wide-eyed and frozen in shock. He's changed, no longer in the soiled, blood-stained clothes from the night before, but a fresh black T-shirt, his leather jacket, and dark jeans. For a solitary heartbeat, I think he's here to save me. To break me out. To take me away from this place and set me free.

But nothing's ever been that easy, has it?

His muscles are coiled and tense, and the words Augustine just said echo in my ears.

He showed up. Sold his soul.

What has it cost him to be the one standing here?

We approach the foot of the bed from different sides. I try not to look at anything else. The white sheets, the two pillows. I hate that I think of Daniel's words from before—the ones about my mom. The things she must have done, the men she must have let inside her in order to support me. She'd probably think little of something like this. Perhaps she'd tell me I should be grateful it's only one man doing the fucking, and that it's a man I know and am attracted to. A man who, just hours ago, I'd been down to do this with willingly.

I know it's just a sick manipulation tactic on Daniel's part, but *god*.

It's effective.

When we reach the bed, separated by nothing but an arm's length of hot, stuffy air, Dimitri slips off his leather jacket, tossing it up near the pillows. I watch him look at the bed, shoulders tight, and visibly gather himself. A lot like I'm doing. It's hitting me that Dimitri has his own issues performing in front of a jeering crowd.

Issues that I've exploited before.

"Pop that cherry!" someone shouts from the crowd and all my bravado threatens to crumble. That's when Dimitri turns toward me and cups my cheeks. All my questions about what he's doing here and how this happened die before they ever make it to my tongue, stolen away by the strangeness of the cold plastic he's pushing into my ears. Wireless earbuds, I realize. The sound of music fills my head, blocking out the crowd, the intrusion of the cameras, my own panicked thoughts. Instantly, I'm brought back to a safer place. A *good* place.

"I had all these plans…"

"Plans."

"Yep. I had a playlist. Couldn't let my Lady lose her virginity to shitty music, could I?"

I'm not losing my virginity in any traditional sense. This isn't my first time with a man. But it is my first time with Dimitri, and despite Daniel's comment about not being able to bill me as a virgin, it appears he tried, anyway. From the few taunts I've heard, it's clearly what these rough men have paid for. Come and watch the sweet little North Side virgin get defiled by the dregs of a South Side thug.

He stares into my eyes as his hands slip away, and even in the face of everything happening around us, I manage a smile for him that's small and vaguely agonized.

Thank you.

Taking a deep breath, I reach up to tug on the hem of his shirt—a question. He comes easily, curling forward to take my mouth in a testing kiss. I don't know how it is for him, but for me, it's a lot like being back in his bedroom once I close my eyes. The music is Dimitri to the core—sad and angry and frantic. I have this thought that, later, I want to ask him why he chose these songs.

Then I remember there won't be a later.

After this, I'm leaving South Side.

I'm leaving Forsyth.

I'm leaving the Lords.

It gets easier then to slip into the lack of awareness of the surrounding crowd. Dimitri is solid and warm against me, spine bowed as he kisses me, his lip rings smooth against my tongue when it tangles with his.

I still flinch when his hand drags up the back of my thigh.

Dimitri pauses for the barest breath, but keeps going when I show no protest. It's just that as he slides that palm up, grabbing my ass, I can feel the skirt going with it. I can feel that the other men are seeing.

He uses his grip there to turn me to the bed, guiding me to sit on the edge. When he pulls back, I chase his mouth, desperate to remain in the safety of the moment he's helping me fabricate. When I open my eyes, he's getting to his knees, both hands sweeping up my thighs. His dark eyes hold mine, tongue flicking out to fidget with the ring in his lip, and the look he's giving me is saying volumes.

He's asking me to be good.

He's telling me it's time.

He's wondering if I'm ready.

Drawing in a breath, lean back on my palms and ease my thighs apart.

The corner of his mouth tugs upward.

I still close my eyes as he pushes up my skirt, because there's no hiding here—not physically. His hands splay my thighs apart, and I know the entire room is getting a full, unobstructed view of the crotch of my panties.

My thighs twitch when I feel warmth, and then pressure, and then dampness against my center. I don't need to open my eyes to know his mouth is there, tongue pressing right into my clit.

It's the strangest thing.

I wouldn't think I'd be able to feel any arousal here, among these loud, brash, disgusting men. But as soon as he touches me, I can feel the electricity building slowly at the base of my spine. He calls it up with the way his hands massage my thighs. A pointed tongue prodding me through spit-dampened cotton. Fingertips teasing at the elastic of my panties. A thumb tucking itself between me and the cotton, rubbing slowly over my folds.

I open my eyes to watch him then, to catch sight of his black demon gaze through the fringe of his lashes as he sucks me through my panties. The sight of him watching me back shoots a bolt right through my belly. The way I buck into his mouth is pure, animalistic instinct. His eyes fall closed on a groan that I can't hear, but can acutely feel. It rumbles around my clit, pulling a sound from my chest.

He rears back to replace his mouth with a broad palm, giving my entire pussy a long, sweeping rub. I can't entirely ignore the flashes of movement in my periphery, the leering men in the distance over Dimitri's head. But *god*, I try.

When his hands come up to tug at the waist of my skirt, I struggle to be good. To let him drag the fabric down my thighs and over my knees. To lay there in my panties and feel whole and untouched by the gazes upon us.

It gets a lot easier when he returns to my mouth, tasting like fabric and my body's response to him. His kisses are deep, bruising, as his hand works itself between my legs, wedged between our bodies. It seems nothing but natural when he shoves it inside my panties and runs his fingers along the places I've become slick for him.

When he sinks a finger into me, he pauses, his lips lingering against mine. It could be a tease—Dimitri likes to kiss that way, where it's hard to tell if he's coming or going—but I see it for the question he means it to be.

I answer by tucking my hands beneath his shirt, sweeping my palms along his smooth, toned back. He lets me drag it over his head before recapturing my lips.

I can't hear what the men are saying, but I think I can feel his reactions to it when the kiss grows strained. When his finger twitches inside of me. When the muscles in his back go taut.

He pulls away, standing between my thighs at the end of the bed, and I can't place the look in his eyes. It's shuttered and empty and impossible to decipher. With no warning, he grabs the sides of my shirt and rips it open.

Instinctively, my arms fly over my chest, the panic spiking so fast that I don't have time to bat it down, to push it away, to process the fact this was inevitable. These men are going to see me naked, whether I like it or not.

Dimitri pins me with his dark gaze, and then gently wraps his hands around my wrists and pries them away. It feels unutterably cruel, and for a second, I wonder who this is. Dimitri? Or Rath?

I don't give him any resistance, but I do slam my eyes closed, desperate to get lost in the music again.

I feel his tongue before I feel his lips, it's pointed, wet tip making a slithering loop around my peaked nipple. His hand slides up my ribs, cupping my breast in a palm as he sucks me. It's not long before I'm arching my back into it, mouth parted with my increasingly shallow breaths. He eases my shirt away as his mouth assaults my breasts, switching from one to the other, pulling the fabric from my arms and discarding it elsewhere.

His hands grab my breasts and push them together, and it isn't until he mouths at the skin between them that I open my eyes to watch.

To watch as his eyes flick up to mine.

To watch as he brushes a soft kiss over the 'R' he carved there.

To watch him say this isn't Rath I'm dealing with.

"Because Dimitri never would have done that to you."

It's hardest when he shimmies my panties over my hips, sliding them down my thighs. I want to curl into myself, but he's there to force me open, putting me on display. I understand why he's doing it, but I still feel the sting of it.

The kindest thing he's ever done is move down my body to bury his face between my thighs. I curl my hands into fists in the bedsheets. Dimitri—Rath— he's always been exceptional at this, tongue exploring my folds and crevices, mouth closing around my clit as he flicks it.

I know the people want a show, but all I can do is gasp and twist the sheets as he works me, hands pushing my thighs wider and wider, until there's a burn in my tendons, and I know the second he lifts his head, there'll be no part of me hidden to the creatures beyond our bubble.

When he does, I just lay there, splayed out like a science experiment.

Let them see.

Let them see the way my toes curl when he reaches for the button on his jeans, flicking them open, tugging the zipper. Let them see the way my teeth sink into my bottom lip when he shoves them down and pulls out his hard, flushed cock. Let them see the way I rise to the sight of it, curling forward to take him into my mouth. Let them see it all. His fingers tangled in my hair as he grabs the base of his dick and pulls it from my mouth, only to feed it back to me. The way he holds me at a distance, making me strain for it, only to thrust it deep, leaving the taste of him on the back of my tongue.

Let them see the way he looks when he's ready to fuck me.

He pushes me back, the knot in the back of his jaw taut and ticking as he crawls over me, dick in hand. It's as he's rubbing the head of it through my folds that I find my gaze unconsciously wandering. I lock eyes with a guy in the front row. He's probably in his thirties, wearing a backward baseball cap, a hand down his pants as he watches me back, mouth curving into a sickening smirk. I try to look away—to look anywhere else—but instead I end up meeting another man's gaze.

Daniel.

One of his arms is crossed, the hand of the other touching his chin as he watches me and Dimitri through sharp, penetrating eyes.

Dimitri must feel me seize up, because suddenly he's wrenching my chin to the side, making me look at him. His lips move, but his jaw is too tight to read them. It doesn't actually matter. I can tell by the flash of possessive fury in his eyes exactly what he's saying.

Eyes on me, Cherry.

That's exactly what I'm doing when he pushes inside, but it'd be impossible to look anywhere else as he slowly fills me, face hardening with every inch he sinks into me. My mouth falls agape, heels digging into the mattress as I rise to meet him. His back is tense under my fingertips, and for the first time, I wonder what he's hearing. Are they going wild? Are they asking him to fuck me harder? To make it hurt?

If they are, he doesn't listen.

He bottoms out and stalls there for a moment, uniting us into one heap of charged flesh, and then he pulls back and drives back inside.

It has no right to feel this good—not in this room with these sweaty perverts' eyes boring down on us—but it does. I tip my hips up to him, an instinctual offering, and Dimitri takes it, planting his fists into the mattress to fuck into me with short, punching strokes.

But he doesn't look satisfied.

Not until I wrap my legs around him.

It's like science then. Like chemistry. He hovers his mouth on mine as his hips push into the cradle of my thighs. And it might not be the comforting safety of that bedroom that may or may not have ever existed, but there's still comfort here. There's still safety.

It's not long before his mouth descends to my neck, sucking his mark into the skin as his muscles pull and shift, driving him into me at an increasingly punishing pace. It feels like it goes on forever, our skin growing slick with sweat, but the passage of time means nothing here.

Dimitri begins getting a little rougher, fingers digging into my flesh, teeth nipping at my skin, bones grinding against bones. I can't tell if he's lost in it or just reacting to the energy of the room, but I pant into his shoulder and watch his body move with intent—with purpose.

He's trying to make it quick, I realize.

I card my fingers through his hair to soothe him, but it just drives him harder into me. When he lifts his head to take my mouth in a hard kiss, it knocks one earbud loose.

The sounds of the room come to me like a shock. There's yelling and laughter and groans and breathing so heavy that I'm repulsed by the knowledge I'm sharing the air.

But there's also Dimitri, voice shredded and deep as he pushes it into my mouth. He's grunting, "Come on, baby. Come for me."

It's not that he's fucking me, and I don't think I can even credit the grinding rhythm of his pelvis into my clit. It's the naked desperation in his voice—the knowledge that he wants my pleasure more than his own—that begins my climb. Something sharp and sweet and full of promise swells in my center, and I chase it, moving with him, heels digging into the curves of his firm ass.

I tear at his back, feeling just as desperate as him, and it has to hurt. It has to fucking *burn*, the way I'm dragging my nails down his shoulders. But the only response I get is a long, ragged groan as I frantically try to get him closer, to fold him inside of me and *take*.

The orgasm clutches at my belly and explodes outward, igniting in a million sparkling points of light. I throw my head back and keen as I shudder, falling apart beneath the mouth pressed to my throat.

"Dimitri…"

He answers with a strained, "Fuck," and slams into me, rearing up to fix me with a fiery gaze. "Where?" he asks, teeth clenched tight. "Where do you want it, baby?"

Anywhere.

Everywhere.

I can't bring myself to answer. I tip my face up to him instead, running my tongue along my bottom lip, and he instantly takes the cue.

He grabs the base of his dick and lurches up, pumping it in a tight fist. Before I can push up to take it, he's kneeling over my chest, stripping his hardness with a fierce expression. When his hand tangles in my hair to lift my head—to position me for his come—I let my jaw fall open and extend my tongue in welcome, barely flinching when the first rope of spunk bursts from the tip.

He makes a frayed, guttural sound as another surge of come lands on my lips, and then he uses the head to push it inside, rubbing it on my tongue.

I know it's over when the tight, corded muscles in his forearm ease. I still suck him clean, and the truth is, it's not about the roar of voices or Daniel's menacing gaze on us. I do it to drag it out a little longer, because something just transpired between us. And only us.

I'm not on this bed alone, and the sweaty man next to me sacrificed himself to keep me safe—whole. He couldn't save me, but he rescued me when no one else could.

I don't belong to Daniel, or the men in the audience, or the perverts at home.

I belong to the Lords.

32

THE GIFT

I'VE KNOWN TRISTIAN since I was nine years old, so when I say I've only got—at maximum—ten minutes head start on him, that shit is precise. I can only imagine his face when he walked into that room at Ray's and found out I'd dipped. The guy's probably going to put another bullet in me.

I'm barreling toward the brothel, regardless, pumped full of antibiotics and whatever else Ray had in those other IV bags. If it had anything to do with pain management, then it's not strong enough to wobble a mouse. My side is a tender, throbbing mess of hurt that explodes with every dip and bump. I gnash my teeth and go faster, because I know by now that the only way to get through pain is to get *through* pain.

The Velvet Hideaway is gasping its last breaths of life for the day. When I pull up, skidding to a dusty stop in front of the gate, it's obvious that whatever crowd was here for the show is long gone. It's been fourteen hours since Rath returned to the cabin, saying nothing as he and Tristian loaded me into that Jeep. It's been twelve since Ray first caught me in a wheelchair, following a harrowing entrance into his underground clinic. It's been ten since the x-rays and the tests and the determination that all this pain and suffering isn't going to kill me—just end my career for the season.

It's been four hours since Rath informed me what my father's done.

I spent most of that trying to get away from Tristian, who—let's be real—probably spent those four hours trying to figure out how to get away from me.

If my calculations are right, then the show happened two hours ago, which makes me too late, too tired, and too pissed to care that I probably look like a walking corpse as I angrily hobble up to the doors of the brothel.

As soon as I get inside, I recognize the regulars still milling about. The Velvet Hideaway is never closed, but there are the quiet, unhurried hours of the night, much like this, when men have found a woman to take to a room and hunker down the moon with. Once, freshman year, I used up a credit on a slender brunette. It was back at the old place out on the avenue, so it was nothing like this. The converted motel was trashy and a bit too obvious, but the back office was comfortable and familiar to me, too many years spent stomping around inside it, being told to sit my hyper little ass down and keep my goddamn mouth shut for five minutes.

My eyes skip around the room, trying to suss out where to point myself when Auggy steps in front of me.

"Killian?" she asks, taking me in with a slow, worried expression. "Honey, I heard you were hurt."

"I'm fine." The pain throbs like a motherfucker, and even though Ray thinks I won't need surgery, he still didn't sound a hundred percent on it. "Where is he?"

She knows who I'm talking about. It's clear in the way her eyes go shuttered. "You're here for the girl, too, aren't you?"

Clenching my jaw, I repeat, "Where is he?"

"Counting cash." She means in his office, near the back of the house. I push past her, but she snags my elbow, the sudden jolt making pain sear up my side. "Killer, don't do anything you'll regret. She's not worth it. She's just a who—"

I spin around, using my precious last nerve to snatch her by the throat. "Go ahead and call her a whore," I sneer, "I fucking dare you."

Her throat bobs beneath my palm, eyes wide and scared. "But you can't honestly—Killian, she's your stepsister."

"She's my Lady!" My voice clips off, because *fuck*, screaming is apparently not something I can do with this hole through my side. "She's *our* Lady," I stress, releasing her with a shove.

Auggy looks scared and hurt, but I don't give a shit. I came down here for a reason. I walk toward the office in the back, holding my side as I push through the pain. I'm not surprised to find Pretty Nick standing guard at the door, but I am surprised to see Rath here. He's sitting against the wall close by, head tipped back, eyes closed as his jaw works tightly around a piece of gum. His hair is a mess, falling into his eyes, and his hand is motionless around the gun it's holding, loose and casual as it rests against his knee.

Pretty Nick straightens as soon as he sees me, holding up both tattooed hands. "I didn't lay a finger on her."

"Lucky for you," I say, watching as Rath's head snaps up to meet my gaze, "my boy already told me that."

If not, he'd already be dead.

"Look, Killer, I got no interest in your weird family drama," he assures me, rolling his eyes as he slides away from the door. "I don't get paid enough for this shit." He's lying—he absolutely gets paid enough for this shit—but he doesn't want to get involved.

Smart kid.

As soon as Pretty Nick saunters away, Rath pushes to his feet. He's wearing nothing but a t-shirt and jeans, and despite the tension in his shoulders, he looks exactly like a guy who's soaking in some afterglow.

I give him a nod. "You good?"

He shakes his head. "Christ, Killer. Aren't you supposed to be strapped to a bed or something? You look like you're about to drop."

"I'm not," I argue, and I don't know how I look, but that's how I feel. "Where is she?"

His eyes slide to the door beside him, jaw clenching around that piece of gum as he bites out, "He said he wanted her to stick around until he was sure we made enough." It's clear what he thinks about this, the flash of spite in his eyes hot enough to burn this place to the ground.

He'll have to stand in line.

A ripple of white-hot fury makes my stomach twinge, but I ignore it, snatching the gun from Rath's hand as I barge through the door.

Inside, Story's perched on a chair against the wall, arms wrapped tightly around the knees she's got tucked to her chest, face buried in her arms. She's wearing an oversized leather jacket that I instantly recognize as Rath's. For some reason, the knowledge that she's wrapped in his jacket eases some of the tightness in my chest. I know there was a time the thought of him and Tristian having her would make something wild and selfish thrash around inside me, but I can barely remember it. Now, it brings me an acute relief. She's cared for, protected, even when I'm laying on a gurney ten miles away, by two of the best and most capable men I know. What could ever be bad about that?

My dad is behind the desk, head snapping up when the door bangs loudly against the wall. I see Story's flinch from over his shoulder—see her bolt up from her seat—but I don't take my eyes off him.

"You're a real sick fuck, you know that?" I hobble into the room, arm curled around my side. "Did you really think I'd let you get away with this?"

"Son." He looks idiotically relieved to see me, giving the stack of money a tap on the desk, making it nice and tidy. "I was just about to come see you myself. Ray made it sound like you'd be incapacitated for a bit." His eyes take in my slumped posture, head shaking. "As if that's ever stopped you before. I don't even want to ask how sloppy you were for Ugly Nick to get the jump on you like that."

"I'm not here to talk about the Nicks." I wave the gun at the money on the desk, feeling stiff and belligerent. "I've got more pressing matters."

He leans back in his seat, and behind him, Story watches me, eyes wide. "I can see I've made some mistakes."

"You're fucking right, you did!" Chest heaving, I finally let myself look at Story. "Go out to Rath."

Before she can, my dad stands up, blocking her way. He throws me a heated look. "The mistake wasn't what happened tonight," he clarifies, voice low but deadly. "It was letting you think she belonged to you. I don't know where you got this idea in your head—"

"She does belong to me," I argue, feeling fit to explode at the way he's holding her back. "You can marry her mother, molest her, stalk her, threaten her—I don't fucking care. None of that makes her yours."

"Oh?" The expression on his face is one I'm used to. It's the look of an irritated parent humoring their child. "And what makes her yours, Killian? A contract? A few nights living under your roof?" He scoffs, planting both palms on the desk to level me with a glare. "I want to be perfectly clear. You may hold my assets by housing Story and Ms. Crane, but they always have, and always *will*, belong to me."

I don't realize Rath has entered behind me until he speaks, voice low and full of threat. "Ms. Crane doesn't belong to anyone. Not anymore." I'm not sure if Rath really believes it or not, but the fucker sure sells it. It's the way it should be, anyway. Ms. Crane didn't stab her old man to death just to be passed to another captor.

Even though that's what happened.

My dad's eyes flick over my shoulder, flashing in amusement. "Is that what the old hag wants you to think?" He barks a laugh. "Oh, boys. Delores Crane was working girls on the avenue before either of you were protein in your daddies' ballsacks. The only thing standing between her and every twitchy celebrity, politician, and husband in this town is *me*." He raises an eyebrow at Rath. "You think she wants to be free? Even if she knew how to be—and she doesn't—she wouldn't last one day out here. She's got too much dirt on the people running this town."

"They can fucking try us," I spit. "Ms. Crane is ours, and so is Story."

"You're being ridiculous." Sighing, he gives the money another tap. "But I do share some blame here. I should have put my foot down about this before you boys cornered her in the laundry room that night."

Story snaps to attention, giving him a stunned, disgusted look. "You *knew* about that?"

He doesn't turn to look at her. "Did I know about the goings on in my own home? Of course. Should I tell her, Killian?" He gives me that infuriating, patronizing look. "Should I tell her about all the nights before that? The way you'd sneak into her room and—"

"Shut up!" It doesn't really matter to me. Story must know by now the things I used to do to her while she was sleeping. It's just that I can't take her pale, mortified expression when she realizes he knows. It's too late for that now, though. She ducks her head, burying her face into her palms.

"I was hoping it was just teenage hormones," he continues, sounding disappointed, "especially considering I needed her virginity intact for the patrons who were interested. Truthfully, I didn't care that you were slinking away at all hours to rub yourself off into her mouth. If anything, the little tales of your exploits just cultivated more interest."

"Oh, my god." Story's cracked whisper is muffled by her hands.

"But I admit, I was hoping to see you form healthier attachments." His gaze slides away, briefly contemplative. "Especially after your mother. You saw how that worked out, didn't you?"

"Shut up," I say again, but my voice is weaker this time, barely a thread of a hiss. "You don't get to talk about her."

"*Healthy* attachments," he stresses, "like the ones you have with the Mercer boy. That's an alliance worth making." I don't miss his glance behind me. "I mean no offense, Rath. You've been an enormous asset and I've always been quite fond of you, but aside from the street smarts and intimidation, you don't bring a lot to this organization." To me, he adds, "Frankly, I'm worried about your future if you keep collecting all these problematic associations."

"Frankly, you can eat a bag of dicks." I adjust my grip on the gun at my side, lip curling. "You're going to leave Story and Ms. Crane alone."

"Am I?" he asks, looking unimpressed. "Maybe you haven't been hearing me—"

"I've heard you just fine," I argue.

There's a pause where he just stares at me, eyes going hard. Then he's sliding open the drawer and pulling out his own gun, sliding out the clip, and shoving it back in with a harsh 'click'.

"I've tried to teach you, son. Life is about making decisions. *Hard* decisions. You think I enjoyed what happened with your mother?" There's this look he always gets in his eyes when he talks about her, and I can't fucking stand it. It's cold and hollow, and it's impossible to miss the flash of grief it swallows. The worst part about it is the knowledge that he probably did love her. "Because I didn't. You must know that. But I had to make a decision, Killian. A *hard* decision." Looking me in the eye, he twists just enough to raise the gun, pointing it at Story's head. "And now, so do—"

I lift the gun and shoot him in the shoulder.

My reaction is so quick and impassive that none of them see it coming. It cracks through the air like lightning, and Story lets out a bloodcurdling scream. In a flash, Rath is over the desk, tackling her to the ground, shielding her with his body.

Kind of a lot of fuss, considering.

My dad falls back into his chair, and he doesn't cry out. No. Paynes don't cry out. We gnash our teeth and look at our assailant as if he's personally affronted us.

Been there, done that.

"What are you doing?!" His growl tears from deep inside his chest, ragged and tremulous as he clutches at his shoulder.

"Making a decision," I reply, motions loose and casual as I approach him to pick up the gun he dropped on the desk. "Sorry. I interrupted you, didn't I? You were going to tell me to choose, right? Her or you?" I tuck his gun away into the waist of my pants, swallowing against the tide of pain. Over in the corner, Rath is tucking Story's head beneath his chin and telling her that everything is fine—everything is chill—but all I can do is give my dad a shrug. "It's the funniest thing, though. Wasn't really all that difficult."

Someone bursts into the room then, and it's a good thing I've been keeping track of the time, because otherwise I'd be pulling some stitches to whirl around and raise the gun at them.

Ten minutes.

Like clockwork.

"Oh, shit," Tristian says, sounding out of breath as he takes in the scene. The gun in my hand. The scent of sulphur in the air. My father cringing as he clutches his injured shoulder. "Did you shoot your dad?" he asks, voice full of baffled excitement.

I spare him a glance over my shoulder. "Yeah."

He nods, eyes fixed to the blood running down my dad's arm. "Nice."

"Who the hell do you think you are?" my dad grates out, struggling to his feet.

Sneering, I answer, "I'm a Lord of Forsyth University. Heir to this goddamn throne."

My father's jaw sets as blood gushes through his fingers. "No one's going to accept a coup from you. Three spoiled little shits who couldn't find their asses with both hands and a compass."

"It's not a coup," I assure him, lurching forward to press the barrel of the gun to his forehead. "This is a message—to you, South Side, the other Royals, and anyone else who needs to fucking hear it. If the Lords or their Lady are threatened again, it doesn't matter who the threat is coming from. They'll be shot on sight." Pausing, I take a moment to impress, "If they're *very* lucky, that is. And if they aren't," I jerk my head to the man standing behind me, "I'll just let Tristian set them on fire."

He gives a tight, pained, humorless laugh. "You think that's what this throne needs? Three psychopaths?"

I reach out to fist his shirt, my hand squelching in the blood-soaked fabric. "We're exactly what you shaped us to be, dad. Never forget that." I throw him back and he flails against the chair, grunting in pain.

Breathless, he bites out, "Whoever sent Nick to kill you should have done a better job."

"Whoever sent Nick to kill me better get the fuck out of Forsyth, because it's not just me they're going to have to deal with." I wipe my forehead, and blood smears across the back of my palm. "They're going to have to deal with all of us; three psychopathic Lords and one seriously conniving Lady."

Tristian extends a hand to Story, who's been speechlessly watching the whole scene. She's not shaking anymore, but she still looks shell-shocked, colorless, and off balance. Despite that, she still reaches for his hand without reservation, allowing him to carefully guide her over a puddle of blood.

"Consider her debt paid," Tristian says, lip curling as he pulls her automatically into his side. "Else, I'll tell my dad exactly what you think of Mercer money."

"And Ms. Crane is done with you," Rath adds, looking my dad in the eye. "You think we're psychopaths? Motherfucker, you haven't seen shit."

Tristian gives him a cold grin. "It's true. She uses metal utensils on Teflon pans. In forty years, we'll all be full of cancer. Downright diabolical."

But my dad is hardly listening to them, eyes fixed on me. "Killian, if you walk out that door—"

I don't give him the chance to finish. "Take the L, dad." Hobbling out of the room, I add, "I'll have Auggy call Ray about your wound. Consider it the last of the mercy you'll see from us."

We leave the Velvet Hideaway amid a crowd of nervous onlookers, Rath propping me up as I shuffle heavily toward the foyer, Tristian and Story hand in hand. The whores and the Johns all move aside as we pass, their faces drawn and worried as their gazes peek down the hall behind us. We probably look like a bunch of fuck-ups, one of us ruffled and fucked-out, the other curled and hobbling, another so impeccably clean and styled that it could only be the result of a deep neurosis. And then there's Story—our Lady—looking weary and blank as she walks her way out of the hell she'd always been intended for.

I suppose I see that now.

To my dad, it was never about having a family, or giving me a gift, or even possessing his own personal little slice of sick perversion. I wonder now if it was even about marrying her mom. Maybe Story has always been about this for him. About owning something pure and unsullied in a world where so few things are, just so he can turn a profit on it.

When we get outside into the chilled night air, it's to the sight of our four cars, all lined up together near the gate. My Range Rover, Story's Charger, Tristian's Porsche, and the Jeep from the cabin that Rath drove up here. For a moment, it looks so ridiculous that it pulls an agonizing laugh from my chest. I should read it as a sign that we're all too connected, too fucking fused, to operate as anything but a unit.

Instead, it just makes something black and ugly twist in my chest.

We stand there a long moment behind our cars, none of us knowing what to say.

It's Story who breaks the silence, clearing her throat. "Ms. Crane. She's…"

"South Side's most notorious madam," Rath answers, posture somehow both loose and closed as he lights a cigarette, the flame illuminating his face in a brief flash. He exhales, nodding up at the mansion. "At least, she used to be. Now she's just," his face tightens, "someone people like Daniel want to pump for dirt. Because that's what she has. Dirt, on every skeevey old fuck in this town."

"That makes sense." Story gives me a quick look, and I know she's remembering that discussion I had with Auggy the first time I brought her here.

Ms. Crane, she's realizing, is the woman all the girls had been asking about. Not because they wanted to use her. Because they loved her. "Tell her I said…" Story pauses, like she's trying very hard to choose something appropriately sentimental to say. In the end, she breathes a laugh and raises an eyebrow. "Tell her she's a crabby old bitch and I'm glad to have known her."

So.

I guess we're parting ways now.

Neither of the others look surprised, Rath just giving her a single, heavy nod. "I'll let her know." He doesn't sound happy about it, but I can see that this is a whole thing.

A thing where we acknowledge she's leaving.

Where we tell her we're letting her go.

When Story starts shrugging out of his leather jacket, he scoffs, reaching out to close it. "I hear Colorado gets cold. Keep it."

Her shoulders slowly deflate, and she ducks her head, pulling the jacket tight around her instead. "Thank you." Rath takes a drag of his cigarette and looks away, as if this is nothing.

She turns to Tristian next, starting, "About the car—"

"No." His blue eyes bear down on her, daring her to say what she clearly wants to. "Take it. It's paid for, and I don't know anyone who'll get as much use out of it as you."

She looks conflicted and all tangled up as she chews on her lip, twisting to send the car a covetous glance. "It's too much."

Tristian reaches up to brush a knuckle under her chin, giving her a sad smile. "I think we both know it's not even close to being enough." Something passes between them—a long look, full of back and forth and a hurt that might be too deep to heal.

To him, she says, "I'll treat her well."

He passes her that winning Tristian Mercer smile I know is as fake as the man he inherited it from. "I know you will."

When she turns to me, I just cast my gaze to the distant lights of the city that'll be mine someday. "Don't look at me. I never gave you anything."

Not yet.

Not until I find Ted.

She steps in front of me and I can't look at her, because I don't know what the beast inside me will do. It's a tossup between throwing her in the back of my truck, kissing her black and blue and bloody, and clutching her to my chest and begging—fucking *pleading*—with her to stay here. To stay mine. To stay *ours*.

None of them is acceptable, so I keep my eyes trained to the distant glow, telling that beast within to shut the fuck up and let this happen. It's harder when she strains up to brush a kiss over my jaw, pain shooting through my torso as I struggle to remain agonizingly still.

Her voice is soft, a whisper against the rough stubble. "Yes, you did."

I don't look away from that point in the distance until I hear her footsteps recede. The sound of a car door opening. The cushioned, mechanical sound of it closing.

Tristian, Rath, and I have been friends for longer than most, but when all three of us start moving at the same time, like someone's cut our strings, I know that we'll never be as close as we are at that exact moment.

Because they were wrestling with the same beast.

We each get into our cars, one by one, and crank our respective engines. One direction leads to the glow of the heart of Forsyth, and the other leads to somewhere else.

When we start filtering out onto the highway, the three of us go left, and Story goes right.

For once, no one chases her.

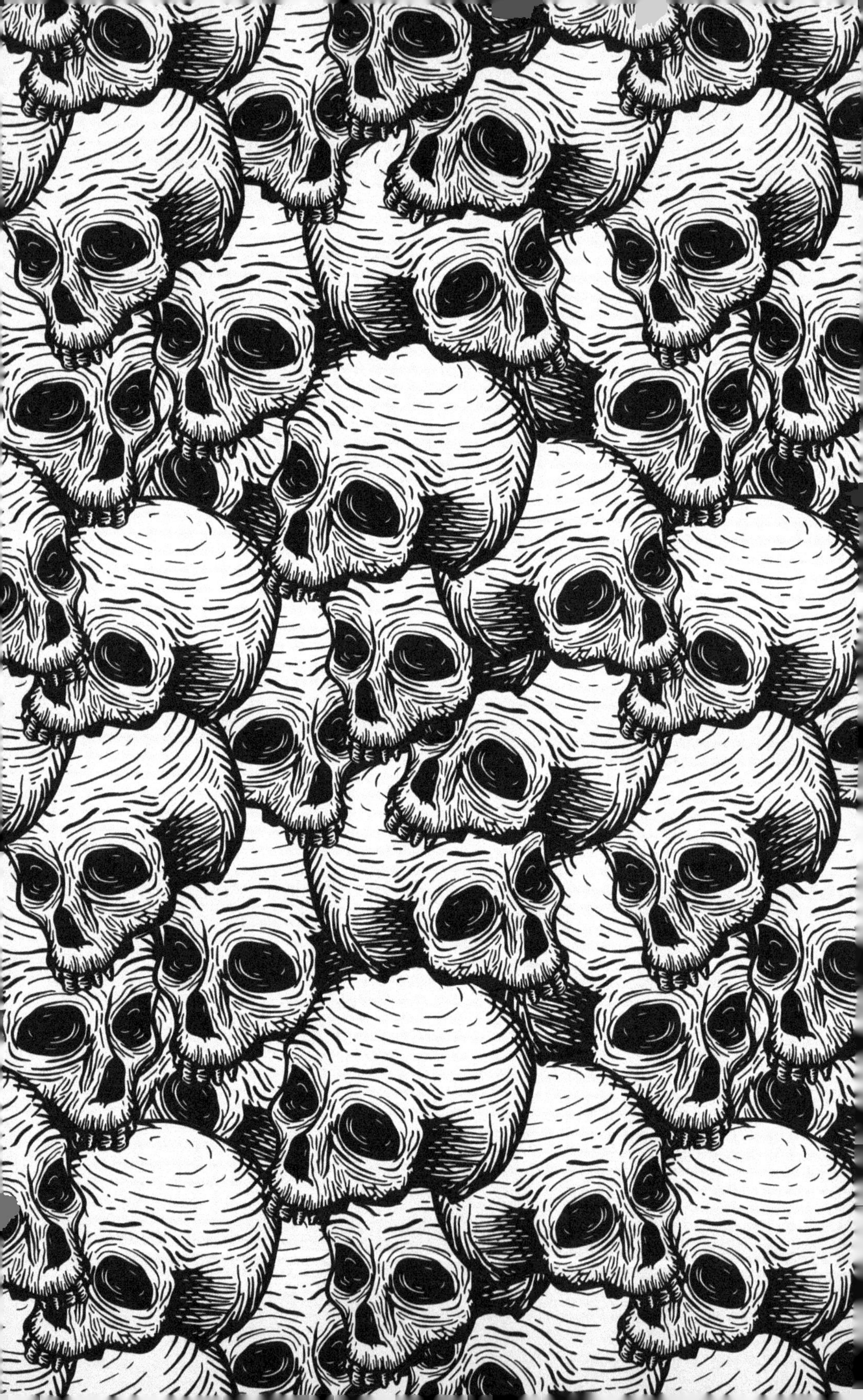

3 3

F R A M E

THE BROWNSTONE IS quiet and dark when we arrive, and I can tell from the look on Killian's face when he all but pours himself out of his truck that we shouldn't have let him drive. Fucking hell, we're a mess.

Rath and I get him through the door, huffing and already exhausted, and I take one look at that flight of stairs and wilt at the thought of lugging him up it.

Killian pants out a tight, "Fuck that, put my ass on the couch."

I look at Rath and he shrugs. "Works for us."

We get him settled—for a given value—and spend a long beat standing around the den, wondering what happens next. I've already checked on my sisters for the third time in one night. Killian is lying there with a pinched grimace on his face, but he's alive. Rath is more quiet than he's been in weeks, so there's no telling what's going through his brain. And Story—

My thoughts pull up short, because Story is no longer a factor in my rundown of people I need to check on. I'm going to have to break that habit.

I purse my lips, digging my phone from my pocket.

Maybe I can break the habit tomorrow.

Rath looks at me from the corner of his eye, and it's a testament to how well he knows me that he asks, "Where is she?"

Thumbing the app open, I check her little dot, something heavy settling into the pit of my stomach when I realize where she is. "She just crossed the county line, westbound on the interstate."

Rath nods, carding his fingers through his hair. He's probably thinking the same thing I am; that Colorado is lame and really fucking far away. "Want to get drunk?"

I throw my head back, pushing out a long, hard sigh. "Jesus Christ, yes."

That's how we find ourselves ten minutes later, slugging down shots of whiskey as Ms. Crane, dressed in a floral bathrobe and fuzzy blue slippers, brings us out a tray of beers.

She grins manically as she waddles over, setting it carefully on the table. "Tell it again."

I don't think I've ever seen this old bat *pleased* before.

It's fucking startling.

Rath pulls his shirt off, throwing it on the floor, and when he reaches for one of the beers, I can see a row of scratches going down his back. I wonder how much of an asshole it'd make me if I looked up the video of them fucking.

Probably a pretty big one.

Rath uses the edge of the table to whack the top off his bottle of beer. "Fucking capped him right in the shoulder. One shot. Probably hit some bone, too." He doesn't grin as he says it, tipping the bottle back and downing half of it in a few quick gulps. It's not like he's *not* pleased about watching Killer shoot his dad, because not one among us isn't.

It's just that it's difficult to muster any real enthusiasm.

Ms. Crane must sense this, because she gives Killer a thoughtful look. "He isn't going to take it lying down. Your old man's generally used to being on the other side of the gun."

Killian's rubbing the bridge of his nose, eyes closed, jaw sharp and taut. "I don't fucking care."

"You're going to," she says, head shaking as she picks up Rath's shirt from the floor. "If it were me, I'd find him and end it quick. Put a bullet in that fucker's head and call it a day."

"Not all of us can be quite as deranged as you." My words lack any of their usual heat, and from her expression, I think Ms. Crane can tell.

"I'm deranged?" she scoffs. "I've seen quivering come bubbles more stable than the three of you." She slaps Rath's legs. "Get your goddamn feet off the table, you degenerate. Spend three minutes in a fuck show and think you're something special."

Rath presses the cold bottle to his forehead, legs falling heavy and limp to the floor. "It was more than three minutes."

"So where is she?" Ms. Crane asks, collecting our bottle caps. "She busted up, any? I know how Daniel's paid boys can get." She would. She spent years cleaning up after the shit they did to her girls. She's probably as happy about Ugly Nick lying on a slab somewhere as she is about Daniel getting capped by his own kid.

Killian bites out a terse, "She's gone, Dolores, and we don't want to talk about it."

Ms. Crane pauses, looking between us. I see when it dawns on her. "You let her go?"

I swallow another shot of whiskey and admit, "It's what she wanted to do."

Her face screws up. "Since when has that mattered?"

"Since now," Rath says.

"Hm." Ms. Crane looks between the three of us, a flash of something subdued overcoming her features. "So what now? Getting a new Lady?"

Ms. Crane has a vested interest in our vested interests. She stays with us because it's safe, but right now, shit is looking anything but.

"We have no idea who put the hit out on me," Killian says, ignoring the question about the Lady, "or who's really been stalking Story all these years. My dad is a fucking asshole, but he's not a liar. Not to me. If it were him, he'd own it. All this sneaking around and threatening people under fake names...it's not his style." Killian slides his gaze to her. "Living with us is dangerous, Ms. Crane. If you'd rather find somewhere else—"

He's cut off, because all of our phones begin buzzing. My first instinct is that it's Story. Maybe she changed her mind. Or worse, maybe she's in trouble. But when I look at the screen, I just see a call from Pretty Nick.

Rath groans. "What does this asshole—"

The room falls into a cloud of hushed tension as we all open the message.

A photo.

The first thing I see are tits, and the three letters carved in the valley between them.

K

T

R

The second thing I see is all the blood, fear rolling like pure ice up my spine.

Rath rushes out, "It's not her," and lurches forward in his seat. "It's not her. The hair is blonde. It's just hard to see over all the blood. It's…" He swallows. "I think it's Viv."

The message that came with the photo says:

Thought you'd want to know bossman is on a rampage about this. He says he saw the same marks on your girl earlier. If I were you, I'd start hiding. Shit's about to get heavy.

I look once again and confirm that he's right. Under all the blood, I see her: pretty, beautiful, obedient Vivienne. Her body is splayed out on the floor, head propped against a concrete wall, arms limp, palms out. The word 'whore' is written sloppily overhead in blood.

The three of us share a grim look.

"Barons?" Rath wonders, eyes troubled and weary.

I shake my head. "They don't care about South Side spats."

"No. This is a fucking frame job," Killian says, glaring into his phone's screen. "We know who did this."

"Who?" Ms. Crane asks, forehead puckered as she peers at my phone.

"Ted." Killian takes a long swig of his beer before answering. "Someone who's going to seriously fucking regret it."

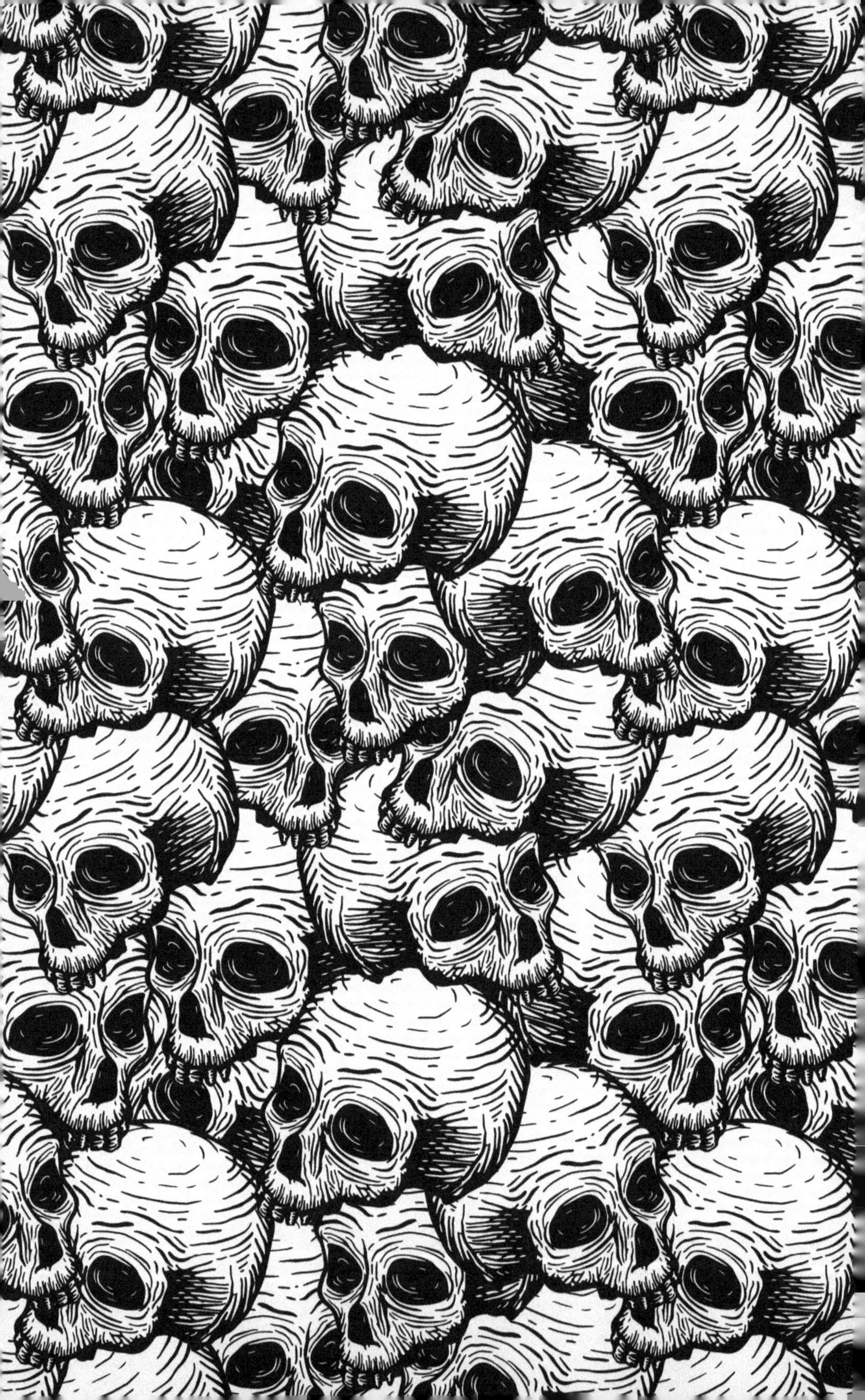

3 4

HOME

THERE'S NOTHING LIKE being on the open road, window cracked, hair whipping in the wind. Sometimes, a lot like that night we ran from the alley, I can still hear Jack's laughter, always so excited about making an escape. I swear I could hear it now, Jack laughing it up as I speed away from Forsyth, telling me I'm *'a real bad bitch, girlie'*.

I drive for what feels like hours, letting the promise of any destination lift the heaviness that's gripping my chest. I've felt like this once before. It must have been over four years ago that my mom came home to our dreary apartment, gushing about the man she met. This man was nice and sophisticated and wealthy, and he had a son around my same age, and he was going to *save us*. He was going to give us a nice home and a happy family, and for the first time in my life, I felt something I'd given up on so long ago was within reach. I'd been so naively optimistic, infected by her enthusiasm. I didn't ask questions. I walked into that restaurant with a light heart and a shy smile.

It's hard to look back on it, knowing everything I do.

So I look forward, instead.

The LDZ skull swings from my rearview mirror, Dimitri's jacket keeping me warm enough that I don't need to bother fiddling with the temperature controls. In some ways, it feels good to take these parts of them with me—the light and the dark—even if I don't think I deserve them. In other ways, it just makes it impossibly harder to keep my foot on the gas pedal.

But I do.

I think of Dimitri's words to me that night in the cabin, about how being their Lady is more than a title. It's something I've become—something I can't shake off. I think of Killian's words as we lay in front of the fire, his quiet request that I pretend with him, just for a moment. I think of Tristian's face the morning after, how incredibly maskless it was when he spoke of the promise he made to take care of me—when he spoke of breaking it.

I think of my Lords and the way they've orbited me for the last few months, and I think to myself, *I'm a goddamn Lady.*

I can do anything.

So I shift up a gear and go faster, speeding toward something full of all the promises men like Daniel never planned to deliver on.

I'm ready to finally go home.

I REACH MY destination in that gulp of time between night and dawn, the world barely threatening to stretch awake around me. It's colder than I'm expecting when I climb out of the car, everything misty and chilled. I spend a long moment staring at the house I'd shared for so long. I get a prickle on the back of my neck, like I could look over my shoulder and see Jack in that back seat.

The truth is, even though so much has happened since I left, it's the same as I remembered.

Walking up the steps and touching the knob, I spend a moment wondering if it'll open for me. Maybe they're not here. Maybe they're busy moving on while I'm moving back. I don't let myself doubt for too long. It's not very Lady-like.

The door's unlocked, allowing me to push it open and enter.

This is as I remember it, too, except for the bright lights and the way it sounds. This isn't a dead house full of dead things. It's just past four in the morning and it's perfectly alive.

It doesn't take me long to find them, sprawled and lazy on the couches, bottles of beer and booze laid out around them. I'm not sure why, but I think I always knew they'd be here, awake and waiting for me. I watch them for a beat, not revealing myself until it becomes a physical impossibility to remain silent.

"I choose where I sleep." Three heads swing around at the sound of my voice, faces showing varying degrees of stunned disbelief. "I choose who I fuck, when I do it, or if I even want to." Shrugging out of the jacket, I stand there in the schoolgirl skirt and top that I'd really like to burn some time.

Perhaps I'll ask Tristian to help me.

"I choose what I eat, what I wear, and where I go."

Tristian is halfway out of his seat before I raise a hand, stilling him.

"In return, I won't talk to other guys. You can still track me. We can keep up appearances for the sake of being Royals." I look at Dimitri, who was slumped back in Killian's usual leather chair when I arrived, but is now pitched forward, elbows resting on his knees. He's shirtless, his gaze almost too intense to connect with. Although I'm grateful for him showing up tonight, it doesn't make what happened to us less traumatic. "No more cameras. No more mind games. No more punishments." I watch Killian, who's laying on the couch, clearly still in pain but drowning it in whiskey. He's shirtless, too, his griffon and lion and patched up gunshot wound on full display. Despite it all, he watches me with those careful, calculating eyes. "And whatever you have planned for Ted," they exchange a look and I snort, "and don't pretend like you don't have one—I want in. I want to be a part of it. Equally."

Tristian lowers himself back into his seat slowly, and I can tell from the tired glaze of his eyes—from the way his shirt is wrinkled and rumpled—that he's three sheets to the wind.

But not drunk enough to skip negotiations. "You choose *who* you fuck?" he asks, and there's a question within his words he's not asking.

I know them well enough to suss it out myself. "Among the three of you," I clarify, voice going low and careful. "No one else."

Dimitri's tongue peeks out to fidget with his lip piercing in a way I refuse to admit drives me crazy, even though it absolutely does. "Anything else?"

"Well…" I bite my lip, shifting uncomfortably. "I'd still…expect the same out of you."

Dimitri runs a thumb between his piercings, agreeing, "Okay."

"And there's one more thing." Killian's frozen as he stares at me, and even though his eyes are heavy, I don't see him blink once. I say this more to him than the others, and for good reason. "Daniel's not going to be paying my tuition anymore."

As I expected, Tristian is the first up. "I can—"

"No," Killian says, cutting him off. His eyes never leave mine, and I'm grateful for it, because he sees the exact thing I don't want. Tristian throws his money around like he can buy anything he wants—cars, influence, forgiveness, affection. I've taken all I can bear to. "We'll figure it out," Killian says.

"I'm going to do it myself. I need to." I duck my head, only to catch sight of the outfit again. I grimace, gesturing to the staircase. "I'm going to go get cleaned up, try to get some sleep in case I want to catch a class today."

They all give me slow nods, like maybe they're still trying to figure out what the thread of the conversation is. It's very possible I might need to have it again later, when they're sober and less freakishly agreeable. What I'm asking for is logical, humane and appropriate.

It's not going to be easy.

Still, I linger for a moment, not partial to the idea of just leaving it like this. When I start toward Tristian, he shoots a look at the others and rises, shoving his hands into his pockets. One of them emerges with the black wrist cuff, and he stares at it, turning it over in his hands. It isn't until he fixes me with a quick, reluctant look that I realize he's unsure if I want to wear it anymore. Their mark.

Their brand.

Wordlessly, I extend my wrist.

He releases an exhale, shoulders sinking with something like relief as he loops it around, snapping it shut. Tristian opens his mouth, likely intending to say something.

I kiss him before he can ruin the moment.

He rumbles into my mouth, arms winding around my waist and hauling me up against him. The good thing about Tristian is that it never really hurts with him. Dimitri will bite and Killian will bruise, but Tristian only wants to control and be seen doing it. He does it now, with the press of his body and the force of his hand, tangled in the back of my hair. He deepens the kiss like he owns it, and when I push back—*mine, too*—he grunts, crushing me closer. Tristian tastes like beer and pure, dark thrill, the promise of illicit touches and scorching flames.

I only push away because he lets me, his glazed eyes fixed to my mouth as I turn to Dimitri.

Dimitri does *not* rise to meet me. He leans back in the armchair, legs spread, black eyes sparking with a hint of wicked challenge. When I accept it, climbing fluidly into his lap, his mouth parts in surprise. He hides it quickly, opting to curl a hand around my neck and pull me down for a kiss. The good thing about Dimitri is that he teases me until I want it so badly, the thought of getting it is enough to make me fly. He tries it now, mouthing at my bottom lip, the hand on my neck keeping me at a distance until I lick out to taste him. He tastes like whiskey and the sharp edge of a blade, the promise of lazy mornings and pitch black nights.

"I doubt you want to hear it," he says against my mouth, nudging my lips with his, "but you were so fucking good last night."

He's wrong, because hearing it brings back the memory of him moving in me, and nothing more. I won't let anything else invade it. "So were you," I say, letting him feel my grin.

When I rise from his lap, his black eyes follow me like a laser, fingertips brushing over my bare thighs.

Killian is waiting for me, and before I've even perched on the couch at his side, his hand is fisted in the fabric of my shirt, tugging me close, just as demanding as ever. He gives it a sharp yank and crushes my mouth to his in a way that must hurt his wound, neck straining up to take charge of the kiss. It hurts with Killian like it always does. It's intense and pointed, and sometimes it's terrifying, but other times—times like this—it's exhilarating and so easy to get lost in that I'm jarred out of it by the pained sound he makes.

I realize I'm pressing into his injured side, and I jerk back, startled. "Sorry," I breathe, inspecting the patch of bandage for any damage.

"Fuck it," he says, trying to pull me back. But I take his hand in mine, keeping this kiss shallow and slow, and I hope I'm showing him that it doesn't *always* have to hurt. That the tenderness he shows me when I'm unconscious beneath him has a place here, too—if he wants to give it. Killian tastes like vodka and moonlight, nights so quiet that anything more than a breath could shatter it.

When I pull away, he doesn't let go of my hand, tethering me to him like two links on a chain. "Wait," he says, but it isn't until I turn to him, our hands suspended over the distance between us, that he asks, "What was it I gave you?"

It's not an easy answer. Killian Payne shared his home with me—more than once. He taught me what it means to be ruthless for the people I care about, and sometimes even *to* the people I care about. He gave me the knowledge of what it feels like to know someone would kill for me. Care about me. Perhaps even love me. In some ways, he gave me Dimitri and Tristian, as well.

But in the end, the best thing Killian ever gave me was something that went against his very nature to offer. I tell him my answer as I retreat, my fingers dragging against his until the connection breaks.

"A choice, big brother."

A THANK YOU
FROM ANGEL

So, this continues on from where the last letter stopped in the back of Lords of Pain.

I'll admit it. The success of Lords of Pain stressed me out. 2021 was a hard year for everyone. We were caught in the middle of pandemic. Things were kind of reopening. We had vaccines. And Sam and I were tight in the middle of both the fourth book in the Preston Prep Series (Heston) and also Lords of Wrath.

In ten years of writing and publishing I had never experienced the enthusiasm of readers like this. I was so scared we would mess it up. Like really scared. We were holding firm to the main reason we decided to write dark bully romance, "Don't Hold Back," because we both felt like this was a missing component of a lot of books in this genre. The HEA comes too easy. As you all know, we're never easy on Story. Especially in Lords of Wrath. But that's the amazing thing. You all were there for it, and still are. Lords of Wrath exceeded all of our expectations and gave us the go ahead to build a Samgel universe of dark, complicated, sexy, dangerous depravity.

It didn't hurt that Dimitri Rathbone is so deliciously hot. Never have so many readers fallen for a cover model made of hopes, dreams and computer AI pixie dust.

Around this point is when readers were requesting signed bookplates. So we sent out 250. It wasn't enough. We sent out 500 more. That wasn't enough. And we had to really reassess the best way to get this into our readers hands. We hadn't settled on the Kickstarter yet, we were feeling out a few options, but that demand for bookplates, bookmarks and other Lords related products made us realize we had to come up with a plan! Little did we know what it would lead to.

A THANK YOU
FROM SAMANTHA

MAN, WE WERE really working through some shit with this book. Sometimes I re-read it and go, "Who wrote that? Someone should check on them, ask them if they're okay." Haha.

Hahaha.

(We were probably not, but whatever.)

But Wrath was especially hard on Angel, so this thanks is for her, for pulling through and always being the baddest bitch. You inspire me every day, creatively and professionally.

And also because even after 14 years of friendship, you're still very scary.